BRIDE TAKES A LAIRD

Highland Vows & Vengeance
Book 2

by Kara Griffin

ARE YOU SIGNED UP FOR DRAGONBLADE'S BLOG?

You'll get the latest news and information on exclusive giveaways, exclusive excerpts, coming releases, sales, free books, cover reveals and more.

Check out our complete list of authors, too!

No spam, no junk. That's a promise!

Sign Up Here

www.dragonbladepublishing.com

Dearest Reader;

Thank you for your support of a small press. At Dragonblade Publishing, we strive to bring you the highest quality Historical Romance from some of the best authors in the business. Without your support, there is no 'us', so we sincerely hope you adore these stories and find some new favorite authors along the way.

Happy Reading!

CEO, Dragonblade Publishing

**Additional Dragonblade books by
Author Kara Griffin**

Highland Vows & Vengeance Series
Bride Takes a Scot (Book 1)
Bride Takes a Laird (Book 2)

About the Book

Laird Magnus Cameron is more than irked by his king's command to accept a border baron's daughter for his wife. He has more problems at home than dealing with his trivial overlord's demands. The inconvenience disrupts his duty as the laird to his clan, but at first glance, Magnus cannot deny his attraction to the winsome beauty Kendra of Clan Graham.

When Kendra's father accepts a bride price from their black-hearted neighbor, she must find a way to return the coins. Only her father's ailment prevents him from remembering where he put them. Can she find the lost coins before her father's lands are besieged by their warlord neighbor? Kendra prays for a miracle and is saved when the king commands that she marry a man of his choosing. She hadn't expected her miracle to come in the form of an utterly handsome Highland Laird—Magnus Cameron.

When all he wants to do is delight in the presence of his bonny wife, Magnus is beset with finding his brother's murderer, scuffles with the Chattans, and petty clan matters. Her kisses and caresses allow him to forget the troubles that thwart him but his duty as laird comes first. When Kendra returns to her family's land, Magnus is faced with making a difficult decision—confronting his enemy or winning the heart of his wife.

Will these Highland vows and vengeance hold the promise of love and redemption for Magnus and Kendra?

Character List

CAMERON CLAN

Magnus Cameron – Hero
Stanton – Father
Faye – Mother
Hugh – Grandfather
Ned – Brother/Steward
Wyren – Brother/Commander-in-arms
Marny – Sister-in-law
Jake – Brother
Ellen – Servant
Clarence – Healer
Winston – Squire
Sigge – Wolfhound/Pet
Craig – Gatewatchman
Hayden – Soldier
Osmond – Soldier

HOUSE OF GRAHAM

Kendra Graham – Heroine
Rupert – Father
Catherine – Mother (deceased)
Aston – Brother
Norman – Steward
John – Father's Attendant/Squire
Linet – Maidservant

Peter – Stable master

King Alexander of Scotland
Queen Margaret of Scotland
Edmund – King's Chamberlain
Ellish Heatherington – Neighbor
Aldo – Gaming Master
Mary – Myltenhus Owner (Stew House / Brothel)
Geoff Chattan – Rival
Rodrick Chattan – Rival

CHAPTER ONE

Lochaber
Highlands, Scotland
Mid-March 1260

T HE BODY WAS found on the ground in the shadow of the great mountain just before the sun rose over its peak. High atop the mound, wisps of mist stretched downward like fingers reaching over the pinnacle. Magnus stood beside his brother's body and gazed forlornly at the sight of the ghastly remains. His brother had been missing for over a month. Searches had ensued when no one had recalled seeing Ned in over a fortnight.

Magnus, as the laird of the Cameron Clan, had been busy helping with the sowing of the harvest and handling other important clan matters. He hadn't noticed Ned was absent until he visited his cottage to gain an accounting of their coins and stores. Ned, their clan's steward, kept their clan's accounts and records of all the land's holdings.

Magnus's brethren stood silent as the winds from the high crags whipped at their tartans. It was a bonny place to die, where the valley sprouted with the first buds of the season. The sound of the waterfalls cascading over the rocky expanse lent to its serenity. Beyond them, pinewoods stood proudly towering high above, watching over his brother's body and protecting him from the sun and elements. Dying at such a place would allow one's soul to enter heaven even if they were besmirched by minor sins.

At least that was the conviction of those within his clan.

He stood rigidly, peering at what remained of his brother. If only he had noticed his brother had gone missing sooner. The trek from their land was laborious and it had taken them most of the morning to reach the isolated location. Beside him, Clarence knelt and surveyed Ned's body. A healer of renowned ability, Clarence could tell how a person died and whether there was foulness involved. With no others to rival his skills, Clarence was unsurpassed in his vocation. The man was somewhat eccentric in his abilities. Nevertheless, he was an important member of their clan.

"What say ye, Clarence? Was Ned murdered or did he perish from the elements? I must have your answer." Magnus waited impatiently for the healer to respond, but the cantankerous man scoffed.

Clarence's bushy eyebrows rose as if the answer eluded him. "I cannot tell ye that, Laird, by viewing him in this condition. He is nearly all bones now and there is very wee insect activity so the death was not recent. There is little to show if he was cut for his blood dried up. Aye, what with the way the wind blows here, 'tis likely he has lain here for nearly a month."

"It does not appear that he was disturbed by animals and the body is intact." Magnus found that odd since the area was known to be visited by wolves and other roaming animals.

"'Tis strange indeed but perhaps none caught the scent of his corpse. He was shielded by the mountain too. I shall inspect his garments later when I get him back and try to assess if he received any wounds." Clarence rose and stood beside him but he continued to stare at the ground. "'Tis something odd about your brother's death for he was not alone when he died."

Magnus frowned and tried to discern what Clarence was looking at. "I see naught. How can ye tell that?"

Clarence motioned to the ground. "Ye see the hoof prints? There were more than one horse in the area. Aye, he was left to die. Might have been dead already afore he was placed." He shrugged. "I shall inspect his body at my cottage and might have an answer for ye in a day or two. Och, I suspect treachery, Laird."

Magnus grunted. *Was his brother murdered? Why would anyone want to kill Ned?* "I want an answer at the soonest. Until we know the truth, we cannot retaliate."

Clarence mumbled, "Aye, aye, there will be vengeance if Ned was indeed murdered."

"Aye, vengeance," Magnus stated with vigor. "I want to know if there is an enemy about." He wasn't aware of Ned's involvement in anything untoward. Ned rarely left their clan's holding and he knew of no one his brother might have visited in the area. Though Ned was fond of drink and overimbibing, Magnus trusted his brother. Yet it was only at their father's insistence that he had given Ned the position as their steward. At the time, he had been uncertain if Ned could handle such a tiresome and important duty.

Clarence motioned to the soldiers beyond him. "Easy now. Take care when ye lift him onto the cloth and cart. Have him taken to my cottage." He turned back to him. "My condolences, Laird, on the loss of your brother. I will work hard to get ye an answer at the soonest." With that, the old healer turned on his foot and marched to the lane that took them around the high bluff of the mountain.

Magnus stood there for a time, saddened by the loss, and perplexed by what had happened to his brother. He couldn't take much time to mourn Ned because there were too many duties awaiting him and, as laird, those came first. With that thought, he mounted his horse and followed the trail of soldiers on the path. On the trek back home, he considered how he would tell his parents and other siblings about Ned's death. They would take the news hard, especially his mother, who adored Ned.

Crossing the wooden bridge over the waters of Loch Eil that led to his home, *Eilean nan Craobh*, he stopped by the gates and dismounted. Their fortification was located on the island of the trees, home to all Clan Cameron, where a small tower sat within a large walled enclosure. Enemies were kept at bay by a deep trench of water surrounding the stone curtain. Numerous cottages speckled the hills between the trees within the walls on the small island but their clan spread far beyond the fief and island.

When necessary, his clan retreated inside the walls for its protection. His family had held the lands as long as anyone could remember, since the inception of their clan. Now that Magnus was laird, he hoped to enrich the fortification and make his home even more impenetrable. Their land's location put them in a perilous position, being centered betwixt many northern clans that would sooner war with them than make an alliance. Wars arose over the simplest matters from a stolen sheep to an overtaking of land. No matter was too trivial for any clan to rise up against their rivals.

There was one clan in particular that instigated Magnus's ire—the Chattans. That clan was a thorn in his arse because they squabbled over land that had long been held in the hands of Camerons. The ongoing disagreement caused minor scuffles so far, but the Chattan's audacity was becoming more irritating by the day and their strife would escalate. Even if he wished for peace, Magnus was certain it would take a great deal to accept any offer of a treaty from that knavish clan.

Magnus paced before the gate and the noise from his clansmen and women, animals that scurried on the lane, the horses hitched to carts and reins held by his soldiers, all muted. He paid no attention to those around him, the weight of his news sat heavy upon his chest. He suspected that once he crossed the threshold, life would be forever changed. Their clan would be affected by the loss of his brother. Until they knew what happened to Ned, suspicions and rumors would abound. He detested the thought of the turmoil that would erupt but he'd deal with his clan's disorder.

"Laird, there ye be," Craig, one of his trusted guardsmen, called. "Ye received a missive from the king. The messenger arrived early this morn." The gate watchman held out a sealed parchment.

"My thanks." Absently, he took the parchment from his guard. Magnus continued to peer beyond the tall, blond-haired man whose beard was trimmed short. His soldier's dark eyes scrutinized him.

Craig cleared his throat. "Laird, is there anything I can do...?"

"Keep the gates closed. Until we know what happened to Ned, we will be guarded and diligent. And I want to know who comes and who goes." Magnus regarded the grim face of his soldier as he shoved the missive inside his tunic. He would read the message later and didn't consider it important, at least, not as significant as the burden he now faced. By now, the news had spread like wildfire through his clan and probably beyond his borders.

"Aye, Laird. Do ye believe the Chattans were behind Ned's death?"

"I know not but if they were, they'll regret it." Magnus couldn't reason why the Chattans would harm one of their clansmen. Their rift hadn't escalated to war yet, but would eventually. There was no cause for the Chattans to want to murder his brother.

Craig waited for him to pass and signaled to the guardsmen to close the gate. The creak of the iron and grunts from his soldiers sounded and both gave Magnus the solace of protection. He couldn't give thought to their strife with the Chattans until he knew how his brother had died and so he put aside his conversation with Craig.

Magnus walked apprehensively, almost leisurely, toward the keep. With his horse's reins in hand, he continued on but dragged his feet. He was in no rush to get inside to impart the atrocious news.

Winston, his attendant, sprinted forth with his dog, Sigge, following. Sigge had been given to him as a gift from his younger brother Jake, who often brought home strays and animals akin.

Winston and Sigge had become inseparable and both were loyal to him. Now, the tall lad shook his shoulder-length brown locks from his face and awaited his direction. The lad had a pleasing demeanor in his brown-eyed gaze and a dedication in his mannerisms and heart.

Magnus handed the reins of his horse to him. Winston was apt at his duty and always prepared. His pet was faithful but when Winston whistled, Sigge trotted off to follow the young soldier. Sigge's disloyalty always showed whenever Winston was around.

At the steps, Magnus hesitated for a moment in an attempt to calm himself, but he drew a resigned breath and marched inside. With a quick stride, he hurried to the great hall, wanting to impart his news mainly to get it over with. Magnus was uneasy about telling them the news of his brother's death because he knew they'd hold him accountable.

His father stood by the hearth and his mother sat in a wooden chair near him.

His mother glanced at him expectantly. She pressed the long length of her brown hair behind her shoulders and then folded her hands in front of her.

"Have ye found him? Please, tell me that he is safe." His mother gained her feet and stood before him.

Magnus was dejected that with his next words, he would break his mother's heart. "Da...Ma... We found him and I am sorry to tell ye—"

He hadn't finished telling them the news when his mother shrieked and sobbed into her hands. "Oh, God, nay. This cannot be. We cannot have lost Ned. How could ye let this happen? Ye are the laird and should have protected your brother. This is your fault. I hold the blame on ye and ye will not gain my forgiveness." She reached out and slapped him hard across his face.

Magnus tensed but said not a word. He didn't even bother to soothe the sting of his mother's ire. His cheek enflamed and reminded him of his role as the laird. He was accountable for the safety and well-being of every living soul within his clan. His mother had every right to show her anger—anger that also wound its way through him for his ineptness.

His father set his arms around his mother's shoulders to offer comfort. "He is with God, Wife, take comfort in that."

Magnus gave them a few moments to mourn. Soon enough, he would need to answer their questions—questions for which he presently had no answers.

His father called to a servant and had his mother taken to their bedchamber. Magnus waited for her to leave and when she cleared the doorway, he slunk to the table, poured himself a cup of good strong ale, and downed it.

"Your ma does not know what she says. Mourning speaks for her."

Magnus grunted. "Aye? But she is right because I am responsible for all the clan. It is my duty as the laird to ensure their protection. 'Tis my fault that Ned has died. I should have been aware of what he was…" He discontinued when his father shook his head and set his hand on his shoulder.

"Son, now ye let mourning speak for ye. Ye are not responsible for anyone's actions but your own. Do not hold guilt in your heart. Ned was a man, accountable for his own life. What happened to him?" his father asked sadly.

"We do not know yet. Clarence is looking Ned over for injuries. It is not known whether he was killed or died from other causes. The healer suspects foulness though."

His father patted his shoulder. "Forgive your ma for her anger. Ye know how she doted on Ned. She will grieve for some time."

"As will we all." Magnus poured his father a cup of ale and handed it to him, then poured more for himself. "Until we know for certain, we should keep our gate closed. I ordered the watchmen to do so."

"Aye, that is wise. I cannot help but wonder why Ned left the holding. He never does…did. It seems strange that he would do so and then be found dead. Why would anyone want to kill him?"

His father motioned him forward and they sat at the large trestle table in the center of the hall. With the cup held in his hand, his father lowered his head and shook it dejectedly.

A banked fire sent warmth to him as Magnus took the seat closest to the hearth. For a moment, he let the heat calm him. He was tired from the journey as well as from the sad affairs. Blearily, Magnus stared at the banners situated high on the walls in the chamber. "I thought the same thing, Da. It is odd, his behavior." He sipped his ale and couldn't form more words to offer his sympathy or accountability.

Magnus hadn't thought his brother had the wherewithal to handle the important position when his father forced him to accept his brother as the steward but he and his father rowed about it. Ned had proved him wrong and they'd settled into a routine until recently. His brother had begun to shirk his responsibilities by not showing up for meetings, and making excuses for the delay of accounting of their coin and stores. His ineptness led Magnus to believe that he had made a mistake by allowing his brother access to their wealth.

His father groaned and rubbed his hands over his dark-haired, bearded face. Of his four sons, Magnus most resembled him in likeness with the same thick, dark brown hair color, and likewise with the greenish-brown shade of his eyes. His brothers more appeared like their mother, bearing lighter brown hair and blue eyes.

He and his father also shared similar traits of honor, dedication, and assertiveness.

Magnus supposed that was why he was chosen to become the laird and not one of his brothers. Not that they didn't possess honor, but Magnus exuded confidence which his brothers did not. No one was more dedicated to the clan than he was. He'd aspired to be the laird and worked hard to be named as such by their clan's council since he was knee-high. From the time he was five in age, he'd been raised and instructed by the elders and spent every waking moment being counseled by them.

"Ye are quiet, son. That tells me much is on your mind."

"Aye, with spring soon to warm us, there is much to prepare. Now, I must deal with this treachery, if Ned was murdered. And there's the Chattans to consider. Our rift with them escalates. I will have to confront them eventually because it has become troublesome keeping them off our land." Magnus set his cup down and felt the parchment jab him inside his tunic. He pulled it out and set it next to his cup.

"What is that?"

"A missive from the king." Magnus stared at the message and hoped its contents were unimportant. Whatever the king wanted had to wait. He was in no mood to deal with Alexander at present.

"What does it say?" His father reached for the missive, but Magnus clutched it before he could take it.

He might as well read it now and cracked the wax seal to open the parchment. His eyes scanned the briefly written lines. "Damnation, I do not need this right now. The king demands my attendance in Edinburgh in all possible haste."

"Why?" His father scowled and snatched the missive from him, scratching his head as he read the words.

"It does not say but only that I am to leave posthaste." Magnus retook the missive from his father and crumbled it in his hand. He then tossed it into the fire of the hearth with satisfaction because he wasn't about to leave his holding. At least, not now with so many issues plaguing him, and not until he had answers from Clarence.

"Ye cannot dismiss the king, son. Give yourself a day or two and then leave." His father grunted. "Alexander will not be put off and the last thing we need is to incite the king's ire."

He wasn't pleased with having to go to Edinburgh, but what could he do? Until he left to meet with the king, he would see to his other duties. Magnus intended to get his answers from Clarence on the morrow and when he returned he'd set out to find Ned's assailant, if there was one to be found.

The Chattans wouldn't cede and battles would force them to stand down. With the sowing almost completed for the early crops, the soldiers needed to return to arms training. While he was away, he would have his brother, Wyren, their commander-in-arms, ensure their soldiers trained hard and were readied for war. As he thought of his brother, Wyren and his wife entered the hall. His sister-in-law carried their wee bairn in her arms.

"I just heard," Wyren said. He guided his wife, Marny, a dark-haired, brown-eyed woman, who recently birthed a bairn, to the table. Marny was from a neighboring clan but had settled in when she'd married his brother. She was a sweet-tempered woman and well-suited to his brother's confident nature. That Wyren always remained calm when under pressure made him the perfect leader and commander-in-arms. Magnus somewhat envied that trait in his brother. He wasn't as patient or understanding.

His brother's bairn, though, had a cranky disposition and often cried, so unlike his docile parents. Hale fretted and wiggled in his mother's arms. Marny tried to soothe their son, but the wee one was not so easily comforted. "Hale needs to be changed. I shall see ye at home," she said to Wyren, kissed his cheek, and left hastily.

Wyren kept his gaze on the entrance as his wife left before he returned his attention to him. His brother yawned widely, stretched, and took a seat next to their father. "I vow my bairn is intent to make me deaf and prevents me from ever seeking my bed again. Aye for I am akin to the living dead. He will not cease crying and he's kept me up over half the night. Do we know what happened yet...to Ned?"

Magnus shook his head. He remained silent and took a deep breath to settle himself. When his brother stared hard at him, he spoke, "This is all I know." He hastily told Wyren how they found Ned and what Clarence had told him. "Now, I have no time to await Clarence's findings because I must leave for Edinburgh. Ye will ensure our soldiers are ready. After we bury Ned, I want all the steward's records brought to me. Have them put in my solar."

Wyren bowed his head. "Aye, Magnus, as ye wish but I say we do not await Clarence. Let us go now and find out what happened to Ned. We will light a fire under Clarence's arse and get our answers now."

Magnus rose and followed his brother from the hall. With him, Wyren and their father walked on either side of him. The healer's cottage sat near the center of their holding, close to the tower fief. None spoke until they entered the healer's domain.

In the small room where Clarence attended the injured and infirm, his brother lay on a high table. Ned was practically unrecognizable. Magnus's stomach twinged but he withstood the urge to gag at the odor and view. He was used to witnessing death and the horrors of war, but those experiences compared little to the sight of his brother's lifeless body.

Nearly twenty candles lit the chamber and sent a glow to the far reaches of the room. The healer stood by the table and held the tunic Ned had worn.

Startled by their abrupt arrival, the healer gasped when he turned to them. "Oh, Laird, I did not expect ye so soon. Ye frightened me."

"I am to leave the holding without delay and cannot await your findings. What say ye, Clarence? Was he murdered?" Magnus approached and stood beside him.

"Ye have not given me much time, Laird, but I say he was murdered. Aye, ye see here," Clarence said and held up the stained tunic. "There are slits in it where he was stabbed. Looks to be the size of small blades. Likely daggers. There is blood staining his tartan too. At first, I thought perhaps the recent rains soiled his garments, but at closer inspection, 'tis blood. Your brother was indeed murdered. As ye know, I thought him dragged to where he was found. Someone killed and dispatched him there so he would not be found. 'Twas an isolated spot."

"Aye, and afar from our lands. There was no reason Ned would have gone there unless he planned to meet someone,"

Wyren said.

Magnus couldn't listen to conjecture. When he found proof of his brother's murderer, he'd act. "Prepare him for burial. I want him laid to rest this night because I leave for Edinburgh on the morrow. As much as I would like to find his murderer, I cannot delay my journey to meet with the king."

Wyren set his hand on his shoulder. "His murderer cannot hide from us. We shall find whoever did this to Ned."

Magnus's gaze shifted to his father and the healer. "Wyren and I will dig the grave. It is our duty to our brother." He and Wyren stepped outside and avoided some of his clansmen who stood on the lane who watched the healer's cottage as if expecting news but Magnus knew the findings would be given later. On the way to where they buried their dead, he snatched a shovel from beside the stable. His brother also grabbed a shovel and together they hastened toward the back of the fief.

There, by the high back wall, was situated a burial site where they buried the closest members of the Cameron clan. He and his brother remained silent whilst they dug and didn't cease until the hole was deep enough. The rich scent of soil and the freshness of the water floated around them. Being on an island, they couldn't dig down too deeply because of the risk of reaching the water below. Once they had the hole ready, they jumped onto the surrounding land.

Standing at the edge of the grave by the time they finished the chore, Magnus watched solemnly as his family gathered. At early eve, just before the sun settled beyond the mountainous peaks in the distance, all within his clan assembled. His closest clansmen: Hayden, Osmond, Craig, and Winston carried his brother's body toward the grave. Magnus wouldn't allow emotion to control him and he stood with a steeled regard.

Ned was wrapped in their clan's tartan, the red and green hues blending as Magnus's eyes threatened to tear. His brother was placed on a wooden board which they used to lower him into the hole. After, Hayden and Osmond took the shovels and made quick work of filling the hole. There was no clergyman to speak Godly words or to send Ned onward to Heaven. Whatever prayers were spoken had to be done privately.

His family stood together solemnly and his mother wept with deep sobs and gave him glances of disdain. His father stood beside her, holding her. His brothers Wyren and Jake watched as the last bit of dirt was added to the mound. Magnus placed a big rock atop the grave. Then one by one, the rest of the clan added their rocks atop to ensure the protection of his brother's body.

Craig stepped forward with a large goblet in his hand. His guardsmen held jugs of ale. They filled his goblet to the rim. When the men within the clan noticed Craig, they moved forward and stood around him.

Magnus gave the signal with a nod of his head. "My brother Ned was murdered. Someone killed him, for what reason we know not. I pledge to all within our clan that I will not cease the search for Ned's murderer until I can enact vengeance for his death." His words came with the vigor of his promise.

The sound of his clansmen's grunts and cheers of acceptance reached him. Craig handed Magnus the goblet. He took a swig then handed it back to him. Craig drank and passed the goblet on until each man within their clan partook of the cup. Their tradition instilled his promise and his clansmen's acceptance.

Vengeance would be his and none of his clan would allow him to forget the vow he'd made on this dark day. Magnus especially because he took the vow to his heart as laird.

Vengeance for his brother's death would be his and his alone.

CHAPTER TWO

East Dunbartonshire
Glasgow, Scotland
Mid-March 1260

THE WRETCHED MAN rode his horse forward and forced her and her maid Linet to stop. All Kendra Graham hoped to do was enjoy the warmth of the morning on her ride through the countryside. Having been cooped up most of the winter, now Kendra wanted to be outside. With the many difficulties she'd dealt with over the past months, she needed the solace only the outdoors would bring.

Even though the day had warmed enough, the sun remained behind dismal clouds. Still, it wasn't completely unpleasant—until she was intercepted by her horrid neighbor. Kendra sat upon her mare and raised her face to the sky with a hasty prayer that he wouldn't detain her. She didn't want to make idle chatter with the nefarious Lord Ellish Heatherington who'd stopped her just at the pass that led to her family's land. There was no way to reroute around him and as much as she would like to ignore the man, she couldn't be rude.

"Mistress, I am surprised to find you out here alone. Should you not have an escort?" The aged man had dark wavy hair with gray-streaked throughout. His face was marked with holes and sparsely covered by whiskers. Though he was garbed in expensive materials, she thought he appeared much like the warlord he professed to be.

"Good day, Lord Heatherington. As you can see, I am not alone and have my maid with me. Our escort rode ahead and I should like to catch up to them. If you shall excuse me." Kendra tried to revert her horse to round him, but Heatherington blocked her path. Sky Dancer, her usually sweet-tempered mare, snorted and twitched her brown tail. She was just as displeased to be held up by the horrid man.

Her maid glanced at her with fearful eyes and Kendra tried to ease her by putting a small smile on her face. Linet always hid whenever Heatherington was near. The man had made unpleasant advances toward Linet and many times Kendra had intervened. Heatherington was a scoundrel and a knave. She disliked him immensely.

Heatherington continued to prevent her from moving around him as he directed his horse to block her as he ogled poor Linet. "My offer still stands, Mistress, and I shall be happy to take your maid off your hands. I hear you are in need of coins… Perhaps if I doubled my offer? She would make a good addition to the maids at my fief." His grin widened with odious snideness.

Linet gasped and her blue eyes rounded at her. Kendra hoped she didn't fall off her horse in a faint, but graciously, Linet shifted her horse to hide behind her.

Kendra wasn't in the least threatened by the knave. On many occasions, she'd dealt with him and he'd always acted somewhat respectfully toward her since he hoped to make her his wife.

"My Lord, you cannot purchase my maid. Regardless of how much coin you offer, I will not sell her into servitude." She disbelieved he'd learned about her family's coin shortage and that he had the indecency to mention it. Was the fact that they were practically destitute common knowledge?

"I say, that is rather disappointing but alas, it matters not because she shall soon be in my home." He feigned a pout but then his grin widened. "Mistress Kendra, I profess that you are as beautiful as I remembered. Your hair must be spun from gold and your eyes are as pretty as a bluebell. A man would be rewarded beholding such beauty each day and I am delighted to be such a man."

Kendra wondered what he meant when he said Linet would be a member of his home. But with his obtrusive words, she scoffed under her breath at the man's forwardness. He always spoke expressively and poetically but his words were far from complimentary. They were meant to be pretty, but his tone made them ugly and his voice even grated her every nerve. She never allowed his false flattery to turn her head. There was nothing she could use as a retort to his overly poetic words, and she tried her best not to glare at him.

"Are you as gleeful as I am by our forthcoming wedding?" Ellish bowed his head. "I shall invite all the peerage. At least those who have not instigated my wrath. It will be a grand event and perhaps I will even invite our king to attend. What think you of that?"

Kendra tried not to look daggers at the man, even as she knew his words were nothing but lies. "We are not betrothed, My Lord, so I bid you to cease any arrangements. As I have told you repeatedly, I will not marry you." He was the last man she'd ever marry. Heatherington knew how she felt about him because she had for the past two years rejected his numerous pursuits with every excuse imaginable.

Still, he'd persisted.

"I am gladdened to announce that yestereve your father finally agreed. Why, only yestereve he accepted my bride price of ten pounds. Now, we can forget this madness and get on with our marriage. I plan for our wedding to occur at the end of the spring season and then you will finally be mine." He grinned with a wicked tug of his lips and continued to ogle poor Linet. "As will you."

Was that true? How could it be? Would her father actually betroth her to such a detestable man? Even now, in spite of his state of mind, he had to understand that Heatherington was not only arrogant and vile in thought and word, but that he was also the most unattractive man she'd ever looked upon. His thinning dark hair always appeared damp, his chin weak, his body lean with nary a muscle to show for his prowess at arms, and worse, he was well over two scores in age. Besides his dubious looks, he was known to be quite vile with a temper and cruelty toward his servants. She could only imagine how he would treat his wife—a wife she'd never be, she vowed. Kendra had done her best to rebuff his advances, but the man wouldn't take no for an answer.

She had always hoped to marry a man the complete opposite of Ellish.

"Surely, you speak falsely, my Lord. My father would have told me if he made an arrangement with you and he swore not to."

He snickered. "Did he now? I lined your father's coffer well for your hand and I expect your submission," his tone turned from sweet to sour.

Submission. Kendra's stomach flipped and she thought she'd be ill. Somehow, she suppressed the urge to gag. Her father wouldn't do such a wretched thing without conferring with her. God, she hoped he hadn't, and for ten measly pounds? Being bartered for so little made her sick to her stomach. She peered ahead and hoped to see her father's soldiers, but no one was there.

"I must go before Papa sends the sentry after me. Good day, Lord Heatherington." Overwrought, she yanked on her horse's reins. Unused to such harsh treatment, her mare reared onto her hind legs. Kendra grabbed Sky Dancer's mane tightly and managed to keep her balance to avoid falling off. Surprised, to see her horse's legs pinoining around his head, Heatherington moved out of her way. Good. Kendra leaned over her horse's neck and rode hell-bent toward home.

"You don't think he's telling the truth, do you?" Linet asked when she caught up to her. Her maid's long auburn tresses whipped at the breeze of her movement.

Kendra turned to look at Linet and noticed the tears in her pretty blue eyes. "Lord, I hope not. And worry not, Linet, because I would never give you to Heatherington no matter how many coins he offered for you. Let us ride on and I'll find my father and ask him."

Linet was her only friend, the daughter of the maidservant and the steward of their manor. She had lived in their home since the day she was born and had been Kendra's ever-present companion for most of her life.

Inside the gate, they dismounted and waited for one of the grooms to take the horses. Linet stood beside her, silent and pensive. Kendra shifted her gaze about the baily and wondered where everyone was. At this time of day, there was always activity—men emptying carts from the fields, guards standing about jesting or discussing the day's events, and children running amok with their mothers chasing after them. But today it was eerily vacant. It was quiet too and only the sound of the wind whipping the pennons atop their manor could be heard.

"Where is everyone?" Linet asked and drew closer to her. "Is there trouble?"

Kendra was unsure, but then she spotted John, her father's attendant. "Oh, John, what is happening? Is there danger?"

John, a young soldier who was old enough to join the other men-at-arms, stayed within the manor and acted more like her father's manservant than a soldier. His almost-black hair covered his eyes and she couldn't tell if his gaze bespoke danger or not. When he reached them, he took the reins of her horse and Linet's.

"Mistress, I was about to send men out to find you. Your da is missing again. I sent a search for him and all are looking beyond the walls. Worry not, for he'll be found quickly. I suspect he hasn't gotten far." The young man assigned to keep watch over her father had a difficult task before him, especially since as a soldier, John was often called to perform his other duties that were more in keeping with his duties as a guardsman.

Kendra raised her hands to her chest as a twinge of pain settled there. "Oh, nay! Wasn't the gate's guard keeping an eye out?" She had directed that the guards keep her father within the walls, but somehow he managed to sneak by them. This wasn't the first time he'd absconded past the gate.

"They were distracted when a woman was knocked down by one of the soldier's horses," John explained. "I heard the commotion and left the manor to give aid and when I returned, your da was gone."

The more John spoke, the more daunting the news grew. "Oh, gracious, is the woman unharmed?" Kendra hoped she wasn't severely injured.

"She received a few bruises for her carelessness. But when I returned to the hall where I'd left Lord Rupert, he wasn't within. I searched the entire manor, around it, and nearby. He was nowhere in sight so I sounded the alarm."

"My thanks, John. I shall go in search of him too." Kendra was about to set off to look for her wayward father when the soldiers' shouts came from the gate.

"Looks like they found him, Mistress." John released the horses' reins and turned to make a mad dash toward the gate to reach Lord Graham.

"Hold the horses," Kendra directed Linet, then rushed after John. There by the gate, her father stood with his head lowered. She put a smile on her face and hurried forward to link her arm with his. "Papa, I worried for you. Come, let us get you inside."

Her father said nothing but strolled silently next to her with his silvery-haired head lowered in defeat. When they reached the courtyard, he said, "I only wanted to walk about the grounds. Why did they drag me back?"

Kendra couldn't answer because her father wouldn't like her response.

As she walked Papa to the house, John led their horses away and the men who had searched for her father returned to their duties. They entered their home with her maid following. Linet took her cloak and set off to let Gilda, the maidservant, know they had returned.

Inside the great hall, their footsteps echoed in the now practically empty room. No tapestries adorned the walls to buffer the sound. The room felt cold as if no one lived there. She guided her father to the small trestle table where only four chairs flanked the wooden surface. Once, there had been a grand table that had sat at least twenty, situated in the center of the large room with smaller tables positioned around it. She'd sold the beautiful table that had been made especially for the hall when the manor was built, along with any other items that could fetch needed coins. Kendra settled her father in a chair and then took the seat opposite of him.

Gilda hurried into the hall and set a basket of warm bread in the center of the table. The maid hastened to the buttery and retrieved a pitcher of ale and cups for them. "The midday meal shall be ready soon."

"Our thanks, Gilda." She turned her attention to her father to address his disappearance. Papa, you know you shouldn't leave the grounds. Remember, we talked about this."

"Aye, but I just wanted to stretch my legs." He grunted. "You shouldn't be telling me where I can go. I am the lord of this manor and your father, and I bid you to remember that."

Kendra pressed a gentle hand on his arm. She didn't let his bluster bother her. He sometimes lashed out but she did her best to keep him calm. "Aye, but you know that I worry about you. You promised me that you wouldn't leave the walls." Before she continued to reproach her father, the manor's steward strolled into the room.

Linet's father, the steward, Norman, approached. "Mistress, I need to speak to you."

She sighed wearily at Norman's sorrowful gaze. He appeared displeased and she suspected that he hesitated to come forward. It wasn't that she disliked the steward, but he always brought bad news and she'd had enough bad news already that day.

After she poured her father a cup of ale, she addressed him, "Good day, Norman."

"I would like to meet with you this afternoon to go over the accounts."

Kendra trusted the steward and had since she reached an age of understanding, and oversaw the keeping of their manor's accounts. Norman realized that she was just looking out for her father when she'd done the recounting. She ensured his accounting was accurate and that he hadn't thieved. There was never a miscounting—not that she suspected he would ever take coins from their coffers. When she'd turned ten years of age, she'd insisted that her father teach her to add sums and count coins. Strangely enough, Kendra excelled at figures and she enjoyed the tasks. It truly was her way of looking out for her father. They'd spent many hours together which brought them closer. Her mother had passed when she was very young and in teaching her, it afforded her father time to spend with her. Kendra cherished those times.

In recent years, Norman often came to her when her father was intent on using their wealth on unnecessary items. She had maintained her ability to rein in her father's spending, a feat that often exhausted her. In the last year, she alone was responsible for the discouraging downfall of their wealth. Kendra had used every pound, shilling, and pence in her quest to find a healer who might cure her father's ailment. All the coins paid were wasted on hair-brained remedies and unsound advice. Nothing helped and her father continued to be forgetful and worse, he declined.

"Will you make time for me, Mistress?" Norman asked.

Kendra pulled herself from her overwrought thoughts and nodded. "Of course, Norman. I will make myself available whenever you wish to meet. Just find me when you have a moment."

The steward bowed to her, backed up a few steps, and hastened for the hall's exit.

She took a warm roll from the trencher in the center of the

table. Her father peered far off as if his mind was elsewhere. "Papa?" He seemed in a daze and she wondered where he went to in his mind when he was like that.

He came out of it a moment later. "Your cheeks are bright, dearest. Were you out riding?" Her father smiled winsomely at her as if he'd forgotten she was reproaching him for leaving the manor grounds. Perhaps he had.

Kendra decided to let the discussion go for now since it was unlikely he'd remember that he'd promised to stay within the walls or even that he'd left them.

She took a bite of bread, swallowed, and nodded. "I was. It is a beautiful day and warm. Looks like it shall rain later. I crossed paths with Lord Heatherington. He tells me that you accepted a bride price from him. Tell me that is not so." Kendra reached across the table and gently shook her father's forearm when he didn't answer. "Papa, did you?"

Her father shook his head. "I do not recall doing so but I might have. I seem to remember him visiting yestereve. Was it yestereve?"

Kendra gasped. "Oh, Papa, you didn't. Please tell me that you didn't accept his coins. You must return them at once and reject his offer. I will not marry the man. He is old and vile."

He muttered under his breath.

She couldn't understand his words and set a hand on his arm again. "Papa, I cannot marry Heatherington. You know that I detest him. He is an evil man. Where did you put the coins? I will have Norman return them at once with your regrets."

Her father shrugged and his bushy eyebrows rose. "Hmm. I cannot recall where I put them." He smoothed his hands over his tunic and patted his thighs as if he were searching for them.

"What do you mean you cannot recall? Have you lost them?" Kendra's shoulders slouched with the weight of his words. "Oh, Papa, what are we going to do? We need to find those coins because if we do not, I shall be forced to wed him." The anguish of her situation reached her throat and her words came heavily as if they choked her. It took all her will not to sob outright or pound the table in anger with all the force of her fist. Ire rose to her cheeks and heated them.

"Worry not, dearest. We will find them."

She despaired that if she couldn't find Heatherington's coins, she would have no choice but to marry the blighter. If there were enough coins in her father's coffer, she would use them to repay the knave, but their stores and wealth had dwindled to almost nonexistence.

Kendra had so much to worry about: their empty coffers, her father's failing health, and now, she had to worry about herself. No one was going to save her. She was doomed.

Thomas, the gate watchman, strode into the hall. When he reached the table, the tall soldier bowed. "My Lord, Mistress, this missive just came from the king. I thought it important enough to bring posthaste."

"Give it here, Thomas," she said and held out her hand. Kendra wasn't about to let her father receive such an important missive—from the king no less. Thomas placed it in her hand, bowed to her, and turned on his heel.

She called out to the guard before he could flee. "Await, Thomas. Did you witness Lord Heatherington here yestereve? Did you see him give my father coins?"

The guard shook his dark head. "Nay, Mistress, he didn't come when I was on duty. I will ask the other guards if they saw Heatherington."

"Please, do, and if they did, have them come to see me at once." The guard nodded to her and left. Kendra returned her attention to the missive and opened it. The king's words were brief but made her stomach clench. Had she just thought she was doomed? She hadn't expected things could get worse, but apparently they could. "Oh, nay, this cannot be."

"What does our fair king want, dearest?" Her father's muted blue eyes stared at her.

"He bids you to bring me to Edinburgh and that he intends to marry me to one of his followers. We are to leave at all due haste for the wedding which shall take place immediately." Kendra scrunched her eyes at the words that wavered before her eyes. The madness of the day was getting worse with each breath.

"Well, then, dearest, our troubles are solved. You won't have to marry Heatherington after all. We will leave to meet the king on the morrow." Her father stood and set his hand on her shoulder. "Worry not, fair lass, all will be well. I find I'm tired after my walk and will seek rest." He stood and left her without another word.

John, fortunately, had returned from the stables in time to escort her father to his solar. She nodded to him, and her shoulders eased, knowing his attendant would look after him for a while.

Kendra sighed heavily and muttered aloud, "My problems grow even more troublesome."

She went to her bedchamber to pack her belongings and as she did so, she realized that she wouldn't return home from the king's castle. With her father aging and ailing, she had to find a way to keep him with her.

Would her husband allow her father to remain with her? Lord, she hoped so.

With her brother away, there was no one else to care for her aged father but her. She wouldn't leave her beloved father unattended especially since her elder brother had hailed off to be in the English king's regiment of soldiers. Who knew how long he would be away and when or if he would return?

Being situated near the border, Aston, her elder brother, hoped to appease both kings to the north and south. Henry, King of England, continued to plague the Welsh and tried to overtake the lands to the west. Wales continued to thwart Henry, but now infused with more soldiers, England would soon make progress in their endeavor, she mused. Henry wouldn't cease his attacks until he gained the reward. Aston had professed that one day, they might need Henry's aid or approval especially since the border region changed hands from time to time. So Aston had joined the South in their war.

Kendra didn't much listen to the political news rife by the border. She had enough worries at home, keeping her father safe, avoiding Heatherington, and ensuring her family's manor didn't become insolvent or go to ruination. Her father overspent with little thought about where the coins were coming from or how they'd be replaced. Then their situation became even more dreadful when she had to sell off most of their property to find the necessary coins to pay the healers. The past year had been hard on her but she'd continued to search for a cure. Somehow, they would make do with the coins that remained which now might need to be used to repay Heatherington.

Kendra packed two valises full of her garments and belongings. Since it was unlikely that she'd return to her family's manor, she ensured she took anything that she cherished. On the chair by the window, she retrieved her mother's shawl. The soft, worn material eased her discontent when she pressed it to her face. She caressed her skin with it and swore she could still smell her mother's scent even though her mother had passed when she was no higher than a man's knees.

Little remembrances kept her mother alive. She had missed having a mother to confide in and there weren't many women within the keep that she befriended except for Linet and the manor's maidservant Gilda and in the village nearby, there weren't many women her age to make friends with, and those who lived close were too busy with the upkeep of their homes. Likewise, Kendra had too many duties keeping her busy to spend time entertaining. From sun up to sun down, she ensured their home was kept in order, kept her papa safe, organized the payment for goods, and oversaw the accounting of their fortune—or lack of fortune.

But that was all about to change. Who would take care of things now?

After she finished packing her belongings, she retreated to her father's bedchamber. Outside the doorway stood John, ensuring her father stayed within. "Lord Rupert is asleep, Mistress."

She bowed to him and set her hand on the latch. "Go on, John, and seek your bed. When I leave, I shall lock his door."

"Good night, Mistress," he said and bowed before leaving.

Kendra was saddened at the thought that she had to lock her father in his bedchamber at night. But it was for his safety and ever since he'd gone off in the middle of the night, they had to be sure that he stayed within. She always checked that the door was unlocked in the morning. So far, her papa was unaware of the lengths she went through to protect him.

After she entered, she grabbed a satchel and packed several tunics, tartans, and a light cloak for him. His snore startled her and she peered across the bedchamber. Kendra loved him and she was the only person who truly cared for him besides John. It was her duty to see that he was protected. With his ailment of failing memory, she worried. Was his time coming to an end? That thought had crossed her mind repeatedly the last few months and she'd gotten no answers from the many healers she'd hired.

When she finished his packing, she did a thorough search of his bedchamber for the coins. She searched the table where he attended to correspondence, the table beside the bed, the various trunks where he kept his belongings, even amongst his garments, and found nothing. She checked beneath his massive bed, behind the secret wall panel in his room he thought she wasn't aware of, and the small jeweled coffer that sat on the window ledge. Nothing. There were no coins to be found. Kendra sighed heavily. Where in God's name did he put them?

Quietly, she closed the door to his chamber, locked it, and hung the key on the hook next to the threshold. She went to the kitchens behind their home. Inside the small stone cottage, a good-sized worktable sat beside a hearth that took up one side of the room. On the other side, wooden shelves lined one wall to the other. On those shelves usually sat sacks of grain, and all the items needed to prepare meals for all those within the keep's walls. Their stores had diminished and hardly any sacks took up the shelving but soon the crofters would send more to replenish their stock once the crops grew and were harvested.

The manor's main maidservant and cook sat having her nightly brew. Gilda smiled widely when she saw her. Kendra was grateful to the woman because she worked tirelessly to keep them fed. Most of the servants had been let go when their coins dwindled and she was unable to feed extra mouths, but Gilda never complained regardless of what had been asked of her.

"'Tis a fine night this. Good eve, Mistress," she said and hurried to fill a cup for her. "Linet has turned in for the night if you needed her." After she set the cup in front of her, she pressed back the curly waves of her faded reddish hair and peered at her with inquisitive blue eyes. Nothing much got past Gilda. She probably already knew they would leave, but Kendra was disheartened to speak of it.

"Nay, I am about to turn in myself." Kendra sat for a moment and took a breath. It had been a day, the most hellish that she could remember. She raised her cup and took a small sip of the potent drink. Gilda made a brew that was made from herbs and other items—her secret recipe.

"How are you, Gilda? Do you need anything?" The woman was a godsend and was married to their steward. Both she and Norman were loyal and took care of them. What would she have done without them? It was down to their good grace that she and her father survived the past few months. Linet, too, had been invaluable and Kendra would probably have fallen apart if it wasn't for her support and friendship.

Gilda shook her head. "Oh, nay, nothing. Norman told me about your father going missing earlier. I took him a bite to eat for his supper and settled him with a goodly cup of brew."

"You are kind to us. My thanks. I just left Papa and he's sound asleep."

Kendra set the cup down, got up from the table and began rummaging through the kitchen stores to find things she could pack for the journey to Edinburgh. She packed two loaves of clapbread, wrapped several strips of salted venison, and a jug of cider in an oversized pouch used for such journeys that was kept by the stores.

"Are you going somewhere?" Gilda asked as she watched her from the table.

"On the morrow, Papa and I are leaving for Edinburgh. I shall not return and I am unsure when Papa will. Will you look after the keep whilst we are away?"

Gilda drew in a breath and rushed to stand near her. She patted her shoulder. "Oh, Mistress, I am saddened to see you go. Why will you not return?"

Kendra muttered the king's request. "I shall be married and will live with my husband. Aston likely will not return for some time. I'll speak to Thomas and shall have the guards close up most of the keep to prevent our home from being ravaged until my brother can return."

Gilda dabbed at her eyes. "I am happy to hear that you will marry, Mistress, but I shall miss you. Like a daughter, you are to me."

Speaking of daughters, Kendra needed to ask Gilda if she would allow hers to leave their keep. A wave of guilt washed over her at the thought, but she knew she'd be completely lost otherwise. "Would you mind terribly if I took Linet with me? If she agrees, that is."

"Try and keep her from going and I promise you, she'd be weeping for days. I am sure she will be pleased to attend you. I'll have her ready in the morning before you set out."

"My thanks, Gilda, for all that you have done for me...for us." Kendra bowed her head to the woman and hastily left the kitchen with the satchel of supplies in hand.

Tears gathered in her eyes at saying farewell to the kindly woman who had looked after her most of her life. Kendra pressed her eyes and sniffled her tears away. She wasn't usually a weeper and rarely cried but the sentiment of leaving those she loved, the home she cherished, and what she was familiar with, threatened to send her into hysterics.

As she passed the manor's entrance, she placed the satchel of foodstuff on a small bench just inside the doorway so she wouldn't forget it on the morrow.

Then there was one more chore to be done before she could seek her bed and that was meeting with Norman. She found him in the small workplace on the main floor of the manor. Atop his worktable sat jars of ink, a scatter of quills, and several volumes of the manor's expenses and income. Lately, the sums added were minimal and dismal. Their discussion was short-lived and expected. Norman handed her a small sack which held five coins.

"I fear that is all that remains, Mistress."

She firmed her lips, nodded, and returned the coins to him. "Keep them in case you need them for the manor. I doubt we shall need them at the king's castle. Whilst we are gone, you'll see to the crofters' payments. Do not threaten them though if they are unable to pay until after the harvest season. Safeguard the coins you receive and we'll figure out what to pay later. I will send a missive when I get to where I am going." Kendra didn't like the unknown but for now, she couldn't worry about it. Until she married whoever the king betrothed her to, she would make the best of the situation.

"Very well, Mistress. I'll look after the manor and will take care of things. Worry not."

"You are a good man, Master Norman. I thank you." Kendra knew the promissory notes were piling up and many were overdue. Somehow, she had to figure out how to pay the merchants. But that was a problem for another day. At present, she worried about Heatherington, her papa's ailment, and Dear Lord, the king's command that she marry.

After speaking with the guard and steward, she finally sought her bed. It was well after dark and she was overtired and overwrought. In bed, she tossed and turned, plagued with the thoughts of who her new husband might be. She hoped to find a little happiness and solace in her new life. What she wouldn't do for a little peace.

CHAPTER THREE

MAGNUS WAS MISERABLE and discontented. The trek to Edinburgh was hampered by spring rains that dampened his tartan. By the time he reached the gates to Edinburgh Castle, he was soddened through and somewhat cross. The weight of his vow to avenge his brother and the gloomy dismal rain dampened his spirit and temperment. He was in no mood to attend to whatever duty the king required of him, entertain his sovereign, or participate in the revelry that would keep him from his sacred duty.

He'd only brought Winston, his attendant, with him. With the death of his brother, he thought it best to leave his soldiers home protecting his fief and clan. Until he learned the truth behind the treachery, he would be cautious. Now he rode up a small rise, which took him between two tall stone turrets and through a gatehouse. At the gate's entrance, Magnus dismounted, removed his satchel, and waited for Winston to take the reins of his horse.

"I will await you in the stables, Laird. If ye need me, just have someone fetch me."

He nodded to his attendant and said to the guard by the castle's entrance, "The king has called for me. Magnus, Laird Cameron."

At once, he was led inside. His boots muddied the entrance of the castle as he followed the escort. He was met by the king's chamberlain, a burly man who was overzealous in his greeting and demeanor. "I am Edmund, the king's manservant. Welcome, Laird Cameron, we are excited to have you here. The king will be pleased that you have finally arrived. He is expecting you. Follow me and I will take you to Alexander." Edmund led him through the hallways to the king's private chamber and knocked at the door. "His Grace should be within."

Someone inside the chamber called "entrance" and the chamberlain opened the door, waving him forward. Magnus noticed the page who stood alone beside a great chair near a table, but the king was not in evidence.

"I will find Alexander and let him know you are here. Take rest from your travel." Edmund twitched a finger at the page who scurried forth and poured him a cup of ale.

Magnus took the drink from the page and settled into a chair facing the plush seat by the table. He suspected that was where the king sat and no others partook of its comfort or the authority it imparted. The king's chamber was otherwise sparsely furnished, except for some chairs and tables situated around the small area. A window with a view to the courtyard took up one wall and the others had tapestries hanging from the ceiling.

Edmund left hastily and Magnus leaned back in wait for the king.

Many moments passed and he enjoyed the solitude of the chamber which left him to his thoughts—the many that pressed him. He was able to shake off the cross attitude he'd picked up on the way to meet with Alexander and wasn't filled with such angst.

A door creaked and his eyes shot to a wall panel where the king made his entrance. Magnus rose, bowed, and stood awaiting the king's greeting. "Sire…"

Alexander crossed the chamber with a quick stride. He waved off the page who awaited his command and poured himself a cup of ale. The king appeared weary and rubbed his hands over the red hairs of his beard and then flapped his hands at the page. "Be gone."

The page left with a bang of the door.

Silence overtook the chamber as Magnus surveyed the king's mood. Alexander ignored him as he set his cup to his mouth and drank deeply before finally setting the cup on the table. Then he thumped down in the overstuffed chair across from him. Magnus's curiosity was piqued but he wasn't about to question his overlord before being given leave to do so. He had to remain patient and wait for Alexander to tell him what he wanted from him—a feat to be sure, since he wanted to find out what was so dire he needed to arrive so quickly, and hopefully then, he could be on his way.

The king waved a hand at him. "Cameron, I am pleased you came hastily. Sit down." He considered Magnus thoughtfully. "I heard about the passing of your brother. You have our sympathies, mine and Margaret's."

By now word of his brother's death had probably reached the border of Scotland. Magnus bowed his head to his sovereign and retook his seat. "My thanks, Sire."

"I expect you are needed at home, but this could not wait. I have asked you here this day because..." Alexander appeared to hesitate. "I mean to unite the lands of Scotland's Low and Highlands. 'Tis time to put our beloved Scotland to the test and take the lands held by Norway. I mean to see our borders extended to the very north and west, with your aid."

Magnus remained silent as he listened to the king's rambling.

"The first step in my plan is to unite northern and southern clans. I want you to take a wife from the border region. With Scotland united, the overtaking of Haakon's lands will come easier. With the arms of our brethren, we will face Haakon's fleet of men easily and extend our borders."

He tried not to scowl at what Alexander had just told and asked of him. His king wanted him to marry. Magnus hadn't considered such a request but before he could reject the king's offer, Alexander cleared his throat and leaned forward.

He continued in a softer tone, "I confess, there are benefits to your marriage. For one thing, you will reap the tithe on your land for one full year and I will forgo your land's tax. Additionally, you will find yourself married to one of our most bonny lassies. With that, I will give you the ability to choose your bride. All you must do is defeat by way of hand-to-hand combat the other grooms."

As Alexander continued to ramble, Magnus's frown furrowed his brow even further and he felt the pull of it between his eyes. The shock of his king's request nearly forced his mouth to hang open, but he held firm.

"Other grooms?" he asked with a little animosity in his tone.

"Aye, I have asked the same of Lairds MacKendrick, Buchanan, and Mackintosh. With these marriages, I hope not only to unite the clans but also to bring about peace in the northern region. I'm aware of your discord with the Chattans."

Magnus grunted. "Aye, still they pester us with minor scuffles."

"This is your opportunity to win over the Mackintoshes to your side. That they sit betwixt your lands, the Mackintoshes have made a complaint that they have suffered from the affray betwixt your clans. I mean to see an end to your discord."

"Ye know, Sire, that Clan Cameron supports ye and supported your father as well. The Chattans give ye no loyalty. I expect our strife to rise and there might be a possible war betwixt us. *Och*, I will not allow the Chattans to take a single trace of my land." He hadn't meant to put such vehemence in his tone, but that couldn't be helped.

Alexander nodded. "I have heard of the discord. If you need my support when the time comes, you have only to ask. The Chattans have made it known they do not support me and I have yet to deal with them. Rest assured, they will be dealt with."

"I trust not the Mackintoshes because they're aligned with the Chattans."

"Aye, still, the matter will be put aside for now," Alexander said.

He studied the king's manner and although Alexander was a young king, he still had two years before he'd reach an age where he could fully take the crown. Presently, he ruled the kingdom with the aid of advisors and a large council. Magnus wanted to stress the urgency of dealing with the Chattans, but it would come off sounding more like a plea and he wasn't about to beg the king for aid. His soldiers were capable of handling the Chattans for now.

Magnus sighed deeply and had no words to rebuff what the king told and asked of him. He wanted to refute the marriage and all the trappings of giving his accord to his king, but he was in no position to do so. The king had his support regardless of what he'd asked of him.

He changed his expression to one of acceptance and jested with Alexander. "Who are these brides? Are they worth accepting or are they hags who ye seek to be rid of?"

Alexander slapped his knee and bellowed a laugh. "You see, I told my chancellor that of the four of you lairds, you, Magnus, were the most agreeable. The brides are from the Forrester, Graham, d'Avranches, and Scott families. They are the most winsome women within the land and rival the queen's beauty, if such a thing is possible."

Now the king jested. Though Queen Margaret was somewhat bonny in her body shape, she was dull in her appearance. Definitely not the fairest lass in the land, at least, not in Magnus's opinion, but he wasn't about to say so. "When will these marriages take place?" Magnus hoped he had time to return home so he might find his brother's murderer and perhaps return when he had more time to deal with the king's request.

"Within the sennight. You will stay here in the castle and a few days hence, we will have a gathering. There will be a feast where you shall meet the lasses and perhaps get to know them before you must choose one of them. The following day, the battles will commence and the brides chosen. The marriages will take place immediately because I am soon to take my leave of

Edinburgh."

"Ah, the reason for the haste. Ye are leaving Edinburgh, Sire?"

"Aye, for I must. I promised my wife that I would take her to England to see her family. She wishes to have our bairn there."

Magnus grunted at that. The king didn't seem pleased at having to visit England. Hell, no one from Scotland wanted to step foot on English soil, let alone visit for a time. He had heard of the king's disagreements with Henry, the King of England, Margaret's father, had simmered but there seemed to be peace amongst them. Magnus didn't envy his sovereign's inlaw but the king must have settled his troubles with Henry since he was taking his wife for a visit.

"*Slàinte*, Sire, on the forthcoming birth of your bairn."

Alexander nodded at his cheers to his news. "Aye, I need an heir and hopefully my wife will do her duty. Now that I have your accord, we should discuss the details further."

Magnus was no fool; he could tell there was something the king wasn't telling him. Alexander averted his gaze. "Your war with Norway… How do ye want our involvement?"

The king chuckled. "Well now, I will likely need foot soldiers, many, for Haakon, once he learns of my plan, will send his army to defend his lands. We will need many boots to keep those lands from him. I deem Haakon doesn't deserve to keep his lands for he is more interested in religious matters than that of his countrymen who are left to their own, way up in the north."

Magnus heard Haakon had left the mainland and absconded back to Norway. He hadn't returned and yet his fleet of ships continued to control the northern coastal routes. Magnus hadn't given his allegiance to Haakon but supported the Scots in recent years. If his king needed his arms, he wouldn't deny him.

"Aye, I will give you additional men for your cause, but there's no need for a marriage. 'Tis the truth, Sire, I have no time to attend to a wife and only recently became the laird of my clan. I thought to marry someday, but presently, I am more concerned for my clan's safety and finding out who murdered my brother."

Alexander stared hard at him. "I understand you have much on your young shoulders, yet who does not? We all have duties but still maintain relations with our wives. Appease me, Cameron, for I want my clans united and the only way to do that is through marriage. You will wed one of the chosen lassies and I shall hear no rebuke. I will have your agreement now." The king's tone rose slightly and it was hard to argue with his authority.

Magnus gripped his knees, grimacing deeply at having to concede. "I can do naught but agree then. Of course, I graciously accept your offer, Sire."

The king shot to his feet. "Good. Then there is much to celebrate. You will not be disappointed, Cameron, with your bride. I promise you that. I will have you taken to a chamber where you can rest from your travels."

Magnus grunted. Until he sought vengeance for his brother's death, he would not celebrate his marriage. The woman was nothing but a means to placate his king—nothing more.

CHAPTER FOUR

THE JOURNEY TO the king's castle finally ended just before the sun sunk low in the sky. Weary from riding in the rain and stopping little to rest wore Kendra out. Her father appeared confused as they approached the castle. Likely, he had forgotten again where they traveled to and why. She leaned to the side and patted his hand in the hope of settling him. Twice on the trek, her father asked where they were going. Kendra repeatedly told him that the king called for their attendance and that she would soon be married.

There seemed to be a good many people at the castle. As she rode through the two towers that flanked the gates, she noticed the many men about and the number of horses that were placed in a makeshift corral near the entrance.

Kendra slid from her horse's back and stood near her father as he dismounted his horse. John and Linet retrieved their baggage as they waited for someone to come forward. John wouldn't let her maid carry the heavy baggage and held four satchels whilst Linet held the satchel with the remaining foodstuff and her own.

A man greeted them with a wide smile. "Welcome, welcome. I am our great king's chamberlain, Edmund." The robust man smiled. "Come this way and tell me who you be."

"Good day, Sir. I am Kendra and this is my father, Lord Rupert Graham." She bowed to him and waited for his direction.

"Mistress Kendra, we are pleased you are finally here. Come, we shall have you taken to a chamber where you can make ready for the night's festivities. There is no time to dally. No time at all."

He walked quickly and she followed the man inside the castle. Along the tapestry-covered hallways and lavishly furnished passageways, she kept silent. Her father held on to her arm and now patted her hand in his attempt to soothe her. He always could tell when she was riled. Kendra's shoulders tensed and her stomach was in a taut knot. Until now, she had avoided the king's court, although from what she heard, the queen often entertained, much to the king's disgruntlement. Fortunately, her father rarely visited Edinburgh, Parliament, or the king himself. In recent years, he tended to stay at their manor. In his weakened state, she was gladdened he hadn't traveled much.

At a chamber, the chamberlain opened the door. "You are fortunate to have arrived in time, Mistress. I was about to send out the sentry to hurry you along, hoping you were on the road here. There is not much time to rest, I am afraid, because the king will soon meet with everyone. He has stated that he will have a private audience with all before the night's festivity. I shall await here while you ready and then take you to his private room. Make haste."

"All? Who else is the king meeting with?" she asked becoming confused at the purpose of her wedding.

"Our king is marrying off several of the ladies from Scotland's border region. Amongst you, there are three others. This night, there will be a feast and you shall meet the other lassies and the men. Now hurry, because no one keeps the king waiting."

Once the door was closed, she rushed behind a screen and changed out of her damp overdress. Fortunately, she had brought a few of her more acceptable gowns. Linet handed her a gown and asked John to help her father get ready. Kendra took little time to change and wash. Her hair was a mess and there was nothing she could do about it except pull half of it back and tie it with a ribbon.

When she finished, she despaired about what she would do with her father while she attended to the king. He had to appear with her and she vowed to keep an eye on him. But John would also attend and that relieved her somewhat.

"I shall stay here and unpack and ready the chamber for sleep. Go on," Linet said.

"Very well, Linet. Hopefully, we are not overlong. Papa needs his rest. If I can, I'll send him along earlier in the evening."

Within minutes, she opened the door and they followed the chamberlain to a room near the great hall. Inside, she met the gazes of the other women and men whom she assumed were the other brides and grooms. She hoped her expression didn't show her regard for the Highlanders. Kendra swallowed hard at the thought that they, she and the other women, were to marry the obstinate-looking men.

She found a vacant chair in which she settled her father. "Papa, stay here with John. Do not move from this chair and do not leave this room." She looked at her father's attendant and he understood her direction.

Her father nodded and another servant hastened forward and gave him a drink. She refused the drink that he likewise offered to her.

Kendra moved across the chamber and stood near the other women. She recognized one of the women, Isabella of the Forrester Clan, whose family lands bordered her clan's property. She had met the woman on occasion in the village when she visited the merchant stalls. The woman stood alone, a little ways from where she and the other women waited. Kendra bowed her head to the women and smiled.

Her gaze slid again to the men who stood with them awaiting the king. They were attractive, strong-looking, and were most fierce in their stances with their arms at their sides and their legs braced. It was as if they were prepared for a fight. The men's faces, though grim, were also handsome. Gracious Lord, she was to marry one of them. Her cheeks heated but she withstood the urge to fan herself.

A thud sounded and the king and queen entered the chamber. The side door slammed shut behind them. Alexander stopped near the men and spoke to them briefly, although she couldn't hear what he said. The queen fell in behind him and they walked toward the dais. Margaret was richly garbed and appeared beautiful, as well as a queen should be. Alexander, King of the Scots, was a striking figure, and yet nowhere near compared to the Highlanders with their dangerous manner. Even so, there seemed to be a bit of nobility about the men with their staid gazes and haughty demeanor.

Kendra waited for the king to speak as did everyone in the hall. The silence of the chamber gave the atmosphere a certain apprehension. She shared a glance with a pretty woman who stood near her.

The king cleared his throat before speaking. "This is a day of import, and I am pleased to see you here. This evening, we shall have a feast with dancing and merriment. I will give you this time to greet each other and become familiar. Before the night ends, the selections will be discussed and finalized on the morrow. I bid you now to eat and drink."

She took a glance to ensure that her father remained in the chair she'd put him in. He sat beside another older man and they conversed. John remained ever watchful behind him.

Kendra hadn't felt so awkward in such a long time. She wasn't coy but she wasn't outspoken either. In waiting for the men to make their introductions, she lingered by the lovely lady next to her and they glanced at each other again.

"I have not met you before. I am Sorsha d'Avranches."

Kendra dipped her chin. "I'm pleased to meet you, Mistress d'Avranches. I am Kendra of Clan Graham."

The woman smiled and it reached her eyes. "Sorsha, please. I used to be Lady Chattan. Are you as delighted as I am to have been chosen by the king?"

"I suppose I am," Kendra said and hadn't spoken falsely. Although the choice of groom daunted her, at least now she didn't have to marry Heatherington. She offered up a quick prayer that whomever she married was noble and kind. The last thing she wanted was to end up with a man akin to her odious neighbor.

"We should go and greet the men." Sorsha set off, leaving her alone.

Queen Margaret approached and Kendra curtseyed low until the queen spoke, "Mistress Kendra, attend me. I have heard that you are a spirited woman from some of my courtiers and I should like to get to know you."

Kendra waited a moment before rising with a smile fastened on her face and then kept her gaze on the queen's plainly adorned head. Margaret wore a simple wimple fastened with a band of gold over her brown hair. "My Lady, I am…" She didn't know what to say. "…am humbled and pleased to be here."

Margaret tucked her arm with hers and pulled her to follow. "Walk with me about the chamber so we might speak in private."

She did as the queen requested and kept her gaze on the floor as she walked. Kendra didn't want to step on the queen's toes, or God forbid, trip her. Laughter and voices rose around them.

"You look beautiful, Mistress Kendra, with your golden hair, and I am certain you have already caught the eyes of many of the grooms. Have you selected the man you wish to wed?"

Kendra shook her head. How could she make such a choice when she had yet to speak to any of them? "Nay, I shall speak to them and hopefully influence the man I wish to—"

"Do you see that man there," the queen said cutting her off, as she pointed to a tall, dark-haired man. "That is Laird Cameron. 'Magnus' to his friends. He is a reserved man and speaks little but he's a favorite of mine and it distresses me that he is so serious. He claims that he has no time for frivolities. The man has many burdens on his shoulders as the newly proclaimed laird of his clan. I deem he needs some joy in his life and a vivacious woman to appease him. Are you up for such a challenge?"

"If my lady wishes it so, then aye, I am up for the challenge." Kendra wasn't sure what the queen wanted of her but she wasn't about to gainsay or deny her.

"If you make him smile before this night is through, then he shall be yours."

"Mine? But is not the choice his? The king said—"

"He *did* say that," she said cutting her off once again. Margaret laughed, her light snicker drew the attention of her husband. "Oh, but it is the Highlanders' choice. Nevertheless, we women have a way of getting what we want in the end and influencing such matters. Do we not?"

Kendra nodded quickly at the queen's supposition. "I shall do my best, My Lady, to make him smile."

"Go then and greet him. I shall be watching. Remember, just one smile, Mistress Kendra, and he is yours for the taking." Margaret dislodged her arm from hers and waved her forward.

Kendra was about to cross the gleaming floorboards to approach Laird Cameron, but then the double-wide doors suddenly burst open. Servants bustled about the adjacent room and she stood in awe of the great hall's splendor. Three large candelabras held enough candles to send a glow to the far reaches of the room. Foodstuff in trenchers, baskets, and trays lined the table and the scent of freshly baked bread and roasted meat filled the air. She whirled around at the sound of music when the first strings of a harpist began playing.

Never had she been at such a feast. Her father had never had the wherewithal to pay for such a lavish event at their manor home and most of the festivals and holy days were spent in Dunbartan's village. Now there were a good number of people moving about the chamber: servants, family, the king's attendants, the brides, and the grooms. Kendra felt out of place but she kept her eyes on Laird Cameron and considered how best to approach him. In truth, she wished she could fan herself because, honest to God, all the Highlanders were intimidating with their good looks, hard manners, and steely bodies.

Before she could intercept Laird Cameron, a man with light brown hair that reached his shoulders approached. Her breath caught a little at the sight of him. He was extremely handsome, with a lean but muscular body.

"Mistress," he said and bowed his head. "I am Laird Mackintosh. 'Shaw' to my friends."

"Laird Mackintosh," she said and bowed. "Shaw." He had a charming disposition about him and his smile surely could melt a woman's heart. "I am Kendra of Clan Graham. Are you enjoying the king's festivities?"

He nodded. "'Tis the truth, I would rather be home but *och*, at least ye ladies are pleasing on the eyes and I am not put off from taking one of ye as my wife."

At that moment, Sorsha drew near. She deftly distracted Laird Mackintosh from attending to Kendra and in a moment they joined the dancers on the floor.

Kendra moved to greet Laird MacKendrick, but he seemed so formidable that she absconded just as quickly and went to meet another of the grooms, waiting for him to finish his conversation while keeping her eye on Laird Cameron. Somehow, she had to figure out how best to fulfill the queen's request to make him smile—or even meet him—but he had yet to make eye-contact or even glance at her.

Through the open doors of the great hall, she glanced around to locate her father to make certain he'd stayed where she had put him. A slight panic overtook her when she noticed that he was gone from his seat. Before she could move off to find him, another man appeared to notice her and approached.

"Mistress Kendra," he said as if he'd already been introduced to her, and bowed. "I am Breckin...Laird Buchanan."

"Laird Buchanan, it is a pleasure to meet you." Although she wanted to run off to find her father, she had to greet the man to maintain politeness. She lowered her chin and took a breath as she curtseyed. Buchanan was far more intimidating than the rest of the men with his piercing blue-eyed gaze and broad shoulders.

Kendra found herself stepping back, just to put a little space between them.

"Do ye wish to dance?" I fear I might step on your toes, but the king insists we join in."

"Oh, I am sorry, Laird Buchanan, but I must go..." She grabbed her skirts and lifted them a little so she wouldn't trip and hastened away. Her gaze shifted from one end of the large hall to the other in search of her father. Where was John? He was supposed to be looking after him. A terrible pain twitched her stomach at the thought that he'd gone off again. How would she ever find him in an unfamiliar and extensive castle?

As she roamed the large hall, her eyes darted to the corners and beyond. Finally, she spotted him, lingering behind the buttery with John next to him, and with a great sigh of relief, she approached and took his arm. "Papa, I told you not to leave your seat. Come, and sit back down. Let John get your drink. John make sure he stays at the table, please." She led her father back to the table and gently pushed him into the seat when they reached it. John hastened after them and set a cup before her father.

"I was but refilling my drink, Dearest."

"Let John attend to you. Now, promise me, Papa, that you will not move from this spot. I do not need to worry for you when I have other..." Her words trailed off when her father nodded vigorously.

"I will not move," he said and lifted the cup of ale John had fetched for him.

Kendra searched amongst the revelers and found Laird Cameron. He stood out as he was taller than most of the men and she walked toward him. When she reached him, she turned to face the center of the room. "Good eve, My Lord."

He bowed his head but kept his eyes on the room. Kendra drew a slow steady breath and was disheartened that he wouldn't even look at her. Gaining his interest would take more thought and courage on her part.

A servant passed by them and offered a drink. The Highlander shook his head.

"Are you not thirsty?" she asked, making small talk.

"'Tis naught but watered-down ale."

Kendra smiled at the sound of his voice. It was rugged, deep, and affecting. The timbre of it was a little raspy and manly, yet appealing. He didn't smile but turned his head and finally gazed at her as she asked, "Perhaps you prefer a stronger drink?"

"A strong ale would be preferable, but I doubt there is any to be had."

She peered up at him. His height put him well over a head taller than her. Like the other men, he was muscular and strong. But he was definitely more pleasing to look upon than Lord Heatherington or the other men who were offered as grooms. In truth, he was probably the most handsome man she'd ever beheld. His light greenish-brown eyes remained on her. The slight frown he wore and the tightness of his lips on his whisker-free face framed by long, thick brown made him appear stern and somewhat intimidating. He rubbed the nape of his neck with his large hand as if he was restless.

Kendra folded her hands in front of her and tried to appear demure and unaffected—a most difficult thing to do in front of this man. "Is that a challenge, My Lord?"

"Laird Cameron," he said with a genuflect, "'Magnus' to ye, lass. And aye, perhaps it is a challenge. If ye find me a good strong cup of ale, I will offer ye my favor."

"I am Kendra, daughter of Rupert Graham. If I find you a cup of strong ale, will you dance with me?" She raised her eyes to regard his mesmerizing greenish-brown and lingering stare.

"I would—"

She didn't give him time to finish his words. "Await me then and I shall return." Kendra rushed from the hall and stood outside the door. In the long hallway that led to the exit of the keep, she peered about for a servant but saw the chamberlain walking toward her. *Excellent.* Just the man she needed.

Edmund stopped before her. "Mistress, are you in need of

aid?"

"Sir, I hope you can help me." Kendra curtseyed to him and smiled.

He bowed in return. "Aye, Mistress, I am at your service. What do you need?"

"I need a cup of good, strong ale. Not for me, you see, but for one of the grooms. He says the hall's ale is weak and I promised to bring him a cup of strong ale." She rambled her explanation.

"Let me see what I can find, Mistress. Await here."

The chamberlain set off and she lingered by the hall's entrance. Time seemed to drag while she waited for his return. Kendra paced the hallway and studied a tapestry that spanned the wall. She noted several missed stitches in the battle scene which didn't appeal to her at all. Noise from the hall drew her regard because she was uncertain if her plan would work. She hoped that she didn't miss the opportunity to impress Laird Cameron.

Finally, the chamberlain returned with a cup on a small tray. "Mistress," he said and held the tray out to her. "'Tis from the king's private barrel of ale, much stronger than what the kitchen serves."

"You are a godsend, Chamberlain Edmund." He blushed at her compliment. Kendra took the cup and thanked him. She entered the great hall and marched to Laird Cameron. With little fuss, she handed him the drink. "I believe this ale is stronger than what is being served. It's from the king's personal barrel."

He peered at her with disbelief. Laird Cameron took the cup, sipped the drink, then downed it, and nodded to her. "This is much tastier than that swill they are handing out. I believe ye met my challenge, Mistress Kendra. Shall we dance?" He set his empty cup on a nearby table and took her hand.

The touch of his hard manly hand brought her eyes to his. She lightly gripped him, but his hold was gentle and not at all as strong as it could be. The chords of the music started and a new song began. It was a softer, slower tune. She faced Laird Cameron and smiled. He had yet to smile at her but at least he was no longer scowling.

They began the dance and she rounded him, moving her feet to the steps of the melodic sounds around her. They shuffled toward each other, setting their palms in each other's hands, and reverted around each other in the spatial pattern of the dance. Touching his hands drew her gaze to his eyes again. She'd never seen such a becoming shade. They weren't green nor brown but a rich shade that blended the tones.

His skin was warm, rough, and yet, the contact was tender.

Unbeknownst to her, behind her, an older man danced with his wife. His movements were rather unskilled and chaotic, and his leg stuck out. Kendra stepped back and the man tripped her. She went flying in the direction of Laird Cameron. He caught her and held her close, his nose almost touching hers, his lips but a breath away. His touch and the way he held her lightened her heart and spurred her trust in him, trust mingled with a passion she'd never felt for anyone before. It swirled through her. Kendra couldn't take her eyes from his.

The music came to an abrupt stop and all gaped at them. Kendra's face heated at being the focus of everyone in the chamber. Magnus's scowl could have felled the poor older man who had tripped her, but then he returned his eyes to hers and his frown lessened. "Lass, I believe ye are falling for me," he said almost with a humorous lilt.

The music began once again and all those around them returned to their partners. Kendra gasped and he helped her to straighten to her feet but continued to hold her in his arms. He made no move to right her or release her. His strong hands held her waist and he peered at her with such a smoldering gaze, that a warmth rose to her chest. "Perhaps I am, Laird Cameron. Maybe I can get you to fall for me too."

"Is that a challenge, Mistress Kendra?"

She couldn't hold back her smile. "I do believe it is, Laird Cameron."

Laird Magnus Cameron's laugh reverberated in the room and

was heard by all, even over the soft sounds of the harpist's music. The queen watched them with a smile and she bowed her head to her. Kendra had just chosen her future husband and she wasn't displeased by it at all.

CHAPTER FIVE

T HE GLOOMY MORNING was spent trying to allay her father's emotions. He threw fits over the food he was served for his morning fare and stated that he knew not where he was, or who she was, for that matter. It took a great deal of coercion to get him to calm down and to keep her tears at bay. It was so unlike her father to behave so irrationally and that troubled her. He was getting worse. Not only did he have moments of forgetfulness, but now he appeared to be so unlike the gentle, sweet-natured man, she knew him to be.

With the rain lessening to a drizzle, John suggested a good walk would do wonders to ease her father's discontent. John helped her to settle him and they now walked about the grounds around the castle. That gave Kendra time to make ready for the day's activities—the day of her wedding to a Highlander. As if she didn't have enough trepidation in her heart.

Linet helped her to dress and chose her favorite frock. The light-blue linen gown with flowing sleeves wasn't too cumbersome. She wrapped her neck in an ornate leather strap and set a matching one around her upper arm. Instead of putting her hair beneath a wimple, Linet parted it in the middle, braided it, and wrapped it into a coif to which she tied with another thin piece of leather.

"'Tis your wedding day, Mistress, and you should look your

best." Linet fussed over her and she loved her for it.

"Linet, please… How many times must I tell you to call me Kendra? We are friends and even though you take care of me, I don't want you to be so formal."

"Whilst we are here in the king's castle, Mistress, we shall maintain…" Linet finished her hair and patted the blond coif. "…a demeanor beholding your station."

"Very well, but it hurts my ears to hear you call me 'mistress'." Her nerves had gotten the better of her not only because she dealt with her father's outbursts, but also because she would be bound to a man this day. She'd eaten little fare and paced the chamber they stayed in, until a knock on the door jarred her from her ruminations and caused her to jump off the floor.

"My but you are jittery this day. I cannot imagine why…you are only getting married." Linet teased her. "Go on, Mistress, I shall gather our belongings and tidy up the chamber."

"Pray for me, Linet, because I am going to need it."

Her dear friend smiled and pulled her into an embrace. "You shall be well. Worry not." Linet turned her, took her shoulders, and guided her to the door. "Any of those handsome Highlanders would do well for a husband and they'll be fortunate if they get to choose you. Now, put a smile on your face, be brave, and try to appear winsome."

Kendra snorted a laugh. "How is it you always make me feel not so distressed?" She reached the door and ambled through it. Along the way to the outside where the bouts would take place, she met up with the other ladies offered as brides.

She was hopeful that her choice of husband would win the brawl that day. If she had to choose one of the Highlanders for her husband, she hoped Laird Cameron would win her hand. Not only was he handsome, but his demeanor well suited her. He had a seriousness about him but she'd noted the edges of his mouth moving when he tried not to smile. The queen had challenged her to make him smile, but she'd done more than that—she made him laugh.

His laughter lightened her and she sensed that Magnus rarely showed that side of himself to anyone. She'd brought out a mirthful sense in him, a lighthearted mien. Ever since, she'd found herself smiling too, for no good reason but the memory of their encounter.

The rain had ceased and the small puddles all but dried now on the walkways. She stood with the small crowd of people awaiting the second brawl of the day. The first fracas seemed to go quickly and was but a blur to her. MacKendrick and Mackintosh fought almost brutally in their attempt to win the first choice of bride. Kendra winced quite a few times as she watched. How wretched it was to witness two grown men fighting. Even though to her it was most barbaric, those around her cheered with enthusiasm. The cheers and jeers alluded to the fact that most thought Mackintosh hadn't given his all in the fight. MacKendrick easily won and chose Lady Isabella as his bride.

Edmund, the chamberlain, bellowed, "The draw for the next bout has taken place. Those fighting are to be Cameron and Mackintosh, and shall commence shortly."

As Kendra waited for the announcement of Magnus's fight with Laird Mackintosh to begin, she watched Magnus who stood afar from her. He appeared impatient and paced before the marked square where the fighting took place. Mackintosh stood a short distance away and he kept glancing at her. Lord, she hoped he didn't want to choose her. Shaw was most charming, but Kendra admitted Magnus had more appeal. Magnus seemed to be studying his opponent too. Shaw wore the marks from the first brawl and she hoped that he was too tired from fighting with MacKendrick to win the battle with Magnus.

Queen Margaret, with her small entourage, walked toward Shaw. Kendra kept her gaze fixed on them because it appeared the queen was having a private discussion with him. When Margaret walked away, Shaw marched off in a different direction and looked angry. In fact, his stride was almost furious.

Margaret glided regally toward her and when she reached

her, she stood next to her and faced the Highlanders. Kendra curtseyed to her and tipped her chin. "Good day, My Lady."

The queen shielded her mouth with her hand and spoke low, "Laird Cameron, my good friend, is ready to fight for his woman." Margaret's smile widened. She tapped her arm and turned her head. "There is no doubt that he shall win. I asked him if you were to his liking and I gained his promise that he would choose you."

Kendra's body stiffened with both excitement and trepidation at the woman's words. "I thank you, My Lady, for your benevolence." She couldn't believe the queen's audacity, but then she found herself wanting to smile. Who but Margaret would insert her wishes upon them? "What if he chooses another just to spite me?"

Margaret snickered. "Magnus knows better than to incite my wrath."

"I certainly hope so, My Lady," she retorted and laughed lightly. Kendra found the queen's trickery amusing and she supposed Margaret would find a way to get what she wanted. Fortunately for Kendra that was her hand in marriage to Magnus.

The horns sounded and the call for the brawl was made by the king's chamberlain. She bowed to the queen who set off to join her husband on the dais.

Magnus made his way to the center and faced Shaw.

Kendra joined the other ladies who gathered on the far side of the square. Sorsha linked her arm with hers. She set her hand on her forearm because the lady was just as tense as she was.

Sorsha whispered, "Do you know that they have known each other most of their lives? Their clans are close in proximity but they're not in an alliance. They usually keep out of each other's way."

"It sounds as if you know them well." Kendra leaned her head closer when she spoke.

"My husband was a comrade of Shaw's and I know him very well. I haven't been in Magnus's company much but I tell you both will want to win this fight. A Highlander never wants to lose. It appears Magnus is in a fighting mood this day."

Kendra wondered why Lady Sorsha was offered as a bride and what had happened to her husband. She couldn't be forward by asking, and instead, she turned her gaze to Magnus. "I hope they do not kill each other because not only am I fond of Magnus, but Shaw is a charming man who doesn't deserve to be thrashed."

Sorsha nodded. "Very true. This fight will impact us both for I've heard the queen wishes we wed them. I wouldn't be disappointed with either of them as a husband. We shall see what happens."

She didn't know what the woman meant, but wouldn't ask. Who did Sorsha want to win? Had she hoped Magnus won so he would choose her? Kendra wasn't about to tell her that the queen had taken the glory from the fight. Now if only Magnus won and chose her as the queen predicted.

Alexander stood on the dais and when all silenced, he bellowed, "The second battle will commence. Those fighting are Cameron and Mackintosh. I remind you, there are to be no weapons but hand-to-hand combat only. You will fight in the square to the finish. If you step out of the square for any reason, you shall be declared the loser. If you falter and call a truce, you will forfeit the fight. The winner of the match will choose his bride." The king backed up and waited for the chamberlain to signal to the troubadour.

Kendra's breath ceased in her throat when the two men met in the center of the square. They both appeared formidable in their tunics and tartans, were brawny, and stood as tall as each other. If either of them held their swords, she'd probably be of a fainter heart. Still, her hands trembled and a rush of panic rose within her. She was near enough to hear them.

"Shaw," Magnus said, greeting his rival. "Let us make a good showing."

"Magnus." Shaw chuckled and said, "I hope ye are ready to be flounced. You'll wear a few bruises before I am through with ye."

The horn blew and Magnus charged at Shaw. He tried to grab him, but Shaw was quick on his feet and eluded him. Magnus circled Shaw and threw the first punch. The sound of his fist hitting Shaw's face made her flinch. Shaw retaliated and struck Magnus several times before he was able to shove him away. Magnus growled and scrambled forward. His fist made contact with Shaw repeatedly and he grunted. Magnus's face reddened from Shaw's retaliatory strikes. The crowd cheered but Kendra couldn't make a sound. Her throat had gone completely dry but her eyes watered and shimmered with tears. She wanted to weep at the cruelty of it but somehow maintained her decorum.

Shaw wasn't about to give up easily and continued to bait Magnus. Both now had blood on their faces from cuts on their noses, lips, and chins. The rest of the fight was a blur to her because they wrestled, threw punches, tripped, kicked, and flipped each other within every space of the square. The crowd appeared pleased by the fanatical and passionate way the men fought. Most shouted in glee when a strike rendered an opponent to sway on his feet.

Magnus licked at his bloody lip and seemed to grow tired of the fight. He marched to Shaw and threw his arm out. His fist settled in the center of Shaw's face and when he drew back, Magnus shouted an expletive. He flexed his hand and shook it. Shaw laughed but then fell to his knees. He tried to stand but he was a wee bit shaky. Magnus took the opportunity to end it and punched him again. Shaw landed on his backside and promptly fell back and groaned. He lay there with his eyes closed, and yet, Magnus's opponent wore a smile on his face. Magnus frowned at the man.

Kendra's heart clashed in her chest. The fight was brutal and she felt every punch in the pit of her stomach. Why in heaven's name was Shaw smiling? Magnus had beaten him, but she suspected Shaw hadn't given his all. Instead, it was as if Shaw cared not that he lost. Had the queen told him to lose on purpose? Margaret alluded to that fact, but Kendra couldn't believe Shaw would so easily allow his opponent to win.

The horn sounded and the chamberlain announced the end of the bout. Magnus waited by Shaw and when his opponent opened his eyes, he threw his hand down to help him up. Kendra moved closer to the square within hearing distance, folded her hands, and placed them on her chest where her heart thumped madly.

"Ye were a worthy opponent, Shaw. Sorry about that last punch, but I wanted to get this over with," Magnus explained.

Shaw bellowed a laugh. "Aye, and I am gladdened ye did because we could have gone on for a time. Let us go forth so the king can make his damnable announcement and I can get a bloody drink."

They stood before the dais and when asked who he selected for his bride, Magnus stated in a clear unwavering voice who he wished to wed. "I choose Mistress Kendra of Clan Graham, Sire."

Kendra didn't know whether to shout with glee or faint dead away. She was pleased to hear her name, and yet, she was apprehensive about marrying such a strong, warrior-like man. Hadn't she professed to want a man the complete opposite of Heatherington? Well, Magnus was indeed that very likeness.

"Well done, Cameron. This eve we will hold your wedding. Remember, there will be no annulment pleas. You will consummate your marriage and you will uphold the promises you made." Alexander motioned to Margaret and they left the dais.

"Next time I meet ye in combat, ye can be sure ye will not fare as fortunate as ye did this day," Shaw said with terseness, shoved Magnus's chest, and marched away.

Magnus made his way toward the castle and looked confounded by the entire ordeal.

Kendra rushed after him. He looked like he could use a drink and a cool wrap for his hand. He turned to her and his mouth widened in a swollen-lipped grin.

"Oh, how awful, Laird Cameron." Kendra sidled next to him and gave him a pitying look.

"Magnus," he said. "Call me 'Magnus,' lass."

She smiled at him and nodded. "Come then, Magnus, let us get you cleaned up and I am sure you could use a drink too." Kendra grabbed his good hand and led him into the castle.

Magnus allowed her to lead him through the hallway to an antechamber of the great hall where some washed in a basin before meals. The basin appeared to be filled with fresh water and had clean cloths folded neatly beside it. Kendra forced him to sit on a chair next to a screen by pushing on his muscular chest. Hardness met her fingertips and she smoothed her hand over his tunic for a moment. He sat back and watched her with his light eyes.

She ambled to the basin and said over her shoulder, "I heard what you proclaimed when the king asked who you chose."

"Aye," he said gruffly.

"Are you going to ask me for my hand? Or are you assuming that I will agree to be your wife when we are at the altar?" She stood by the basin and dunked a cloth in the water. She'd teased him and hoped to hear him laugh again but she knew sure enough that she had no choice in who the king gave her to. Kendra had meant her remarks as banter, but his manner was far more serious.

Magnus scowled deeply and stared at her. To appease her, she supposed, he decided to give her what she wanted. "Mistress Kendra…"

She wrung out the cloth and waited with bated breath for his proposal.

"Um…Mistress Kendra, I would be pleased if ye would accept my offer of marriage."

"I shall gladly accept your offer, Magnus." She held the cloth and approached him. With a gentle hand, she dabbed at his bloody lip. The care she took in tending to him caused him to close his eyes. Being close to him again sent a tingle through her body. Excitement meshed with longing. Both rarely felt emotions swarmed her.

His words came in almost a whisper as he sat back and seemed to enjoy her ministrations. "I haven't been cared for in such a way since I was a lad but then, my mother's servant, Ellen, always nursed my wounds. I never coveted a woman to look after me, but I'm coveting it now."

Kendra sighed softly, disheartened to hear that he'd been tended to by servants. How sad that his mother didn't care for him. Or perhaps she had died and he'd been left motherless like her. She'd have to ask for more details, but later, when she knew him a bit better.

With her hand pressed on his cheek, she dabbed the now-dried blood from his face. She set the cool cloth on the other side of his cheek that swelled and pressed gently.

"That feels good, lass."

As tenderly as she could, she had him cleaned up and soothed in no time. "Before we settle this contract, you should know that I am not a wilted flower to be stomped on by her husband. I am an intelligent, caring, trustworthy woman, and I expect to be treated as such. What I am not is a simple-minded, tenderhearted lass who is easily squashed. I shall not weep and carry on over insignificant matters. I will not demand that you love me. I understand the contractual joining betwixt us."

Her tirade brought forth a light chuckle from him. "Aye? That is good to know. Ye needn't sing your praises to me, lass. I do not mistreat women, wives, or otherwise, and I abhor a weeping woman so that appeases me. Tears will not sway me to give in when a command is necessary."

"I have never used tears to get my way, Magnus, and I do not plan to start using them now. But I suggest that you ask, not command, when it is necessary to direct me." She nodded and returned to the basin. After soaking the cloth and wringing it out again, she moved back to him and continued to soothe his injuries. Magnus held up his hand which now showed a bruise from striking Shaw's face.

"Oh, I dare say you might have broken a bone or two in your

hand." She left him again and retrieved a different, thicker cloth, soaked it with water again, and wrung it out. Kendra took his hand and with the lightest touch, wrapped it in the cloth. She held his hand and peered at him with concern. "You might want to have a healer look at your hand."

Magnus appeared taken aback and his grip on her hand tightened. Kendra was extremely gentle and as his hand sat in hers, she reveled at the touch of his skin. The contact was warm, hard, and strong. Perhaps she was exactly what he needed: a woman to care for him, one who wouldn't weep, one who was trustworthy, and one who didn't require love. He might get used to such care…eventually, she hoped. As for love, she found herself thinking she could easily love him and she doubted it would take years to do so.

Kendra leaned toward him and pressed back the dark locks of hair by his forehead. "I am gladdened that you won the brawl, Magnus, and I thank you for choosing me." Her soft voice seemed to allay him and he closed his eyes briefly again.

Magnus then gazed hard at her and with a shiver, a rush of warmth swarmed her. He pulled her to sit on his lap and he kept his hands firmly on her waist. "Aye, ye are welcome, lass. I believe I fell for ye as ye predicted last eve. I want to kiss ye."

She could barely draw a breath as mesmerized as she was by his words. Magnus appeared to be awaiting her response and so she said, "I want you to kiss me."

His face shifted nearer to hers and his nose practically touched hers. He set his mouth on hers and gently kissed her lips. Magnus briefly pulled away at the touch of their lips but then set his mouth back on hers. Nothing mattered at that moment except for the kiss he shared with her.

Kendra placed her arms around his neck and pressed her body against his. He tightened his hold on her and she marveled at the hardness of his arms. Everything about him taunted her to want more—more of his touches, his care, and his body. She returned the kiss and the soft mewing sound from her throat stiffened him.

She felt him flinch.

Magnus heightened the kiss and he used his tongue to deepen the desire that surged between them. The pleasure of it nearly forced her to groan. No man had stirred her desire like Magnus had. For all the torment she'd endured over the past year, finally, something had gone her way. She'd marry the handsome Highlander and before the sun set that day, he'd be hers.

CHAPTER SIX

THE GREAT HALL was crowded when supper was served. Kendra prepared for her wedding and wore her favorite gown, a tan overdress with billowing sleeves that had many pleats about the waistline and a modest bodice. Sewn at the edges was a pretty lace and the garment was belted with a thick band of brown silk. She rarely wore the dress but hadn't had many occasions to wear it and she felt so becoming in the elegant gown.

She stood next to her father's chair, where she'd settled him with John standing behind him. Earlier, during the brawls, John had kept her father safe and she'd found them in their chamber when she returned. Hopefully, her father stayed put when she was called for the wedding. He smiled and seemed content but likely he didn't know where he was or why. She wished she was as eased, but alas, the next moments were about to change her life forever.

Queen Margaret approached and Kendra bowed and greeted her. "My Lady, good eve."

"Your wedding will take place shortly. Oh, this is exciting and I am glad you chose Laird Cameron. He is such a worthy man and I trust you will please him. We're just awaiting Alexander, but he is meeting with his advisors and shall come shortly. Will your father be joining us?"

Kendra moved closer to the queen so her father couldn't

overhear her. "It is best that he remains here. Our servant, John, will look after him while I attend the wedding. My father has been absent-minded recently and confused. I don't want him to wander off or become upset when I'm taking my vows."

Margaret took her hand and squeezed it. "Oh, Mistress Kendra, I am sorry to hear that. I too had a relative that happened to and witnessing his madness was difficult as I am sure it is for you. Such a shame when their minds don't hold memories. I shall bid a servant attend to him and bring him supper and keep his cup filled so you need not worry." She walked off and left the hall.

Kendra appreciated the queen's empathy. She turned and searched the hall for Magnus, hoping he had come early so she could talk to him. Before the ceremony, she wanted to speak with him about her father. She hadn't gotten a chance earlier when she had tended to his wounds because right after their kiss ended, he left her abruptly. She hoped he hadn't changed his mind. Was he disappointed with their kiss? Vulnerability sank her shoulders and until she spoke with him, she felt helpless.

Magnus appeared and stood by the buttery. He'd changed his garments and wore a tan colored tunic and a red woven tartan with a dark green plaid. Magnus must have bathed because his hair was clean and curled at the edges and his face was smooth and free of whiskers. His handsomeness ceased her breath, even with the slight swelling of his lip and bruising beneath his eye. Kendra was awed by him, his manner, and everything about him.

She couldn't believe she would soon marry him. He took a drink from a passing servant and his eyes found hers. His gaze lingered as if he called her to him but he made no movement to motion to her. Kendra nodded to John and the servant who was assigned to her father's table. She ambled to where her future husband stood.

"Laird Cameron, might I have a word with you before the ceremony?"

"Certainly, and ye should call me 'Magnus.'"

"In private?" She sighed, because the conversation she wanted to have with him was of a serious nature. Kendra tensed knowing she would have to ask him the unthinkable. What man would permit their father-in-law to accompany them home after the wedding? She prayed he would understand.

Magnus grabbed her hand and led her into the hallway. He continued and directed her outside onto a short stone-walled balcony. The late afternoon air chilled her but fortunately, the rains had stopped earlier that morning. With the trepidation of what she needed to ask him, she'd become overheated.

"I should apologize for earlier…" His voice was raspy and deep. "A laird should be noble at all times. I shouldn't have kissed ye or been forward before our wedding." Magnus peered beyond the balcony with his eyes focused on the trees in the distance.

Kendra tilted her head to the side. It was as if Magnus had repeated a mantra. Either that or he took his duties as a laird to heart and was gallant. Taken aback by his apology, she set her hand on his arm, gladdened to know what had caused his abrupt departure. "You haven't changed your mind then? Do you still intend to marry me? You left so abruptly and I thought that you—"

He turned his head to her. "If I'd stayed, ye would've been in danger. The last thing I wanted to be was unchivalrous toward ye. Say ye forgive me, lass." He peered now at her, waiting for her to speak.

Kendra swallowed hard. What did he mean by danger? Had he meant that he couldn't control himself during their kiss? If that was so, then she had hope that their union would be passionate. She smoothed her hand on his arm. "Of course I forgive you."

"What did ye want to discuss? Ye haven't changed your mind, have ye?" He set his hand on hers and gently brushed it away.

She shook her head confused by his brisk manner. "Nay, nay, of course I haven't. I just…"

He continued to gaze at her with a smoldering look in his eyes. At that moment all she could envision was their earlier kiss. How she wanted him to do so again but he was too noble for that, she supposed. Lord, how the man kissed her, and she was just as wanton in the return of it. Kendra wanted to ask what bothered him, but she decided to stick with the plan and discuss her father's situation and her needs.

He nodded to her. "Go on, lass…Kendra. What is it ye wanted to discuss?"

Kendra took a deep breath. "I must ask you something and I worry that you will disagree before I might explain."

"I will not stop ye. Say what ye will and if it is within my means, I shall not disagree."

"My father is ailing and I had hoped to bring him with me when we travel to your home. There is no one at our keep to look after him, no family that is, but me. My brother has gone off to war and until he returns, my father has no one but me to care for him. I cannot leave him alone. Can we bring him with us when we leave?" She rushed through the explanation and ceased abruptly.

His brows furrowed slightly and he shifted back a step. "He ails? What is wrong with him? Will his ailment delay our travel? I cannot afford any detainment in returning home."

"He is well except that he is forgetful and often he doesn't remember where he is or such matters. Bodily, I deem he is capable and I don't believe he shall cause any trouble or delay on the journey to your home. His attendant John will look after him."

"Family is most valuable. Of course, your father is welcome to stay with us until your brother returns. I have a large family and clan. Ye both will be welcomed, protected, and cared for." Magnus stepped toward her and raised her chin with the tip of his finger. "I do not like though that ye worry for him."

Kendra kept her eyes on his. "I cannot help but worry for him. He is all I have and I thank you for allowing him to come. It would have distressed me so to leave him behind. Magnus, I vow to make a good wife for you."

"I do not doubt it, lass. After this day, ye will have me too.

Remember that. We will do well together. I should explain that as the laird, I have many duties to see to and am often kept busy. There will be times when I am away from the holding for a length of time. It is unfortunate, but we may not spend much time together."

She put distance between them as his words came with sternness. "I thank you for explaining, but it is not necessary. I understand that you are a busy man as the laird of your clan. When you need me, I will be there for you."

"We should return. Kendra…?"

She stepped away but turned back to him. "Aye?"

"I had not thought about taking a wife and never needed anyone," his voice pitched. "I doubt I will need ye, but it is good to know ye will be there."

"In time you will come to value our marriage and perhaps one day, you will also need me."

"Perhaps," he granted. "But I already value you."

His declaration pleased her. They returned to the hall when the chamberlain approached and announced that their marriage would take place in the king's antechamber. Guided by two servants, they were led to the room through a wall panel adjacent to the great hall.

Inside the small chamber, the king and queen attended. There were no others present except for the chancellor who wore stark black vestments. He appeared as aged as Saint Michael and his baritone voice droned on about their marriageable duty to each other, to God, and what marriage meant. His demeanor was almost judgmental and he scowled with unease. She wasn't sure if he was judging her or Laird Cameron.

Kendra gave the appropriate responses when she was asked if she agreed to marry Magnus. "I, Kendra of Clan Graham, take you, Magnus of Clan Cameron, to be my husband…"

He likewise agreed when asked if he would uphold his duty to her. "Aye. I, Magnus of Clan Cameron, pledge myself to ye, Kendra of Clan Graham."

The chancellor then motioned to her. "Do you wish, Mistress, to speak of your vows to Laird Cameron?"

She shook her head. "He is already aware of my vows to him." Kendra had said all that she needed to when they were on the balcony. What more could she ask of him since he allowed her father to go with them to his fief?

Magnus gave a slight shake of his head to the chancellor when he was asked. He, too, had spoken his vows to her on the balcony. Magnus took his duty as laird to heart and she suspected she'd see little of him. He had even spoken of such matters, so there was nothing left to be said. What saddened her a bit was that he'd practically said that he didn't need her. She would make him need her one day even if it took years for him to admit it. It was unlikely that they would ever come to love one another. Love marriages were rare and most opted for the protection of a contractual agreement and that was exactly what she was getting.

What had she hoped? Had she had her heart set on a love match? Kendra wasn't usually caught up in emotions or sentiment but the thought of having her husband love her would verily enrich her life. His kiss and their banter led her to believe that there might be something between them—something more than duty and honor. She might've been wrong about that.

A moment later, the Chancellor announced they were husband and wife. Magnus gave her a modest kiss on her lips and barely grazed her mouth with his. Kendra was disappointed because their kiss earlier was much more affecting. She'd hoped he'd at least press his lips against hers for more than a heartbeat.

The queen squealed and clapped her hands. "I know you two will do well together. When we return from England, Lady Cameron, I just might ask Alexander to bring me for a visit."

Kendra bowed to the queen. "I should like that, My Lady."

"Come, we should make ready to leave," Magnus said in his no-nonsense tone.

She was shocked to hear they would leave immediately. "But can we not stay the night and leave on the morrow?"

Magnus shook his head. "I only explain because we are newly married. I will not do so in the future. My return is pressing and I cannot linger. I will have the horses readied. Get your belongings and your...father. We leave shortly. I will not be delayed." He rushed away before she could object.

Kendra returned to her father and asked John to stay with him until she returned. She then hurried to her chamber and collected her and her father's garments. Linet was a great help and had most ready. With the valises stuffed, she hastened outside with her two attendants and father and found Magnus standing with another man.

"Winston, this is my wife Lady Cameron. Ye will ensure her protection on the way home." He turned away and tied a satchel she supposed was his to his horse.

The man, Winston, appeared young and probably had only just reached manhood. His hair was much longer than her husband's and hung over his shoulders in dark straggly strands. "Milady," he said and bowed.

"It is a pleasure to meet you, Winston." Kendra released her valises when he reached for them. "Is there a reason we must hurry to your home?" she asked Magnus.

"Our home now," Magnus said. "There is a reason. Aye, we need to get home so I can find my brother's murderer. I have delayed long enough." He didn't explain further and turned away from her again.

Murderer? Kendra suspected now was not the time to ask questions and would find out soon enough what had happened to his brother. When she reached her father and tried to guide him to his horse, he balked. But then she explained. "Come, Papa, we need to go. I married as the king commanded and Laird Cameron has agreed that you can come with us. Is that not wonderful news?"

"Nay, I should return home. You are married now and should follow your husband. I do not wish to be away from my lands." He shimmied backward with wide eyes, his gaze somewhat alarmed.

"You are coming with me. My husband said we could have a visitation. Do you not want to see me settled before you return home? John will be with us and Linet." Kendra softened her explanation because her father would get angry if she told him the real reason that she insisted he go with her. If he returned to their lands, it was probable that Lord Heatherington would seek to harm her father for accepting the bride price coins and receiving no bride. "We shall be together until Aston returns."

"Very well, but as soon as I hear that your brother has returned, I shall make the journey home. 'Tis where I belong."

Kendra nodded. "Thank you, Papa, for understanding, and for coming with me. It will make my leaving you so much easier to bear."

Her father pressed his hands on hers and bobbed his head. Kendra guided him to his horse and was relieved that he understood and ceased being angry. John nodded as if he grasped her silent signal, a dip of her chin, for him to keep watch over her father.

Magnus had their belongings put on the horses and his comrade handed her father the reins of his horse. Her husband didn't help her mount her horse but sat steadily on his mount awaiting her. Everyone took to their mounts and they waited for Magnus to direct them.

"Will the journey take long?"

"Long enough," he said and led the procession through the castle's gates.

Kendra wasn't concerned for herself but for her father. She could ride all day and make no complaints even if she suffered. But her father hadn't had much use for riding lately, especially with him ailing. Their guards kept her father inside the gates of their home ever since he'd gone missing. She rode next to her father and prayed they would reach Magnus's lands before there were any mishaps.

Magnus led their group through the forest, hills, and brown

fields, and rarely glanced back at her. Whenever they stopped to rest, he kept his interaction with her to a minimum. Being married, she realized, wouldn't change her life at all. She would be left on her own with no one to account to, just as she had existed at her father's manor. Kendra wasn't too daunted by that and she wouldn't be a distraction for her husband. He was the laird after all and the most important man in his clan. She understood what that meant and as much as she hoped to have his adoration and attention, she realized that was unlikely.

THE LONG DAYS of riding took its toll not only on her, but her father, and Linet as well. John, Magnus, and Winston didn't groan or walk like stiffened elders when they stopped to rest. During the nights, they slept in areas surrounded by pines and woodland. Magnus handed her a heavily woven tartan, which she assumed was his. He'd told her to use it for sleep. When she tried to hand it back in the morning, he shoved it back at her.

"Ye may keep it."

He was kind and courteous and a man of little words. Kendra used the tartan to keep herself warm during the days, especially when the winds grew brisker and the air colder. It seemed Spring turned back to Winter the farther north they rode.

Throughout the journey, she kept quiet and rode along silently. Whenever Linet tried to speak to her, she waved her off. Kendra didn't want her husband to overhear any conversation she'd have with her friend. It seemed to her too that he wanted them to refrain from speaking. His focus and his guardsman's were on the trail and their surroundings. Magnus was in protective mode and she wouldn't be a distraction.

The closer they got to Cameron land, the more detached Magnus became. Kendra was saddened at the thought that her husband had little joy in his life. He wore a serious expression on his handsome face and was as staid as any laird, she supposed. One day, she vowed, she would make him happy and he wouldn't be able to cease smiling.

Kendra realized by the time they reached the gates that she needed him to want and need her, just as much as she needed him. Whether he wanted her was another matter altogether. There was something about him that drew her empathy, the longing for his touch, and her need for his approval. How could she fulfill her vows and he, his, if he hardly interacted with her?

CHAPTER SEVEN

A S THE GATES came into view, Magnus's first thought was that he could now get back to finding his brother's murderer and seeking vengeance. He would settle Kendra and her father and then meet with his brothers and find out what they had learned, if anything, about Ned's last actions and days. His brothers, Wyren and Jake, were tasked with asking questions of Ned's closest comrades. They should have made some progress by now since it had been over a fortnight since he'd been gone.

Throughout the ride home, he'd thought he might have a run-in with the Chattans, but fortunately, they stayed on their lands. His wife kept to herself and spoke little to him. She was a demure lass and had such a grace about her. Magnus realized the more time he spent with her, the more he appreciated her reserved nature. He couldn't help but also notice her beauty. She appealed to him with her fair hair, bonny blue eyes, and tempting body. Yet he couldn't allow her to distract him. His duty was of the utmost importance and nothing would detract him from it, not even a wife.

With her father and his soldier along on the journey, he couldn't do as he'd hoped and consummate their marriage. Did he want to now, with the vow of finding Ned's murderer hanging over him? He'd been ordered by the king to make the marriage legitimate and—he nodded to himself—he would see to it and soon. Once that duty was fulfilled, he could attend to the pledge he'd made to his clan—finding Ned's murderer.

At the gate, Craig, the gate watchman bellowed, *Let Us Unite*, bowed his head, and bade the others to open the gate. Magnus was gladdened to see they followed orders and kept the gates closed whilst he'd been away. He returned the chant they often used to greet each other or to call the Cameron soldiers to arms.

As soon as they reached the keep's courtyard, Magnus dismounted. He helped Kendra from her horse and gave her a few moments to stand before he released her. Holding her lightened him and even though riding through the gates had tensed him, he felt comforted being close to her which was a strange sensation since he'd never sought reassurance from anyone.

"There is no room for your father in the main keep. He will need to stay elsewhere." Magnus peered about his home, searching for Wyren or his closest comrades. He wanted reports as soon as possible and needed to find out what had happened while he was away.

Kendra took hold of his tunic sleeve and stopped him from moving away. "I don't want to be separated from my father. Can we not stay in a cottage nearby?"

Magnus shook his head. "My wife stays with me."

"But Papa will be confused. I will worry for him and cannot look out for him. He'll wander off and get lost," she explained in a tone that thickened with emotion.

"He will stay in a cottage near my grandda's and has his attendant to look after him." Instead of giving her the details, he motioned her forward. Magnus would command, need be, that his grandda would look after her father too. His grandda boasted about being bored since leaving the keep and the men would get on well together. At least, he surmised they would, given they were around the same age. He wondered briefly how old Kendra's father had been when he'd sired her. Lord Graham had to be already aged then and appeared more akin to her grandfather rather than her father.

"I cannot agree to that," she said softly. "I must look after him. He is my responsibility."

"And ye are *now* mine. I am also *now* your responsibility, Kendra. Best ye remember that. He will be safe enough. Ye worry too much." Magnus peered at her hand, still clutching his garment, and decided to explain. "My grandda, Hugh, is aged and lives in a cottage at the far end of the island but his mind is sound and he is spry for his age. He is more than capable of looking after your da and would be honored to be given the task. There's an empty cottage next to his that your father and his attendant can stay in. Worry not for him."

"I like not that you deem it a task. My father was once a spry man too and noble. Now we are asking your grandda to watch him as if he is a child."

"I am only trying to relieve your concern. My grandda will befriend him and your da will enjoy staying in the cottage. They will do well together."

"Will my father be safe?" Her eyes implored him. "I don't want him walking off. He's done so before and was lost. He is in an unfamiliar place, even so, he'd often become disoriented at home, and being in an unknown place will likely unsettle him." She released his tunic and stepped back, lowering her eyes.

Magnus didn't like the look of defeat on her bonny face. He raised her chin with the tip of his finger. "The island is mostly walled in and the exits are guarded. Your da cannot get out without someone seeing him or allowing his exit."

A small smile settled on her sweet lips. "Very well, but can we ensure the guards keep him within the walls? Papa has been known to wander and when he wants to abscond…"

"Fear naught because my guards are most effective at their duty. Come, we'll take him to my grandda's now, and after, I will have my brother alert the guards," Magnus instructed Winston to bring Lord Graham's satchel and to follow. The attendant, John, rushed forward to take his master's belongings from the soldier. Magnus walked along the lane with Kendra and returned the greetings from his clan with a nod. Behind them, her maid, Lord Graham, his attendant, and Winston trailed along.

Kendra, he noticed, smiled at the passersby but she held on to his arm in a death grip. "Your land is beautiful and serene. But are all within your clan of a stern nature? Why are they so angry? Or is it me that causes their displeasure?"

"Ye could not displease anyone, lass. Nay, there is another reason for their hostility." Magnus hadn't noticed the sternness of his clansmen and women until she pointed it out. He knew well why they were ireful. "They are not usually of foul temperment but they have good reason to be angry. One of our clansmen was killed recently and his death has not been avenged."

"Your brother," she said and turned her face to him. "I am sorry, Magnus, that you lost your brother. You don't know who killed him?"

"Nay, not yet." He didn't elaborate or say anything else about Ned's murder. The last thing he wanted to do was frighten her. Who knew if they had a knave within the clan? Until he found Ned's murderer, he would be diligent and would ensure she was protected. He considered putting Winston on duty to see to his wife's protection when he wasn't around. Magnus had to give it more thought before he decided.

To lighten the mood, and to give her something else to think about, he took her hand and said, "My clan is large, but my direct family members mostly live within the fief. My mother and father live there, as well as my brother Jake. There's a handful of servants who also reside within. Wyren, my other brother lives with his wife, Marny, and their bairn, Hale, in a cottage close by."

"You are fortunate to have family surrounding you. It's always been Papa, me, and Aston. Aston wasn't ever home. My father either until recently."

"Ye were left alone?" Magnus didn't like hearing that.

"I had servants who looked after me."

"Your mother?" he asked, knowing the possible answer, but still, he wanted her to tell him.

"She died when I was very young. Papa never remarried and said that no other woman would hold his heart. It had always been the three of us. Papa was often away but age recently has kept him at home. Aston travels now and offers his sword."

"If it is family ye want, lass, mine is rather large and intrusive. I warn ye, my mother will be most attentive as she is with all her children, except me. I am certain ye will like her. My da too for that matter." He released her hand when they had to divert around a tree that sat in the middle of the lane that led to his grandfather's cottage.

The walk didn't take long. Ahead, the one-room dwelling sat a stone's throw from the wall's back gate. His grandda sat outside with his back against a thick tree trunk with a stalk of wheat sticking from his mouth. Hugh Cameron was usually cantankerous, but this day, he appeared relaxed and agreeable.

"Grandda, I have brought you some company," he said as he approached and helped his grandfather to stand by taking his hand.

"Magnus, my lad, ye are home at last. 'Tis sad tidings for your ma still mourns Ned. I doubt she shall come out of it anytime soon. How did your travel to Edinburgh go?"

He bowed his head to his elder. "The king insisted that I marry. Aye, this is my wife, Kendra. Kendra, this is my grandda, Laird Hugh."

"Laird Hugh," she said and genuflected to him.

"Married? Och, well this is wonderful news. Remind me to tell ye the one about the laird and his new wife," his grandda said and grinned. He was always one for telling a jest and had the best stories, some of which were rather raucous and not for tender ears. His grandda tossed the stalk of wheat to the ground and stuck out his hand. Kendra placed her hand in his. His grandda raised her hand and almost kissed her knuckles. "What a bonny lass ye have wed, lad. Milady, please call me 'Hugh' for I have not been the laird for a good many years."

"Only if you call me 'Kendra'."

His grandda chortled. "And who is this man?"

"This is my father, Lord Rupert Graham."

"Lord Graham. Have ye come to see your bonny lass settled?" his grandda asked.

"Rupert," her da said and extended his hand. "'Tis the truth for I know not why I am here or who these people are. Have I been summoned?"

Kendra took her father's hand and seemed to try to soothe him. "Nay, Papa, you're here to help get me settled before you return home, remember?"

"Oh," Rupert said and his gaze meandered around him.

"I want him to stay in the empty cottage next to yours, Grandda," Magnus explained. "There is no room at the fief and Kendra will be comforted to know ye will help his man look after him." He motioned to his grandda and pulled him aside so Kendra and her father couldn't hear him. "He is a wee bit maddened, disremembers, and oft wanders off. She worries for him. Will you look after him whilst he is here, as a favor to me?"

"Of course, lad, of course. I had a comrade once who had the same malady. Poor chap died only a year later when his memory faltered. Worry naught for her father. I will ensure he is kept safe."

Magnus returned to Kendra. "Lord Graham, this is where you will stay whilst ye are here. There's plenty of room for ye and your attendant. My grandda will show ye around, too."

"I shall come and see you on the morrow and make sure…" Kendra said to her father, but he disregarded her and stepped inside the cottage without a farewell. The attendant followed. Kendra's gaze lowered. She appeared to want to weep at having to leave her da and yet she forced herself to remain strong. A sense of pride hit him when he noticed her strength.

Magnus held out his hand. "Come, let us get ye settled and have some supper before we turn in for the night. I'm sure ye will want to rest after the long journey." She walked beside him and he sensed she was tense. He would be too if he was going to a new home where he knew no one. With that, he wrapped his arm around her waist and slowed his pace. "I promise ye, sweetheart, my family will come to care for ye. They are loyal to me and all within our clan."

"I am certain that I shall like them," she said and kept her eyes lowered.

Her maid and Winston followed but kept a few paces behind.

"Winston, will ye show Mistress…" Magnus had forgotten what her servant's name was.

"Linet," Kendra supplied.

"Oh, aye, Mistress Linet where the maidservants stay. There's a cottage behind the fief where the servants reside. Ye can find a bed there. And Winston, bring our satchels after and put them in my chamber."

His attendant nodded and motioned to the maid to follow him.

Alone now, at the fief entrance, he opened the door and guided Kendra inside. At the hall's opening, he noticed his parents at the large trestle table. Supper had just been laid in the center and the scent of pottage wafted to him. He was hungry and looked forward to a good meal.

"Perfect timing. We'll eat before we settle in our chamber." Magnus cleared his throat and called to them. "Ma, Da… I would like ye to meet my wife, Kendra."

"Magnus, lad, ye got married? This is quite a surprise. Is that what the king wanted? Oho, dear lass, welcome. What a lovely woman ye are." His father stood and extended his hand.

Kendra clasped his father's hand and smiled.

His mother also stood but she wasn't as pleased with his news. A solemness remained in her gaze. "Did the king know anything about Ned's murder?"

"Nay, Mother, the king knew of it, though, and passed on his condolences. Alexander asked me to take this lovely lass's hand in marriage, amongst other things," Magnus said, but would wait to explain the other matters the king bade of him.

Kendra bowed. "Milady Cameron."

"I am Lady Faye. All call me 'Lady Faye'." His mother dipped her chin but remained unsmiling.

"Lady Faye, I am pleased to meet you." Kendra slightly curtseyed to his mother.

Magnus motioned to his father. "This is my da, Laird Stanton."

"Laird Stanton, it is my pleasure," Kendra said.

His father shook his head. "Stan will do well enough, lass, for I am not the laird any longer, not since my son recently took over. I'm gladdened for it."

Magnus chuckled because his grandda had just retorted the same to her.

The door banged and his brother Jake entered. He had a falcon perched on his shoulder and grinned in greeting. "Magnus, ye finally returned."

"Oh, dear lord, get that vile creature out of here!" His mother shrieked at his brother and frowned. "How many times have I told ye not to bring those foul animals and birds in here?"

The falcon flapped its wings but stayed resting on his brother's shoulder. "I am not keeping him here but am taking him to Vincent. It has a wounded wing and cannot fly. I will leave right after supper."

Magnus appreciated his brother's care of animals and he'd often taken those that needed care or aid to Vincent, a healer of animals and the stable master. Even as a wee lad, his brother brought home any animal that he'd found. Usually, his mother forbade him from keeping them inside but if Jake had his way, he'd keep them all. He introduced his brother to Kendra, "And this is Jake, my youngest brother. He has recently become a seasoned soldier within our regiment of men."

She bowed her head. "Jake."

"Welcome, Milady. Magnus, it is good to have ye home." Jake took a trencher and piled on bread, cheese, and pieces of meat he'd probably give to the falcon. "I am going to head to

Vincent's and then the garrison and will stay there this night." Jake bowed to him and left.

"He's been staying more oft in the garrison of late," his da said.

It was time for explanations. His parents implored him with their gazes to explain what happened in Edinburgh and there was no time like the present. "Alexander married off several Highlanders to border lasses. I got to choose my bride," he said and kept his gaze fixed on Kendra. "I was fortunate to win her hand."

Magnus motioned her to the table. He sat next to her, and they ate and made small talk. He gave the details of his meeting with Alexander and what the king had asked of him and the clan. His father of course was inquisitive and asked Kendra questions about her family, where she lived, and how she was raised. Satisfied with her answers, he finally quieted. His mother spoke little which was so unlike her, but he suspected mourning kept her silent. Usually, she was the talkative one, and his father was the quiet one.

After the meal, Magnus stood and waited for Kendra. "I will show ye where we shall sleep."

She followed him to their bedchamber on the second level of the fief. Magnus had a spacious solar and was given it when he was named the laird. He often held meetings within the antechamber and attended to many of his duties there. To the one side, the vastness afforded a large bed, trunks, a good-sized hearth, and a table with a chair. An arched opened wall led to the area that had an extensive table where he handled correspondence or met with Wyren, or previously, with Ned, to go over clan matters. He opened the door for her and motioned her inside.

Kendra was quiet and he suspected that she was apprehensive. He crossed the chamber and when they reached the bed, he pulled her to sit next to him. "No one ever comes in here. Ye will have some privacy. If ye want to put your things in a trunk, there is an empty one there," he said and pointed to the one next to the hearth.

"What is all that?" she asked and rose. She motioned to the numerous manuscripts that sat on the table in the antechamber. The manuscripts were piled high and overtook the surface of the table and among them were varied-sized coffers in which their coin was kept.

"The keep's accounting." He said no more, but seeing the manuscripts reminded him that he needed to go through them. Now that his clan was without a steward, he needed to replace Ned at the soonest because he had no time to devote to such a tiresome task. Until he could do so, he would keep the records in his solar for safekeeping. The weight of such a momentous task caused his concern. He should see to it soon because it was important to know where his clan stood on their wealth.

Kendra crossed the chamber and turned back to him. "It is a pleasant room."

"Would you like a bath? I can have the servants bring a large tub for ye to…" Magnus didn't continue his words when she nodded. "I will see to it. Why do ye not get settled and take your rest? I must go and meet with the clan."

Her voice came low, "I shall see you…then."

He didn't understand why she suddenly became coy, but then she was in his private room, in an unknown place. He supposed it would make a woman anxious. He crossed the floor and reached her. Magnus pulled her against him. His mouth found hers and he gave her a sensuous kiss. He didn't want to cease kissing her soft lips, but he'd never finish his duty if he stayed. There were too many things he needed to do before he sought his pleasure or rest.

Magnus pulled away from her and smiled. "I shall see ye soon, sweetheart." As he walked to the door, he chuckled to himself and shook his head. His wife's kisses would definitely be a distraction. Whenever he touched her, his body came alive. Desire almost overrode his good sense because he was willing to forgo his duty just to spend time with her. Even now, he didn't plan to be long at his tasks.

On the way to his brother's cottage, he stopped at the kitchen, an overly large stoned building that was divided into various rooms. The large, main room held two hearths for cooking, tables, stools, and all the tools needed to prepare meals for the fief and their soldiers. The scents of meat and stews wafted through the chamber. He stopped before Ellen and directed a bath be sent to his chamber. Kendra's servant stood with Ellen and said she would see to her lady. He thanked them and didn't waste time in his effort to get his duties completed.

Outside, Magnus headed for Wyren's cottage. He rapped at the door and waited. He could hear his infant nephew's wails from within. His brother opened the door and waved him inside, but Magnus shook his head. "'Tis probably better if we speak out here where we can hear each other." He had jested but his brother frowned.

Wyren stepped through the doorway, with his bairn in his arms, and closed the door behind him. He turned to him and yawned widely, covering it with a quick hand. "Take him for a wee bit." He thrust Hale at him.

Magnus grunted at being forced to hold his nephew. Hale squirmed in his hold until Magnus told him to cease. At once, the bairn's wails ended and he peered at him as if he knew who he was. "Aye, he already obeys his laird." He chuckled at his jest and still, the bairn remained quiet.

"Can we make this hasty? I need some shut-eye."

"Is Hale still keeping ye awake at night? What is wrong with him? Is he sickly?" He held Hale in the air and eyed him. "He appears healthy."

Wyren scowled and pressed his hands over his face. "There is nothing wrong with him. He is a bairn and just a wee bit fussy. All bairns are fussy. He shall settle down soon. I just want him to sleep through the forsaken night." He yawned again. "God willing."

"I sure hope he does for your sake," Magnus said as he leaned against the large stone that abutted his brother's cottage and settled Hale in the crook of his arm.

"Aye, so ye have returned, eh? Ye were gone longer than I expected. What did Alexander want?" His brother pressed his eyes and then rubbed his palms over his face.

Magnus grunted. "More than I was willing to give. He forced me to take a bride."

Wyren chortled loud enough to be heard by the clansmen and women in the nearest cottages. "A bride? Ye jest? And what did ye say to that? Did ye outright laugh in his face?"

"What the hell do ye think I did? I married the woman and I am…" Magnus took a breath to settle himself and glared hard at his brother who continued to laugh. He shushed his brother and inclined his head to Hale who had closed his eyes.

"Och, laddie, ye be blushing. I take it ye find this woman that Alexander married ye to, to your liking?" Wyren grinned as if he thought their conversation was comical.

"Aye, liking is putting it a wee bit mildly. There was also the benefit of no tax for a year though we must supply the king with soldiers when he deems to take Haakon's lands. I do not suppose that will be for a while though since the king will be traveling to England for a long visit."

"Your travel to Edinburgh was of importance then. Are ye happy ye are married? Ye did not answer me." Wyren shoved his shoulder.

"Aye, Kendra is a bonny lass, reserved, graceful."

Wyren raised a brow. "That is not what I meant. Are ye attracted to her?"

Magnus scoffed. "When ye see her, ye will get your answer. Now tell me, have ye found anything out about Ned's disappearance or his murderer whilst I was gone?"

His brother shook his head. "'Tis strange. I questioned all of Ned's friends, the watches, the sentry, and others. None recall him leaving the fief around the time he disappeared. I tried to gain a sense of his last days here and no one remembers who he was with or what he was doing. 'Tis as if he vanished until ye found him by the mountain. Whatever happened to Ned took place outside our walls. I have had the entire keep's lands checked for any sign of blood or scuffle. I plan to head to the village to find out if anyone saw him there."

"That is a fair idea. I will go with ye when ye trek to the village."

Wyren laughed. "Are ye not going to be too busy with your new wife?"

"Is there anything else?" Magnus asked, ignoring his brother's banter.

"Nay, nothing much happened whilst ye were gone. Ma has not been herself and mourns. Da told me that she hasn't left the keep and stays within. He worries that she will make herself ill with her bereavement."

"I noticed the sadness in her eyes," Magnus said lowly. He was distressed that his mother was brokenhearted and knew she would remain so until he could enact vengeance for Ned's death.

Wyren leaned against the low-lying wall and crossed his ankles. "The crofters continue the seasonal planting. We began the shearing of the sheep, about half were done and the wool will fetch a good amount of coin, the wall has been fortified, and the soldiers trained. All was quiet."

Magnus leaned against the wall next to him. His brother handled his duty well and that surprised him because Magnus didn't like giving up control. Yet he'd had no choice and the clan hadn't fallen apart during his absence. "I see that the gates were kept closed."

His brother nodded. "Aye, we kept them closed as ye bade. They were only opened for the sentry but otherwise remained shut. On market day, we allowed the clan's men and women to exit the back entrance."

"I will meet ye on the field in the morn to see how the training is going. Is Jake doing well? That lad has grown and surpassed us in height." Magnus chuckled.

"Jake is a toughened soldier now, likely our fiercest. He is getting proficient with the sword. Perhaps we should promote him now that he's a seasoned soldier and put him over some of the younger lads."

Magnus agreed with a nod. "He could do with the added responsibility. I'll consider it."

"Aye, I have a few lads that could do with his guidance." Wyren pressed his hands on his face and yawned again.

Magnus turned and had almost forgotten that he held Hale. He set his nephew in his brother's arms and nodded. "I hope ye get some sleep this night."

Wyren chortled and opened his cottage door, jarring his son. "Unlikely, not with my son's wailing. I hope ye get some sleep this night too but with a new bride in the marriage bed, I doubt ye shall." Wyren bellowed with laughter and slammed his door shut behind him. Hale's wails began again the moment the door closed.

By the time he finished his conversation with Wyren, the sky had darkened. Magnus left his brother and strode back to the keep. It was quiet and his parents probably sought their beds. Inside the hall, he retrieved a pitcher of water and two cups. Taking the steps, he hurried to his bedchamber. He was impatient to see Kendra again. It had taken all his will to leave her while he gained his report.

He thrust the door open and expected to find Kendra in bed. Instead, she sat in a chair and he startled her. She nearly shot to her feet but then, seeing it was he, eased back in her seat. Magnus set the pitcher and cups on a small table near the bed and crossed the chamber. Being married was going to be a great disruption especially since he couldn't, or rather, didn't *want* to keep his hands off his lovely bride. The thought of consummating their marriage tensed his body. But before the night was through, he would get to touch her as he pleased. Finally.

CHAPTER EIGHT

KENDRA GASPED WHEN the door burst open and at the unexpected intrusion. She hadn't expected Magnus to return so soon. She'd had enough time to bathe, don her nightrail, and settle in the chair near the hearth. As she sat by the fire considering her father's situation, she used her fingers to detangle her damp hair. Being clean and in fresh garments lulled her. She was more tired than she thought from the journey, her worry over her father, and the night to come. The marriage bed was somewhat of a fear of hers—because she wasn't privy to what would happen.

"I thought ye would be asleep. Did I frighten ye? I apologize if I did."

She shook her head. "I just…wasn't expecting you back so…soon." Kendra smiled at the sound of his raspy voice. How could so few words appease her? But his voice lightened her and that he was caring enough to apologize for startling her, eased her spirit.

"I only needed to get a report from Wyren, my brother, who is also the commander-in-arms." Magnus pulled his upper tartan from his body as he crossed the chamber. "I think I will partake of your bath water." Before he reached the basin, he began shedding his garments and left them on the floor behind him in a trail as he walked until he stood before the basin naked with his lovely backside on display. He turned his face to peer at her.

Kendra was sure her cheeks were as bright as a smith's poker for she had never seen a naked man before. She had to take a breath to remind herself that Magnus was her husband now and she shouldn't be embarrassed. The incredible sight of his body drew her sigh though. "The water is probably cold by now. Do you want me to have some water heated for you?"

"Nay, I will not be overlong and only want to wash." Magnus stepped into the bath and sat back with his legs bent, his knees sticking above the water level. He barely fit in the large tub.

"Do you wish me to bathe you?" She had heard that most wives bathed their husbands and some wives even bathed guests that visited their keeps. She hoped that wasn't something they did in the Highlands and that it wasn't expected. Still, Kendra wanted to be a good wife, no matter what that entailed.

"If ye wish," he said and motioned her to him.

Kendra knelt next to the tub and picked up the cloth she had used to wash. She lathered it with the bar of soap she'd retrieved from her belongings. Then she set it on his chest. As she ran the cloth over him, she couldn't help but notice the taut muscles of his body. Everywhere she touched was firm. He was utterly male, strong, and marred by scars.

Magnus closed his eyes and relaxed back. She took advantage of his inattention and peeked at his midsection. What she could see beneath the water made Kendra's cheeks grow further enflamed. Abashed, she slapped the cloth on his knee and washed one leg and then the other. When she glanced back at Magnus, he was staring at her. His greenish-brown eyes deepened to a greener shade.

Kendra smiled. "You are finished, unless you want me to do your backside. I mean, your…"

Magnus leaned forward. "Just my back, sweetheart."

She gently swiped the cloth over the hardness of his back and glided her fingers over the texture of his musculature. Her face was so close to his that she felt his breath on her cheek. Kendra had never seen such a well-bodied man and that she was married to him pleased her. He definitely wasn't akin to Heatherington in any sense. She quickly gave a prayer of thanks to God for that.

Magnus set his hand on her arm and forced her to stop. "That's enough."

"Let me get you a drying cloth." She hastened to the trunk where she had put her belongings and retrieved a large cloth she used for bathing. It was still slightly damp, but it would do to dry him. She hurried back to him and held it open for him to step into. She averted her gaze and blushed madly when he rose and had no qualms about standing before her in the nude.

He took the drying cloth from her, stepped out of the tub, and patted himself. Kendra retreated to the bed, sat upon the bed covers and kept her gaze averted. She had no notion of what to do. Should she instigate their relations? What was expected? She had no knowledge from which to draw upon, so she decided it was best to let him initiate any passion between them.

Magnus didn't bother putting on a garment but sat on the side of the bed. He appeared just as daunted as she was. Kendra wondered what he was thinking, but assumed it was probably the same as she was—about their marriageable consummation. Only he probably had experience from which to draw upon. Most men did, didn't they?

"Did you—?" she said.

"Are ye—?" he said at the same time.

Kendra chuckled and lay back. "This is rather silly, is it not? I should warn you, Magnus, that I have no experience with matters betwixt men and women in the bedchamber."

"I should hope the hell not," he said and shimmied next to her. He leaned his back against the bedframe, a large poster bed that took up most of the space on one side of the room.

"I am not afraid," she whispered.

Magnus set his hand on her face and turned her to look at him. His eyes bore into hers. "Ye could've fooled me, lass. Just looking at ye pleases me. The rest will come easy. Trust in that."

"I do trust you, Magnus, it's just...you will have to tell me what to do. I wish not to disappoint you or be inept at it."

He grinned and then set a light kiss on the side of her face. "There might be pain for ye when I join with ye the first time. I will try to be gentle." He continued to place light kisses on her face and then slid his lips to her neck. The sensation of it gave her a shiver.

Kendra enjoyed his closeness and his attention. "I can bear it."

Magnus smiled. "Ye are a brave lass." His hand pressed down the length of her nightrail. "Let us get ye out of this." He helped her remove her garment and shifted it over her body until he pulled it over her head. His hands grazed her skin and sent rivulets of pleasure through her body.

Kendra had never allowed anyone to see her unclothed. Her skin flushed and she couldn't look him in the eyes. A chill shook her and a smattering of goosebumps flushed her skin. She wanted to hide beneath the covers.

"There is no need to be coy with me, sweetheart. In time, ye will not hide from me."

She set her arms at her side because it was as if he'd read her thoughts. "I don't mean to hide. It's just...in this instance, I find I'm being cowardly. I am sorry..."

He chuckled and kissed her lips. "Do not be. This is a new experience for ye and I want ye to enjoy yourself."

She gritted her teeth as his hand pressed her shoulder and slid down the length of her arm. "I do not know if that is possible. The unknown makes me uncomfortable." Kendra shivered and she noticed his sigh. It wasn't that she was cold, but just a strange sense that chilled her from within. Perhaps fear gripped her but Kendra was rarely afraid of anything and she didn't know why she showed such distress now.

Magnus settled next to her. "We'll go slow and I vow to ye, sweetheart, by the end of it, ye will enjoy it." He wrapped his arms around her and set his chin on the top of her head.

Kendra almost gasped aloud when his muscular body

touched hers. It was as if his entire body pressed against her as he embraced her. His skin was hard, hot, and warmed her. With his hands splayed over her back, he pressed her against him, thoroughly hiding the front of her from his view. She felt his need jabbing her leg, and even though she promised herself that she wouldn't fall apart, she was coming close to doing so. But she wasn't an emotional woman and instead of becoming undone, she decided to take control of her situation.

She pressed her hands over the muscles of his chest. Kendra decided she wanted to know every part of him and in learning that, she would take her mind off the inevitable. As her hands perused him, she used her legs and feet to likewise feel the thickness of his calves.

Magnus groaned. "Ye are making it hard not to take ye without preparing ye."

"Will you just kiss me so I don't think about it—?"

He set his mouth on hers and didn't let her finish her words. That was enough to turn her mind to mush. The man surely could kiss. His mouth turned over hers, and at first, his tongue gently twirled with hers. The longer they kissed, the more fervent she became. Kendra didn't know what came over her, but she couldn't get enough of the kiss, his touch, or the feeling of his body against hers. She held him in a tight embrace and let herself go.

Magnus dislodged their mouths and pressed her back against the mattress before sliding down her body to take her breast in his mouth and Kendra gasped. White-hot fire shot to where his tongue caressed. She nearly screeched as pleasure simmered between her legs. He continued to tease her and used his hands to caress every part of her. She enjoyed their love play until he reached to press his fingers within her. Then she shrieked because it was unexpected.

"Let me make ye ready, sweetheart. It will help to ease ye when the time comes." Magnus returned his mouth to hers and as he busied her with his mouth, he pressed his fingers inside her.

Kendra spent all of two seconds focused on his touch there until the desire for his kisses reverted her attention. Their kisses grew hotter and deeper, and swarmed her with a need she had never known existed. Magnus spread her legs and before she knew what he was about, he shifted his body and entered her.

He wouldn't cease kissing her and kept his mouth against hers. Kendra moaned and thought to stop him, but it was futile now. Her fingers clutched his hair and she held him close. He pressed onward and suddenly a stitch inside her caused her to gasp. She drew in a big gulp of air and pressed her hands against his chest and pushed him gently in hopes that he wouldn't continue.

Magnus petted her and spoke encouraging words. She had no notion of what he said because she was too focused on what he was doing to her. The pain he spoke of was minimal and only slightly uncomfortable.

"Do ye want me to cease? If ye do—"

She wanted to be brave so she shook her head. "Nay, I'd rather get on with it."

"Good because I don't think I could stop now that I…" Magnus moaned and drew a heavy breath. He leaned his head against hers and that was when she realized how raspy his breath was.

Was he uncomfortable too? Kendra was about to ask him that when he brushed his lips over her face and smiled.

"Ye are so tight, sweetheart, I am sorry that I hurt ye. We will give it a moment."

She frowned at him and shook her head. "You didn't hurt me, Magnus. Is it over? A moment for what?"

He grinned. "A moment until we seek pleasure, and nay, lass, it's only just begun."

Kendra disbelieved him. "This will not work, Magnus. I do not think we shall get pleasure from this act."

He chuckled. "Aye, we will."

Magnus shifted his body and the movement of him sliding from her and then gently easing within her again caused her to suck in a breath. She didn't realize she was panting until she closed her mouth. He took it slow but gradually increased his thrusts. Kendra didn't know when, but she wrapped her legs around his hips and squeezed his biceps with all her might. She held on and tried to meet his thrust. How wonderful it was, the twinges of desire so thoroughly numbing her to any thought. She reveled in his movements and hers.

It was as if they were entwined in a sensual dance. The bed rocked with such force that the wood thumped against the stone wall. Before long, their motions were wild with passion and overrode any sense of decorum. Kendra grunted from the force of his thrusts and watched his handsome face. He was focused, determined, and utterly attractive. She was so damned glad that she had chosen him for her husband.

Her culmination swarmed within her and she didn't understand what was upon her until it washed over her like rays of sunshine. Kendra tilted her head back and she was uncertain if she'd shouted to God. Pangs of pleasure started between her legs and spread through her body like wildfire. She almost wept at the sheer delight of it. The feelings were so intense that she squeezed her eyes closed, gripped Magnus, and shouted an unladylike expletive.

Kendra felt as though she floated back upon the bedding and opened her eyes.

Magnus stared at her with his becoming eyes. He had somewhat of a smile on his face. His movements then became rather slowed.

"Ye are bonny, sweetheart. Aye, and mine." With that, he jerked his body and rammed her with hard thrusts. He continued to shift against her until he leaned his head back, exposing his manly neck, and grunted.

Magnus froze and seemed to harden—his arms, legs, torso, every part of him stilled. A lingering groan came from between his lips. Kendra pressed her hands over his body, hoping to further fuel his pleasure. She shifted to keep him where he was and smiled up at him. Her mouth settled on the side of his neck and she placed light kisses on his damp skin.

He lowered his head to her chest and moaned. His hot breath fanned her breast. Kendra entwined her fingers in his hair and pressed him to her. Never had she felt closer to anyone before. Magnus calmed and shifted to lay next to her. He caressed her body with his large hand stopping at her throat. His thumb stroked the pulse there and he smiled.

"Kendra, I suspected ye were going to be good, but damnation, that was better than good." He grinned at her and set a kiss on the side of her face.

"I don't know why I was scared. It was not so bad." She had meant to tease him.

"Not so bad, eh?" He laughed. "Just wait, there is more to loving than what we just did, lass." He raised his brows and wore a devilish grin.

"More? I disbelieve you, Magnus, because that was incredible. Will we do that often?" Kendra wanted more. She couldn't believe husbands and wives did such things to one another.

"Aye, if ye want to. I know I do." Magnus set his leg over hers and yanked her hard against him. "For now though, we should get a wee bit of sleep. Wake me if ye want more," he teased.

Kendra closed her eyes and her body lulled not only from the sensual love she'd shared with Magnus, but also from the journey, and her worries about her father. She heard Magnus's light chuckle as she stretched and settled in his arms. Realization dawned on her that she was no longer alone. Even if she spent little time with him during the day, he was hers at night. His light snore sounded and she sighed happily. She had Magnus when the moon rose and that had to be enough for her for now.

CHAPTER NINE

MAGNUS HELD THE door latch and peered back at his sleeping wife. He didn't want to leave Kendra, but there were duties to see to, and being laird meant that he couldn't linger in his bed. Quietly, he closed the door and took the stairs to the great hall. There, he grabbed a hunk of bread, shoved it in his mouth, and washed it down with half a cup of ale. Later, he'd return for the midday meal since he hoped to check on Kendra then.

Being home brought a sense of peace to him but it also reminded him that he was no closer to finding out who had murdered Ned. That duty was far more important and he needed to make progress soon.

A coldness had settled in the hall and he started a fire in the hearth to warm it. With the logs set with kindling, the spark from flint easily ignited it. None had risen yet but when they came to the hall, at least it would be warm. Magnus had hoped to see his mother so they might put aside their differences over Ned's death, but he'd have to return later to see her.

He stepped through the entrance of the fief and felt the brisk breeze on his face and on the skin of his unclad legs. His tartan was thick enough to keep his body warm but did little to protect his legs.

Outside, the day was a wee bit chilly and cloudy. He hurried to meet Wyren who stood by the field holding Hale in his arms. Wrapped in a tartan and tied to Wyren's body, Hale was cradled securely, and for once, content. Magnus bellowed a laugh.

His brother glared at him and shushed him.

Magnus kept his voice low. "Is he not a wee bit young to start his training?"

Wyren scoffed. "Aye, that he is. Och, my wife told me to take him out so she could get a wee bit of rest. My poor lass hasn't gotten a good night's sleep since he was born. 'Tis the truth neither of us has gotten more than a wink of sleep since the last full moon."

"You should seek the healer or midwife's advice. They will tell ye what ye can do to make him sleep at night."

"I just might take your advice. I set the men to their training schedule for the day."

Magnus turned and faced the field. More than two scores of soldiers sparred on the field. He spotted Jake right off and watched him. His brother was a large man, likely less than a hand taller than he was. Jake was good with the sword but given time, he would get better. "Should we make Jake a leader soon?"

Wyren shrugged. "I am not certain he is ready."

"Why?" Magnus was surprised by Wyren's objection. "I thought we agreed last eve that we would put him over some of the younger lads?"

"I get the feeling he is holding back. Something is off about him and he has been quiet of late. Give me more time to assess him." Wyren untethered his son and held him out. "Take him for a moment, will ye?"

"Very well." Magnus held Hale at eye level and grinned at the handsome bairn. He much looked like his brother with light hair. His eyes were still dark but appeared to be lightening. After he settled Hale in his arms, Magnus raked his eyes over the field and was pleased with the efforts his soldiers were putting forth. As he stood with his brother watching the various bouts and tarries, Hayden, one of his most trusted guardsmen approached and stopped before him.

"Laird." He waited for permission to speak.

Magnus nodded to him. "Hayden, how goes it?"

"I finished the first round of my training earlier and was up just as dawn broke."

"Aye, that is good. I am sure Wyren could use help with the lesser-skilled soldiers if ye want to join him in leading the men this morn." Magnus continued to watch the soldiers and didn't notice Wyren settle by a tree. His brother appeared to have fallen asleep, and likewise, his bairn. Hale slept heavily in his arms. He motioned to Hayden to follow him and they stood far enough away so they wouldn't disturb his brother. Magnus kept his voice low so he wouldn't disturb the bairn.

"We should give him a few minutes."

"Aye, he's been plagued with no sleep. I have stepped in for him when I found him sleeping on duty." Hayden chuckled. "'Tis the truth I did not have it in my heart to wake him. Laird, Wyren asked all the soldiers if they noticed anything odd about Ned before his disappearance…"

"Did ye notice something? Speak it and tell me what ye know."

Hayden fingered his dark beard and grimaced. "I did not think of it until now but… Ned was acting strangely then. I asked if he wanted to go to the village with me to partake drink at The Tavern, but he said he was too busy. Later that week though, I saw him there. He was involved in a dice game but did not see me."

"Was he wagering?"

Hayden shrugged. "Probably, because most games are wagered. I did not see him after that, here or in the village. That was right around the time that he went missing. I regret now that I did not speak to him or find out why he was being evasive."

"My thanks, Hayden, for coming forward. Wyren and I are going to the village later. I will ask if anyone saw him around that time. I need ye to relay a message to the gate watchmen. All need to be told… My wife's father is to be kept within the walls. Tell them not to allow his passing through the gates." Magnus described Kendra's father to him. He had almost forgotten his promise to Kendra. If anything, he would ensure the man stayed within the walls so she wouldn't worry about him.

"I will do so at once, Laird." Hayden bowed and retreated to the lane that led to the gate.

Magnus returned to Wyren and shoved his leg with his foot. His brother opened his eyes and stretched. "We should make for the village soon if we want to get back before dark."

He helped his brother to rise by taking his hand and yanking him upward. Wyren stood, took his son from him, and staggered toward his cottage. He walked beside him and his nephew remained asleep. When Magnus was about to say something, his brother shook his head so he remained quiet. At Wyren's cottage, his brother entered and returned within a moment without Hale.

"Let us go."

"Were ye able to settle him without waking him?"

"Aye, och I deem my bairn likes the sound of swords for he fell asleep within minutes of us being at the training field. Marny will be fortunate if he stays asleep until midday." Wyren motioned him toward the stables.

Magnus found Winston and Sigge outside the entrance of the stable, and his attendant was giving his warhorse a good brushing with a wad of hay. In the adjacent corral, a handful of horses stood by a lone patch of grass that had sprouted, each trying to nibble the newly sprung blades. Their tails flicked and they blew air through their nostrils, sending wafts of steam in the air. The stable master, Vincent, was nowhere to be seen and must have still been inside the stables.

He nodded to his attendant. "Winston, saddle my horse, lad, and then ye should join the soldiers this day and get in some training."

"Do ye not need me to go with ye, Laird? I should protect your back."

"Nay, I appreciate the offer, but Wyren is going with me. We're off to the village and will return before nightfall. Go and try not to enjoy yourself too much. After ye finish training, ye will stand guard at the fief and watch out for my wife." Magnus laughed when Winston tossed the hay aside and returned a brief moment later, with his saddle and hurried to finish his tasks before he ran off. Sigge barked and ran after him in their excitement to get to the field.

Winston surpassed the lads his age at arms which was why Magnus had chosen him as his personal attendant. Since Winston didn't need to train on the field all day, he found other things for him to do. That got him thinking that he might need to put Winston in charge of a fledgling group of young ones just starting, once the business of finding out who murdered Ned was finished. For now, he would command that Winston protect Kendra when he was not within the walls. If there was a foe within his clan, he wanted his wife protected.

HE AND WYREN rode toward Fassiefern, a small hamlet on the north shore of Loch Eil that had a tavern situated in the village's center. Many travelers stopped on the way to the north at the tavern. It was a good resting place of spectacular beauty.

Magnus chuckled when he viewed his brother who'd let his horse's reins loose. Wyren closed his eyes and slouched as the horse trudged along. At least his brother could get a wee bit of shut-eye on the trek. He took hold of the reins and guided his brother's horse along.

The afternoon cooled with a hearty wind blowing from the west but the sun shone when the clouds grew sparser. Magnus eased at the beauty that surrounded him. Sounds of siskins, bullfinches, woodpeckers, and crossbills sounded in the woodland along the trail. The views of the Suileag River came into sight and he breathed deeply taking the pristine air into his chest. Not only did the view of the bonny land ease him, but the sound of the running water lent to the ambiance of its serenity.

"If Ned was wagering at dice, I know a man that we can talk to when we get to the village. He'll know where the games take place."

Magnus shot his gaze to his brother. "I thought ye were asleep."

"Nay, just closing my bleary eyes, *och* but I am awake. I trust not riding through these woods. The Chattans are oft near here and I would not leave myself open to attack." Wyren took hold of his horse's reins and picked up his pace. "Come, the sooner we get there the sooner we can return." He rode past him.

Magnus signaled to his horse to pick up the pace and trailed his brother. At the village, many hawkers had called it a day and closed their carts and huts. At the end of the lane sat the white-washed stone building of the tavern with its worn wooden signage. Simply called *The Tavern*, it was owned by a member of the MacDonald Clan who welcomed anyone be they aligned or a rival of his clan. Tom was more after the patron's coins rather than their friendship.

A small hostel afforded them a place to secure their horses while they visited the village. There, they tethered their horses and paid for a small helping of feed. Magnus wanted to get his questions answered so he could return home. He wondered briefly how Kendra was getting on, but he shouldn't worry about her. She was safe and with his family. Besides, he had told her that he was often away and that he wouldn't see her much.

Near the building, Wyren stepped over a gully that had formed from recent rains and opened the door. Inside the stale odor of ale drifted to him. Magnus drew in the scent. He liked the tavern's ale, for it was dark and tasted less sweet than other ales and the head was much creamier. He ordered their drinks and found an unoccupied table nearest to the small hearth at the far end of the room. The Tavern had a dozen tables and a high trestle table where patrons could stand or where they ordered their drinks.

Magnus peered about the establishment and noticed a door across from them. He tilted his head, silently alerting Wyren of its location. "Do ye think that is where they wager?"

"I would say so. *Och*, let us wait until the servant comes."

A few minutes later, two large tankards of ale were set before them. Wyren put a coin into the hand of their server, an older voluptuous woman who kept her eyes averted. "Is there by chance a game of dice being played this day?"

The server shook her brown-haired head and hastened away. He hadn't seen the server before and she must be newly employed at The Tavern. Magnus disregarded the server and picked up his cup. He drank deeply until he almost emptied the tankard. "They serve the best ale here. Do ye see that friend of yours? Perchance he can tell us if there's a game of dice happening."

"I do not see him. Let us wait a wee bit. Maybe he will come. How was your night? Was your wife as pleasurable as ye hoped?"

Magnus chuckled. "Aye, she was." He didn't elaborate because it would be unseemly to do so. Yet he grinned at the remembrance of the passion he'd shared with Kendra. It almost made him wish he hadn't left her early that morning but he looked forward to the night to come.

As Magnus sat there, his back was to the patrons. His brother motioned to the server who came and hastily refilled their tankards.

"Did ye hear what Hayden said? If Ned was wagering... I wonder where he got the coins? Ye do not think he took from our coffers, do ye?"

Wyren scowled hard at him. "I should hope the hell not. Have ye looked at the manuscripts yet and done an accounting? Surely they should be current and only the sums from when Ned had gone missing have yet to be added."

Magnus grunted. "When have I had time? As soon as we

buried Ned, I hailed off to Edinburgh. Now I am trying to find out what happened to him. I'll get to it soon. If Ned used the clan's coffers to pay for his wagering, I will curse him in hell."

"Rest easy, brother, we know not if that is the case." Wyren chuckled. "I never would have thought that Ned had the bollocks to take the clan's coins. He was too pigeon-hearted and tied to our mother's apron to do something so clever or ballsy."

Magnus bellowed a laugh. "Aye, maybe he did not. I will find out though soon enough when I have time to look at the manuscripts."

"There is my comrade," Wyren said and stood. "Await me here. I'll find out if any games are being played in the village." He moved away and met with a man across the tavern. The man was a short stout man who wore no particular clan's tartan. The vagrant spoke to his brother but Magnus couldn't hear their words. Wyren gripped the man and lifted him off the floor. His brother set the man back on his feet, smoothed his tunic, and ambled away.

"Come, there's a small barn behind the hostelry where they partake of dice and debauchery. We should find our answers there."

Back outside, Magnus followed his brother to the hostel. They reverted around the building and crept toward the old barn in the distance. It appeared to be falling down with broken pieces of wood nailed over the gaps and holes in its sides and roof.

When they reached the door, Wyren yanked it open, practically removing it from its worn hinges. "After ye, brother."

Magnus stepped inside and Wyren followed. He unfastened the loop of his dagger's sheath and set his hand on the hilt. He didn't much care for the look of the place or its occupants. The smell alone in the barn was rancid and he couldn't even begin to guess what or where it came from. There was little candlelight to brighten the confines, but near the game, at least four candles sat on wooden crates.

A group of men shot their gazes at them but they returned

their attention to the game at hand.

One man strolled toward them with a glare in his eyes. "This be a private place. Ye be trespassing. Ye best be leaving afore Aldo comes."

Wyren scoffed and then grinned. He held a pouch of coins and shook it, and the tinkle of them drew the man's gaze. "I am looking to place some wagers. I heard there was a game of dice happening here. *Och*, if ye don't want my coins, say so now, and we shall be on our way."

"If ye be willing to part with your coins, step this way." The man turned back to those immersed in the game and held his arm out as if guiding Wyren onward.

Wyren turned and spoke low, "Ye go on and question the others whilst I keep this knave busy and maybe I shall come away with some extra coins." His brother flashed a wily grin.

Magnus lingered by the group of men. He asked if anyone knew his brother Ned. Two men shook their heads. A man who stood by an old pen trudged toward him. He appeared to want to talk so Magnus drew him away from the others.

"Did ye see Ned of Clan Cameron here about a month or so ago? He's about my height with lighter hair. He went missing and we found him dead, but we are trying to trace his last moments."

The man bobbed his head. "Aye, I know Ned Cameron. I saw him here oft. He played dice with that man," he said and pointed to another man who seemed to be in charge. "I heard he owed a good bit of coin to Aldo, at least, half a dozen shillings. I do not think Aldo ever collected the debt though because Ned never showed up for their meeting."

"He was going to meet Aldo to repay his debt?"

The man bobbed his head again. "Aye, I went with Aldo to meet him at The Tavern. We waited but he never showed. Then about a sennight later we heard Ned was dead."

"Had Ned lost before to Aldo?"

"Oh, aye, he was not good at wagering and lost a good bit of coins to him. The last time he was here, he said he was going to recoup what he lost, but in the end, he ended up losing. We all felt bad for him. *Och*, that's what happens...the luck of the roll."

Shouts came from the players and Wyren held his hand out. The man, Aldo, placed a few coins in his brother's hand and he appeared disgruntled by it. Wyren always had a lucky hand at whatever he played, be it dice, cards, or even archery. "My thanks, sirrahs, for the coins." He turned away and patted the seam of his tunic to ensure the coins were secure.

Magnus motioned to his brother with the tilt of his head. They retreated from the old barn and outside, he stopped and waited to see if anyone followed. Knaves akin to those inside the barn might want to recoup their losses, and by that, Magnus suspected they could be set upon on their ride home. But the barn door remained closed and no one followed. He hastily told Wyren what he'd found out.

"So Ned had wagered and lost. If he did not meet with Aldo then mayhap our coffers were not completely depleted."

"God, I hope not. I will have to look into it when I get home. I vow, I trusted Ned and didn't check the manuscripts or coffers. The thought never crossed my mind that he'd do something so indecent. I never should have listened to da and made him our steward." Magnus's chest tightened with woe. He should have been more diligent in double-checking Ned's accounting and hadn't ignored his untrusting nature. Why had he been so bloody daft and staunch?

"We do not know if Ned ruined us yet. Let us head home and find out."

Magnus fumed. Even though the man told him Aldo never collected the coins from his brother, he had to wonder how many coins had Ned lost to him prior. And what if Aldo had murdered his brother for the unpaid debt? He wasn't about to trust the word of the man or his croony. They could have murdered his brother. Until they had proof though, he would stay his hand and wait. Yet impatience wore on him to get the matter settled and behind him.

Never had he thought Ned would steal from them. Yet he did not know if that was certain. It would take him more than a fortnight to go through the accounting of their stores and coins. He hoped with all his heart that his brother had not been deceitful and caused his own death. If that was so, then his vengeance would be for naught.

CHAPTER TEN

KENDRA WRAPPED THE bed cover around herself, ambled toward the antechamber, and picked up a manuscript. She opened it and perused the writing. She had wanted to tell Magnus that she could aid him in the accounting of his stores and coins but then thought better of it. Men often scoffed at women who claimed to have such knowledge. Many times, their steward had disbelieved her ability until he'd recounted the numbers himself. The last thing she wanted was for Magnus to think her daft. She placed the manuscript back on the pile and sighed.

A knock on the door startled her and the sound nearly made her drop the bed covering. Kendra approached the door and called, "Who is there?"

"It's me, Linet. I thought—" She opened the door and Linet almost fell through the threshold. "Good morn, Kendra. I thought I'd check on you. How did your night go?"

Her face warmed at the thought of telling Linet what happened between her and Magnus. "I was so tired and got a good night's sleep. And you?"

"I slept soundly too, but you know that is not what I meant. How was *your night?*"

"I was not disappointed." That was all she was going to offer as an explanation.

Linet laughed. "I'm not surprised to hear that. Your husband is verily handsome and I suppose he's a good lover."

Kendra feigned outrage at Linet's teasing and moaned. "And you would know because…"

With a wave of her hand, Linet crossed the bedchamber to the hearth where she knelt to stoke the fire. She gazed at her from her position on the floor. "You only have to look at him to realize he would be good in bed. Well, I am not the demure maid you deem me to be." She laughed and rose to her full height. "Now, let us see what we can do to make you presentable. Are you sore?"

Kendra's cheeks burned and she turned away. "A little, but it's subsiding."

Linet approached the basin and picked up the pitcher. "I'll get fresh water and we'll have you soothed in no time." She left the chamber.

Kendra laughed to herself thinking about Linet and her comment. Just how shameful was Linet, and who had she been wanton with? Kendra would have to pry it from her because Linet never revealed much about herself. It wasn't that her friend was secretive, but she was quiet and kept her matters private. Many times, Kendra had to question her repeatedly to get her to confess her thoughts.

Kendra hurried to remove the bedding and she rolled it into a clump. She blushed mightily at the thought of what she and Magnus had done the night before. Yet, she looked forward to their next encounter. Magnus had said there was more to the sensual act and she longed to find out what that was. He was already up and about when she'd awakened and she wondered if he was still within the keep's walls. Would he come and greet her or should she seek him out? Marriage and wifery were positively unknown realms to her.

The door opened and Linet entered carrying a pitcher set against her hip. She reached the basin and put the pitcher on the floor. Then she dumped the old water out of the window casement before she refilled the basin. "I'm sure you'll want to check on your father this morn. Let us get you dressed so you can be on your way."

Kendra took a clean cloth and pressed it over her face. Sleepiness instantly abated. After she was clean and soothed, Linet helped her pull on a blueish-gray overdress. She slipped her feet into her boots while Linet combed her hair.

"There, I tied it behind your neck. It's chilly and you should leave your hair down to keep you warmer."

She always listened to Linet's sound advice when it came to matters of dress and hair arrangement. Linet always appeared put-together even in her plain frocks with her red hair. She admired Linet's hair and wished hers was as bright and becoming.

"I should go." Kendra picked up the laundry from the floor and headed for the door.

"Leave that, I'll take care of it. I'll have someone come and take the tub away too. I know you have much on your mind and I am here to help you, so let me."

Kendra set the laundry on the floor next to the door and retrieved her shawl in case she needed it. "I am glad you are here. It would be lonely without you." Kendra embraced her and felt eased. "But you should come with me. I don't want to walk to my father's cottage by myself."

"Very well. Let me take the laundry to the kitchen and I'll ask Ellen if someone will see to it and the tub too." Linet snatched the pile from the floor and waited for her to open the door.

With apprehension, Kendra left the chamber and strolled with slow steps to the great hall. Linet followed along silently. Kendra hadn't expected to find anyone there, but Magnus's mother was eating her morning fare.

"Good day, Lady Faye."

Linet set the launder by the entrance and hastened to the table to fill a trencher for her. Kendra eyed her but smiled. Linet went beyond and treated her as the lady of the keep but Kendra wasn't comfortable with that honor. In her mind, the role of lady still went to Magnus's mother.

At the same time, while Lady Faye lived there, she would have to curb her tendencies to take charge. She'd been the lady of her father's manor for so long that Kendra was uncertain it was possible to behave otherwise. Still, she would try.

Musing on this, Kendra took a piece of warm bread and smeared it with a jellied relish.

"Lady Kendra, good morn." Faye poured herself a drink and filled it nearly to the rim. She lifted the cup and took a small sip to keep it from overflowing.

"Please, Lady Faye, call me 'Kendra.' It is still morning? I thought I had slept away the morn and apologize if you awaited me. I was overtired from the events of the past sennight and the journey." She set to eat a bite and poured half a cup of mead into a clean goblet.

"Oh, I am sure ye were tired from your journey. It is rather a long way from Edinburgh. Did I see laundry in your maid's hands?" She set her cup down and gave her full attention to them.

Kendra nodded and felt her face heat. She didn't want to have to explain why the bedding needed to be laundered and hoped Magnus's mother didn't ask. "I thought to have the bedding washed but Linet shall take care of it."

"There is no need. Ellen has a group of lasses that come each day to help her. Oh, here is Ellen now." Faye turned in her seat and waved the maid forward.

A woman near Lady Faye's age approached. She had a pleasing demeanor and her grayish-blue eyes peered with kindness. Her hair was the shade of hay when autumn was in full. Kendra dipped her chin to the woman and smiled.

"Ellen, this is our new lady… Lady Kendra, Magnus's wife. She has left laundry there by the entrance, will you see to it?"

Ellen smiled. "Oh, 'tis a pleasure to meet the laird's wife. Welcome, Milady. If ye need anything, ye have only to ask. I shall see to the washing for ye."

"I do not wish to give you more chores, Ellen, or the maids that help you. I am used to looking after myself for the most part.

Linet will help me, if you'll only direct us to where you do the washing. You met Linet last eve?" Kendra finished her drink and pushed the goblet away from her. It was so sweet that she puckered her mouth.

Linet stepped forward and stood beside her chair. "Good day, Mistress Ellen."

"Oh, aye, and what a sweet lass. Good morn, Linet. Ye be fortunate to have her, Lady Kendra. But I have several lassies who help me, so worry not about the wash. I will see to it. Besides, ye are now our laird's wife. We must take care of ye and ye shall allow us to do so," Ellen said. "The bedding will be laundered and replaced before ye seek your bed this night."

"You are kind. Is the weather fair? I had hoped to visit my father this morning."

Lady Faye seemed to shrug and didn't answer.

Ellen folded her hands in front of her and nodded. "It is a wee bit chilly but fair. I heard that your father stays near Laird Hugh in Old Angus's cottage. He shall find our laird's grandfather good company."

Kendra rose. "I shall go then. My thanks, Ellen, for your aid. Do you wish to accompany me and Linet, Lady Faye? We can take a nice stroll and you can show me around, and perhaps I'll find Magnus on our walk."

"Oh, nay, I do not leave the keep, not these days." Magnus's mother lowered her eyes and sighed sorrowfully. "Your husband was up early and is likely about his duties. Magnus takes his position as our laird very seriously. I rarely ever see him as I doubt ye shall."

"Thank you, Lady Faye, for telling me. I wondered and shall see him later then." Kendra grew concerned for a moment but would speak to Magnus later about his mother's odd comment. Questions rankled her. Why didn't she leave the keep? Was her son's death dispiriting her? Was it possible that something could be done to brighten the woman's mood, or was she always so melancholy? With hope, Kendra wondered if she might somehow aid her if Lady Faye allowed her to.

She left the keep and stood outside the entrance where she gazed about and watched the faces of the clan's people. It struck her that everyone wore such serious or melancholy expressions. There was no joy in their faces, only sorrow. Winston, the lad who had journeyed with them to Magnus's home, stood near the entrance of the fief, and bowed to her when she eyed him.

Linet sidled next to her. "How sad they appear. There is a darkness about the people here. You can feel it."

"I believe they are in mourning but I could be wrong. Perhaps they are always dour or maybe Magnus's brother's death has affected them greatly."

"How did he die?" Linet asked.

Kendra shrugged. "I hoped Magnus would tell me, but he hasn't spoken about it. He too seems to mourn his brother deeply. He must have been greatly cherished or perhaps his death was disheartening? I suppose someone will tell us when they are ready to." She wanted to find out the answers to those questions. "Come along then and let us get to the cottage."

Linet linked her arm with hers as they usually did when they walked about. They set off toward the back of the fief. Winston walked behind them in the same direction. Kendra thought nothing of it and paid him no mind.

Though it was sunny, the wind whipped at her. She pulled her shawl around her and walked toward the back of the fief. Kendra missed her home. Though she was often alone there, except for Linet's good company, she was just as alone here. She supposed there wasn't much of a difference in her life but she hoped to find friendship and a closeness with Magnus's family.

A woman dropped a basket of wool on the lane. The wind easily swept some of it away and the woman shouted. Kendra and Linet hurried to help retrieve the bits of wayward wool. When they had gotten all the wool back and pressed it deeper into the basket so the wind couldn't scatter it again, the woman smiled up at her from her place on the ground.

"Glory be, I thought I had lost the day's collection. My thanks, Mistress."

Kendra returned her smile. "You are more than welcome. I think we got it all."

"I do too. Thanks to you," the woman said as she pushed herself to her feet and positioned the basket on her hip. "Good day." She hastened away.

Kendra walked on and saw Hugh's cottage in the distance. She thought to visit Hugh since his home was first as she passed. When she reached it, she knocked at the door but no one answered. She opened the door, stepped inside, and Linet followed. The cottage was clean and somewhat tidy, especially given that an elder man lived there. The bed was made and there was a tin cup on the table. Laird Hugh must have gone out. Yet she hadn't seen them on her walk.

She retreated from the cottage and opened the door to the next one. That cottage too was empty. Kendra thought to take a moment to search through her father's belongings again. Surely, the coins he'd accepted from Heatherington had to be amongst his possessions. She'd found nothing when she searched her father's bedchamber before they left for Edinburgh. That meant that the coins had to be either on his person or within his possessions.

"What are you looking for?"

"For the coins Papa took from Heatherington. I need to find them soon so I can send them back before he makes threats."

Linet rushed forward and helped to search among her father's garments. "I'll check his clothing."

Kendra removed his garments from the satchel, set them in a pile for her and Linet to search, and felt along the seams. *Nothing.* She found two small satchels he used when he was about the keep and emptied them. All she found was a string, a small dagger, and a collection of small stones.

"Where did you put them?" she said aloud as if expecting an answer.

"Nothing's here in his garments," Linet said.

Then Kendra checked his bedding, thinking that if he had the coins, he could have hidden them there. He probably didn't know the significance of the coins or how important it was that they were returned. She lifted the stuffed mattress, felt along the coverings, and beneath the bed. *Nothing*. Kendra despaired that if she didn't find the coins soon, they would suffer some horrid slight from Heatherington. The man wasn't one to go against and he would be irked if he was deceived. Would he try to overtake her home? Kendra needed to protect her family's servants and kinsmen.

She stood in the center of the cottage and couldn't find anywhere else to check where her father would have hidden the coins.

"What are you doing in here?"

Kendra whirled around, startled, as her father and Hugh entered the cottage. She shook off her despondent mien and smiled. "Good day! I thought I would come and see how you were getting on, Papa."

"Who are you, lass?"

She narrowed her eyes at her father's question. "It's me, your daughter…Kendra. I wanted to make sure you were settled and to ask you about the coins again. We must find them."

Her father traipsed past her and sat at the table. He poured himself a cup of ale from a small jug that sat in the center and disregarded her. He grumbled something, but she couldn't make out what he'd said, though "coins" was one of the words she could discern from the rest of his mumbling.

Kendra glanced at Hugh before she rushed past him to the table. "Papa, please speak to me."

"I do not know you, lass, or about these coins you speak of. Be gone with you. Get out." He turned his back to her.

Kendra wanted to weep as great sorrow lodged in her throat. Her father did not recognize her. The way he spoke to her nearly crushed her heart.

"Aww, lass, come outside with me." Laird Hugh motioned to her.

Kendra was weary and sad but she nodded. "I'll be outside. Will you stay with him until John returns, Linet?"

"Of course, Kendra. Worry not for him. Where is John?"

Laird Hugh heard her from the doorway. "He's gone to fetch foodstuff from the kitchens for our midday meal. He should return soon."

Kendra stepped outside and peered at the man, forlorn. How had her father failed to recognize her after only a night's absence from him? "My thanks for seeing to my father." She fought back tears. "He is declining, is he not?"

Hugh scrunched his face in a manner that alluded to the dislike of their discussion. The wisps of his gray hair tousled from the wind. "Your da has been aloof all morn." Another, stronger gust of wind forced her shawl to fall from her shoulders. Laird Hugh picked it up and returned it to her. "Here, Milady, ye best keep yourself warm. Listen to me, aye, a comrade of mine had such a malady and it took him from us long before we understood that he ailed in his body. An ailment of the mind is a saddened state of affairs. Ye should prepare yourself."

"I know that he has not long in life and accept that he may be taken from me. But there's more to it. Please…if my father speaks of coins, you must tell me what he did with them. You see, he was given coins in error. He misplaced them and I need to find them. He should not have accepted the coins and I mean to return them to our neighbor."

"*Och*, do not worry, Milady. I will tell ye if he says anything. He has not mentioned coins. I took him for a walk to the stream and meant to keep him busy. He keeps asking why he is here."

Kendra's heart ached to hear that. "He should not go beyond the walls."

"Worry not for I was with him. He was reminiscing about your dear mother earlier."

She was surprised to hear that. Her father hadn't spoken of

her mother in years. "What did he say?"

"He said he missed her and longed to be with her." Hugh sighed wistfully.

"Do you think he shall be with her soon? I fear his days are numbered."

Hugh shrugged. "Who knows how long he has left in this realm? We shall aim to make his days pleasant whilst he is here. Are ye excited for Bealtuinn?"

"Bealtuinn?" she asked, not sure what he was speaking of.

"Oho, ye might know it as Roodmas for the church frowns upon us calling it Bel-Fire. Aye, they have renamed it to 'Feast of the Finding of the Holy Cross.' Blasphemous, I vow, that they stole our fair celebration for their own."

"I fear we did not much celebrate holy or festival days where we lived."

Hugh scowled. "Ye did not? How dreadful, lass, that ye didn't get to join in the festivity. Soon, the men will go in search of the woods needed for the great fire. They'll also be putting boughs on the lassies' window casements and doors to keep them safe. I heard tell they will choose a winsome lass by the name of 'Gloria' as the May Queen. She shall lead the marches in song and the spirit of the Goddess."

Kendra smiled at the man's enthusiasm. "It certainly sounds merry. I look forward to it."

"Aye, 'tis rumored that Winston might make an appearance as the 'green man' and a marriage might take place before the great fire. All shall delight in that. It might even take away the despair that the clan is suffering through right now."

"Does Winston want to marry Gloria?" Kendra was fascinated by Hugh's talk.

"Aye, aye. The lad has been in love with the lass since he was knee-high. She has finally accepted him."

"Magnus didn't tell me about the festival or Winston's forthcoming marriage. I will be happy to witness their union and the other events. When will it be?"

"Less than a sennight away, Milady, on May first."

Kendra set her hand on her hip and continued to question the elder. "Why is the clan so forlorn? Is it because Magnus's brother died?"

"'Tis so and most mourn the loss. Ned was a good sort and friendly to all. He had a way about him that put people at ease, unlike Wyren and Magnus. Now that Wyren has married, most find him more approachable, except some of the soldiers who are in awe of him. And all are leery about approaching Magnus. He has always had a formidable mien about him. That is why the council elected him as our laird. No one would dare cross him."

Kendra supposed that was true and she remembered what the queen had said of him: *He's a reserved man and speaks little. He is a favorite of mine and it distresses me that he is so serious and claims that he has no time for frivolities. I deem he needs some joy in his life.*

Her husband definitely needed to smile more and she thought perhaps that she might bring him a little joy. That was, if she could find some joy within herself. If she didn't find Heatherington's coins, there would be hell to pay and their lives would be filled with misery. Kendra couldn't allow the loss of her family's holding. Somehow, she had to hold on to it for Aston.

"I dare say you are right. Magnus does seem capable of scaring anyone. I found him somewhat daunting when we first met."

Hugh chuckled. "And now, Milady?"

"He seems to want to please me. I do not fear him now."

"Await me," Hugh said and lumbered through the doorway of his cottage. He returned a moment later and took her hand. In it, he placed a brooch. "This was my wife's, Magnus's grandmother's. She said it had magical powers and drew me to her. Perhaps it will help ye to win my grandson's heart even more."

Kendra was in awe of his gesture. "I cannot accept this, Laird Hugh. Please, keep it."

"There has been no other lass that I wished to gift it to. You keep it, Milady. I vow it will draw my grandson's regard, just as it drew mine toward my dear wife."

"Should you not give it to your daughter? Lady Faye is your daughter?"

He bobbed his head. "Aye, she is indeed. Faye has other items that belonged to her mother. She won't miss it, and besides, she already caught her husband's adoration."

Kendra clutched the beautiful brooch which appeared to be a thistle flower entwined with silver vines and had a purple amethyst jewel embedded in the pewter. "It is beautiful."

"Wear it, Milady, on Bealtuinn, at the festival. Pin it to the Cameron tartan for I am sure it will bring your husband joy."

"I promise, I shall. Speaking of Lady Faye… She mourns her son and says she doesn't leave the keep. I worry for her." Kendra placed the brooch inside the seam of her overdress to keep it safe until she returned to the fief.

"My daughter doted on Ned and his loss greatly affects her. She will ease with time."

"I got the sense that she didn't dote on Magnus." Kendra shouldn't be so forward by speaking of such matters with the man, but she hoped to gain an understanding of Magnus's relationship with his mother.

"Magnus was taken from his mother at a tender age. She never had the chance to adore him and she's always been distant toward him. Of her four sons, both Magnus and Wyren were born for the duty of the clan. Ned and Jake had their mother's love for they were spared the responsibilities that the others were not."

"That is sad." Kendra didn't know what to say. Her husband hadn't had his mother's care and had been raised for his obligation to his clan. The insight of his rearing explained much about his manner. "Thank you for explaining. It is getting late and I should say my farewell to my father." She left Hugh and stepped inside her father's cottage.

By then, John had returned and set on the table a large trencher of food. Linet placed food on smaller trenchers and fixed her gaze on John. Kendra smiled at the thought that her friend had often reacted as mirthful when John was near. Linet hadn't said she cared for John but it was evident in her look and smile.

Kendra approached her father and set a hand on his shoulder. "Papa, I am leaving now. I will come back later."

"Dearest, when did you get here?" Her father seemed surprised to see her.

"I...sometime ago. Laird Hugh tells me that he took you on a walk beyond the walls."

"Aye, lass, and he said he would take me fishing at the loch that he favors on the morrow. I have not been fishing in years and long to enjoy it again."

"I am certain you shall have a good time." Kendra set a light kiss on his slightly whiskered cheek and hastily left the cottage. Outside, she stood by the door and wiped at her eyes. Tears sprang to her lashes and she couldn't help but feel sorrow. Her father's memory returned in short bouts, but the fact that initially he hadn't remembered who she was sank her heart.

She waited for Linet who came outside a moment later.

"We should get back to the fief." On her return to the keep, she spotted Ellen walking with a young maiden. They both carried hefty baskets of laundry. She hurried forward and took Ellen's basket. "Let me carry this for you, Ellen."

Ellen rasped with heavy breath. "My thanks, Milady. Supper will soon be served. Cook has made a delicious pottage with rabbit and fine vegetables. It smells heavenly. Where has the day gone?"

Kendra entered the back of the keep and set the basket with the one the maid had carried. Ellen was correct. The day had flown by. She wondered if she would see Magnus before she sought her sleep. He had to have left the holding because she hadn't seen him on her walk about the keep's grounds. How she wished he had woken her this morning and told her that he'd be gone. But she realized he wasn't used to answering to anyone, let alone a wife.

Ellen rushed to the small table in a pantry room and collected a clean pitcher. "I must see about setting the table for supper. Cook must have the meal ready by now."

"I'll take the pitcher and you see about the supper." Kendra took the pitcher from her and hurried to the great hall. It was more crowded than it had been the night before. Lady Faye and Stan sat at the table. A woman walked by the large hearth, with a crying bairn cradled in her arms, trying to soothe him. Jake stood by a window casement with his back to everyone. There were also three other men in attendance.

"Oh, there ye be," Stan said, stepping forward. "Come and I will introduce ye. All, this is Magnus's wife Milady Kendra." He motioned to each of the people and said, "This is Osmond, Hayden, and Craig, the laird's closest guard. There, by the hearth, is Wyren's wife, Marny, and their bairn, Hale."

"Good eve, everyone," Kendra said. She stood by the buttery and filled the pitcher with ale from a barrel then rushed to the table and set it before Stan. Afterward, she approached Marny. "It is a pleasure to meet you, Marny. Magnus told me that you had recently had a bairn. He is a handsome lad."

"He is rather bonny, is he not? But he's got a cantankerous disposition like his great-grandda," she said and giggled.

"Do you mean Laird Hugh?"

Marny nodded. "Aye, tell me that he is not the most grumpy man alive?"

Kendra shook her head. "He has been nothing but kind to me and my father."

"I jest with ye. Laird Hugh is a kindly man but he can sometimes be blunt." Marny jostled the babe. "I vow nothing I do soothes Hale and he wails most of the day."

"May I hold him?" Kendra asked. Marny held out the bairn and she took him. The bairn gazed at her and though his crying ceased, he continued to whimper and she rocked him. Within seconds, she found herself humming to the babe. Hale settled and looked content. How she wished all it took was a soft melody to settle her but it would take more than a song to make her troubles disappear.

CHAPTER ELEVEN

O N THE TREK back to the keep, Magnus was displeased that he hadn't questioned Aldo about Ned's wagering. He should have gained his perspective and what Ned had told him about his repayment. Perhaps he would have alluded to where Ned was getting the coins from. It could have also led to a hint as to what happened to his brother. He would need to revisit the village again and soon, to question the knave.

Winston wasn't at the stable when he reached it but then he remembered telling him to be at the fief watching over Kendra. He patted Sigge's head and ruffled the fur of his hound in greeting. Wyren took the reins of his horse and said he'd get the beasts settled.

On his way to the keep, Magnus took a calming breath and appreciated the night's tranquility. All had sought their supper or slumber and the sky darkened with speckles of stars spread across the sky. Such a night would normally soothe his agitation, but with so much on his mind, he barely allowed the beauty of it to affect him.

He took the steps of the tower keep and entered. Voices from within the hall alerted him that many had gathered. There was talk but no laughter. Perhaps one day there would be laughter within his hall again. Once he learned who had murdered Ned and sought vengeance, all would be righted and normalcy would return—whatever that normality was. He was uncertain if there ever would be peace within his clan again.

Magnus stopped short at the hall's entrance when he spotted Kendra by the hearth. She held his brother's bairn in her arms and was so focused on the babe that she didn't notice him. He watched her with interest. How bonny she appeared holding a bairn. It gave him hope that within the next year or two, they would have a child of their own. Magnus hadn't much thought about being a father or having a family but now that he married, it was something that suddenly struck him. If he was going to be the kind of father he hoped to be, he needed to make changes, not only to himself but to the hierarchy of his clan.

Marny sat in the chair by the hearth and appeared to be sleeping. His brother entered and bypassed him, making his way to his wife. He lowered his head to speak in Kendra's ear, then took the babe from her. She smiled and gently placed her hand on the babe's head. How appealing his wife looked and how pleased he was to be home. He stepped forward until he reached her.

She turned to look at him with a welcoming smile. "Magnus! You are back."

Magnus wanted to grab her and pull her into his arms. He wished to kiss her with enough passion to brighten her fair cheeks. Lord, she was lovely. But then he realized everyone in the hall was looking at them and Magnus suddenly became reserved. He presumed his family hoped to get a glimpse of his relations with Kendra and he would leave them wondering. So he took her hand and gave it a light squeeze, letting her know that he was pleased to see her.

"Sweetheart, ye…are here…" He wanted to tell her how bonny she looked, but instead, he said, "What did ye do this day?"

She smiled lightly and squeezed his hand in return. "I visited my father, enjoyed speaking to your grandda, helped Ellen a little, and walked about inside the walls."

"And what do ye think of our home?" He didn't smile or frown but hoped she found their land as beautiful as he did.

"It is quite pleasant here, from what I saw of it. Perhaps when you have time, you can give me a tour?"

Magnus lifted her hand. "I would be happy to…when I have the time. I saw ye holding Hale. Ye look bonny holding a bairn. Are ye amiable to becoming a mother?"

Kendra pressed the long length of her blond locks behind her shoulder and nodded. "I had not really thought about it but aye, I should like to be a mother one day. It is a wife's duty, is it not, to provide her husband with an heir? I shall do my duty one day. Do you hope for a large family?"

He waved to his family, beyond them at the table, and grinned. "That is what I am used to, but we will be blessed with whatever God deems we deserve."

"I am sure we will have at least two or more. That is my hope."

"God, how ye please me," he whispered in her ear as he leaned close. "I shall show ye my adoration later." Magnus guided her to the table and settled her in a chair. He sat at the head of the table and listened to the discussion going on around him. Yet, he heard all of two words of it because he was focused on Kendra. Though she appeared pleased to see him, there was a note of sadness in her eyes. He would find out later what had distressed her.

The meal was served and all ate, conversed, and partook of ale and wine. That his family gathered for the meal somewhat surprised Magnus. They hadn't eaten together in some time. Supper ended and all left the hall. Kendra set her supper dagger on the trencher and peered up at him. She seemed to be waiting for him but Magnus had finished eating long ago.

"Shall we set off to bed?" he asked.

She nodded and demurely, rose from her seat. He walked behind her as she took the steps to the upper floor. Magnus appreciated her body and the way her shoulders moved when she walked. She had a gracefulness about her and was almost regal in her movement. He found himself completely enthralled with her.

Just inside their bedchamber, he didn't wait but pulled her into his embrace. He pressed her against the closed door and kissed her. Lord, how he wanted to ravish her, but he maintained a little control.

Her response was just as filled with desire. Her hands gripped his garments, and he tried to untie the strings of her bodice with frustration. Once he successfully undid the ties, he shifted the material away from her shoulders. Her overdress fell to the floor in a heap. She was clad in an alluring chemise that covered little of her and did nothing to hide her attributes from him.

Magnus stood before her, staring into her lovely blue eyes. "Sweetheart, undress me. I long to feel your hands on me and cannot wait." That certainly was true. Numerous times throughout the day, he had envisioned undressing her, her disrobing him, and the joining of their bodies. Lord, he was smitten with his wife, and he was damned satisfied by that.

Kendra's hands shook when she unfastened his tunic and pressed away his tartan from around his body. She used both hands to take hold of his belt and unfastened it. With little care, she let it fall from his hips and it clanked on the wooden floorboards. Magnus should have removed his sword, but he was too anxious to have her. He lifted her in his arms and carried her to the bed. There, he set her gently in the center and leaned back to gaze at her beautiful body.

He pressed a hand over her naked leg until he reached the hem of her chemise. His hand slid beneath the delicate fabric and eased it upward until he cupped the weighty flesh of her breast. She was endowed with ample breasts, more than enough to satisfy a man. He shifted forward and kissed a nipple through the thin material of her garment. Though he was anxious to be with her, he delighted in teasing her and reveled at the sound of her winsome murmurs.

She reached out to touch his hair and shifted her fingers to glide and take hold of the strands. With force, she pulled his head to hers. Magnus took it as her signal to want to be kissed. He set his mouth on hers and pressed his lips lightly at first. But then desire wound its way through him and he soon had her tongue responding to his. Lord, the kisses were hot and sultry. He kept up the torment of it which spurred an insatiable lust within him.

Magnus had never acted without honor with a woman and he was hard-pressed to maintain such now. Something within him turned his touches and movement to fervor. His hands roamed her skin, effectively squeezing her gently, gripping her legs, and bringing her closer to him. He pressed his length against her thigh and groaned at the hardness of his center. A throb taunted him to take her but his sweet wife shrank away from him.

At that moment, Magnus realized how forceful he was being and eased away from her. He'd forgotten how little experience she had. "I seem to be in a rush…"

"Magnus, don't…stop."

"Was I hurting ye?" Lord, he hoped not. "I apologize if I was."

"Nay, I liked what you were doing. Please, kiss me again."

"I want to do more than kiss ye. I want to hear ye shout my name when ye come undone. Say that ye will." He pressed the row of his knuckles over her soft cheek and waited for her promise.

"I shall if it makes you happy."

Magnus rejoined their mouths and kissed her with gentle passion. Their lips enmeshed and became torrid. He wanted to be tender but desire swarmed every part of him. The intention to take it slow was short-lived. He couldn't wait and moved his hand to her center. The warmth of her core beckoned his fingers and he readied her. She was tight and wet, more than ready for him. He pulled away from her and shifted her legs wider so he could join with her. As he set his erection at her center, he watched as her eyes darkened with passion. With little effort, he slid the length of himself inside her and groaned at the exquisite sensation of her surrounding him.

Pulses of her desire urged him on. It took great will not to thrust madly inside her. Magnus's legs shook with the need, but he wouldn't allow himself the pleasure. Not yet. She needed loving, a gentleness that spurred her lust and passion. With deliberate strokes of his length, he teased her, prodding her to meet him. She lifted her body to take him in and he moaned at the exquisite trembles of his body. The pleasure was there for the taking, but still, Magnus held back. He wanted Kendra to succumb to him, to meet her end before him, and to receive the bliss he was certain that awaited her. Bliss certainly awaited him.

She thrashed about and gripped his thighs as she propelled her body toward him. Their clashes became maddened then, each taking what each wanted and needed. She gasped and called his name in a breathy whisper. Hearing his name on her lips sent his culmination to overtake him. They met their ends together, both rasping and in thorough harmony. There was no greater rapture than that.

Magnus gently eased from her and set his head near her shoulder. His lips grazed the tender skin below her ear and he tried to calm his racing heart and breath. She placed her hand on his face and eased her fingers over his cheek. Magnus shifted to his back, kept his gaze on the beamed ceiling overhead, and considered how easy it was for her to enthrall him. He wasn't displeased by that, but he had no power to resist her or the promises made by her body.

When he peered at his wife, he found her watching him. "Have I told ye, sweetheart, how bonny ye look this day?"

She giggled lightly. "Aye, you did but you need not say such sweet words to me."

"Every lady should be told so each day, especially by her husband. I meant to tell ye that and more when I first saw ye in the hall." Magnus pressed a kiss on the side of her face and reached his arm across her torso.

Kendra shifted from beneath his hold, left the bed, and retrieved a cloth. She used it to clean him and her and returned it to the basin. When she came back to him, she didn't dress in a nightrail but pulled the covers over her naked body. He almost grinned thinking how easy it would be for them to join again later in the night.

"How was your trip to the village? Did you find out anything about your brother's death?"

"I found out some information that might be useful. What about ye? How did your visit with your father go?"

"My father at first failed to recognize me. I fear one day he won't and never shall again. That saddens me, but what can I do?"

"I'm sorry, sweetheart. Your father seems like a good man and 'tis disheartening to see him affected so greatly by this malady."

She wrapped her arm around him and snuggled closer. "Your grandda gave me a brooch this day. He said it belonged to your grandmother."

Magnus leaned upward and frowned slightly. "He did? I am surprised because he vowed that he would never part with my grandmother's brooch. He said it beheld magic and that the wearer would receive love from the man that she admired. Many a time around the night fires, my grandda told the story of how my grandmother had an old crone cast a spell upon the brooch so she could win my grandda's affection."

Kendra snorted a light laugh. "I disbelieve in magical charms, Magnus, but to appease Hugh, I accepted it. He told me to wear it at the Bealtuinn festival."

"Oh, aye, the festival approaches. I wish I could find Ned's killer before Bealtuinn. It would help the clan accept his death and perhaps lessen their mourning. I fear they will not want to celebrate unless I fulfill my vow of vengeance."

"You vowed to seek vengeance for his murder?" She gingerly roamed her hand over his torso and he flinched at her light touch.

"Aye, and it is a vow I take most seriously."

"I do hope you find out who took him from you. What if you do not find his murderer? Will you go to your death, the end of your days, seeking to fulfill this vow?"

Magnus wondered that too, but he didn't answer only grunted. "I should give the soldiers the next few days off so they can collect the wood and boughs for the great bonfire."

"If anything the festivity might lighten everyone. It saddens me to see your people in such mourning but I will probably be in the same spirit when Papa passes."

He slid his hand to her shoulder and pressed her back. "All hearts mourn when we lose someone close to us but we all die eventually, sweetheart. When your da's time comes, we shall send him to heaven with reverence as is his due."

Kendra placed her hands around his neck as he leaned over her. She clasped her hands and peered at him with sadness. "When his time comes, I want to take him back to our manor where he can be laid to rest with our ancestors. It is only right to honor him in such a way."

"Mayhap that is so, but he may not pass for years and by then your brother might return." Magnus was dejected hearing her say such a dreadful thing. She wanted to go home. Kendra hadn't exactly spoken those words, but he sensed a bit of homesickness in her. He wasn't sure if he could take her there and risk her not wanting to return with him. Yet she had spoken her vows before the chancellor and the king. She wouldn't go back on her vows now. No matter what happened, he was unwilling to lose her.

Magnus yanked her body closer to him and he set his mouth on hers. He couldn't get enough of her kisses, touches, and love. He would spend the night showing her how much she affected him even if it took him until sunrise.

CHAPTER TWELVE

KENDRA DIDN'T WANT to leave the bed and tried not to make any movement. She stayed still and watched her husband sleep. Magnus had his eyes closed and his dark hair covered some of his face. She longed to brush the strands of his hair aside and caress the light whiskers that formed overnight on his cheeks.

They had been married for almost a month and still, she had not figured out what kind of man he was. Magnus was kind to her, but he kept himself shielded, protecting himself. The only way she found anything out about him, was by questioning him or others. He often eluded her questions and never supplied her with or offered her information. That saddened her, that he felt the need to keep his emotions and thoughts to himself. Hopefully, one day, he would share things that bothered him or information without being asked. But she suspected that she'd be old and gray when that happened.

She stretched and pulled the bed covering over her. Magnus's arm roamed the cover and he set it over her and pulled her closer. Kendra wrapped her arm over his waist and leaned her head against his. "Good morn, Husband."

"Is it?"

Kendra laughed lightly. "Aye and from the view of the window, it appears to be sunny outside. Perhaps it shall be warmer this day. Does that please you?"

Magnus grunted. "If 'tis sunny now, wait an hour and it shall be raining."

"We should rise." She tried to dislodge his arm, but he was unmovable.

"Nay, not yet." He pressed her chin up with his fingers and gave her a light kiss. "Ye are right though, because duties await me and I cannot linger in bed as I want." Magnus rolled away. He stood, marched to the basin, washed, and dressed. He glared at the antechamber and sighed. "I should get to those manuscripts but have no time this day." The accounts were important and really needed to be handled. Yet Magnus detested numbers and having to do sums. Eventually, he would undertake the massive chore, but not this day.

"Should not the keep's steward see to the accounts? You do have a steward, don't you?" Kendra stayed abed and watched him with interest. He moved with confidence and the muscles in his legs, arms, and torso exuded strength. He wasn't burly, just strong-bodied.

"My brother Ned was the steward and since he died… I have yet to replace him but have no time at present to handle that or the accounts. I need to and soon." Magnus groaned. "I detest having to go over the accounts and sums. I am more apt with my sword than with parchments and figures."

Kendra climbed from the bed and reached him. She straightened his upper tartan and pressed the fabric of it, smoothing the wrinkles. "Magnus, you have such weight upon you. You should leave the clan's problems at the door."

"But I am the laird and the duty falls upon me…"

"Aye. Aye, it does, but once you are beyond our chamber door, you are no longer the laird. You are just a man, Magnus, seeking his rest with me, your wife. If you want peace, that is what you must do. Leave those problems at the door. Think of this room as a sanctuary of sorts."

He didn't hold back the frown that settled on his face. "There is no peace for me, not until I fulfill my vow to seek vengeance for my brother's murder. And there will never be peace for me, a man, who is named laird of this clan."

She pressed a hand on his face and he almost leaned into her touch, but he kept still. Kendra needed to understand the pressure he was under. "You deserve a little freedom, Magnus, surely?"

Magnus shook his head. "Nay, my clansmen and women have more freedom than I do. I am the laird, Kendra, and ye should understand that my ruling of this clan comes first. It comes before my wants, my needs, my peace." He stepped back from her. "I need to attend to my duties which are the sole reason for my existence."

She pressed her lips together and considered his words. Why would he make such an outlandish comment—*the sole reason for his existence*? How could she ever make him understand that he was more than a laird? Kendra needed to give it considerable thought. "I had hoped you would show me around this day. I long to see your lands."

"I must first gain reports and check on a few matters of importance. If I have time, I will find ye later, mayhap after midday." He reached the door and gazed at her with his greenish-brown eyes deepening as if he was sorry, but said nothing more.

Magnus's eyes seemed to implore her as if she was able to aid him before he closed the door behind him. She wished that were so. Her husband would not deny his duties and she realized that she did have the means to help him. Kendra draped a robe around herself and strode to the massive table that held the many manuscripts, opened the first volume and continued with the next and the rest until she'd sorted them by seasonal references. Later, when she had more time to devote to the task, she would go through the figures and enter the slips of parchment that had yet to be entered. Then she would take account and figure out if all was in order.

Linet hadn't come to see her as she usually did in the morning. Quickly, Kendra dressed and hurried to the great hall. By the time she reached it, all had gone about their day. It was later than she'd thought and she had missed the morning meal. But she found Marny who had just entered the fief.

"Oh, good morn, Milady," she said and repositioned Hale, who whimpered.

"Please, Marny, we agreed that you would call me Kendra. Come, join me, for I need company. It is too quiet in the hall."

Marny sat across from her at the table and took the cup Kendra handed to her. With Hale settled on her lap, she patted his back though he continued to fuss. "I am gladdened ye are here because I was a bit lonely. Wyren set out early to the training field."

"We are now sisters—well, sisters-in-law—and, I hope, friends. I never had women friends at my home unless you count the manor's maid but she's endeared to me and I cherish our friendship."

"Ye speak of Linet. I met her yestereve and she is a kind lass." Marny smiled. "I had three sisters and three brothers. I was never alone until I came here."

Kendra took a thin slice of bread and smeared it with a fruit spread. "Do you not see them now that you are married?"

"Oh, nay, and I haven't seen them since my marriage. The Camerons do not allow visitors and I do not have permission to leave the walls to visit my family even though they don't live too far away."

"That is disheartening, Marny. Perhaps in time, we can change that."

Marny scoffed. "There is no changing my husband's mind or the laird's. Wyren is commander and his foremost skill is protection. He will never allow me to leave the land unless he is there to protect me, and even then, he would be too cautious to take me so far from our keep."

Kendra patted the table and nodded. "Then that is what we shall do. We'll get him to accompany you for a visit to your family."

Marny chortled lightly. "Wyren would never agree but I am

not too distressed by it and do not miss my family overly. 'Tis the truth, it is kind of good having a wee bit of peace except for Hale's wails. And now, I have you to talk to."

Kendra smiled slightly. "Now that we're alone, can you tell me why Magnus is so…serious? He rarely smiles or seeks pleasure, and by that, I mean doing what he wants and not what is expected of him. He said his sole existence was his duty to his clan."

Her newfound friend shrugged her shoulders. "I have not spoken much to Magnus but from what I understand, he was born to lead the clan. He was raised for the position of laird by the elders so aye, perhaps his existence is only that—duty." Marny leaned closer and spoke low, "Wyren, my husband, was raised to lead the soldiers, that left Ned and Jake. Magnus and Wyren were held to strict daily regimens, whereas the two latter brothers were left to their own. I fear they became less important and probably realized their insignificance."

"Which means they were not held to account for their actions as the two elder brothers were?"

"Rightly so. And 'tis rumored that Lady Faye spoiled her two younger sons. Ned was, from what I heard, hard to get along with. He thought nothing of shouting at you when he didn't get his way, as if he was a child."

Kendra was surprised to hear that because from what she'd heard since her arrival, all held Ned with esteem. That didn't seem to be the case. "And Jake, what of him?"

"Everyone taunted him. He was mocked and teased as a lad until he grew. Once he surpassed most in height, the teasing ceased. He now spends most of his time testing his sword. He is most serious about being the best warrior amongst the Camerons."

"Jake has given himself a goal to achieve like his brothers." Kendra pressed her hand on her heart, distressed to learn of Magnus's brothers' lives and his. From appearances, the Camerons seemed to be a caring family and devoted to each other. But from an insider's view, there was discord aplenty.

"My thanks, Marny, for sharing that with me. I think my husband is saddened by Ned's death and he mourns his brother."

Marny shook her head. "Not sad, Kendra, but honor-bound. He holds himself accountable for his brother's death and seeks to avenge him. Until he does, he will not receive his mother's forgiveness, and possibly not even then, because Lady Faye does not forgive easily."

Kendra folded her hands and considered what Marny had told her. Would Magnus care if his mother forgave him or not? Regardless, she had a hefty problem on her hands since she'd taken an oath to bring him happiness. How in God's good grace could she achieve that?

Before she left the hall, Kendra posed one last question to Marny. "Is there someone about whom I can trust to help me with a situation? One of the soldiers, perhaps?"

"What do ye need?" Marny bobbed Hale on her knee now and kept him from crying.

She quickly explained how she wanted to help Magnus with the manuscripts, but that it had to be kept secret. "I need someone to get me the count of the livestock and stores."

"Oh, I am certain Winston would help ye. He is the laird's manservant and is often about. I deem he might be honored if ye were to ask him."

"My thanks, I shall speak with him. I want to get outside and perhaps take a walk and visit my father before I return to my chamber." Kendra rounded the table and pressed a hand on baby Hale's head. "I wish you luck in getting him to nap this afternoon."

Marny chuckled. "I shall need it."

Kendra left her and stepped outside. She found Winston standing on the step and almost bumped into him. He held out his hands to keep her from falling down the step but hastily removed them.

"I...I apologize, Milady, for touching ye. I...shouldn't

have…" Winston's face brightened with shame. He stepped aside to allow her to pass.

"Good day, Winston, I appreciate your protection. Will you walk with me? There is something I wish to speak with you about. It is rather private."

The strapping young soldier nodded. "Aye, Milady, if ye wish me to. The laird asked me to stay close to ye whilst…" his words trailed off as she watched him expectantly. "Ah, what I meant to say is that he asked me to keep ye safe when he is not within the keep."

She smiled to appease him, but his words concerned her. "So he has left the walls? Is there a reason why I need to be kept safe?"

Winston shook his head, his dark locks disordered from behind his ears. "Nay, of course not, Milady. The laird only means to keep ye safe and as your husband, he deems to do so."

"I need your favor…" Kendra walked beside the soldier and quickly explained what she wanted him to do. "You see, I wish to surprise Magnus, and I don't want him to know what I am doing until it is done. Can you handle this task for me?"

"I cannot go against the laird, Milady. What ye ask of me goes beyond my duties to him. My laird might deem it as disloyal."

Kendra stopped in the lane and faced him. "He is troubled, Winston, and I mean to help him. I must have your trust and as your laird's wife, do I not get to make requests of you? Are you not as devoted and loyal to me as you are to him?" She kept her expression serious and had hoped to sway the soldier by insulting his honor.

"*Och*, Milady, our laird has never been married before and I do not know what my duty to ye is or should be. Yet I see the way he looks at ye and I suspect he cares for ye. If ye promise not to reveal how ye came about the information, I should be able to help ye. And whilst I seek your answers, ye must promise to stay inside the keep's walls." Winston whistled and a large hound came barreling from the lane directly at them. By the dog's wagging tail and wiggling body, she could tell he didn't mean any harm no matter how fearsome he appeared.

"Oh, is he yours?" She petted the dog's head and knelt so she could allow him to get her scent. "You're a handsome dog, aye you are." The hound was huge with scraggly grey hair and his long tail flapped eagerly. Though he appeared mangled, he was still handsome in her view.

"This be Sigge, the laird's hound."

"He belongs to Magnus? Why don't I keep him with me whilst you are attending to your, ah...task? During my walk, I promise not to leave the walls. I intend to visit briefly with my father and then I shall return to the keep."

"Very well, Milady. I would feel better if Sigge stayed with ye. I'll return shortly." Winston sauntered away and disappeared beyond the keep's tower.

Kendra called the dog to her and he followed. She traipsed to the end of the lane where Hugh's cottage sat. Neither her father nor Hugh were home or nearby and must have gone fishing as they'd mentioned the day before. As much as she wanted to search for her father and Hugh, she would keep her promise to Winston and not leave the walls.

She returned to the keep and continued her assessment of the manuscripts. Sigge lay on the floor beneath the table and stretched out with his head settled on her foot. Kendra found the volume that went from the present back to the previous summer season. She decided to use that volume to assess the numbers and go from there. Her eyes perused the accounts of livestock, grain stores, meat stores, each clansmen's holdings, and the clan's coins. When Winston returned with the latest count, she could figure out if there were any discrepancies.

Her back ached from sitting still most of the afternoon. Kendra stretched and left the chair. Sigge lifted his head briefly and then settled back. She walked to the window and gazed through it at the clan's people near the keep. The door opened and she almost jumped. Magnus had returned. She had thought it might be Winston, but surely, he wouldn't enter without knocking.

Sigge groaned but didn't move from his spot under the table.

"What are ye doing, hiding in here?" he asked and set his discarded tartan on a trunk.

"I thought to take a rest before supper. Are you through with your duties for the day?"

Magnus sat on the edge of the bed and removed his boots. He shuffled back and leaned against the bed's headboard. His brows rose and he almost smiled. He twitched a finger at her and patted the bed covers beside him. "Come here, sweetheart."

Kendra did as he bade and she sat on the edge of the bed. He pressed his hand on the side of her neck and pulled her forward for a kiss. She set her palms on his chest and kissed him back.

Sigge crawled from beneath the table and stood by the door. It was Magnus' turn to groan as the dog whined to leave. Kendra tried to get up to let his pet out but her husband held her fast. But then a knock sounded and again, Magnus groaned, but this time he let her go so she could hurry to the door to open it. Winston had returned. She tried to give him a subtle warning that Magnus was within, with wide eyes.

"Milady…"

She shook her head, silently letting him know it was not a good time. Sigge forced his way past her and reached the soldier.

Winston was astute. He quickly hid the parchments behind his back. "I just wanted to… I had hoped ye returned to your chamber and wanted to make sure ye were within the keep."

"Who is there?" Magnus asked from the bed.

"Just Winston, making sure I am where I am supposed to be."

"Tell him to go away."

"I shall find you later," she whispered and closed the door. She returned to Magnus. "You didn't answer me. Are you finished your duties for the day?"

"That depends," he said and pulled her over his body. "…if ye want to spend a wee bit of time with me."

Kendra giggled when he pressed his hands on her backside and yanked her hard against him. "I could be persuaded…" She didn't finish her words but set her mouth on his.

His hands roamed her body and he took little time removing her garments. Kendra helped him and pulled his tunic over his head. She set a smattering of kisses on his chest and straddled his hips. Face to face, she sighed at the desirous way he gazed at her. His greenish-brown eyes darkened. She took her time taking him in and caressed the sides of his face.

Magnus shifted her and she spread her legs to give him easier access to her. He entered her and she leaned her head against his. Gently, she rocked against him and as she did, he pressed his hands on her breasts. Their movements, in unison, were slow and oh-so-affecting. Kendra's legs shook and though she wanted to wait to reach her pinnacle, her body gave over. She drew in a breath and latched on to Magnus as ecstasy took control of her.

"Ye are so bonny, sweetheart, when ye reach the wee death," Magnus said and held her face. He kissed her passionately, turning his mouth over hers, sweeping his tongue against her lips, and sending more warmth and pleasure through her.

Kendra wouldn't let him shift her and she set her hands on his shoulders. She leaned upward and with effective strokes of her body, she met his hardness, fully encompassing him. Magnus pressed his face against her shoulder. His open mouth against her skin heated her with his heaving breath. Her body met his forcefully, keeping the pace of his thrusts until he shouted his release and tilted back his head. She leaned forward and set a gentle kiss on his throat, the side of his neck, and his muscular shoulder.

She didn't move off him directly after but continued to hold him. "What did you mean by 'wee death'?" Kendra almost laughed at his words but really didn't understand why he'd spoken them.

"'Tis what the French call *la petite mort*, aye, the wee death…when ye come undone amid passion. Ye reached it, aye?" He spoke so fervently that she believed him.

"I certainly did. Then I hope to reach wee death often," she said and lightly kissed his lips.

Though she might not have Magnus's attention during the day, she had his full attention in bed. That soothed her and she knew she would have to make do with that for now. In time, he would leave his worries at the door, he would smile and laugh, and he would find peace within their bedchamber. Kendra vowed it would be so.

CHAPTER THIRTEEN

THE LAST DAY of April was busy for all the clan's men and women. Magnus gave the men time away from training, farming, and other employment to take care of the Bealtuinn festival needs. He rose early, gave Kendra a lingering kiss, and hastened through the door. With a spring in his step, he reached the outside and forwent eating his morning meal. He would partake of it at the barracks where he would direct the events of the day. There was much to do to ensure the rites and celebrations were handled accordingly.

As he approached the building that housed his soldiers, he met up with Wyren who conversed with Jake. They needed to leave soon to worship at the old stone so they could return before the afternoon and evening festivities began. Magnus was impatient to get going.

"We should forgo the celebration."

Magnus turned and found his father standing behind him. "We cannot."

"Your mother is in deep mourning and says that until your brother's death is avenged, the clan should cease any merriment or gatherings."

He sighed and glared at Wyren who he hoped would take his side but his brother remained silent. "We have never, regardless of any deaths, withheld the festivity of the bel-fire. Besides, Da, we don't know yet if Ned deserves vindication. I will leave on the morrow and learn more, but until we have proof that Ned wasn't dishonest, we will go along as we have always done."

"Why do ye deem he was dishonest? Is there something ye are not telling me?" his father demanded.

Magnus was unsure of how much to tell his father. At this point, he would divulge as little as possible. "There are some disparaging facts that have come to light recently about Ned. I want to find out if they are true before I either avenge him or end my vow."

"Ye do not intend to tell me what those disparaging facts are, are ye?"

"Until I learn the truth or more, I shall await to reveal the matter."

His father nodded, appeased with his explanation. "I shall tell your mother what ye have decided."

"It is my duty as laird to investigate this matter. I will not make rash decisions, and for now, we will partake of the festival. Besides, we could use a wee bit of merriment." Magnus shrugged at the scoff his father made under his breath.

There was no way to sway his mother to accept Ned's fate or that he might have been culpable for underhanded dealings. This day was not a day to consider such ramifications or dastardly deeds done by Ned. It was a day to celebrate the rites of marriage, the beginning of new life, and the hope for future blessings.

"Let us ride out," Magnus said and Winston handed him his mount's reins.

As the procession of men rode through the gates, the women who were assembled gave them bunches of flowers tied with ribbons to place on the old stone. As his men rode by, they tucked the gifts to the goddess securely inside their tunics.

They rode toward a small village near Kilmallie where on the north-eastern side of Loch Linnhe sat the great old Charra, an ancient stone where they often worshipped. When they reached the stone, which was taller than most of the men, they left their horses to graze in the adjacent field. All approached on foot, silent and reverent. Magnus motioned to his men who stepped forward and placed the flowers, trinkets, and other bestowments at the base of the stone.

All bowed their heads, each reflecting their thoughts to their ancestors, Gods, Goddesses, and the Catholic God in prayer and devotion. Most sought the blessing of the Mother Goddess for it was only due to Her enlightenment that they achieved the continuation of their people, the enrichment of their crops, and the essence of their woman's affection.

Magnus prayed for redemption for his brother's death and that God would lead him to the culprit and enlighten him of the truth behind Ned's dealings. He also gave thanks for sending him Kendra, for the bairns they would soon have, and for his family and clan who he lived to serve.

When the devotion was completed, Osmond and Hayden retrieved the goblets and brew. It had become their custom to take a drink at the stone as an offering of their commitments. Osmond drank deeply from the goblet and refilled the cup with the potion that he likened to that of the spirit of their ancestors.

"Here, Laird, take a good swig of this. It'll wake ye and thicken your blood." Osmond handed him the goblet.

Magnus set it to his mouth and drank. As the liquid coursed through his body, a deep burning settled in his chest which reminded him of the pleas he'd just made at the stone. He burned for justice, salvation, and ultimately happiness with Kendra. When he finished the drink, he poured more "spirit" into the goblet and handed it to Wyren. Each man partook of the drink, and after each had drained one goblet full of the harsh liquid, they stood around silent and insightful.

Winds whipped the field's grasses and pressed their tartans to their bodies. None wanted to move from the sacred place that held such meaning for them.

That was, until Hayden broke the silence, "Drunkenness is next to Godliness, aye?"

The men shouted their agreement with cheers and all bellowed in jubilation.

When the men calmed, Magnus held up his arm. His men neared and all stood and waited for his direction. Winston handed him a parchment that listed all the items and tasks they needed to accomplish before sundown.

Twenty men were chosen to go and search for the sacred woods that would be used for the massive bonfires. Their customs dictated they use the nine sacred woods from alder, ash, birch, hawthorn, hazel, holly, oak, rowan, and willow trees.

"Winston, are ye certain ye wish to marry the May Queen, Gloria? There's still time to change your mind." Wyren bellowed a laugh when Winston sneered and shoved his chest.

"My bonny bride will have no other but me, so I am willing to accept her."

For his brash comment, he received several strikes from their comrades to his shoulders and back offering congratulatory banter. Magnus tried to hold back his smile because it was good to see his men making merry again. They had been too solemn of late.

"Winston, will ye be garbing yourself as the green man?"

His soldier nodded vigorously. "Aye, I am prepared to make a showing as the green man."

His brethren chortled and ruffed up Winston with jabs, pokes, and light punches to his body. Winston's grin was wide at being the focus of the men's jubilation.

Magnus cleared his throat to gain their attention. "Winston, ye will take many men with ye to collect the boughs and garlands. When ye return to the fief, ye can attach them to the windows and doors of the maidens. There's a good amount of men who are marrying during the festival." Magnus watched as the procession of bachelors passed by him. Their grins and jests lightened him. Though he hadn't been able to reap the benefit of his marriage at the celebration, many considered marrying on the first of May a blessing. Families allowed the courting rites of their lassies and negotiations of marriages were well settled before and at the end of the day.

"Wyren, will ye find a few men to ensure all hearths are darkened before the bonfires are lit this eve? Once we light the two bonfires, we'll allow the farmers to bring the livestock through." Magnus noted his brother's acceptance of his task.

Wyren nodded and pointed to some of the men standing around him and spoke low, giving them directions for their task. The men scattered to perform their duties. Those who remained in the area to collect wood and boughs would return later. The rest of them took to their mounts and headed for home.

Of all the rituals and rites of the festival, Magnus found the blessing of the fire to be the most coveted and sacred, but the worshiping at the stone was just as poignant. When the fires were lit and as the animals passed between the fires three times, they would then be put to the summer pasture where the animal's fertility would be ensured. Some years they had doubled their livestock numbers. He hoped to do so again this year.

Magnus returned with some of the men and rode through the gate of his home. He left his horse in the large corral to give his warhorse time to settle before he was taken to the stable. His gaze lingered over the grounds of his home. The womenfolk set up tables, strung banners, and pennons from cottage to cottage. There were games set for the children, and barrels of ale situated along the lane for the adults. A platform was erected near where the bonfires would be lit for the musicians, a bunch of rowdy men who were well known to partake of the barrels more often than they should.

Magnus hurried and ate his mid-day meal and then continued with the preparations. Near dusk, he marched toward the keep's tower and awaited Kendra, who was to join him. His home took on an ethereal appearance with all the decoration and the clan's people adorned in their best garments. That night the Camerons would celebrate and nothing would stop them from enjoying the festivity, not even his mother's mourning.

Kendra appeared and stood by the door of the keep. Magnus stopped short when he got a glimpse of her. Clad in the overdress she'd worn at their wedding now, she'd draped it with the Cameron tartan. Pinned to it was his grandmother's brooch. The late afternoon sun shone on the silver and sent a glint at him. His breath about ceased at the sight of her. How fortunate was he to win her hand? Magnus thought that perhaps he should send a missive to the king, thanking him for forcing him into the marriage.

Kendra approached and stood before him. "We never had festivals like this near my home."

Magnus raised his hand and used his knuckles to caress her soft cheek. "Come, after they light the fires, we just might sneak off and do our own sort of celebrating." He smiled and she clasped his hand.

The minstrel began singing: *Nine woods in the cauldron, burn them quick and burn them slow, bring on the maidens, here we go...*

Magnus wrapped his arm around Kendra and guided her along the lane. They passed his clan's men and women who sang along to the minstrel's tune. Two soldiers ran along the lane and when they got to the wooden structures, they set their torches to it and the flame took hold. A long moment passed before the wood ignited and sent a glow about the faces of his clan.

"How beautiful."

"The fires are bonny, but we use the sacred woods which represent protection, wisdom, healing, power, and success, amongst other things. I have joined this festival since I was born, and likewise, all of my clan. Not a year passes that we do not light the fires."

"Still, it is incredible. I wish I had such merriment whilst I was growing up."

He nodded and understood because now that Christianity had taken hold, most people only partook of the rites of their religion and celebrated the Feast of the Finding of the Holy Cross. Priests performed mass outside where many gathered around a bonfire and the land was blessed. Magnus was glad they didn't have any clergymen on his land presently because that allowed them to continue to revere the old rites. But his clan probably wouldn't ever cease celebrating the old ways along with the new.

Winston's marriage was held between the two bonfires. Men carried Winston down the lane and shouted for all to make way. His soldier was garbed as the green man, completely covered in leaves, twigs, and moss, which represented the forest's cycle of life, death, and rebirth. What skin showed on Winston was painted with the bluish-green hue of the leaves. All gathered and some of the women tossed flowers before the bride as she marched with her family to her destiny. Each proclaimed their love and agreement to wed. Their union was announced by the bride's father and all the clan cheered. He'd never seen his soldier look so pleased. Kendra likewise smiled and seemed to enjoy the ceremony.

Men marched toward the fire and lines formed for the running through the flames. A man backed up and then sprinted toward the fire. He jumped over it, through the high-licking flames, and fortunately came away unscathed. Some were less fortunate and their tartans caught alight. Instantly, they were put out and suffered some minor burns on their skin, but nothing major.

Kendra's eyes widened at the fanfare. Her mouth hung open as she watched the men take their turns. "Tell me you will not jump through the flames."

Magnus chuckled. "I haven't jumped through the flames in a long time. Aye, for I leave it up to God whether He will bestow good fortune on me. I believe He has. The men think the flames will bless them with good fortune," he explained. He laughed when Jake ran through and jumped so high that the flames had no chance of catching him.

"It is good to hear you laugh, Magnus. I wish you were always so lighthearted." Kendra leaned against him and grinned.

"This day always brings me joy."

"Is it the only day?"

"For now," he said and turned, guiding her away from the revelry. Magnus returned to the keep, to a table sitting near the entrance. "Let us have supper and then we will take a walk in the woods."

"Beyond the walls? Really? I want to see what your land looks like."

Magnus pulled a trencher from the small stack in the center of the table and set it before her. He took one for himself and piled it with mutton, sweetcakes, and raw carrots. Kendra spooned pottage onto hers and they ate silently. He hadn't taken her beyond the wall before and was not too concerned because this night the woods would be filled with his soldiers.

While they ate, his closest comrades joined them at the table. Wyren and Marny sat across from him and Kendra. Hale was tucked in his father's hold. Winston sat with Gloria. Hayden and Osmond took up the rest of the space. Sigge wasn't far behind and sat next to him, thumping his tail against the ground, vying for his attention and pieces of his mutton. Magnus petted him and gave him what he wanted. His dog gulped down the food thrown at him. Before long, Jake strolled along and joined them too. Magnus thought to give direction now for the morrow since it was unlikely he would see them after they finished the meal.

"On the morrow, we will leave to confront Aldo and find out the truth behind Ned's death. Wyren, you'll stay here and look after the keep. Ye will need to ensure our men are ready to face any threat from the Chattans. Winston, since ye are newly married, I give ye leave from duty for the next day. After that, ye will ensure Kendra's safety whilst I am gone. I'll have my da watch out for her until ye return to duty."

All stared at him. He felt Kendra's eyes piercing him but he needed to assert his dictate. "I will take Jake, Hayden, and Osmond with me. The three of ye select one other to go on the trek. There will be six in all. I will select a small regiment of men to accompany us as well. We know not what we will face when we confront Aldo, but I want answers and I mean to get them."

His men grumbled and grunted. As each left the table after their supper, they stepped before him and bowed their heads in silent acceptance of their mission. Not that they could refuse, but the men he chose to attend him were the most trusted, fiercest soldiers, within the clan. His brother Jake seemed surprised that he'd asked him along. This was the first time he'd take him on a mission but it was time for his brother to show his mettle.

When his brother stepped before him, he stopped him. "Jake, I hope ye know that I value ye and wanted ye to gain experience before I asked…"

"Ye do not need to explain, Laird. I am ready to serve and protect ye now. My sword is sharp as well as my mind. We shall find our foe and I will be gladdened to be there when ye do."

Magnus was taken aback by his brother's pledge. It was the most he'd spoken to him at once in a long time. He rose and clasped his brother in a brief embrace. "My thanks, Jake. Do not linger out here all night. Ye need a wee bit of shut-eye before we head out."

His brother nodded and set off.

Magnus waved to Wyren and Marny as they left to put Hale to bed. Now he sat alone with Kendra and he rose to stand behind her. She left her seat and turned to peer at him.

"You are leaving again. How long will you be away?"

"Probably a few moon rises. Come," he said and took her hand. He guided her toward the gates. They continued onward until he stopped on the wooden bridge that led to the island. The moon, now higher in the sky, shone on the waters that flowed beneath it.

Magnus kissed her cheek and took her hand again. They traipsed along and when they reached the darkened woods beyond the land's embankment, he pulled her into his embrace.

"Magnus, there are others about."

"Aye, it's part of the rite. All within the wood this night will couple with their women. Next winter there will be a great many

Cameron bairns born." He grinned, thinking about that and hoped that perhaps he and Kendra would be blessed to welcome their first child.

Kendra wrapped her arms around his neck and he lifted her into his arms. When he found the perfect spot, a soft, grassy place between the thick trunks of pine trees, he set her down. Magnus was careful when he disrobed her. Her overdress was of delicate materials and he was careful as he unpinned the brooch he so remembered from when he was a lad. When she was only clad in her shift, he leaned back and removed his garments. The crisp air of the night did nothing to cool his ardor for he was filled with lust and longing.

Magnus wanted their time together to be special. He wasn't sure when he'd see her again but it would be a long while. Too long.

He lay beside her, gently caressed her, and aroused her body to respond to him with light moans. She was soft and sweet. Kendra tried to pull him to her for a kiss, but he pressed her back. "Let us take it slow. We should enjoy this time together."

In the dimness of the woodland surrounding them, he could barely see her. Magnus wanted to bring her pleasure and so he set his mouth at her apex and used his tongue to lash at the heat of her vagina. In his ministration, he heard her rasps, murmurs, gasps, and moans. Then, she succumbed to the pleasure and thrashed about. He grinned to himself, but now, he was hard and hot for her.

"Magnus, please, let me." She straddled him and gyrated her hips to take him in again and again.

As he lay back, enjoying the pleasure of his wife's body, he pressed his hands on the dewy grass near him before he lifted his hands to reach out to Kendra's face. He pressed his dew-covered palms on her cheeks. She peered at him inquisitively.

"'Tis believed that if ye wash your face with the early morn dew, ye will be blessed with good fortune." Magnus settled his hands on her hips and pulled her toward him. The movement of her body against his sent him reeling once again.

"I already received good fortune and need no more," she whispered.

Her words pleased him and he was caught up in the desirous motion that it only took a moment for lust to engulf him. His moan echoed in the woods along with those of many men that night, purposely pleasing the Goddess Flora who would ensure the transition of the season of rebirth.

After their romp in the woods, Magnus held her hand on the return to the keep. They didn't come across anyone on their walk back. At the keep, he led her to their bedchamber and they readied for bed. Magnus undressed and waited for her to do the same. Once she was settled, he joined her and held her close. He thought about the excursion on the morrow and what he needed to do. Would he finally gain the answers he sought about Ned's death?

CHAPTER FOURTEEN

ON THE JOURNEY to Fassiefern, Magnus somehow contained his fury. They didn't leave the holding until well past midday. He'd wanted to leave at first light but several of his soldiers hadn't arrived at the gate as instructed. Others were sent to roust the men, and finally, when all assembled, he led the group onward. When they reached the thickly pine-covered land on the lane toward the village, he slowed his pace.

Two men lagged behind and retched in a thicket of yews. Served them right for imbibing too much the night before. Magnus grunted and hoped they had headaches and sore stomachs, for it was well-deserved. He considered leaving them behind and selecting others to take their place, but they eventually showed themselves.

"What has ye so agitated, Laird?" Hayden asked. "Are ye thinking about how we will confront this Aldo fellow?"

"Nay, I am piss-arsed that none of ye listened. I bade that all be at the gate early because I wanted to confront Aldo in the early morn. Now, we will arrive later than I had hoped."

Hayden lowered his head. "I should have ensured the men followed your orders, Laird."

"It matters not now. We will adjust our plan and will confront him in the dark of night instead." Magnus nudged his horse to canter ahead of the men. As they rode toward the village, he considered what he'd do. It would be best to meet Aldo when he least expected it and he might as well disturb his trade whilst he was at it.

On the outskirts of Fassiefern, he stopped in a well-shielded area. The thick woodland was abutted with crags that would hide them until he was ready to make his presence known.

"Take rest and make camp." Magnus settled his horse by running his hands over the muscular beast. Not only did it benefit his steed, but the motion also calmed him. He was deep in thought as he considered his plan when Osmond approached.

"Laird, what says ye? What is your plan? Will ye be telling us or will we just be left in the dark?" Osmond stood near him with a scowl on his face.

Magnus wasn't about to allow his follower's blatant provocation. He grabbed his burly soldier by the fabric of his tunic and held fast. "When I want ye to know my plan, I will tell ye." He tossed him back. Osmond lost his footing and fell back on his arse.

His brother Jake offered a hand to the fallen soldier and gave him a reproachful look. Magnus growled low in his throat. Ordinarily, he would not accept a show of disrespect from any of his soldiers but Jake was his brother and he shook his head, keeping his rebuke silent.

All his men kept their distance after Osmond's humiliation. Magnus paced between two trees and tried to settle his ire. While they waited, some rested, some sharpened their swords, and some ate. Without speaking to him, Hayden hesitantly approached and held out a large helping of bread and a flask of ale. Magnus took it and sat next to a tree. The rest of the day passed in agonized slowness. He was anxious to get going and when the sun set and the land dimmed, Magnus called his men to make ready.

"We will go to where they wager, a ramshackle of a barn at the far end of the village. Aldo is likely to be there this time of day in his den of debauchery."

As he rode toward Fassiefern, Magnus blocked out his thoughts and concentrated on the mission at hand.

The lane through the village was empty, save for a few people who walked along. When he reached the old barn, he slid from his horse's back and marched to the old worn door. His men followed closely behind. To catch the men inside unawares, he yanked the door open and they rushed inside. Magnus shot his gaze from man to man until he found Aldo.

Aldo stood at the back end of the barn with a handful of players who knelt on the ground, peering at the dice someone had just thrown. The Cameron soldiers aided his progress and kept anyone from hampering his approach.

Magnus reached Aldo and pulled his sword free. He'd let his weapon do the talking for him. "Tell me about Ned Cameron. I want to know exactly how he came here and all that ye know."

Aldo backed up with his hands held out and fear widening his eyes, retreating to stand near some wooden crates. "I...I do not know any such man."

"Ye speak falsely. Your friend there"—he pointed at the man who he'd spoken to on his previous visit—"told me that my brother was here and that he lost a good deal of coin to ye. That ye were supposed to meet so that ye could collect your take. Now tell me what I want to know."

Aldo pressed his beard with his hand. His black hair lay in straggled strands on his shoulders. His appearance was bedraggled and the stench from him gave a warning that the man hadn't bathed for some time. "He came and wagered from time to time. Ned tried to recoup his losings... *och*, he only lost more."

"Is that because ye tricked him, aye, cheating your way to winning a man's coin?" Magnus grunted at his assertion.

"Nay, nay, I am not a cheater. I swear, by God, I do not commit such a sin. I run an honest business here. Your brother told me to meet him at The Tavern two days hence after he lost, and that he would pay me. I trusted him but he never showed."

"Who did he befriend here in Fassiefern? Was he comrades

with the other wagering fools?" Magnus clipped his words and ire filled him because still, he was getting nowhere in his attempt to achieve his vengeance.

"Ned wasn't comrades with any of these men but he oft sought the night with a woman of ill repute. I do not know her name but she's one of Mary's lassies. Mistress Mary allows men to visit her home to be with the lassies there."

"Where can I find this Mary?"

"Her manor is to the east, located about two leagues or so from the village." Aldo backed up another step. Magnus grabbed hold of him so that he couldn't gain his release.

"If ye speak falsely, I will come for ye."

The man was about to bawl. "I swear to ye, I speak the truth. Ned was my comrade and I wouldn't have killed him over coins. I thought he was good for it."

"How much did he lose to ye?"

Aldo wheezed and gasped when Magnus clutched him with more force. He tried to escape by forcing Magnus's hands away but it was futile. "Three marks. He owed me three marks."

"Damnation, Ned owed ye over four hundred pence and ye had no care? I disbelieve ye."

Aldo gripped his wrists to get him to release him. "I did care, och what was I to do when I heard he was dead? There is no begetting repayment from a dead man."

Magnus shoved him back, then grunted and sheathed his sword. "Do not leave Fassiefern. If ye do, my men will find ye and ye will end the same as Ned with a dagger to your heart." He turned and marched out with his brethren following after they made threatening glares at the men inside the falling-down barn.

Outside, he whistled for his horse. Once he and his men were ready, they headed in the direction of the woman's manor. Magnus hoped to get answers there. Perhaps the woman Ned met knew of what happened to him. At best, he might figure out why Ned was willing to lose such a good deal of their clan's coin.

By the time they reached the distance they'd been told, a

narrow lane afforded them a trail to a large manor home. The windows mostly were darkened except for a few on the lower floor. Smoke wafted from the chimney. The night air swathed the land with a frigidness and their breaths formed clouds of mist. Covered with thick woven tartans, he and his men paid little attention to the cold that settled around them.

Magnus stepped lightly toward the building and when he reached the threshold, he thrust the door open and stepped inside. The dozen men who rode with him wore grins when they were met by the scantily clad women inside. Women of every size and shape were strewn about the room, garbed in see-through garments, chemises, and some in plain braises. None of the women hid their bodies when they entered. Magnus slid his eyes around the abode and searched for someone in charge.

"I deem ye had more than enough revelry last eve," he said to his men. "None of ye will approach these women. Do I make myself clear?" Magnus gave his men the order and waited for the woman supposedly in charge, Mary perhaps, to approach.

His men nodded but continued to ogle the women.

A huge bald man thumped forward with heavy steps. "What do ye want here? The cost for an hour with a lass is a groat for each of ye."

"We are not here to partake of the women's services. I was told my brother Ned Cameron came here and had a woman that he frequented. Know ye of her?"

The man shook his head. "I know not who ye speak of. Many men visit Mary's Manor." He tilted his head at his men and nodded. "Aye, for I see some faces I recognize."

Magnus glared at his brethren, not because they visited a house of ill repute, but because no one told him they had been there before. "Is the Mistress about? I wish to speak to her."

"Mary is busy."

"Make her unbusy. I don't want to cause trouble, sirrah, but if ye don't get Mary right now, you'll have more trouble than ye can handle." Magnus set his hand on the hilt of his sword, blatantly making the threat. "I do not want to draw my sword, but shall if ye need a wee bit of encouragement."

"We want no trouble with the likes of ye. I will ask if she will see ye." The man marched off, thumping over the floorboards, and disappeared from his view.

Magnus kept his hand on his sword and peered about. The men who visited the manor were mostly tradesmen, none to give him concern. Still, he wasn't about to let his guard down.

"Laird," Jake said and stepped next to him. "Allow me to question the woman. I'll get answers from her."

His men guffawed and Osmond chuckled and said, "Aye, Jake, ye be a wee bit green and are wanting more from her than answers."

"He wants a wee roll in the haystack," Hayden said and bellowed a laugh.

"Ye will all remain here. I will question the woman myself," Magnus said sternly.

A short moment later, the man returned. "She'll see ye. Follow me."

Magnus was about to trail the man but turned to his men. "Stay by the door. If I do not return shortly, find me." He turned back and strode toward the back of the manor. The man opened a door and waved him forward.

He entered the chamber and found a woman who was draped with a piece of red silk fabric. She lay upon a long chair and held a goblet in her hand. An unclothed man stood by the window awaiting the woman's direction.

"Stay there until I finish with this man," she said with authority, and to him, "My man tells me that you refused to leave until you spoke to me." She patted the strange furniture she lay upon. "Come, I don't bite unless you want me to." She practically purred her command.

Magnus didn't want to scare the woman, so he trudged forward and sat next to her. "I need to know about my brother, Ned Cameron. I was told he visited here."

"Oh, Neddie. Of course, I know him. Aye, he oft came here. Sometimes, he spent time with Nicola but mostly spent his time with me. You are his brother? Which one?"

"Magnus," he said and watched the woman's face to assess her honesty. If she lied, he would know. He'd always had a sense when someone was lying but given her profession, he wasn't surprised that the woman was crafty.

"Oh, you're *that* brother. You don't much resemble Neddie." She kept her eyes on him and *tisked* when the man by the window moved. "Remain still," she commanded and the man braced his legs.

Magnus shook his head at the absurdity of the man by the window but he wasn't there to condemn anyone, only to find answers. It was true he and Ned had dissimilar looks because his brother was fair-haired and blue-eyed while he was dark. "We found him murdered near the old crag of Lochaber."

"We heard about Neddie's death. I'm sorry for your loss but if you deem we had something to do with it then you are—"

"Nay, I just want to know who he might have interacted with. Know ye that he wagered with a man named Aldo in Fassiefern?" Magnus hoped she'd be forthright and give him information about his brother's activities.

"On his last visit, Neddie was riled and rough. I eased him as best I could. He spoke about a debt that he owed to Aldo but that wasn't what concerned him." Mary set a hand on his arm and sensually stroked him.

Magnus was about to stand, but she clasped his arm and continued, "He said that two of his clansmen were trying to wrest coins from him because they found out that he was wagering in Fassiefern. He worried about it and it took me most of the night to relieve him. When he left, he said he was going to meet his clansmen and deal with the problem. We heard that he was murdered a sennight later. If you are seeking who would do Neddie harm, look to your own clan."

This was disconcerting and hard to believe. Still, he had no other information regarding Ned. Was it possible she was telling the truth? "He did not say who these men were or name them?"

Mary shook her head. "Nay, but he was put out by it and uneasy. He mentioned that he was taken aback that his brethren wouldst extort coin from him."

Magnus frowned deeply at what she'd told him. Who within his clan would do such a thing? The mystery of what happened to Ned further confounded him. He had to find out who tried to extort the coins from him and about Ned's underhanded dealings. Who within his clan had the bollocks to threaten his brother? He was about to make his exit when the woman leaned toward him.

"There's no need to rush off. You are quite handsome, Laird Cameron. Perhaps you would like to join me this night. Free of charge, of course. I can have Odran sent away and we can be alone. Unless you wish to join us." With the back of her hand, she flapped it at the man, who had continued to focus on the window.

"Stay where ye are, Odran. I am afraid, Mistress Mary, that I have no time to take ye up on your generous offer. My thanks for the information." Magnus pulled a small sack of coins from within his tunic and set them on the table by the door on his way out.

He reached his brethren and they fled the manor. Outside, he called to his horse, mounted, and cantered away from the sordid place. As he rode for home, Magnus was weary at the prospect of finding out who wanted to coerce coins from Ned. He believed the mistress because Aldo certainly didn't have the bollocks to murder anyone even if he was owed coins.

Hayden sidled next to him. "What happened? Did ye find out what happened to Ned?"

"Not yet. Soon."

Jake flanked the other side of him. "What did the mistress say? Was Ned there? Was he with anyone else?"

"She said he was there but did not say if anyone was with him. The woman gave little detail." That was all he was about to say on the matter. He'd kept what Mistress Mary had told him to himself. Magnus would speak to Wyren about it, but other than that, he trusted no one. Someone within his clan murdered his brother and he was filled with rage. How dare they try to extort coins from a Cameron? That they murdered Ned over riches infuriated him, but what was worse was that it was done by his clansmen.

The closer he got to home, the more enraged Magnus became. His breath increased and his fingers gripped the reins of his horse with absolute determination. He wanted retribution and his vow to seek vengeance purged through him, heating his blood.

Before they reached the woodland that sprawled over the hills near his fief, he heard the sound of riders a short distance away. Magnus motioned to his men to take cover in case it was a rival clan that rode through. He thought it might be the Cameron sentry doing their nightly duty, but when he took in the form of the lead rider, he discerned that he wasn't from his clan. Was he a Chattan soldier? Magnus was unsure but who else would trespass on their land but the Chattans?

Magnus shouted his clan's war cry, "Sons of the Hounds, Come Hither And Get Flesh!"

The ting of swords being pulled from his soldiers' scabbards rang in the air. Magnus wasn't about to let the Chattans get away with trespassing on his land, and this day, he would prove it.

CHAPTER FIFTEEN

W HEN SHE AWAKENED, Magnus had already left. Kendra
smiled to herself in remembrance of the night she spent
with Magnus in the woods. The May Day celebration was
enjoyed by all and she couldn't wait until the next celebration.
She spent the morning in their bedchamber and entered the
figures from the parchments that hadn't been added. The only
thing left to do was to compare the numbers to the counts
Winston had given her to that of the totals in the manuscripts.
She closed the volume and sighed because she had yet to figure
out how to tell Magnus that she had remedied the problem for
him. He was probably going to be surprised and perhaps
delighted that she had handled the situation for him. She
understood how pressing the matter was.

A knock came at the door and she rushed to open it. A young
soldier stood on the other side.

"Milady, the gate watch asked me to deliver this message to
ye." He held out a parchment.

Kendra thanked him and took it. He turned and left, so she
closed the door and peered at the parchment. Who would send a
missive to her? The writing was unknown and she shuffled
toward the window to better see it. Hastily, she opened the
parchment and read:

My dearest Mistress Kendra, I have heard the most atrocious news that you have married a man bidden by the king. As you know, your father accepted my bride price and yet I have no bride. I request the sum which I paid returned to me posthaste. If I do not receive the coins that I gave to your father by summer's end, I shall take the Graham manor by default. I expect to hear from you soon. ~E. Heatherington

She couldn't catch her breath as she rasped at the words before her eyes. As she'd feared, the situation with Heatherington had escalated and she despaired to figure out a way to repay him. If only her father remembered where he'd put the coins.

Somehow, she didn't fall to the floor in a heap as hopelessness threatened to overtake her. Her hands shook and she crumbled the missive and gripped it tightly in her hand as she paced the chamber and tried to calm down. There was nothing she could do until she found the coins.

Until then, she would consider the matter and try to figure out a way to repay the knave. Somehow, she would think of something to remedy her situation.

The midday meal was likely served and she found she could eat a bite. She hadn't eaten all morning and now she was ravenous. Kendra wrapped her mother's shawl around her shoulders, trying to warm and comfort herself as she made her way to the hall to eat.

When she opened the door, she almost bumped into Linet. "There you are. I wondered why you hadn't come to see me this morn. I was just on my way to the hall for the midday meal."

Linet appeared pretty in one of her favorite frocks, a dark blue overdress with cream embellishments along the edges of the seams. Her hair was even done in a coif. Usually, she wore her hair down. "I am sorry for being tardy, but I helped Ellen this morn prepare for the supper meal and then I went to check on your da and John. I took them bread and a jug of ale."

So visiting John was the reason for Linet's special care with her appearance. Kendra decided not to mention it, however.

Instead, she said, "That was kind of you. How is my papa this morning?"

Her friend's face saddened with the dip of her chin. "We haven't talked about this but… You are aware that he is getting worse? He didn't know who I was."

She nodded and took a deep breath through her nose. "His memory falters. He didn't recognize me either, when I most recently visited. Laird Hugh told me that he spoke of my mother and that he said he would soon join her. Do you think he knows he will soon die? My heart is full of woe because I cannot bear to think of losing him."

Linet set her hand on her shoulder. "When his time comes, you will have the strength to deal with it. More than anyone, you have courage and we shall face the loss of him together."

Kendra wrapped her arms around her friend and briefly closed her eyes. She wanted to tell her about Heatherington's message but didn't want to worry her friend. She was more than enough worried for them both. "I want to weep at the thought of it but you know how I detest crying. Your friendship gives me courage, Linet. My thanks."

"Go on down to the hall and have your meal. I'll tidy your chamber. Perhaps I'll have a bath readied for you and will choose your most becoming gown for this night's supper." Linet pulled away from her and started on her tasks.

Kendra turned away and left the room. On her way down the stairs, she considered her father and decided to visit him. If she had little time left with him, she wanted to spend as much of it as she could with him. She entered the great hall and found Magnus's father standing by the hearth.

After snatching a hard roll from the table, she approached him. "Good morn, Stan. How are you this day?"

His face was grim with a dullness in his eyes. He looked melancholy. "Good morn, lass. If ye were looking for Magnus, he left the keep earlier and I do not expect he'll return until late this eve or mayhap even the morrow. If ye shall excuse me, I was about to take a small tray to my wife."

Magnus's mother had become more miserable by the day. Kendra worried about her too. "Lady Faye hasn't come down for the midday meal?"

He sighed. "Nay, she will not leave her bedchamber now and refuses to do so. I can not get her to eat either, *och* I will keep trying. She has not eaten since yestermorn."

"That is not good. Let me try. Besides, I should like to see her." Kendra took the tray from him and headed to the lady's bedchamber. She knocked at the door but heard nothing from within. As she leaned the tray on her hip, she opened the door and entered. "Good day, Lady Faye." She set the tray on the end of the bed. Lady Faye sat on the bedside and gazed toward the window casement and didn't bother to glance her way. "It looks to be a beautiful day."

"Does it? I did not know it was midday." Her tone implied that she was unaware that morning had passed, and nor did she care that the weather was fair.

Kendra sat in the chair that faced the bed. "Laird Stan was going to bring you food but I insisted he let me bring it. He tells me that you are not eating."

"I am not very hungry."

"You will make yourself ill if you don't eat. I understand that you mourn your son. But he wouldn't want you to sicken yourself because of your despair." Kendra leaned forward. "You must eat."

"What do you know about despair?"

Kendra sighed lightly. "'Tis the truth, I know much about it. My mother died when I was very young and this is all I have left of her." She pulled the shawl tightly around her shoulders. "I cherish this shawl not because it keeps me warm but because it is like being hugged by my mother. Often, I seek its comfort and I assure you, it does ease me. I had hoped… Well, Magnus spoke so fondly of you and I thought perhaps to at least befriend you."

Lady Faye snorted a derisive laugh. "I doubt that, lass. Magnus is not fond of anyone, least of all, me."

"When I first arrived, he told me that I would like you and his father and that you were both friendly. I cannot lose you when we have yet to know each other. Please, at least eat a little."

Lady Faye lowered her gaze. "I am sorry to hear that ye lost your mother, lass. Ye have never had a motherly person care for ye?"

Kendra shook her head. "Not really and believe me, it was rather lonesome sometimes. There were very few women at our manor and I did have a friend...Linet. Her mother was kind to me too. But it has always just been me and my papa. My brother was hardly at home and I rarely saw him. I'm afraid I have little family to speak of and when Magnus told me that he had a large family, I was gladdened because you would now be my family."

"I always wanted a daughter but God only thought to give me sons."

"You were blessed, My Lady. Your sons care for both you and your husband."

Lady Faye reached out and took a piece of cheese from the trencher. "I fear that I might have ruined Ned and Jake with my coddling. My two eldest sons were taken from me and put to training at such a young age. I never got to enjoy being their mother, not like I did with the two youngest." She nibbled on the cheese. Kendra was pleased to see that she finished it and then reached for another piece.

She decided not to mention it. "A mother must bear such heartache," Kendra said. "I hope that I can keep my babies with me as long as possible."

"Ye and Magnus plan to have children soon?"

Kendra smiled. "We do. Before you know it, you will have a wee bairn to hold and coddle. Think of your grandchildren. I will need help and your motherly wisdom too, Lady Faye, so I cannot have you sicken yourself. Please, eat. Go outside and get some air. Return to your activity. That would please Ned, and me too." The mention of grandchildren seemed to perk the lady up and the edges of her mouth shifted slightly upward toward her cheeks.

"I apologize, lass, for worrying ye."

"I want to share something with you…something I have not told anyone except for Linet. Before my father and I left for the king's castle, my father accepted coins from our neighbor as a bride price." Kendra lowered her gaze in shame. "I prayed for a miracle to stop the marriage and then we received the order from the king. Never did I expect to marry someone as honorable as Magnus."

"He is that," his mother said. "Perhaps too noble."

"I am grateful that Magnus chose me. But now the situation grows wearisome and I—"

"Now ye must return the coins to this neighbor?"

Kendra nodded. "I must because the man is nefarious and rather vindictive. If I do not return the coins by summer's end he threatens to take our manor—my brother's legacy—in repayment."

"Then 'tis simple, return the coins. Have Magnus do it when he returns."

"I…I would but I cannot find the coins. My father does not remember what he did with them and I am unsure what to do." She explained how her father's memory failed. "My search of my father's possessions has yielded nothing and I have not been able to find them."

"Oh, dear, that is quite the dilemma, lass. Well, Magnus would pay the man back his coins. Ye have only to ask him."

Kendra shook her head. "I cannot do that and will not be beholden to my husband to repay my father's debt."

"Do not let the shame of that besmirch your marriage. Magnus will understand that ye had nothing to do with the transaction. He will repay your neighbor without judgment." His mother set a comforting hand on her knee.

"I am shamed by it. My father had to put the coins somewhere and I hope to find them. Then and only then, can I right this situation. When I do, I shall return them to the knave and all will be well. I beg you to keep this to yourself until I figure out what to do."

"I shall keep your secret, Kendra, but soon ye must confide in Magnus. He shall see it put to right."

She reached to take her mother-in-law's hands. "And you... Have faith that Magnus will find out what happened to Ned. He will enact vengeance if it is merited. Until then, we must go on."

"I will think on your words," Faye told her. "I know that Magnus is unrelenting and I believe he shall find out how Ned was killed. Go on, lass, I will finish my meal here and then I will come down after I have changed. Worry not, for ye will find the coins or Magnus will see to the repayment."

Kendra headed for the door and smiled at Lady Faye before she left. She hastened her steps and reached the outside. With the burden of her secret released, she felt somewhat better about having told Lady Faye. In revealing her distress, she hoped to distract Lady Faye from her mourning and give her something else to focus on instead. If that didn't work, Kendra knew, having grandchildren to anticipate and live for definitely would give Faye a reason to stay alive.

It was nice to have someone to share confidences with besides Linet. Her friend didn't understand the severity of her situation with Heatherington. Mostly because she hadn't shared the truth of the situation, because Kendra didn't want her friend to worry about the possibility of her own parents being ousted by the knave.

The afternoon had grown warmer and she removed her mother's shawl and placed it over her arm. On her way to see her father at the far end of the island, she smiled and waved to the clan's women. Most were outside tending to tasks. A woman hung laundry on lines of rope next to her cottage. Another woman stirred a large vat set on coals near the stoop of her stone cottage. One woman scattered feed to a quietly clucking flock of chickens and hissing geese. Children raced about, shouting and laughing. People seemed happier than they had before the festival and while she wasn't sure if it was the warmer weather bringing joy back to them, or the continued gaiety from the bonfires, she was glad to see the pall had lifted.

When she reached her father's cottage, again, he wasn't inside. She traipsed to the back of the fief and at the gate, she stopped before the guard. "Have you seen Laird Hugh or my father?"

"Aye, Milady, they went to the loch a while ago."

After he gave her direction, she picked up her steps and hastened toward the copse of trees. Beneath the canopy of the high-leaved branches, she felt much cooler. As she neared the loch, the scent of water and soil engulfed her senses and she could see the brackish color of the water between the tree trunks. Kendra listened for sounds and heard men's gruff voices a little way down the bank. She walked spryly toward them and smiled when she spotted Papa and the laird. They welcomed her.

"I have never seen any place as beautiful as this," she said in awe when she stopped next to her father. Surrounded by woodland, the loch waters flowed leisurely along. The loch was large enough to have to take a boat to the other side and was too far to swim across. On the shore abutting the beach, branches of pine and yews swayed from the mid-afternoon breeze. Just being there sent a sense of serenity through her. "How goes the fishing?" she asked and knelt next to her father.

Laird Hugh took a tartan and set it on the ground next to where her father sat at the loch's bank. "Take a rest, Milady, and aye, it is bonny here. We haven't caught a single fish yet."

"Who is the lass?" her father asked Hugh. Just as he said that her father rose and yanked his stick. A fish flew through the air and landed on the bank before him. Her father grinned and celebrated his accomplishment with a shout. "Aye, look at the size of this one, Hugh."

"We'll have a good supper this night," Hugh said.

As saddened as she was that her father had asked who she was, she was gladdened that he seemed to enjoy being at the loch.

Kendra relaxed back and leaned on the palms of her hands, splayed behind her determined that she too would enjoy being in such a lovely spot.

She spent the rest of the afternoon in their company. It lightened her heart to see her father smile and enjoy himself. By the time they readied to leave and return to the fief, the men had caught four fish in all. John returned before they retreated. He'd spent the afternoon doing a spot of hunting and had used his bow to kill two hares.

Their walk to the wall was filled with enthusiastic embellishments of how large their fish were. Even though the basket Hugh held was quite heavy, the fish were only about the length of her forearm. At the wall, the guard opened the gate and greeted them. She walked them to the cottage and bid the men a good night.

Then she hurried to the main fief and hoped she wasn't late for supper. Inside the great hall, many had gathered for the meal. She sprinted up the stairs and entered her chamber. There, she quickly washed and changed her gown. When she was ready, she rushed to the hall. Kendra didn't see Magnus within and realized he hadn't returned. Saddened, she took her place at the table next to Magnus's usual chair which was vacant.

Supper was a blurred event for her as she couldn't help but be immersed in her thoughts—what to do about Heatherington, how to win Magnus's affection, but the most affecting, her father's possible looming demise.

CHAPTER SIXTEEN

I N THE DEEP woods of the forest near the border of his land, Magnus slid from his horse and held his sword clenched in his hand. With so many trees rooted to the ground, there wasn't enough space to ride through. He tensed with anticipation of battling the Chattans. His men likewise dismounted and waited for his command to attack. They allowed their horses to roam free and the men moved toward the open field nearby to draw their enemy.

The sky lightened as dawn shadowed the land, giving it an ethereal mien. Magnus and his followers reverted silently around the woods to where they'd heard the interlopers. It was eerily quiet. At the onset of a new day, birds were usually chirping and making their calls from atop the tree canopies. Yet, there were no noises from the feathered creatures. Nor were there sounds of scuffles from morning venturers of grouse, wild cats, squirrels, or deer.

His thudding heart overtook his ability to hone in on his surroundings. Magnus took a breath and released a long drawn-out sigh. He kept his eyes trained on the spot where he expected the Chattans would ride through. He listened for the sounds of the trespassers and heard the thud of hoof falls on the forest floor. Then came snorts from horses and muffled voices from men who were unaware that Magnus and his followers lay in wait. He twitched his fingers at his men to indicate their foes were a length before them. Two of his soldiers sprinted ahead and the clang of their swords pierced the air.

At that moment, Magnus shouted and ran forth. He spotted a Chattan follower and clashed his sword with his foe's. After a brief tarry, he was able to cut the man down. The Chattans were akin to ants retreating from their mound in the ground. One after another came traipsing through the woods between the trees.

Outnumbered, Magnus wondered if he should call a retreat. Yet the advantage was still on his side since the men he'd brought were the fiercest amongst his soldiers and the Chattans hadn't been expecting their attack. The clangs continued to ring, shouts reverberated through the trees. When he struck a third man, he heard a Chattan shouting and calling for retreat. The forest quieted a moment later and although Magnus's breath rasped from his exertion, he rose and lowered his sword. Footsteps approached from behind him and he gripped his sword and ready to strike at whomever lurked there. But when he turned, he saw Hayden approaching.

"Are ye unharmed, Laird?" Hayden asked.

"Aye. Round up our men. We need to make sure none suffered injuries and put distance between us and the Chattans. Go." After Magnus instructed his soldier, he walked toward the treeline where their horses congregated on the field, eating the green shoots of grass. His breath calmed and he was pleased with their efforts to keep the Chattans off their land. The Chattan soldiers would return to their laird and tell him what happened that day. But would that deter the Chattans from seeking retribution? Probably not.

"Laird," Hayden called, "Oswald and Jake are injured. Two others didn't make it. Their injuries were fatal. We should probably get Oswald and Jake to a healer."

Magnus marched to the group of men who stood nearby. Jake and Oswald sat on the ground. Two others tended to them and wrapped Oswald's leg and Jake's shoulder. Once their injuries were cared for, at least for now, they retreated from the woods and gained their horses' backs. His followers retrieved the bodies of their fallen brethren and tied them to their mounts. They'd receive the highest praise at their burials when they reached home.

As much as he appreciated battling with the Chattans, he disliked the fact that two of his men had died and two others were most grievously wounded. His brother was carried on Hayden's horse because he couldn't ride alone.

"Laird," Hayden called, "Jake hast lost a lot of blood. He's barely hanging on."

"We'll stop near the border of our land and MacKendrick's. There's a healer there, Lillith, who aids anyone in need. It's much closer and we'll get the men seen to sooner." Magnus took up the rear of the procession. He was concerned for his brother and when he chanced to look at him, his brother appeared to be pitched forward, slouched over and unconscious.

Hayden kept hold of Jake's tartan-clad body and peered at him. "We need to make haste. Jake is not doing well and might succumb before we get to Lillith's."

It didn't take long to reach the stone wall surrounding the healer's cottage. Magnus bade his men to await him by the wall as he approached on foot. He knocked at the door and it was opened slightly.

"What do ye want?" a woman's voice came.

"Lillith, it's me, Magnus. We need your aid." He hoped she'd be amiable to help them. She was renowned for her healing methods and she never refused to help anyone regardless of which clan they belonged to.

"I wouldst gladly aid ye but I have a man convalescing within. He is of the clan MacKendrick if that matters to ye."

Magnus shook his head. "We are not aligned with the MacKendricks but we are not warring with them. I give ye my oath that we will not make trouble for ye or your charge. We only seek your aid for our wounded men."

"Very well, bring them inside." She turned, opening the door more widely before she disappeared from the entrance.

He motioned to his men and signaled to Hayden to bring Jake. His soldier dismounted, pulled his brother from the horse's back, and set him over his shoulder. He trudged forward and entered the cottage. Oswald, with the aid of another soldier, limped toward the building and also entered.

Magnus was about to follow them but turned and said to the remaining men, "The rest of ye settle in until we know how the men fare. Make camp for now. If we are delayed, I'll send ye along home with our dead so they can be readied for burial."

Inside the dark cottage, there were bunches of drying plants hanging from a rope nailed from one wall to another. Scents permeated from simmering cauldrons hung in the hearth and on a long table at the far end of the cottage, sat medicinal jars lined in perfectly aligned rows. Set before them were pestles and healing tools of which Magnus had no knowledge. The woman was apt at her occupation and he admired her for the skill.

Jake was lying on an empty table near the long table of medicinals. Lillith set to work on him and Hayden helped her remove his tunic. She went about her tasks silently and engrossed. Magnus took a moment and peered at the man who lay upon a makeshift cot on the other side of the cottage. He recognized Trevor, one of Declan MacKendrick's guardsmen.

"Will Trevor survive?" he asked Lillith in a low voice.

"He's out of danger for now. It will take him time, however, to heal. Now, about this man…"

"My brother Jake," Magnus supplied.

"He was pierced through his shoulder. It doesn't appear that anything major was sliced. He's lost a good bit of blood though. I'll clean the wound and get him patched up. We must pray that infection doesn't come to his wound."

Magnus paced the small area before the table while she tended to his brother. Jake still hadn't regained his senses, thankfully, and remained unaware of her poking and prodding. When she finished, Lillith covered the wound with a cloth and tied it.

"He will need to stay here on the table. I have given him a dram which will lessen his pain, ward off infection, and keep him sleeping for a while. Now who else needs aid?" Lillith approached and stood before Oswald.

"Let us see what's what." She lifted the hem of his tartan and pressed the fabric far enough upward to reveal the bulky muscle of his thigh.

Oswald drew in a hiss at her touch. "Will I lose my leg?"

Lillith frowned at his leg and focused on the wound. "Ye took a good strike to your leg and it barely bled. There will be a good bruise which will probably take weeks to heal."

"It hurts," Oswald said. "I can barely stand on it."

"Aye, ye shall limp for a time. For now, I will wash your leg with wine and then put some ointment on it to soothe it and a cool compress to ease ye." Lillith crossed the cottage to the back table and turned her back to them. She prepared medicinals for his soldier's leg.

"I am sorry, Laird. I shouldn't have allowed myself to become injured—"

"Ye need not apologize, Oswald. Let Lillith tend to ye."

"Ye should go and return with the men. I will stay here with Jake and that will give me time to recover. Take our brothers home and bury them."

Magnus appreciated his soldier's offer but he didn't want to leave Jake until he knew for certain that he wouldn't succumb to his injury. His mother couldn't stand the loss of another of her younger sons.

Hayden approached and stood next to him. "Go on, Laird. I'll stay with them both and will come when I have news."

Lillith returned from her table and dabbed a wine-soaked cloth over Oswald's leg. "Magnus, ye should go and take your dead home. I will take your soldier up on his offer. He'll be of use to me here whilst I tend to the wounded. When they recover, I will send them back to ye."

"Aye, we will go then. Hayden, if ye need me…"

"I will come, Laird," Hayden said.

Magnus nodded to him, took a glance at his brother who continued to slumber, and turned to the door. Once he was outside, he whistled to his men and readied for the trek home. The men quickly disbanded camp, put out the small fire they'd made, and mounted their horses. They set out for home and he hoped to reach it before nightfall.

The heavens were marked with varying streaks of color as the sun set over the peaks of mountains in the distance. With its brilliance, a smattering of stars made their appearance in the early night sky. They approached the gates and stopped before the guardsmen. After explaining what happened on their trek, the men left to prepare for the burials which would take place after the soldiers' families were told of their demise. With the onset of darkness, they'd bury their fallen soldiers in the light of the morn.

Magnus was met by Winston at the stables as he approached. His soldier had a fat smile on his face. Marriage agreed with him. Magnus quickly told him of the happenings.

"Terrible news, Laird. I'll tend to your horse and will aid the men to prepare for the burials."

"Before ye do, fetch Wyren and have him come to the keep."

"Aye, Laird." Winston disappeared with his horse inside the stable.

Before Magnus could seek his rest, he needed to give the news to his soldiers' families. Giving such dreadful bearings tightened his chest. He never wanted to impart such atrocious news to the families of his clan, but it was his duty as laird.

The families, as expected, were distraught and inconsolable. He slowed his steps on the advance to the fief. Although he wanted to see Kendra, he didn't wish to have to explain, once again, what transpired on their journey. His father would expect an explanation and would want the details.

Magnus wanted to seek his bed, shut his eyes, and have a wee bit of peace. Come the morning, there would be time aplenty to fill his father in on the news. He opened the door to the keep and entered. There were no voices to be heard and he thought all had sought their beds. But as he gave the great hall a quick glance, he noticed his father sitting by the hearth. Magnus took a settling breath and slowly moved toward him. He took the seat across from his father and leaned back, wary and tense in wait for Wyren.

His father inclined forward and stoked the fire. "'Tis a chilly evening. I should have the men bring more firewood."

Magnus barely heard what his father said.

Wyren trudged into the room and sat in the chair next to his father's. "Winston said ye wanted to meet. What happened on your trek? Did ye find anything out?"

"Before we get to that, I must tell ye that Jake was injured in a scuffle with the Chattans. I took him to Lillith, the healer, and she's tended to him. He'll take time to recover, that's if he survives. Hayden stayed with him. Oswald, as well, suffered a battered leg. He stayed at the healer's cottage too." Magnus's words droned out and he couldn't look at his family. He kept his gaze on his knee and waited for their outrage.

"Lillith is the best healer in these parts. She'll have Jake well in no time," Wyren said. He poured a cup of ale from the pitcher that sat on a nearby table and handed it to him. "Looks like ye need a drink, brother."

"Oh, damnation, your mother will pitch a fit when she hears about Jake. I will wait until the morn to tell her for she's gone to bed," his father said.

"Did the Chattans attack or did ye initiate the fracas?" Wyren asked.

Magnus pointed to himself, and after, he chugged the ale until there wasn't a drop left. The drink did nothing to allay him. "Me, for I am at fault. I wanted to insert my wrath at them being on our land. I should've just kept riding... We were headed for home."

His father pressed his hands over his face and spoke in a harsh tone, "*Och*, ye are not to blame, son. 'Tis a sad state of affairs that we lost two men and two convalesce, but at least now the Chattans know we mean business. Mayhap now they'll stay off our land."

They fell into silence. Magnus appreciated his father's and brother's support. Not that it lessened his regret or culpability.

Wyren refilled their cups. "Tell me what ye found out about Ned."

Magnus swirled the ale in his cup and peered at it as he spoke, "Aye, apparently Ned told his mistress—"

"Wait…whoa, what say ye? Ned had a woman?" Wyren chortled. "I disbelieve ye. He wasn't the lover sort of man."

"She wasn't his alone."

"Oho," Wyren said and his mouth hung open. "That makes more sense for Ned would have to pay for a woman. Never saw him with a lass. Go on."

"What do ye mean by that…that she wasn't his alone. Do ye mean she was with others?" His father frowned hard at him.

Magnus nodded. "He paid for his woman with the clan's coin. Ned also wagered and pilfered coins from the clan's coffers to pay his wagering debts. But that is not all that I found out because—"

His father shrieked loudly and jumped from his seat. "He did what!?"

"When Ned last visited his strumpet, he told her that a few men from his clan tried to pilfer coins from him and that they would not bespeak of his losses at the dice games if he paid their demand."

His father retook his seat, leaned forward, and groaned. "God Almighty! Ned thieved from us and used our coins to wager? And to pay for… Cosh, what a mess this is."

Wyren spoke an expletive under his breath too. "Are ye telling us that these scoundrels—"

"Aye, we have a few traitors to uncover within our clan. Not only did they try to extort coins from Ned, but they probably killed him too. Mary said Ned left her that night and he was intent to meet with the betrayers."

"But ye said that Aldo likely murdered Ned because he did not pay him what was owed." Wyren rubbed his face. "This is all so confounding."

Magnus nodded his agreement because he was downright perplexed by his brother's behavior too. "It is highly shocking. Ned owed three marks to Aldo, a good amount, but I do not think the man murdered him. I believed him when he said that Ned never showed up for their meeting. I was able to retrace his steps to Mistress Mary's manor. She is a harlot who entertains men and has a house of ill-repute for the purpose. When I met with her, she said that Ned was a favorite of hers and on their last night together, he told her about the extortion. He spoke of his clansmen trying to take coins from him for their silence. I can only assume that those men murdered Ned when he refused to pay them."

"And ye wish to force these men to come forward? I doubt they will," Wyren said.

"They will not come forward on their own and probably told no one of their misdeeds. We will have to use underhanded means to uncover them." Magnus stood and paced before his father and brother. "I want every single Cameron accounted for. We'll invite groups of twenty to twenty-five to spar with us on the training field. If they are brazen enough to show their faces on my field, we might catch a word or observe their guilt-ridden miens. Once we have met and accounted for all the men within the walls, I shall go and meet with all those outside the walls. We will not cease our search until we have spoken to every single Cameron."

"Son, I understand that ye are angry—"

"Angry, Da? I am more than furious that our clansmen intended to take coins from our clan, from my brother, from me. I am wrath that Ned used our clan's coins for wagering and the use of paying harlots for sex. He was a miscreant of the lowest level. The only reason I seek vengeance now is because I will not tolerate men within our clan who deem to try to take coins from me. Ned does not deserve vindication."

Wyren stood next to him and set his hand on his shoulder. "Be calm, Magnus. We understand and commiserate with ye. It could take time to find these traitors. In the meantime, we will be diligent in our search for them."

Magnus shook his head adamantly. "Nay, it is my duty, and I will not cease my search until I find these men and oust them. They'll be banished for good."

Wyren turned toward the door. "I will go and get as much rest as I'm able. We shall begin first thing on the morrow after we bury our dead."

Before his brother could depart, Magnus stopped him. "Attend me a moment... Only the three of us know about Ned's woman and what she said to me. I spoke none of it with the soldiers who traveled with me."

"Not even with Jake?" his father asked.

"Nay, not even to Jake. It is better that he not know what foulness Ned was capable of. He will probably learn of it soon enough when we confront the men who intended to thieve from us." Magnus knew Jake's fondness for their brother and he didn't want to be the cause of his younger brother's hatred. In time, Jake would learn the truth though, there was no way to shield him from the pain of what Ned had done.

"I vow to keep this to myself and will not speak of it even to your mother," his father said.

Wyren agreed and nodded. "It will be easier to find our traitors, the less others know about this." He marched to the exit, swung the door open with force, and left the fief.

Magnus stepped outside and walked alongside Wyren. Before he sought his bed, he wanted to let the night air calm him and clear his head. His brother walked off toward his home and he continued toward the gatehouse. When he reached it, he motioned to Craig who continued the night watch with a handful of other soldiers.

"Oh, Laird, I am gladdened ye came. This just arrived for ye." Craig handed him a missive.

"My thanks, Craig. I want ye to keep our gates closed. None, not even the sentry, are to exit the walls until I give leave to do so. If anyone comes, I want ye to name those who return."

Craig gazed at him with confusion. "Even the sentry, Laird? Surely, we need to let the sentry do their duty."

"Until I say otherwise, they are forbidden to leave. All are forbidden to leave." He hadn't meant to raise his voice, but he needed to assert his command.

"As ye wish, Laird. I'll keep any from leaving and will let ye know who returns." Craig bowed to him and returned to his post.

Magnus didn't want to give the culprits time to get away. If they got any suspicions that he was on to them, they could easily abscond and he'd have to hunt them down. If the knaves had no choice but to stay within the walls, then he'd find them all the sooner.

As he walked back to the keep, he broke the seal on the missive and opened the parchment. His eyes skimmed over the long lines and his face heated at what he read:

Laird Cameron, I am told by the king's servant Chamberlain Edmund that you wedded Lord Graham's daughter, Kendra. She was promised to me and a betrothal was set with the bride price paid to her father. Since our betrothal is now nullified, I am owed ten pounds which I want returned. If you ignore this demand, I will have no recourse but to take action against the Grahams. Yours, Lord Ellish Heatherington, servant to King Alexander.

Magnus practically burned the parchment with his eyes. He wondered if the king knew about this supposed betrothal agreement betwixt Heatherington and Kendra's father. Then he wondered if Kendra knew of it and why she hadn't mentioned it to him. With fury, he crumpled up the parchment and tossed it into a small firepit that he passed on the way back to the fief.

Magnus decided he'd wait to see how long it took for his wife to enlighten him on her supposed betrothal. He hoped with all his heart that she was either unaware or had an explanation for keeping it from him.

Since Magnus had no time to deal with the lord, he would put him off with a missive and pay the price for his bride. The fact that the man mentioned further action almost made him smile because he would rather take up arms against a nefarious lord by the border than his clansmen, a duty he was most bitter about. But alas, he had no time to scuffle with Kendra's supposed betrothed. His search for the betrayers was most important now. Instead of vengeance for Ned's death, he reasoned his vengeance now ingrained in him the need to unveil his traitorous clansmen.

CHAPTER SEVENTEEN

ORNING LIGHT FILTERED through the window casement, alerting Kendra that it was time to rise. Her eyes shot open and she rubbed the sleep from them. She rolled onto her back and felt Magnus beside her. She hadn't heard him arrive during the night and must've slept like a rock. He lay next to her with his eyes closed, his breathing easy and quiet. She took a moment to gaze at his handsomeness. He wore a bit of scruff on his cheeks. The light beard appealed to her and made him appear even more fierce. She wanted to stroke his face to feel the coarseness of his whiskers, but she didn't want to wake him.

Magnus's eyes flipped open and he stared at her for a moment without speaking.

"Good morn. I was just about to rise," she said but didn't make a move to get out of bed. "How was your journey?"

"Unremarkable."

She disbelieved him because the look in his gaze and his somber tone alluded to the fact that something had happened. He wasn't about to share it with her however and so she didn't press him. The silence of the bedchamber unnerved her. Magnus was being quieter than usual. He seemed displeased with her but he wasn't about to impart why.

"I should get up," she said and tossed the covers from over her. With his sullen mood, she thought it best to retreat from the chamber.

Magnus took hold of her arm and pulled her back. "There's no need to run off."

Kendra thought that he might kiss her but he made no move to do so. To appease him, she settled back in the bed and waited to find out why he wanted her to stay.

"Kendra, would ye ever keep something from me? Something important that I should be made aware of?" His eyes seemed to implore her as his eyes pierced hers, unblinking.

She shook her head. "Like a secret?"

"Aye? A secret. Would ye purposely keep me in the dark about something that ye should confess? Something that perchance ye should tell me as your husband?" He leaned on his side, his eyes continuing to stare at her intensely.

His scrutiny made her uncomfortable and she swallowed before answering. "I am certain that I know not of what you speak of because I wouldn't deliberately keep something from you. Why would you ask such a question?" Kendra's shoulders tensed as she waited for him to answer.

She wondered if he meant the secret of her papa accepting Heatherington's bride price. But then, she reasoned he couldn't know about that. Only she, Linet, and John were privy to that secret and she didn't deem her friends would speak of it to Magnus. Then she remembered she'd told his mother about it and hoped with all her heart that Lady Faye had kept her secret. She didn't want to be a burden to Magnus and have him return Heatherington's bride price. Kendra hoped to solve the problem on her own. He had enough to deal with concerning his clan and his brother's death. If what he'd asked her wasn't about Heatherington, she thought perhaps he'd viewed the manuscripts. Was that what had him filled with angst this morn?

"I only wondered… Never mind. I should rise too. There's a duty I must see to early this morn." He flung back the bedcover and shifted his legs to the side of the bed.

Kendra didn't know what troubled him and until he told her,

she'd be the one in the dark. She hurried and washed and pulled a tan-colored frock over her head. After, she pulled the length of her hair into sections and braided it, then coiled it and secured it with a tie.

Magnus had dressed by the time she'd finished. He marched across the chamber to the antechamber and picked up a volume. He glared at the table and turned hastily toward her. "Have ye touched these manuscripts?"

"Oh, I forgot to tell you… I took care of adding the sums and accounting that needed to be entered since Ned had…" She trailed off and changed her thought. "The manuscripts are current. You need not worry about it now. If you will look, you shall see—"

He cut her off with a bite to his tone, "Kendra, ye shouldn't have done that. It was my…"

She waited for him to finish his sentence but his mouth hung open.

"Your, what? Are you pleased? Appreciative? I know how much the task weighed on you and when I lived at home I often took care of such matters for my father."

"Nay! I am most disappointed. It was my responsibility as the laird of this clan and I was going to get to it. Ye had no right to do so, especially without telling me first. Ye should not have touched these manuscripts. I trust no one to handle the matter but me. And until I put a steward in place, I should be the one to keep track of the clan's accounting."

Kendra tried to resist the tremble that came to her, but her voice shook, "But I was only—"

"Ye disappoint me, Kendra. I cannot discuss this right now because I have men to bury."

She realized how upset he must be with having to bury his soldiers. "I am sorry you lost men. Can I do anything to help?"

Magnus continued to scowl at the accounting volumes and didn't glance at her when he answered, "Nay, there is naught for ye to do. They were my clansmen and their families are suffering at their loss. I must make it right."

Kendra thought perhaps the weight of his men's deaths added to his reaction of her helping him do the accounts. She wanted with all her heart to lessen his sorrow and to help him but he wouldn't allow her to. As his wife, wasn't it her duty to aid him when he needed her? Magnus didn't seem to know that but at the moment, she refrained from reminding him of that fact lest she anger him further.

Without another word, Magnus hastily left the bedchamber, thudding the door behind him.

Kendra tried not to let his disgruntlement get to her but tears gathered in her eyes. She pressed her eyes to abate them. Why he was bothered by her aid daunted her. She'd only tried to help him but he took his duties of being laird to heart. She wished he understood that and that didn't mean he had to bear the burden of everything. If he allowed her to help him, she could ease his troubles. How could she make that known to him?

He wasn't about to listen now. Kendra disliked that he was angry with her but there was probably nothing she could do to make it right or make the hurt recede. The damage was done.

Linet entered the chamber and held a basket of laundry in her hands. She set down the basket and crossed the chamber. "Good morn, Kendra. It's a beautiful day outside. I was thinking of going… Oh, no, what is wrong?" She pulled her into an embrace. "Your face tells me that something troubles you. You look brokenhearted."

Kendra couldn't hold back the sob that escaped her. "I *am* brokenhearted." She quickly explained what happened between her and Magnus. "He is rather angry."

"Fret not. Men often make such a fuss about things they should be doing, and yet, it sometimes takes them forever to handle the tasks. Mama always nags my da to do things but he usually drags his feet. Once Laird Cameron realizes how fortunate he is that you aided him, he shall forgive you."

She snorted a laugh. "I doubt very much that will happen."

"You need to get out of the keep this day. I was going to suggest that we visit your da and John. We could go to the loch and perhaps take a swim for it is going to be a warm day."

Kendra decided she needed to get out of the keep and away from Magnus, at least until his temper cooled. She helped Linet tidy the chamber and they left the fief. On the way to her father's cottage, she tried not to think of Magnus and his abruptness. When he calmed, she would explain and hoped he'd understand that she hadn't meant to overstep but only to relieve him of the plight. Somehow she would gain his forgiveness.

"I wanted to speak to you about something…" Linet slowed her pace, linked her arm to hers, and kept her gaze ahead. "I know not how to brooch this with you so I shall just say it… I married John."

Kendra gasped and tightened the hold of her arm to stop her from walking ahead. "You what!? When did this happen?"

Linet lowered her chin. "At the Roodmas celebration. We did so in secret and professed our vows to each other since there is no clergyman here. I am sorry that I kept it from you. It's just we wanted a private ceremony…"

She understood. "You have cared for John for such a long time, since you were a young lass. I wondered when you would admit it to him. I am happy for you, Linet, and for John. This is wonderful news." Kendra pulled her into a congratulatory embrace and hugged her tightly.

Linet pulled back. "You might not think so when I tell you that we intend to return to your father's lands when he goes home. John has family close by and he only came because Lord Graham needed him. But he wants us to live there and I must go with him."

"You shall leave me. That's what you're saying. As much as that saddens me, your life is with your husband. I understand. Oh, this is especially pleasing news. I am gladdened to know that you married for love. How I wish I had." Kendra reasoned that her marriage was more contractual given the king gave her hand to Magnus. Still, she'd hoped marriage to Magnus would bring them close and perhaps even to love one another eventually.

How wrong she had been because Magnus loved his clan and had no room for her in his heart. Such a feat seemed impossible now. The woebegone nature sat afoul in her stomach and she didn't want to appear forlorn in front of her dear friend. Despair threatened to make her weep or bend over sobbing at the hopelessness of it. She shook it away and tried to appear happy for Linet.

With a renewed spirit, she smiled. "Now, come along, and tell me what plans you have made. You must be excited to begin your life together." She linked arms with Linet again and they ambled forward.

Linet rambled on about her future, but Kendra's mind retreated and she barely heard a word she said. On the approach to her father's cottage, she spotted him outside. He stood next to Laird Hugh and they seemed to be readying to go fishing. Kendra placed a smile on her face and hoped her father recognized her. With all the sadness of the day, she didn't want to be overlooked by the one man who truly cared for her.

"Ah, lass, you are here. We're off to do a spot of fishing," he said, greeting her with a welcoming grin, and her heart soared.

"Good morn, Papa. Do you mind if Linet and I join you?"

"Of course not. 'Tis a fine day for fishing and mayhap a dip in the water for it will soon be warm enough."

She nodded. "I thought the same. Let us go onward then." Kendra unlinked her arm from Linet's and stepped next to her father.

Linet sidled next to John and smiled at him. John's face neared her friend's and he almost pressed his lips to her cheek. Instead, he spoke low in Linet's ear. Kendra couldn't hear what he'd said and whatever it was, made her friend blush sweetly and nod. They made off toward the trees that surrounded the loch.

"John, I must offer my good tidings on your marriage. I am very pleased for both of you."

The soldier's face brightened and he dipped his chin. "My thanks, Milady."

They trudged through the trees and made their way toward the water. Kendra loved the scents of nature as they neared the loch. There was the freshness of the water, the pine odor of the tall trees, and the balance of soil that seemed to penetrate her senses. Being there relaxed her and she let herself forget her troubles of the morning.

Laird Hugh set a blanket on the ground. She and Linet sat upon it while the men tossed their lines into the water. John held a sharpened spear and stepped into the water until it reached his knees. He stood still and waited for the fish to come to him.

While they sat there waiting for the fish to bite, Kendra wished she'd grabbed something to eat before she left the fief. Her stomach rumbled and caught Laird Hugh's notice.

"*Och* ye be hungry, lass? Is that your hunger growling?" He chortled.

Kendra's face pitched from embarrassment. "I was in a rush this morn and didn't eat anything." Her stomach grumbled again. "That must be why my stomach is upset."

"Oh, I have some sweetened bread Mistress Ellen gave me this morn. Ye are welcome to it." He pulled out a cloth-wrapped loaf and handed it to her.

"You are a saving grace, Laird Hugh. My thanks." Kendra pulled a piece of the bread from the loaf and ate it. Her father yanked at his line and was quiet. "Papa, how are you this day? Feeling well?" She wondered if he was clear-headed or if he was inside himself. He seemed to be well and at least had recognized her when she approached him earlier.

"My dear, how pleasing you look this day. One day I hope we have a daughter as fair."

Kendra's shoulders slumped when she realized that he thought he was speaking to her mother. She somewhat resembled her mother, from what she'd been told, with her fair hair and light eyes. "Papa, I'm Kendra... I'm not Catherine."

"You look akin to my wife. Are you certain you are not her?" Her father grunted as if he disbelieved her.

"I am your daughter Kendra." She pressed her hands together and tried not to be solemn. To take her mind off his disremembering, she continued to eat the bread Laird Hugh gave her.

"My wife is the most beautiful, kindhearted woman. I loved her from the moment I spied her in her da's hall. Her father wasn't impressed with me and it took me months to win his acceptance." Her father chuckled and looked far off as his memories took hold.

Kendra had heard him reminisce about meeting her mother before but he hadn't spoken about it in some time. His eyes always shone with mirth when he spoke of the tale. "I am gladdened you did."

"Oho, but her da made me wait to marry her and I confess that I thought he would never allow me to marry my sweet Catherine. Sweet," he said with a guffaw. "She was far from sweet and challenged me on everything. I liked the confrontations and often let her win just to keep the peace. I shall join her soon and then we will be together..." he mumbled and his voice trailed off. Her father grew saddened and he pouted slightly until something caught on his line.

Kendra wondered what he was going to say. But he was now focused on fishing so she let him be. That he spoke of her mother tensed her heart. Her worry for him grew as each day passed. She hoped he lived long enough to see his cherished home and land again.

Speaking of marriage and confrontations reminded her that somehow she needed to make amends with Magnus. He would hear no explanations that morning and she hoped by the time she saw him that evening his anger would have lessened. Perhaps then she could make her apology and get him to accept it. But then she scoffed to herself. Magnus was stubborn and it was unlikely he'd understand why she needed to help him.

The rest of the afternoon passed pleasantly. In the heat of the afternoon, they swam for a bit. The water cooled her and was a little chilly, but it offered a respite from the heat of the day. Six fish had been caught in all when the day drew to a close: three by Laird Hugh, two by her papa, and one by John. Kendra took up the cover from the ground and folded it. Dusk swathed the land and the day's light dimmed. She was hungry and hoped supper would be soon. A queasiness overtook her and she closed her eyes and breathed slowly to abate it. After a brief uneasy spell, she regained her composure and set off toward the fief's walls.

On the way back, she looked apprehensively for Magnus but didn't see him. Would he come to their bedchamber that night? She hoped he would and that his laird duties didn't keep him away. Kendra drew in a resigned breath. It seemed she'd be forever awaiting him.

CHAPTER EIGHTEEN

MAGNUS STOOD BY the garrison and tried to pay attention to what his brother was saying, but he couldn't help but think about Kendra and that she purposely kept from him the fact that she was betrothed when they'd met. That she hadn't confessed when he asked her dejected him. He didn't want his wife to keep secrets from him. There had to be a reason why she'd done so. Eventually, he'd get her to open up about it. Until then, he needed to settle the matter.

Wyren grumbled and shoved his shoulder. "Only two men are missing from the garrison. Since there's no sentry out about our lands, I say they might be the two we search for."

"That makes sense. Aye, have a search made for them and when we find them, I want to question them."

His brother nodded. "I'll see to it."

"I must take care of something, a personal matter, and need two messengers. Pick two of our most trusted soldiers."

Wyren tilted his head to the side. "And where are these messengers headed?"

"It doesn't concern ye. Just have the men await me outside the fief." Without another word, he strode off toward home and entered. Someone was inside the hall and he heard voices. He supposed it was his parents because no others resided within. He'd spotted Kendra earlier headed to the back of the fief so she wasn't inside. Taking the steps two at a time, he entered his chamber, left the door open, and rushed to the table.

There, he picked up a quill and found a blank parchment. After he dipped the quill in the small ink pot, he considered what he'd wanted to reply. He hastily wrote:

Lord Heatherington, enclosed within ye shall find the sum which ye paid to Lord Graham for his daughter's hand. I consider this matter closed and ye will not have contact with my wife or her father henceforth. If I hear that ye try to extort coins from my wife or her father again, ye shall bear my wrath. Magnus, Laird of Clan Cameron.

He reached for the small coffer on the table and retrieved the coins needed to pay the debt. Once he placed the coins in the center of the parchment, he folded it tightly so they wouldn't fall out and sealed it with wax along the seams and in the center with his seal.

Before he left the chamber, he glanced around and noticed his wife had tidied it. His shoulders slumped because he should have just told her what he'd found out instead of trying to get her to tell him. He realized he'd been overly harsh too with her and that tightened his chest. Kendra was a kind-hearted lass and she had tried to help him even though she should have spoken to him about the parchments. With that thought, he returned to the tables and picked up a volume.

Magnus thumbed through the pages and he sighed at the work she'd done. All were correctly inputted, summed, and properly categorized. The discrepancy wasn't as great as he'd thought it would be. Ned hadn't squandered their fortune. He gave praise to God above for that because the coin belonged to the clan and their needs.

How had his wife come by such knowledge? He should've known she would be apt at such a task. When next he saw her, he would have to apologize for being brash and perhaps even thank her for her aid.

He set the volume down and picked up the missive that he wanted to be delivered to Heatherington. Trudging down the stairs, he listened again but didn't hear anyone in the hall. He left the keep and found the two soldiers his brother had assigned to the task of delivering his message. Magnus handed the missive to James and instructed where to deliver it.

The men bowed to him and set off.

Magnus headed for the stable and met with the stable master, Vincent. The man stroked the feathered back of the hawk that his brother had brought to him for healing. The hawk skitted around on the protective cover on Vincent's forearm and eyed him curiously.

"How is he? Almost ready to be freed?"

"Aye, he's sound now, he is. I was awaiting Jake's return and thought he might want to release him. When is he expected home?" Vincent lowered his dark-haired head toward the bird a made clicks with his tongue.

"I know not when he shall return. He's recovering from an injury at the healer's cottage. It could be some time before he comes home. If the bird is ready to be released, I'm sure Jake would want ye to handle it."

"Och, I'll see to it then. Are ye needing your horse, Laird?"

Magnus nodded and wondered where Winston was. "If ye are busy, I can get him. Where's Winston?"

Vincent grumbled. "Your attendant has been shirking his duties of late. Either marriage is keeping him from the stables or he is up to no good."

"I'm sure whatever keeps Winston away is important. It is not like him to shirk his duty. I shall ask him when next I see him." Magnus strode away from the stable master and reached his steed's stall. It took little time to saddle him and get him ready for the trek.

Outside, he mounted his horse and rode to the gate. The watch hastily strode toward to open it and as he rode through, he said, "I will return on the morrow."

Craig, the leader of the gate watchmen, shouted their clan's motto and nodded to him.

Magnus didn't bother to take anyone with him for his trek to Lillith's cottage. The location of the healer's domain was close to the border of his lands and a great distance, at least a few leagues away. As he rode along, he thought about his brother and hoped Jake recovered. Likewise, he suspected Oswald's injury had to be good and healed by now.

From the distance, he noticed the smoke from Lillith's chimney. Blackish-gray smoke wafted into the afternoon's sky. Outside Lillith's cottage, he tethered his horse and ambled up the walkway to the door. He rapped on the wooden edifice and waited. The door was opened a moment later by Hayden.

"Laird, 'tis good to see ye. I'm gladdened ye came." Hayden opened the door wider to allow his entrance.

Magnus stepped inside and clapped Hayden on the shoulder. "'Tis good to see ye too. How are our men?" He saw Lillith tending to the MacKendrick soldier. Jake lay upon a cot next to him. Oswald sat in a chair by a low table and stirred something in a pot.

"Oswald is well enough to return, Laird," Lillith said.

He approached his soldier and nodded. "That is welcome news, Oswald. I'm glad to hear it."

"Och, aye, my leg is just a wee bit tender. I can walk on it now for a short trek."

"Good. And Jake?" he asked Hayden.

"Your brother still has not regained his senses." Hayden's face shifted forward as if he hid his eyes from him.

Lillith continued with her task of tending to the other soldier and said over her shoulder, "Jake lost a lot of blood and I suspect that is what keeps him from waking…that, and fever."

Magnus was disheartened by that news. He stepped toward the cot where his brother lay and studied his face. His brother's eyes remained closed and it only looked as though he was sleeping. He waited for Lillith to finish tending to the

MacKendrick soldier and when she stood, he bowed to her. "Mistress."

"Laird Cameron, I'm afraid your brother has developed an infection and I have had a difficult time keeping him cool. I continue to observe him but he is not out of danger. He shall need to remain here. Oswald is free to go."

"Will Jake survive?" Magnus's body tensed as he waited for the answer. Often infection lingered and took the life when a wound was too severe to mend.

"I cannot say, Laird, but I will do my best to help him."

Magnus nodded, his heart heavy. "My thanks, Mistress, for your care of my men. Is there anything ye need? I can have my clansmen bring whatever ye need... Or should I leave Hayden here to assist ye?"

Lillith wiped her hands with a cloth she picked up from a nearby table. "Your men may leave. I no longer require them. Now that Jake is settled on a cot and the MacKendrick soldier is healing, there's naught much to do. I will take ye up on your offer though, for I need some herbs and such, and have no time to collect them. If ye can have someone fetch them from the woods... I shall need mint, licorice root, willow-tree bark, and honey."

"Of course, Mistress. Hayden will set men to tend to it when we reach home and return within a day or two with the items." Magnus pressed a gentle hand on his brother's head but Jake didn't respond. He hoped he would recover soon. With that, he left the cottage and awaited his men outside.

Hayden ambled from the cottage and rounded the building, then returned a moment later with his and Oswald's horses. "Laird, how goes the keep? Have ye made progress in finding out what happened to Ned?"

"Aye, a wee bit of progress. I'll tell ye later what I have learned." Magnus trusted Hayden as much as he put his faith in Wyren. Although he hadn't wanted anyone within the clan to know about the two traitors, Hayden might have information that could shed light on the situation.

Osward retreated from the cottage and there was no limp in his gait. He mounted his horse and they rode toward the woods that led to their fortification. All were quiet during the ride.

Magnus had hoped to return home by nightfall, and since it was now dark out, they might have to make camp and settle for the night. The trek to his home was more than a few leagues and would take time to reach. After riding for a good stretch, he called a halt.

"Let us make camp and we'll continue onward when there's enough light to see by."

His men dismounted. Hayden set off to find wood for a fire while Oswald retrieved his saddle bag. From it, he removed a bit of foodstuff he'd been given by Lillith.

"She gave this to me before I left the cottage. It should make for a good meal," Oswald explained. "'Tis some pottage in a hollowed loaf of whey bread."

Hayden started a fire and tossed in various-sized twigs and branches he'd collected.

"I am hungry." Magnus settled near the fire and after eating a little, he grew tired. A night's rest in the woods would help to clear his head and give him a good rest. He lay back on the ground and used his tartan under his head. Fortunately, the night hadn't gotten too cold. He'd need no extra tartan to keep away a chill.

As the men settled around the fire, he closed his eyes and thought about his bonny wife. With everything that happened of late, he had put aside his marriage and his wife's feelings. It didn't sit well that he'd seen little of her or had given her his attention. If only Ned's murder or his men being injured during their fracas with the Chattans hadn't taken up his time. He might have enjoyed his marriage to Kendra. There was much to learn about her and the first thing he needed to know was why she hadn't told him about her previous betrothal or how she learned the tasks of a steward.

The sound of a swish alerted him that someone was in the woods. A thumping sound caused his eyes to shoot open. He saw a rock rolling on the ground and it stopped before it reached the fire. His eyes scrutinized it for a moment and then he heard the sound of another whistling through the air. The rock hit Hayden's head and his soldier fell back. He landed just before the fire with a thump on the ground.

Magnus was just getting to his feet when another rock came, sailing through the air with speed. It hit Oswald in the center of his eyes and he pitched forward and fell flat on a patch of grass near their horses. Magnus drew his sword and searched within the dark woods but the obscurity of them hid their ambushers. He turned about, peering around him. Another rock came and hit him on the side of the head and he lost the hold of his sword. He dropped it and it almost landed in the fire.

Magnus pressed his hands on his head, closed his eyes for a moment, and tried to stop the intense twinge. When he opened his eyes again, his view was obscured and hazy. His head throbbed madly and he felt a warm stream of blood flowing down the side of his face.

Magnus fell to his knees, groaned, and tumbled forward, landing on his chest. He shifted his hand to his head and pressed above his ear to try to abate the dizzying sense that overtook him. His other hand felt around the ground for his sword, knowing he needed to protect himself. Voices sounded around him but before he could ascertain the threat, he succumbed to the darkness of unconsciousness.

CHAPTER NINETEEN

SOMETHING AWOKE HER—A bang or shout, Kendra wasn't sure which. She rubbed her eyes and sighed wistfully because she didn't want to awaken. She'd had the most sensual dream about Magnus. His hands roamed her body and she sensed the effect of them on her skin as if it were actually happening. Regrettably, now she realized it had been just a dream and he wasn't in bed beside her. By the sight of the window casement, it was night for the sky was dark. Magnus still hadn't returned and his side of the bed remained unoccupied for the third night.

The banging sounded again. Someone was knocking at her bedchamber door.

Kendra closed her eyes and drifted slowly toward a good slumber and back to the sensual essence of Magnus caressing her when someone shook her.

"Kendra, you must awaken. Something has happened."

She groaned and rolled to her side. "I don't wish to rise, Linet. Go away." Kendra wanted to revisit her dream. In her sleep, Magnus loved her. It was the only place—in her dreams—that he was honest about how he felt about her.

"My Lady, your father has gone missing. You must rise."

She shot up to a sitting position and pressed her hands over her face to abate her drowsiness. "What say you?" Kendra threw her legs over the side of the bed. Sleepiness and the lure of being with Magnus had completely vanished and she stared at her friend. "I'm awake. What has happened to Papa?"

Linet rummaged through her garments and approached with a frock. "Here, put this on. You shall need a cloak too for it is a little chilly this night. Your da has gone missing. John said that they had gone to bed and he'd awakened because he heard a noise. He realized that your da was not in his bed and so he searched the cottage and outside but alas could not find him. The watch has called a search and there are men even now searching the grounds."

"Oh, nay. He's probably just wandering around the fief. We shall find him." At first, Kendra wasn't too worried because her father had gone on a walk before but he'd never gone too far. But as the final dregs of sleep drained away, she realized they weren't at home. It was her worst fear, that he'd be lost on Cameron land, come true.

"Come, we should join the search." Linet awaited her by the door.

Kendra pulled off her night garment and yanked the over-dress over her head. She slipped on her boots and pressed down the tangles of hair that had gone askew during the night. There was no time to make herself completely presentable and she was in a rush to get outside. As she approached the door, Linet set her cloak about her shoulders. Kendra fastened it by tying the strings together at her neck as she proceeded to the steps.

She hastened outside and at the entry, she halted. A brisk wind hit her and she pulled her cloak tightly around her. "We shall search at the far end of the fief." With that, she marched onward and didn't speak to Linet, but only searched amongst the cottages on the way.

There was no sight of her papa. Each step brought a daunting despair that settled in her chest. It was too cold for her father to traipse around in the night. Hopefully, he'd put on his cloak. She worried for him and prayed that he would be found soon.

Half the night passed. Still, there was no word from the

guards and she hadn't found him either. Along with the harsh wind, a dampness settled on the land. By morning, fog rolled on the ground and sent a wearisome message—that something horrible had happened to her father. Kendra lingered by the back gate and questioned the soldier who'd been assigned to the post.

"And you didn't see him leave the gate?"

"Nay, Milady. No one went through this exit."

Laird Hugh stood next to her now, but she hadn't noticed him arrive. He scowled at the guard and pressed him for information. "Ye stayed at your post all night?"

"I only left to seek nature's call, Laird Hugh. I was gone but a short time. Surely, he could not have passed through the gate whilst I was gone."

"We need to search from here to the loch," she said. Kendra was about to run forth when she saw Winston and Craig approach the back entrance. Their faces beheld a grimness and it seemed everything stopped. They walked forward as if they were slowed in time, ghosts in the night coming to tell her disparaging news. Her eyes blurred and she took a breath to settle herself.

"Milady," Winston said, "I am sorry to tell ye…" he paused as if afraid to go on.

"Sorry to tell me what, Winston? Go on, speak the news. Though I cannot bear it, I need to hear the truth." Kendra leaned against Linet and her friend set her arm around her back. She appreciated her friend's support, but she drew away and stepped toward Winston. "Tell me."

Craig the gate watchman pulled Winston back when it seemed the man was unable to speak, and spoke instead. "Milady, we found your da. He was floating in the loch. I'm afeared he drowned. He was gone when we pulled him from the water. I am awfully sorry, Milady, for your loss."

Her breath came hard and fast as if she'd run a mad dash about the fortification. Her chest rose rapidly as she tried to draw in breath. Kendra pressed her hands on her chest and willed herself not to succumb to the heart-crushing pain of their news.

Her papa was dead.

"Milady, I am sorry," Winston said and stood before her. "Clarence, our healer, told us that he didn't last long in the water. His death was hasty and he didn't suffer overlong. Our clan shall mourn Lord Rupert."

Crestfallen, he stepped back. He kept his gaze averted but it was still sorrowful.

"We should return to the keep, Kendra. Come, 'tis grown colder and we should get something warm in you. A good cup of hot mead will ease you and we will sit by the fire," Linet said.

Numb and unaware of those around her, she followed Linet meekly. Each step brought on a lightheadedness and she suppressed the urge to gag. Kendra's hands shook as she pulled her cloak around her shivering body to ward off the brisk chill. Still the cold overtook her and she couldn't avert the shock that wound its way through her and twinged her with unbearable pain.

At the fief, Linet guided her to the hearth where a fire had been stoked. Flames licked the insides of the stone with a good many logs set. She settled in the chair as close as she could get but still, she couldn't get warm.

Voices sounded around her but she didn't listen to or even hear what was being said. All she could think of was that her dear papa was gone. She was alone in the world now. Worse, she felt as though she had no family, and had lost the only man who ever cared for her.

"Get this down you, Kendra. It'll warm you. You're shivering." Linet handed her a goblet of mead. After, she pressed a thick tartan over her lap.

Kendra took a small sip, but the warm, sweet brew did little to help cease her shaking. She held the cup in her hands and closed her eyes, wishing she'd never brought her father here. He wasn't familiar with the land or its people. She felt responsible for his death and it wore on her. Had they been home, she could have kept him safe. He never would have been able to abscond beyond their walls. She'd made certain of it.

Lady Faye entered the hall and shooed all from the room except for Linet. "Go and have Ellen heat water for a bath for Kendra. We'll get her warm and settled in bed. The poor lass is distraught."

Linet left after nodding to the lady.

"Kendra, dear lass, I am sorry for your loss. Come, we shall take ye to your bedchamber where ye can mourn in private. Linet is having a bath fetched and we'll get ye garbed and tucked in for a good sleep. Ye shall feel better when ye awaken."

"I need Magnus. Where is he?"

Lady Faye took the goblet from her, knelt in front of her, and clasped her hands. "I know not where he is. I shall have Winston find out."

"He's been gone for so long. He hasn't returned to the fief?"

"I think not because he would have been alerted of... Ah, well, Winston shall find him. Worry not. We shall have Magnus come to ye soon."

She shivered and unclasped her hands from Lady Faye's. "It doesn't matter if he comes. I want to go home."

"This is your home."

Kendra shook her head. "Nay, this is Magnus's home and yours and the Camerons'. I do not belong here. I need to take my father home so he can be buried next to my mother. I shall leave when the sky lightens."

"Ye should await Magnus. Surely, he will take ye."

She snorted a laugh at that. "Magnus is more concerned for his duties and cares only for his clan. He shan't even know I am missing, I promise you that. Nay, I will leave with my friends and we shall go home."

"What will I tell Magnus when he returns?"

Kendra shrugged. "I care not what you tell him. He didn't want to marry me. Magnus does not need anyone, least of all a wife. I vow he'll be pleased to be rid of me." Her sorrowful mood lessened her faith in Magnus even more. And at that moment, all she knew for sure was that she needed to go home. She had to bury her father and mourn him as a dutiful daughter should.

"If ye insist on leaving then I must send ye with an escort. Magnus will be angry if we allow ye to travel without protection."

She rose and handed the tartan cover to Lady Faye. "We will need a cart."

"I shall have Winston attend to it. Should ye not rest though? Take a day or two to mourn and then ye can go. By then, Magnus might return and he can take ye—"

Kendra shook her head and didn't let her finish her request. It seemed unreasonable and Kendra couldn't see doing this any other way. "We shall not await Magnus. I am through waiting for him and I will have plenty of time to mourn on my way home. Tell Linet that I do not require a bath and have her tell the men to ready my father for our travel home." She staggered toward the steps and hastened up them to her bedchamber.

Quietly, she closed the door behind her, stepped to the bed, and sat on the side. Tears blurred her vision and she hurried to the chamberpot to retch. Every part of her hurt but mostly her heart. At the basin, she used her hands to press her wet palms over her face. Nothing helped to settle her despair. She sobbed and pressed her eyes. Her dear papa wouldn't want her to weep and she tried not to but alas there was nothing she could do to stop her tears from falling.

While she awaited Linet, she considered her plans. The only thing that mattered was getting her father home and putting him to rest, and then she thought of Heatherington. Somehow, she had to find a way to repay the knave, especially since she would reside at her father's manor, at least until Aston returned. She had to ensure her safety and that of her servants and soldiers. She prayed that he wouldn't besiege them or extort them. The missing coins had to be somewhere. She wished with all her heart that her father had remembered where he'd put them but now it was up to her to right the situation. Being home would allow her to continue her search.

As much as she would miss Magnus, she doubted he would care a whit that she left. He was quite angry with her for tending to the manuscripts. And his repeated and frequent absences proved that Magnus didn't need a wife. He'd make do without her. Also, with the despair filling her heart at her father's death, there was little room there for her absent husband or her care for him. She wouldn't allow herself to think about Magnus or how he would react to her leaving. He'd all but broken her heart and nothing he did would change that.

And it was true that Kendra had spent most of her life alone and hadn't needed anyone. Magnus had given her a small glimpse of what having a husband would be like, and yet, in spite of her independence, she'd found she wanted more—love, devotion, and togetherness. She doubted though that he'd be willing to give himself to her the way she'd hoped. She would go on as she had before—without him—and especially, without his love or affection.

Such thoughts deepened her sorrow and she wept uncontrollably.

CHAPTER TWENTY

A SHRILL SOUND awakened Magnus. He groaned and rolled to his side before he opened his eyes. His vision blurred slightly and he blinked to try to see where he was. His head throbbed and caused him to scrunch his eyes against the light of day. Nearby, a group of men stood beside a cluster of horses. They didn't approach and he couldn't discern what they spoke of. He pressed his hand at his temple and felt the lump there.

The last thing he recalled was that he and his brethren were attacked. They were ambushed by hurled rocks that had injured Hayden and Oswald. He remembered them lying unmoving on the ground. Then he too was struck. Who had attacked them? Was it the men who stood nearby? Was it a rival clan, likely the Chattans?

Magnus moaned softly, slowly raised his body to a sitting position, and heard someone behind him clear his throat. He looked around him until he spotted a man standing but a short distance away.

"Finally, ye came to your senses. I thought we might have to roust ye for ye slept overlong. Here," the man said and handed him a cup.

Magnus wasn't sure if he should accept the drink, at least until he was aware of who his enemy was. He shook his head at the man, refusing his offer. "Who be ye?"

"Ye do not recognize me? Aye, for it has been a long time since we met face to face. I'm Geoff of Clan Chattan."

He shook his head. "I don't recall meeting ye at all. Did ye attack me and my men? Where are they, my men? And where in damnation is my sword?" Magnus realized his sword was missing from its scabbard when he reached for it but it wasn't in its place. If he had to protect himself, he wanted to ensure his sword was at the ready. Alas, he would have to make do with the dagger he would retrieve from his boot. Before he made a move to withdraw it, the man spoke again.

Geoff sat across from him and raised a brow. "Think ye we're daft enough to let ye hold onto your sword? We'll return it, but after we speak. As to your men, we left them in the woods. 'Tis a shame that ye do not recall our meeting. Ye spoke to my brother Rodrick about our land dispute and refused to allow us to use your fields. Are ye still intent to keep us from using the land?"

He remembered meeting Rodrick Chattan but not his brother. Rodrick was of an easier temperament and was not as easy to rile. His brother seemed the opposite for the man wore a glare on his face and his words were spoken with callousness. "Why should I allow ye to use my land? It is mine and belongs to Clan Cameron. Use your own damned land."

"Och, we hoped to make a treaty with ye and for your life, we shall be given rights to let our sheep wander the fields betwixt us." Geoff tried again to hand him the cup. "Ye should take the drink. Know that there is no foulness offered here, only good strong ale and good intentions. Surely ye are thirsty. Take it."

Magnus did so and accepted the cup from him. He took a small drink, only enough to wet his throat and to discern if there was something in it besides ale. He set the cup beside him. "If ye want to kill me then do so but I won't be contemplating a treaty betwixt our clans."

"Why the hell not? See here, Magnus, we mean no threat and willst not have this discord between us. My brother was too soft in dealing with ye, aye, but I am not he. I will destroy your entire clan if ye don't make a treaty with me. Either ye accept my terms or it will be the end of the Cameron Clan."

"Ye speak of war." Magnus tried to think clearly but the bump on the side of his head rendered him incapable of putting together his thoughts. If he didn't agree with the man, he'd be killed. To keep himself from being murdered, he nodded. "Aye then, I suppose ye give me no choice but to accept your treaty. Ye want me to allow your sheep to graze upon my land and in return ye shall let me live. Is that correct?"

Geoff nodded. "'Tis correct. Aye, for we cannot help it if our sheep wander onto your land. We will have no more rift between us though. I want your word that ye won't seek retribution against us for our wee attack in yonder woods either. My men did not mean to harm your brethren but only meant to gain their attention. Och, 'tis a shame they were harmed and I deem ye will seek vengeance. If we are to move forward in peace, then ye must agree that ye will not take up arms against us."

Magnus shook himself. He tried to follow along with the man's words. His men were harmed? Were they dead? Geoff sought to save his hide by making him agree not to seek retaliation but Magnus was unwilling to do so until he found out if his comrades were harmed. "What of my men? Do they live?"

Geoff shrugged. "They were alive when last we saw them. Och, who knows what befell them after we left? I will have your vow, Laird Cameron, Magnus... Then we shall part ways. I will leave ye be as long as ye leave me be and allow us to use your field for our sheep."

"Why not use your own land? I am sure your sheep will be just as pleased to graze upon Chattan land even though it probably lacks." He tried to comprehend the need because it mattered not where the damned Chattan sheep grazed.

"Our hills are rocky and barely any grasses grew during the warm season. We have little sustenance for them and as ye know our sheep are our lifeline. Magnus, I seek peace and a truce. Either ye shall agree or we will go forth with wrath. A war between us would be most welcomed for we relish the idea of fighting against the renowned Cameron warriors."

Magnus disliked the man intensely. He scrutinized him, from his dark, curly hair to the fullness of his beard. He was strong in his shoulders, burly in his body, and a bulky man. It wasn't the look of him though that sat afoul with Magnus, but the sheer audacity of him to suggest that he either accept his truce or suffer the consequences.

"I cannot accept your offer until I speak with my clan. Give me a sennight and I shall send a message giving our acceptance or not."

"Very well, *och* ye have a sennight. That will give me time to call up my allies. Aye, for if ye decide against our truce, ye might want to ready your soldiers and call forth your allies. We intend to fight for the use of the land." Geoff said nothing more, but stood and marched off toward his awaiting men.

One of his men neared and tossed his sword a bit of distance from him. The man then turned away and ambled toward his horse. Geoff and his followers mounted their horses and left him.

The sound of the horses dissipated within a moment. Silence abounded except for the light chirp of a bird. Magnus picked up the cup of ale left beside him and downed the remainder of the drink. He groaned and stood. His steps were somewhat sluggish as he made his way toward his own horse, tethered to a nearby bush. He took the reins in hand and walked a little way to further clear his head. The thumping subsided slightly and his eyes no longer hurt.

On his walk, he recognized the landscape. Ahead of him was an old crag where they'd often taken rest on the way home. The old stone was almost completely covered with moss and a few thin branches that must've fallen atop it from the adjacent tree. He knew exactly where he was now and the land that the Chattans so coveted was close by.

His horse snickered as if alerting him that they should make haste. Magnus mounted his warhorse and rode rapidly toward the area where he'd last seen his men. When he reached the spot where he believed they'd been attacked, he noticed no one near. He peered at the scatter of rocks that sat on the ground, most were about the size of one's palm, easily aimed at a target. At least the rocks were somewhat smooth and hadn't cut him. He noted no blood on the rocks except for one.

Hayden and Oswald were no longer there. He sighed wearily and hoped they'd made their way home. Onward, he rode, until he crossed the wooden bridge and reached the gates of *Eilean nan Craobh*. By the gate, he dismounted and waited for his guards to open it. There was no sign of Craig, the leader of the gate watch. He had hoped to gain news from him. Magnus was about to ask the others if Hayden and Oswald had returned but his grandda approached.

"Magnus, lad, ye finally returned. Ye had me worried. I've been awaiting ye and kept watch of the gate for your return. Come, there is much news to impart." His grandda waved him onward and he followed him. "Where have ye been?"

"I will speak of it later. Tell me… What of Hayden and Oswald? Did they return? We were attacked by the Chattans and…" his words trailed off as he detected the troubled look in his grandfather's eyes. "Tell me the news. Are they safe?"

"Hayden is being seen to by Clarance. He took a mighty blow to the head and hasn't come to as yet. Wyren found them when he'd gone in search of ye because…well, ye took overlong to return and he worried that something happened… Ah, I'm afraid Oswald was struck dead. The men are preparing him for burial."

Magnus stopped in his tracks. Oswald was killed? Rage heated him from within. He had promised to consider the Chattan's truce but now that was impossible. Only vengeance would right the wrong done by them. The taking of one of their own assured they'd take to arms and they would war with their hearts for their beloved soldier. Not only did he want to avenge Oswald but also for their ambush in the woods. He needed to speak to Wyren at the soonest to ready the soldiers. He would call upon his allies:

the MacMillans, Stewarts, and the MacDonalds. Chattan's sheep would starve before he'd allow them to graze on his land.

"That's not all, lad. Your wife's da... He drowned in the loch a sennight ago and she took him home. We sent a handful of Cameron soldiers to protect her on the journey. I'm sorry but your lass is gone."

He stared at his grandfather as his news completely jolted him with trepidation. Kendra had left him? She was gone? His chest pounded and he wanted to rush off to find her, to prove his grandda was wrong. Kendra hadn't left him, she wouldn't. She'd taken a vow before the king and queen. She was his wife. She belonged to him.

"She was devastated by her da's death and wanted to have him buried with his wife. Winston went with her, along with a few other men for her protection. Her maid and her da's attendant also left with them," his grandda explained further.

Magnus whirled around and noticed his parents standing on the fief's steps. His mother looked beyond despaired and his father gave him a look of commiseration. He knew in an instant what his grandda had told him was true. When he could, he would go to Kendra but for now, there were too many pressing duties to handle. The first thing in order was the gathering of his men and calling up his allies. Then he'd check on Hayden and have Jake fetched from Lillith's cottage. No one would be at the Chattan's mercy. He'd make sure of it.

Thinking of Lillith reminded him that he'd promised to send herbs to her. When he could, he would have two of his soldiers attend to the duty.

"Magnus, let me take ye inside and have Clarance tend to your wound. Ye need some rest before ye hail off to do your duty. Aye, for ye look dead on your feet." His father took his arm and led him to Clarence's cottage.

Inside the cottage, a foul scent engulfed him. Magnus peered at Hayden's body which lay upon a table, where once his brother Ned had lain. He swallowed hard and prayed that his soldier had thrived and hadn't died from his injury. Hayden couldn't be dead. Emotion threatened to overtake him. Magnus fisted his hands to avert his need to succumb to his sorrow.

"Laird, let us see how bad your wound is. Ye have blood dried on your face." Clarence's bushy eyebrows rose as he pressed on his shoulder and bade him to sit on a stool by one of his tables. He prodded and assessed the wound. "'Tis naught but bluster and ye were only grazed. Ye do not need a stitch. I'll put a healing salve on it and ye should be eased."

"My head aches," he said and closed his eyes briefly.

"Och, ye be fortunate, Laird. I'll make ye a dram to ease your ache." As the healer went about his tasks, Magnus couldn't form the words to ask about Hayden but his grandda tried to relieve him when he crouched near him and gave a reassuring look.

Clarence saved him the trouble of explaining and said, "Laird, worry not for Hayden. He is only in a slumber. He'll awaken soon." After he handed him a cup with the dram, the healer dabbed the salve on the bump on his temple. "*Och*, he came to a short while ago. He might not be on his feet for a day or so, but I deem he should fare well once the headache subsides. At least, that is my hope. But he's not dead, Laird, rest assured."

The tightness in Magnus's shoulders eased. Though he was dismayed by Oswald's death, he was much gratified to know that Hayden lived. When Clarence was through with his ministrations, he'd go and see Wyren. Not only did he need to seek vengeance against the Chattans, but he still needed to find the two traitors within his clan.

Until those matters were concluded, he couldn't seek Kendra, as much as he'd wanted to. Duty and vengeance took precedence over locating his wife, and he was somewhat irked that he needed to fetch her. She'd have to await him.

CHAPTER TWENTY-ONE

East Dunbartonshire
Glasgow, Scotland
September1260

EARLY AUTUMN'S LIGHT shone upon the stones and wooden crosses amid the burial grounds. Kendra stood before the hole that had been dug for her father's final resting place. She peered at the stone carved into a square with rounded edges and etched with *Catherine*, the name of her mother, next to where her papa would be placed. Her parents would be rejoined in the hereafter just as her father had spoken of many times in the last few months. That thought didn't do much to quell her sadness. She already missed her cantankerous papa but she was gladdened to know that he was now with her mother.

After the priest spoke prayers and praised her father, he bade the men to lower her papa into the ground. As he descended into the darkness, Kendra remained still. Her eyes stared without a single tear showing her emotion. She kept herself steeled against showing her true feelings. She had to endure and be strong. Besides, she'd wept most of the way home and her eyes had all but dried up and no tears remained.

Kendra waited until the last shovel of dirt was placed atop the small mound before she headed back to the walls of the manor. The mourners, several Dunbartonshire locals, the manor's servants, soldiers, crofters, and merchants paid their respects. She bowed her head in appreciation for their mournful words as they passed by her to exit. Her mouth had gone dry and she didn't think she could utter a word without sobbing.

Linet stepped forward and set her arm around her shoulder. "Come away now. Unless you wish for more time…"

She shook her head. Kendra took one last glance at where her parents rested in a settled grave and the mounded new one, and stepped back. Linet guided her from the graves and they walked in a leisurely pace toward the manor. There, Mistress Gilda had a light early supper served but Kendra couldn't eat a bite. Her stomach was in knots and flutters. Instead, she took small sips of mead and listened to those around her speak of her parents. Stories were told of how fond her father was of her mother and what a good lord he'd been.

Kendra wondered if the keep's residents worried about who their next lord would be. She worried about that too, and considered writing to the king to give him the news that her father had passed. If Aston was there, he would take on the role of lord, but he hadn't returned and might not, given the amount of time he'd been gone. Would the king place someone else as lord? Perhaps she should hold off informing the king of her father's demise.

Winston approached and interrupted her thoughts. "Milady, now that ye have buried your da, we should make arrangements to return to Cameron land." He spoke low. "I will see to the matter if that pleases ye."

"Nay, I shall not return, at least not yet. You may go, Winston, and take the Cameron sentry with you." She hadn't told the young soldier why she wanted to remain, but she needed time to find the coins and return them to Heatherington. Only then could she return to Cameron land.

She wouldn't tell him that his laird probably wouldn't care if she returned or not, or that their last encounter was filled with his wrath. She firmed her lips at the remembrance of his anger when he'd looked at the steward's parchments. Perhaps she could find a little peace now that she was home—that was, if she could find and return Heatherington's coins.

Undecided, Kendra raised her face to look at Winston. "Give me a little time and I shall let you know when I am ready."

"I cannot return without ye and will await until ye are ready." Winston inclined his head and stepped away.

Kendra didn't wait for the sky to darken before she sought her bed. She left the hall and trudged up the steps as if her feet weighed as much as boulders. Lord, she was tired. Now that she had seen to the duty of burying her father she could finally get some rest.

She opened the door of her bedchamber, and sighed because she had never thought of seeing her room again. Nevertheless, she was home in the bedchamber she'd used since she was a young lass. Being there filled her with both sadness and joy.

She went about readying for bed almost mindlessly and pulled back the covers. Kendra crawled upon the bed and pulled the covers to her chin. Weary, she closed her eyes and fell asleep without a thought.

As DAWN BROKE on the horizon and filled her bedchamber with light, Kendra stretched and threw her legs over the side of the bed. She took a moment to settle a dizziness that came over her. She closed her eyes for a moment to keep the room from spinning but then she hastened to the chamber pot. Kendra fell to her knees and held the pot with shaky hands. With all that had happened, her body rebelled against her. She gagged and drew in deep breaths but nothing helped. Taking slow breaths through her nose finally eased her and she rose.

At the basin, she used her hands to scoop handfuls of water and pressed them on her face. After she washed and dressed, she was ready to plunge forth into a thorough search of the manor.

She didn't care if it took her a fortnight. The coins had to be there somewhere and she meant to find them.

In the hall, she found herself alone. She sat in a chair and scooted forward. There was a trencher of sweetbreads and a fresh pitcher of mead placed in the center. She helped herself to a small piece of bread and half a cup of mead. It was as much as her stomach would allow.

"Milady, good morn." Winston came into the hall and approached.

"Good day, Winston. Before you speak, I should tell you that I plan to stay here for a while. If you would be so kind as to take a message to Magnus when you return to Cameron lands, I would appreciate that."

"But Milady, I thought ye were going to return with me."

"I do not think I can for I have a malady..." Kendra shuffled her chair back and stood. "I am ailing, Winston. Until I feel better, I will remain here. But I do want you to take a missive to deliver to Magnus."

Winston's face reflected his disappointment with a slight scowl on his dark brows. "I live to serve ye, Milady, so if that is what ye wish...but I cannot leave. I'll have another soldier deliver the message to our laird."

"Good. Come and see me later. I should have the missive written by then. The messenger can leave on the morrow." Kendra turned away and left the soldier standing by the table. Her heart ached to tell him such but it was the truth. She wasn't feeling well, though she probably could travel. Her footsteps took her to her father's bedchamber.

Gently, she closed the door, leaned against it, and took in the sight of her father's domain. It still smelled like him: a woodsy and leathery scent that permeated the air. She drew a deep breath and smiled because his scent would stay with her and she vowed never to forget it.

Kendra did a thorough search for the missing coins. The chamber was completely disheveled by the time she finished.

Chests remained open, blankets tossed here and there, chairs askew, and trunks toppled. She'd searched every single spot and found no coins. But she found a small wooden box that contained her mother's cherished items that her father had kept.

Inside the box, there was an ivory comb etched with flowers that had likely cost a small fortune, a scrap of parchment that had the lines of her mother's favorite sonnet, a length of ribbon, and last but most prized, a ring her father had given to her mother when they married. Had he saved it for her? Her father had never mentioned it.

She set the items back inside the box and held it against her chest. When she was able to shake away her sentiment, she placed the box on a table and went about setting the room to rights. As she tidied up the chamber, she found a few items of her fathers that she added to the box: a small gold cross, a braided ring of horsehair that could fit upon a wrist, and a kerchief that her mother had made for him with his insignia embroidered at the corner. The box now contained a treasure that she wouldn't part with for the world.

Kendra left her father's chamber and put the box in her room. Whatever ailed her came upon her again and she lay upon her bed. The room seemed to float before her eyes. A knock sounded on her door and she called out to enter.

Linet crossed the room and reached the bedside. "Kendra, you're still abed? Winston mentioned that you are ailing. Are you ill?"

She nodded. "I have been for a few days now, even before we left Cameron land. I cannot seem to hold anything down and my vision is making everything move."

Linet retrieved a damp cloth from the basin and set it on her forehead. "That should make you feel better. I shall have my mother come to see you. Tell me about your ailment."

Kendra told her how she'd felt and the effects of her dizziness and such. Linet listened patiently and then left the chamber.

She groaned as her stomach rumbled. That morning, she had

eaten very little. Perhaps it was only that she needed to eat. She didn't want to worry Linet or Mistress Gilda.

A little while later, Linet opened the door and called to her. "'Tis just me and Mama. She's brought the midwife with her too."

Kendra tried to sit up but instantly her stomach convulged. She lay back. "I do not think that I need a midwife, Linet. It's just a stomach ailment."

"At least let her check you over. Mama says that it sounds as though you might be with child." Linet smiled widely and sat in the chair closest to her.

Gilda took a seat on the other side of the bed and bobbed her head. "Worry not, lass, we shall see you right. This is Agnes, a friend of mine from the village. I've known her since we were young girls."

The woman, a midwife, was aged with a full head of long, gray hair. She had kind blue eyes though, and so Kendra allowed her to tend to her.

"Be still, My Lady, and we shall find out soon enough if you are carrying a babe."

The midwife's hands roamed her stomach and she pried her eyes open. Kendra felt awkward with the woman's somewhat rough treatment especially when she pressed her fingers on her breasts. She made her urinate in the chamber pot and all the while Kendra's face brightened. The woman though, seemed unaffected by her embarrassment. Mistress Agnes took the chamber pot from her and stood by the window casement. After a long moment, she returned to the bedside.

"Yes, My Lady, I can confirm that you are with child. You must be far along because your belly is quite big. I say you will bear your child before winter ends. You must eat small meals throughout the day and drink no mead for it will upset your stomach. 'Tis the honey that makes you retch. Best to drink ale or water. I shall come and see you in a fortnight or so to check on you." With that, she bowed her head to Gilda and left the chamber.

Gilda and Linet remained silent. Kendra stared at them and was dumbfounded. She didn't know how to react to the midwife's news. That she was with child pleased her but it also saddened her. She needed Magnus but alas, she was on her own for now.

"There, there, My Lady, you have some time to go before you give birth. We shall fatten you up for you must eat. I can make some drams that will settle your stomach too. I'll go and prepare a light meal for you. Rest and stay abed." Gilda left.

Kendra gently pressed her hands over her stomach. "I cannot believe this."

"I am sure your husband will be overjoyed at the news," Linet said. "We should make arrangements to return to him and—"

"Nay, I cannot leave now, Linet. I must find the coins my father accepted from Heatherington. Only then can I go."

Linet sat beside her and clasped her hand. "I understand that you feel it necessary to return the coins but you should be more concerned about—"

Kendra cut her off because she needed to explain. It was time to tell her what Heatherington intended, though she had tried to spare her friend the worry. "If I do not return the coins, Heatherington will besiege us and all within the manor will be in danger. I cannot allow that to happen. Will you help me? Help me search for the coins?"

"Aye, and I'll have John aid us as well. Together, we will search every place we can think of. Worry not and when we return the coins, you can go to your husband."

Kendra nodded. "I will send a message to him for now. Perhaps he will come to me if he is not too busy with his laird duties." But she knew that Magnus had his hands full with finding Ned's murderer and other clan matters. She was but an unwanted diversion, a wife he hadn't asked for. Still, he was noble and maybe he would understand that she needed time at home. Would he come to her? If so, when? She wondered how much time she had.

CHAPTER TWENTY-TWO

BEFORE DAWN, MAGNUS set out to visit Oswald's grave. After crossing the wooden bridge, he skirted the clan's village and reached the short-walled enclosed burial grounds. He stood before Oswald's burial site, knelt, and thanked him for his service to the clan and to him. He'd been a dedicated soldier and comrade, and Magnus had known him his entire life. He'd miss his lifelong friend. That he was killed for such an insignificant reason infuriated him. The Chattans would pay dearly. He'd see to it and soon.

When he left his friend's resting place, he stopped at the barracks and directed two soldiers to seek the herbs Lillith needed and take them to her. As much as he wanted to return to Lillith's to check on Jake himself, he told his guardsmen to return with word of his brother's condition.

With resignation in his heart, Magnus returned to the keep and headed for the training field. There were already scores of soldiers tarrying on the field when he arrived. He joined them for exercise and to rid himself of his intense anger. With a yank of his sword, he gripped it in his hand and marched onto the field.

A soldier near to his age offered to spar with him. They clanged their swords and continued until Magnus lowered his sword and helped the soldier at his feet to rise. His opponent, whom he had battered to the ground, rasped with heavy breath.

Training in arms always relieved his tension and he'd spent most of the day going against any of his soldiers brave enough to test him.

His men needed more training before they would confront his enemy—the Chattans. War would give him the satisfaction of retribution and also would ingrain his wrath at those who trespassed on his land and ambushed him in the woods.

He strolled through the soldiers who remained on the field and commented on their abilities or failures with the sword. Across the field, several men took to the quintains and practiced archery. Arrows flew through the air at the targets. Some hit the center, some did not. Arrows littered the ground and beyond. A group of his soldiers also threw daggers but they were more proficient and seasoned. Most hit the aimed targets and hardly any daggers lay upon the ground.

Wyren approached with his son strapped to his chest. The bairn appeared to be sleeping. His brother chuckled as he approached. "My son is soothed by the sounds of the swords. 'Tis the only time he sleeps soundlessly. I wonder if I should have two men assigned to ply their swords by my bedside?"

Though his brother jested, Magnus didn't laugh. He was in no merry mood. "Have ye found the men yet? The two men who were missing from the count?"

Wyren shook his head. "Not as yet. They are named Gordon and Ezlen. Neither have been seen since Ned had gone missing and were not assigned any duty that would take them from our lands. They must be behind our brother's death."

"I want proof before we condemn them. Have the men continue to search for them. Send men beyond the fief if necessary. I want to question them myself."

His brother agreed with a nod. "What of Hayden? Is he well? Has he awakened?"

Magnus intended to visit his comrade and walked toward the healer's cottage. "I'm on my way to see him now."

"I'll go with ye," Wyren said and shifted Hale's body to cradle him in his arms when he fussed. "*Och*, I should probably take Hale home first. I'll meet up with ye later." His brother set off toward his home.

Magnus continued to Clarence's abode. He rapped at the door and didn't wait to be bid entry. The door opened before he shoved it. Clarence grumbled something under his breath which Magnus couldn't comprehend. Something bothered the grumpy healer but Magnus couldn't guess what or why he was cross. He entered the cottage and saw Hayden sitting in a chair. His comrade's dark hair fell over his eyes as his head leaned forward.

"Oho, so ye finally awakened, aye?"

Hayden raised his face and grinned. "I'm well enough now, Laird. Tell me, when do we seek revenge?"

"Soon enough. The men make ready and Wyren has had them training from sunup."

"Good." Hayden stood and before he left the cottage, he turned to Clarance. "My thanks, healer, for your aid. I'm well enough now."

Clarence guffawed. "So ye say, aye? *Och*, ye might want to wait a few days before returning to duty or training or ye might be wavering on your feet."

"I am well and my head no longer hurts," Hayden said. "I need to get back—"

"*Och*, who am I but a healer…?" Clarence tisked and flapped his arm at them. "Be gone then. I'll likely see ye here again before the day is through. If ye start to see double again, return at once. Laird, keep an eye on him for he is not as recovered as he deems."

Magnus nodded to him. He wasn't about to demand that Hayden stay at the healer's cottage. If his soldier considered himself well enough, then he wouldn't gainsay him.

Hayden stepped outside. "I vow that man is maddened. He wouldn't cease prodding and poking at me. Methinks he hasn't had a live person to tend to for some time." He bellowed with a grunt. "I cannot believe Oswald was killed. When I awakened in the woods, I realized ye were gone. I thought you'd gone for help but when we returned, I wasn't thinking right. Clarence said that Oswald was struck true in the center of his eyes."

Magnus grunted. "He was struck harder than ye were."

"I have a hard head," Hayden said and grimaced. "I will miss my comrade, my brother-in-arms… There was no one I trusted more than him, except for ye, Laird. Until I avenge him, I won't be able to mourn him."

"Aye, me either. I visited him this morn, his resting place. Ye should go and see him. The clan could not await us for his burial and he was laid to rest before I returned." Magnus had left his friend's grave with anger filling him. Since he'd been able to rid it with the use of his sword arm most of the day, he felt much better.

"I understand, and aye, I probably will visit his grave this eve." Hayden walked beside him. "Before the attack, ye were going to tell me what happened at the harlot's home… What did ye find out about Ned's murder?"

Magnus had forgotten that he had yet to explain what transpired and what he'd found out about Ned. He quickly filled Hayden in on what Mary had told him and that they now searched for Gordon and Ezlen. In brief, he spoke of what happened when he was confronted by Geoff Chattan, and lastly, that Kendra had left him.

"I know them both well, Gordon and Ezlen, and cannot believe they would extort coins from Ned. But that is not to say they wouldn't. When we find them, we shall force the truth from them," Hayden said.

"*If* we find them. They've been missing for some time. It is probable that they have left the area and absconded to who knows where…? We may never get the truth about Ned's death. I find I grow weary of worrying about it." Magnus approached the main fief and invited Hayden to supper.

"I am sorry, Laird, to hear that Milady returned to her da's home. But I understand that she needed to take her da's body home. It is only right that the lord be buried on his land. She will return. As to the Chattans, 'tis about time we show them that the Camerons will not be tread upon. We'll make them see that we mean business when we take to arms."

Magnus waved Hayden to enter the keep before him. They ambled inside and took cups from the buttery on the way to the table. Inside the hall, his parents sat at the trestle table. The table was laden with various foodstuffs. He found himself hungry after training most of the day. He piled on stew, bread, and a handful of nuts on his trencher and set it before him.

His mother gazed at him with reproach. Magnus grunted in objection at her look, but she didn't desist. "What is it, Mother? Ye appear to want to say something so speak, go on."

"I am disappointed in ye, Magnus. How could ye let this happen? Ye should go and collect your brother from that healer's cottage. Bring him home. We should tend to him, not some stranger. And I disbelieve ye allowed your wife to leave and have no concern for her. Ye should be riding hellbent to get to her, and yet, here ye are, eating supper as though ye have no troubles."

He sighed and peered at his mother with angst. "Think ye I do not want to go after Kendra? I cannot leave when we are on the brink of war with the Chattans. They insist that we allow their sheep to graze on our land. I will not allow it. Along with that horrid situation, I must find the men who murdered Ned. *Och*, ye are right though. We should bring Jake home. He should be here, tended to by Clarence. I'll see to it on the morrow."

"I'll go with ye, Laird," Hayden said.

His mother pounded the table with her closed fist. "Ye worry about a small tract of land when our clan mourns. Who cares if the Chattans allow their sheep to graze upon our land? Let it be, Magnus, and go and retrieve your wife. Your soldiers can bring Jake home and when ye return, ye can find out who killed Ned. I do not know why ye are making this so difficult."

"I am the laird, Mother, not ye. I make the decisions for this clan and family, and right now the matters that I must handle are more important than fetching a wife who should not have left the holding without my permission in the first place. Now cease haranguing me." Magnus rose and with a pound of his fist on the table, said, "I do not need to hear this cosh, not from your surly tongue." He turned to Hayden. "Be ready at first light and we'll retrieve Jake."

No one spoke to him on his way from the hall. Magnus trudged up the stairs and entered his bedchamber with a thrust to the door. The quiet eased him but being there also reminded him that he needed to get to Kendra. He wanted to be there for her in her time of need, and yet, he was unable to leave his holding at the present. Torn between his duty as the laird and his duty to his wife, Magnus raked his hands through his hair and growled in frustration.

On the approach to his trunk that held his garments, he spotted his grandmother's brooch sitting atop. Kendra had left it behind. He sighed in objection because he wasn't sure what that meant. Did she intend not to return? Or had she left it behind to keep it safe? Regardless, he held the brooch and closed his eyes at the coldness of the metal in his hand. Lord, he hoped she was safe.

He disrobed and got into bed. Sleepless, his mind wandered from one thing to another. But he finally drifted off as he thought of how bonny his wife was, how winsome she was in spirit, how pleasing she was. He missed her. As much as he wanted to be there for her, he admitted that he needed her too. She had a way of solacing him. What he wouldn't do for a wee bit of peace now and with his wife held in his arms.

CHAPTER TWENTY-THREE

KENDRA SEARCHED THE entire manor for the missing coins. Every place where she could think of was checked and rechecked for the misbegotten bride price, even the loosened floorboards in the hall and her father's bedchamber. She removed the few remaining tapestries and considered there might be a hole in the wall where her father might have put them. But there was nothing, no secret hole or place within the manor. All the floorboards were intact and none loosened.

Deep in thought, she hadn't noticed Linet enter the hall. Kendra paced around the small table with her hand beneath her chin as she pressed her other hand at her temple. An ache throbbed there in annoyance at her failure.

"Are you unwell?" Linet asked.

She about jumped knee-high off the floor. "Oh, you gave me a fright. I didn't hear you enter. Nay, I am not unwell. I am feeling much better, only aggravated that I haven't found the coins yet. I must thank your mother for her potion for it has settled my stomach." She continued to traipse around the table and stopped. "We have searched for days on end, everywhere within the manor for the coins. They cannot be here inside the walls. I mean to search for them outside."

"If Heatherington came and spoke to your da, they were probably outside. Maybe he hid them out there somewhere? I'll get John to help us search." Linet left the hall.

Kendra retrieved her mother's shawl and pulled it around her shoulders. The air had chilled considerably since she'd returned home. Though it was autumn, winter wasn't too far off. That reminded her of the bump that now showed at her waist. She was getting bigger by the day. Soon, she would be unable to travel and she drew in a regrettable sigh at that. Kendra had hoped to find the coins and return them to Heatherington before the weather turned or before she was incapable of riding. She had intended to return to Magnus but that he hadn't come or replied to her missives brought on the trepidation that he might not care if she ever returned.

Kendra ambled outside and waved to the soldiers and servants she passed on the way to the stables. Although her father hadn't ridden much before they left to attend the king, he could have been in the stables when Heatherington visited. She hadn't thought to check there but would now.

"Milady, do ye want me to saddle a horse for you?" the stable master asked.

"Nay, my thanks though, Peter." She walked along the stalls and stopped to pet her horse. Sky Dancer, the poor animal, hadn't been ridden for some time but there was nothing she could do about it now that she was carrying a babe. The risk was too great to injure herself or her unborn child. She stroked the horse's nose and turned back to Peter. "Have you let out the horses this day?"

Peter set a bucket down by the trough and strode toward her. "Earlier, Milady, and I just brought them inside. 'Tis a wee bit brisk this day and the air is growing colder. I deem we'll need a good fire this night for it will be freezing afore the morn."

"I think you're right." Kendra walked on and stopped by her father's horse's stall. She opened the gate and stepped inside. His horse was as cantankerous as her papa was and now the beast butted his head against her shoulder and tried to nip her. She pushed him back with a hand to his nose. "I won't be but a moment. Cease being surly," she said to the horse.

A saddlebag hung on a peg on the back wall. She recognized it and remembered her father using it whenever he'd traveled. Kendra lifted it from the peg and it was heavy. She fell to her knees and then settled back against the wall. With anticipation, she clutched the flap of the bag and tossed it open.

As she rummaged through the bag, she found one of her father's tunics, a pair of stockings, a horseshoe, and a small pot that he probably used for stew when he traveled. When she emptied the bag, she shook it and heard the tinkle of something else within.

Kendra pressed her hands inside the bag and found a compartment that was closed with a pin. After she unfastened the closure, she pushed her fingers inside the spacious space. She grabbed a hefty pouch from within and shook it. The knot that kept it closed was difficult to open, but finally, she got it undone. She emptied the pouch onto her lap and it overflowed with coins—at least enough to equal ten pounds.

Tears gathered in her eyes and blurred her view of the coins. She was relieved but also melancholy that she hadn't thought to check her father's saddlebag sooner. All the time she had wasted in search of the coins when they had been there all along. Her father must have put them in his saddlebag when Heatherington visited. That he'd placed the bag there without taking the coins inside the manor perplexed her, but of course, her father hadn't been in his right mind.

Kendra collected the coins and put them back in the pouch then rose and left the stall, ensuring the door was closed so her father's onery horse couldn't get out. With a farewell to Peter, she left the stable and hastened to the hall. There, she wrote a missive to Lord Heatherington for him to come to her. She put the coins in a trunk by a side table and closed it. They would be safe there until she could return them to her knavish neighbor.

John entered and approached. "Milady, me and Linet searched everywhere outside, beneath every rock, by all the walls, and I had men check the small pond. We found nothing."

She raised her eyes to John's defeated gaze. "Worry not, John, I just found them. They were in Papa's saddlebag hanging in his horse's stall in the stable."

John smacked his head with the palm of his hand and groaned. "Why did I not check the saddlebag when I hung it in Lord Rupert's stall?"

"He must've put them in there when he met with Lord Ellish and that's where they were all along. Can you take this missive to Heatherington at once?"

John held his hand out and Kendra placed the missive in his palm. "Hurry now because I want to get this matter settled quickly."

"Aye, Milady." John turned and left.

Kendra took the steps to her bedchamber. Although it was only midday, now that her mission had been completed, she found herself finally able to relax. Tired, she lay on her bed. Within moments, she fell asleep though her slumber was fitful and she dreamed of Magnus. The moments they had shared together flitted through her mind as if she relived them. With a startle, she awoke with tears streaming down her face. Hastily, she wiped them away and suppressed the sob that still thickened her throat. How she missed Magnus. Would he ever come? If he was going to, he would have arrived by now. She lost hope that he was too busy to give her any consideration.

Taking a moment to allow fresh air inside her chamber, she opened the window shutters. The window casement showed a dusky sky with the oncoming night. A chill now filled her bedchamber and she shook herself and closed the shutters. She went to her wardrobe and changed her overdress. After she washed and took care of her toiletry, she left the chamber and made her way to the hall.

Linet and Gilda had set the table for supper. A stack of trenchers sat in the center along with baskets and bowls of foodstuff. Kendra's stomach rumbled and she was hungry. She sat beside the chair her father usually used and peered at the empty seat. If only he was still there, grumbling to her about his day. She missed him as well. Even though she had the servants, soldiers, and the Graham clansmen and women, Kendra felt lonely.

"My lady, shall we join you?"

"I should like that, Gilda. Please, sit with me and have your supper." Kendra spooned the pottage into a bowl and grabbed a chunk of soft bread. As she ate, Norman joined them. He spoke softly to his wife and she couldn't hear what he'd said.

"My Lady, the collection of the crofters' tax is done. I shall send our tithe to the king's men on the morrow. We'll see how much remains after that but I suspect we will have enough to purchase seed for the spring planting and to see us through the winter." Norman accepted a trencher from Gilda and she smiled at him.

"That is good news, Norman. My thanks for handling that. I'm gladdened it's done."

A noise outside the hall alerted her that someone had come. She was about to rise when John entered with Heatherington following in his wake. The man wore a grim look on his face but settled into a more amiable manner when he reached her.

"Lady Kendra," he said and bowed. "It has been some time, has it not? You look as beautiful as ever."

"Lord Heatherington, I see you received my missive."

His head bobbed. "Aye, aye and I came at once because—"

She rose and retrieved the pouch from the trunk by the side table. "As you know, the king gave my hand to a Highlander, and your agreement with my father was nullified. Since you insisted we return the coins to you, I wanted to get them to you as soon as I could." Kendra set the pouch on the table in front of him. "Go on, take them."

Ellish frowned at the pouch and returned his gaze to her. "But My Lady…"

"I want no strife between us, Lord Heatherington. To keep those who reside on Graham land safe, I insist you take the coins. My people will be unharmed and there will be no cause for you to attack us or take arms against any of our soldiers."

"But My Lady—"

She wouldn't allow him to speak. "Just take the coins and be gone."

"I cannot take your coins."

Kendra scoffed at him. "Why not? You wrote to me and threatened to besiege my home. You insisted that I return the coins and suggested that you would destroy us. Now I have returned the bride price as you bade. Why won't you take them?"

"Because, My Lady, your husband already repaid the debt. He wrote to me some time ago and sent me the coins to repay the bride price your father accepted. I cannot take your coins because he told me that he would seek retribution if I did."

"My husband…?" Kendra tilted her head to the side. "Magnus repaid the debt?"

Ellish grinned and nodded. His smile was filled with kindness and not his usual wolfish grin. "Aye, he did. There is no debt, My Lady, to repay. 'Tis the truth, I am not so angry about losing you now. Though I wish we had married for we would have made strong children. I have married another lass and I'm most pleased with the arrangement." He turned and with a wave, walked to the exit.

Kendra followed him. "I am gladdened to hear that you are happily married, Ellish. I shall come to meet your wife when I can. It would be the neighborly thing to do, to offer a welcome."

He took her hand and almost raised it to his lips. "I would rather you did not for she would be envious of your beauty." She stood still and somewhat shocked at the manor's entry and Ellish seemed to hesitate to leave. "If you ever need aid, as your neighbor, My Lady, I will be obliged to come. You have only to send word. I will leave you now." He didn't wait for her farewell but left hastily.

Kendra watched him saunter to his horse, mount it, and ride off. As she stood there, a light snow began to fall. She held out her hand and glanced at John when he stepped beside her. "Did

Magnus tell you that he paid the debt?"

John shook his head. "Nay and I did not think he knew about it. How did he find out? Maybe Heatherington wrote to him or the king might have told him. You'll have to ask him, My Lady, when next you see him."

Kendra's shoulders slumped. If she ever saw him again, she might ask him about it. When next she saw Magnus, she would force him to take the coins. The last thing she wanted was to be indebted to him for her father's misdoing. It was only right that he allow her to repay him.

"Come, My Lady, the snow falls heavier. We should get inside. I think a storm is coming. I'll see to the manor's fires and ensure all is battened down."

"Thank you, John." Kendra returned to the table and finished eating. By the time she sought her bed, John had secured all the windows, refilled the hearths with firewood, and directed the soldiers to secure the walls.

Kendra opened the wooden shutter in her bedchamber and shook as the chill overtook her. She peered out into the night and shielded her eyes against the heavy snow that blew inside. The storm ramped up and the ground was now covered in white. There was no returning to Magnus now. Travel would be impossible.

CHAPTER TWENTY-FOUR

A s Magnus approached Lillith's cottage, a cold wind blew and a light snow fell. He needed to make haste and get back home before it became too difficult to travel. He dismounted near the wall and released the reins of the additional horse he'd brought along for Jake. With a stomp forward, he reached the door, rapped on the worn wood, and the door was opened.

Lillith smiled in greeting. "Laird Cameron, I was wondering when you would darken my doorstep again and here ye are. My but 'tis cold enough to freeze your nose. Come inside and get warm. I just made a hot broth and bread."

Hayden followed him inside and stood near the doorway.

Magnus looked for Jake on the cot where he'd last seen him but his brother wasn't there. "Where is Jake? Has he...?" He couldn't form the words to ask his question. A sense of despair washed over him. If he lost his brother, Magnus couldn't fathom how his clan would react. They still mourned one of his brothers and the last thing he needed was to lose another.

"He's gone to fetch water for me," Lillith said.

"So he has recovered?" Magnus glanced at where the MacKendrick soldier had rested but he too was gone.

"Aye, he is still a wee bit sore but has made little complaint. I deem he is well enough to go home. He might take a bit more time to heal completely though." Lillith busied herself at her table and started to grind herbs in a small vessel. "If ye wish for broth and bread, help yourself."

Magnus shook his head at her offer. "What of the MacKendrick soldier, Trevor, did he survive?" He hoped so because he admired Trevor and thought he was an amiable fellow.

"He recovered and returned home when his laird had the fall festival. I wanted to thank ye for sending along those herbs I had asked for. It was appreciated and helped a great deal in tending to the men. How are ye, Laird Cameron? I heard ye had married At least, that is what Jake told me. Is life treating ye well?"

Magnus grunted at her question. Though he was sound and whole, inside he was hollow and miserable. He still hadn't found the two missing men after searching for them for many moon rises. Not only that, but he despaired at what to do about Kendra. He should have gone to her long ago when he'd first learned she'd returned home. Was his absence giving her the idea that he cared not? He certainly hoped that wasn't the case. Yet there was no time to fetch her, not with his duty to his clan pressing upon him.

"Laird Cameron? Did ye hear me? I asked—"

"I heard ye, Lillith. I am well enough. I need to get Jake and return home before the snow hampers us. How far do ye think he went? I should go after him." As he spoke, the door opened and his brother stepped inside, carrying a bucket of water.

"Magnus, ye are here. I thought I recognized the horses." Jake set the bucket by the door, marched to him, and clasped his hand. "'Tis good to see ye, Laird."

"And ye, brother. I'm pleased ye recovered and appear mended. Are ye well enough to travel home?" Magnus turned his gaze from his brother's head to his feet. Jake's height seemed to have grown even higher and his stare was formidable.

"Aye, I waited for ye and thought I might have to walk home but alas here ye are."

Magnus pulled Jake into a half-hearted embrace. "Aye, we

missed ye. I'm gladdened ye are well now and finally can come home. Ma has not ceased pestering me to retrieve ye. Da was concerned for ye as well, as was the clan."

Jake chuckled. "She would. I'm sorry she harped at ye and for getting myself injured."

"'Twas no fault of yours." Magnus wandered to the door and waited for his brother and Hayden to follow.

Jake stepped to Lillith and pressed a hand on her shoulder. "Lillith, I cannot thank ye enough for your aid. I am indebted to ye and if ever ye need me or any of the Camerons, just send word and we shall come."

"I shall. Go on, men, and leave me be. There is much to do before the snow grows thick and I am confined to my cottage." Lillith turned back to her tables and dismissed them.

Jake's arm fell by his side and he said as he ambled toward the door, "I put a large stack of wood at the back of the cottage near the doorway there. And there's six hares that I caught this morn in the box for your suppers."

"Thank you for your kindness, Jake. Now off with ye. Ye have done enough." Lillith shooed them out the door with a flap of her hand and smiled whilst doing it. She waved from the doorway. "I hope I do not see ye soon. Safe travel home."

"We'll have our sentry check on ye from time to time during the winter," Magnus told her and bowed his head to the healer. He was grateful for her aid and she was most kind to offer her assistance especially since she belonged to the MacKendricks. After he mounted his horse, he signaled to Hayden to take the lead. Magnus rode beside his brother and noticed he had regained his vigor.

"Tell me the news of home," Jake said.

Magnus was dismayed to speak of it but he rambled on and told his brother everything he'd missed during his infirmity but left out the news of the traitors. He told him that Vincent had released the falcon he'd saved. His brother seemed pleased at hearing that news.

Along the way home, there were no sightings of the Chattans or their damnable sheep. Since winter was practically on their doorstep, the Chattans probably forced the flock closer to home where they belonged.

Though it was darker earlier in the day because of the heavy cloud cover and snow, they could see enough to continue their journey. They reached the gates of home before night fell. Magnus was glad to be home again. Now he could handle his duties and make ready to leave to see Kendra. His chest hurt just thinking of her and how much he missed her. He suspected she must be grieving the loss of her father and he wanted to be there to ease her discontent.

"Come inside and see Ma before you retreat to the barracks, Jake. She'll disbelieve ye are home unless she sees ye for herself." Magnus entered the keep with both Hayden and Jake following.

His parents sat at the table and appeared to have just finished their supper. His da sharpened a dagger with a stone and his ma plied a needle to a piece of fabric. When they noticed Jake, they rose from their seats and almost shouted in jubilation at his brother's homecoming.

Magnus bid his parents a greeting and left them to have a private reunion. He ambled toward the chairs by the hearth. Weary from riding all day, he sat in a chair and warmed his hands from the heat of the fire. Warmth permeated him and eased the tightness in his shoulders. It was good to be home, but the solace of it was short-lived since Kendra wasn't there to greet him.

Hayden approached and handed him a cup of ale. "Here, Laird, drink. I'm off to seek my bed unless ye need anything."

"Nay, go on. Thanks for taking the trek with me, Hayden. I'll see ye on the morrow." Magnus watched him leave and then he turned his gaze to the flickering flames of the hearth's fire. The crackle of it allayed him and he relaxed back, happy to be eased, even if briefly.

The voices of his parents and Jake sounded far off as he ignored their talk. Likely Jake told them what had happened to him and how he recovered. Magnus was glad his brother survived the injury to his body. He appeared sound now and would probably insist on taking to the training field as soon as the morrow. That was if the snow ceased and didn't collect on the ground. Training might be delayed for a time.

"Magnus, I need to speak to ye." Jake's voice interrupted his reverie. He raised his face and searched his brother's expression. His tone was most serious and his gaze blank as if what he wanted to say was dire. "Aye? Join me, Jake. 'Tis warmer here by the fire." It was then that he realized his parents had left the hall. Only he and Jake remained.

Jake set his cup on a nearby table, flopped down in the chair across from him, and pressed his hands over his face. "I have thought long and hard about how to say this for a time…"

"What is it?" Magnus leaned back in his chair, not really paying his brother any heed. He suspected Jake would thank him for taking him to Lillith's.

"It was my fault that Ned died. I was with Gordon and Ezlen when they approached Ned." Jake lowered his chin which practically touched his chest.

Magnus's pulse began to race and heat surged through veins. He shifted forward and leaned his forearms on his knees, giving his brother a heated glare and his full attention. "Ye were with them? They approached Ned? Why? Why did you not tell me! Tell me from the start, Jake, and leave out no detail."

"I knew Ned was up to something foul in the days leading up to his death and I spoke to Gordon and Ezlen about it. For days, I followed him and suspected that he had taken the clan's coin. Aye, for I spied on him and saw him lose at dice with Aldo on a few occasions. I was close enough to hear them but he didn't see me because I stayed in the shadows. There was a good many inside the barn that day. When Ned left to repay his debt to Aldo, I asked Gordon and Ezlen to go with me when Ned absconded that last day with the clan's coin. We followed him to Fassiefern." Jake cleared his throat and retook the cup he'd set near him. He sipped at the drink and avoided his gaze.

Magnus said nothing. He wasn't certain whether he was shocked or annoyed at what Jake told him. He waited to hear what else his brother would confess. Though he couldn't believe or fathom that Jake killed Ned because his youngest brother was too honorable to do something so wretched.

Jake set his cup on the floor next to his chair and folded his hands. "I thought Ned was going to meet with Aldo at the Tavern as they had arranged, but he continued riding and went to Mary's. Me, Gordon, and Ezlen went inside the Myltenhus and pretended we were there to be with the women. Ned disappeared for a time but when he reappeared he was visibly upset. He left the manor and we continued to follow him. Near the great crag, we approached him and I confronted him about taking the clan's coin."

Magnus steeled himself, ready to hear the atrocity and happening of Ned's death.

His brother flexed his palms and then used a hand to rub his nape. "I hadn't known that my comrades were aware of our brother's crime. Apparently, they had approached Ned earlier and demanded recompense. Gordon and Ezlen spoke to him again about paying them coins for their silence. Ned scoffed at them and told them to go to hell. Before I knew what was happening, Gordon and Ezlen stabbed Ned with their daggers. Ned fell to the ground. I ran to him and tried to help him but it was too late." Jake's voice deepened with emotion as he recalled the clandestine mission.

Magnus tensed at his brother's retelling of the event. He fisted his hands but stayed seated. There was more to come, he was certain of that.

Jake tried to slow his raspy breath by breathing through his nose which flared at the force. "Ned was dead when I reached him. I saw red at that point and drew my sword. I ran at them and struck them both down. I killed Gordon and Ezlen to avenge our brother. Afterward, I fell to the ground and stared at the bodies around me, unsure what I should do." He quieted and stared at the fire.

"Jake, be calm. Go on and finish the tale." Magnus steepled his fingers by his lips and waited to hear the rest. Somehow, he remained patient and didn't react to his brother's confession.

"When I got my senses back, I dragged Gordon and Ezlen to the water nearby. The river was deep enough to take them away. They floated downstream and eventually I couldn't see them."

"So that's why we were unable to find them," Magnus said, discouraged.

Jake nodded. "Then I returned to Ned and was at a loss as to whether I should take him home or leave him there. If I took him home, I would have to confess that I witnessed his thievery and that I was with the men who murdered him. I couldn't do that to Ma. So I left him by the crag and pulled him near the rock so he'd be protected. I suspected that he would be found within days but no one noticed he was missing."

"Until we went and searched for him."

"Aye," Jake said. "And by then, I didn't know how to confess that I murdered two of our clansmen. But I did so in retaliation of Ned's murder. They deserved to die. If I had known what they were up to, I wouldn't have asked them to go with me when I followed Ned. It is my fault that they tried to coerce coins from him and that he was killed."

Magnus nodded but said nothing.

"If you are going to banish me, then do so now. I admit that I witnessed Ned's death and killed two of our clansmen. I admit that I followed him that day but I intended to talk Ned out of giving our clan's coins to Aldo. I was going to try to help him make restitution and figure out a way out of his mess but then everything went wrong."

"Jake, I must think on this."

"If it means anything, I returned the coins Ned took to your coffer. I didn't want ye to find out that our brother was a thief." Jake kept his gaze lowered and wouldn't look him in the eyes.

Magnus grunted at that. At least his brother returned the clan's coins. That was why the discrepancy of their coins wasn't that great. "For now, say nothing about this to anyone. I need to consider what ye have told me. I will not be rash and make a decision right now on whether to banish ye or not." Magnus couldn't look at his brother, but rose and stumbled toward the steps. He trudged to his bedchamber and closed the door quietly behind him.

Defeatedly, Magnus sat on the bedside and clenched his fists. He was furious with Jake for keeping the matter from him for so long. His brother had put him in a difficult position. As laird, it was Magnus's duty to ensure everyone in his clan acted with honor. Jake had done so when he killed their brethren for outright murdering Ned. Still, the fact that Jake kept secret all that time about what transpired that day sat afoul with him. If he wasn't his brother, Magnus would have banished him on the spot.

A knock sounded on his bedchamber door and it opened slightly. "Laird, sorry to bother ye but a message came for ye. I thought I best bring it to ye posthaste."

Craig ambled forward and handed him a missive. He bowed and then made his exit.

Magnus held the missive and wondered who it was from. He hoped it was from Kendra, letting him know that she was safe. With gripped hands, he cracked the waxed seal, opened the parchment, and read:

Cameron, we awaited your response to our treaty request. Since ye have not responded within the sennight as we agreed, we have taken that as your objection. I have employed my men to build a wall to secure the tract of land we intend to use. If ye cross the barrier, we will take it as an act of war. G. Chattan

His eyes practically set the parchment aflame with his heated gaze. "Well, if it is war ye want, Geoff, 'Tis a war ye will get."

CHAPTER TWENTY-FIVE

Days, then a fortnight, then more days passed, and still Kendra had not heard a word from Magnus. She sent him another missive asking him to come. Deep winter was fast approaching and she'd prayed that he had received the missives she'd sent him but John told her the men he'd sent had yet to return.

Kendra leaned on her bed chamber window ledge and gazed at the landscape of white. Snow covered everything and was deep enough to obscure the track marks made by the carts on the lane. There was no way she could travel in such weather and with her now heavy burden, she was confined to her bedchamber. Linet thought she'd fall down the steps of the manor for she wobbled when she walked. Not only was she hampered from travel, Magnus too must have been hindered. She expected he would await until the snow melted to come to her and that could take until spring. Though she despaired because she wasn't sure if it was due to the weather or his anger that kept him from her.

Her midsection stuck out and she gentled her hands over the material of her overdress pressing the swell of her waist. "Lord, I pray my sweet baby that you are not large but from the sight of my belly, you must be. You're going to be difficult to bring into this world." She chuckled lightly at her speech. The babe was growing steadily and encumbering her as each day passed.

A knock jarred her from her thoughts and she hastily sat in a nearby chair. Otherwise, she'd likely receive another lecture from Linet about leaving her bed. Linet opened the door and used her hip to close it behind her.

"Good day, Kendra. I brought you a light midday meal. Mama says you should eat something because you barely touched your morning meal." She set a tray on a nearby table and sat on the bedside, facing her. "Are you well?"

"I am. In fact, I feel wonderful. If you insist that I do nothing then let me come down to the hall. I can do nothing from there. But there is much to see to before the baby comes and I must handle it before I'm unable. I will let you and John and your mother fuss over me and see to the tasks."

Linet laughed. "Since I doubt that I shall be able to keep you from leaving your bedchamber, then very well. But at least let me guide you to the hall so you don't fall."

"I want to meet with the hawkers this day. Will you ask John to tell them to come?"

"The hawkers?"

She nodded. "I thought to return the coins to Magnus, the ones he paid to Heatherington, but I deem he won't accept them and so I decided to refurnish the manor and put it to right. I sold a good many things when I was trying to find a cure for Papa. Now I can restore my home to its former grandeur."

"I cannot believe your husband hasn't come. I thought he would. Winston is plagued with worry over it. He deems something might have happened to Laird Cameron. He said that he might travel home when the snow melts to find out." Linet pressed her hands over the wrinkles of her dress and averted her gaze.

"All you need to do is take a gander at the snow to know what has kept him. I haven't seen such a harsh winter in many a season. I am sure it is only the weather that impedes him."

Linet raised her eyes and fixed a smile on her face. "If that is what you believe, I hope that is so. I shall tell John at the soonest to have the hawkers come. Mama says the midwife should be here soon for your lookover."

"Good. I'll eat my midday meal here. Return for me and I'll settle in the hall and await Mistress Agnes and the hawkers." Kendra pulled the tray to her and took a chunk of sweetened bread.

"As long as you promise not to take the stairs."

She nodded and set her hand on her heart to assure Linet of her vow.

Linet left her and Kendra spooned in the thick pottage. It was a delicious rabbit stew that was hearty with a thick broth, carrots, and leeks. She ate the entire bowl, set the tray aside, and broke the bread into small pieces. As she ate the bread, Kendra thought over her conversation with Linet and that she too worried why Magnus hadn't come. She told herself that it was because of the snow but realistically, she was unsure if such a thing would keep him from coming to her. Did he not care? With that thought, she wrote another missive, the third she would send to him.

Magnus, I know not what keeps you from me but I hope you are well. Our child grows rapidly within my body and soon I shall deliver him or her. I want to assure you that I am well and hope that you come before he or she arrives. I thought that I wouldst receive a response to my prior missives but alas, you must be too busy to write me. My heart grows weary at waiting for you to come. Yours always, Kendra

She sniffled a tear back as her heart tensed at rereading the words she had written. Why hadn't he responded? If he received her missives, he would have. Perhaps he hadn't received them. The men she'd sent hadn't returned but she thought they might've been delayed because of the snow. That made sense, and so she used the back of her hand to swipe away her tears.

Kendra opened the door of her bedchamber and called for Linet. She awaited her at the top of the steps. Though she was capable of taking the steps, she had promised Linet to await her.

"Let me take hold of you," Linet said and wrapped her arm around her back and held onto her hand. "Take it easy now."

Since Kendra had become confined to the manor and her bedchamber, she appreciated Linet's endearing friendship more than ever. And she was a great help especially now, when it seemed as if half the day passed before she reached the bottom of the stairs. Finally, Kendra waddled across the floorboards and when she reached the table, she was practically breathless. Before she could ask whether John had relayed her messages to the hawkers, he strode inside.

John bowed to her. "My Lady, you look well. The hawkers said they would come later, after they close their carts and cottages. There's nary a person outside this day for there's an icy wind. They'll probably close early."

"Linet, will you have your father come? As the steward, he should be made aware of what coins I want to use. I also wish to make a list of what I want to purchase with the coins." She reached for the pitcher of water that sat on the table and poured herself a cup. Linet left but returned with Mistress Agnes.

"My Lady, you are glowing and appear to be quite the image of health. I shall look you over and should gain a sense of how long you have."

"How long do I have? I feel as though the baby will be here soon."

The midwife nodded. "Yes, but be warned, babies come when they are ready, not when you are. You are as big as a… Well, that is to say, you must be further along than I thought."

All left the hall except for the midwife. Agnes inspected almost every speck of her body and made *tsking* sounds but said nothing as she went about her task. Kendra immensely disliked having the woman touch her but she had no choice in the matter. When Agnes finished with her inspection, she washed her hands in the basin by the buttery and returned to her.

"You will probably have the baby soon, My Lady. Have you felt any pains?"

"Nay, none at all. Is the baby too large? Do you deem that I shall have trouble delivering him? I fear that I might." Kendra had tried not to think of the coming event but it was always the second of the last thought of the night before she closed her eyes. The last was always that of Magnus and she prayed that he was well. She ruminated over his absence and her inability to share with him the joy at the forthcoming birth of their child.

Agnes shook her head. "Of course not, My Lady. God willing the baby slips from you and you have an easy time of it. We shall see. Now, Linet tells me that you won't stay in bed so I'm telling you to stay off your feet and let others tend to you. Once the baby comes, you will be tired and will relish the opportunity to rest."

"I promise that I shall. Thank you, Mistress Agnes. I will call for you when it is time."

After the midwife left, Kendra pressed herself upward and rose from her seat. She crossed the hall to the table where she kept parchments and ink. When she retrieved the items she needed, she returned to the table, sat, and set out to make a list of the items she wanted to replace. First thing in order was trying to regain the massive hall's table she'd sold. Hopefully, no one had purchased it from the hawker. Her father would be happy to know their home would be returned to its former prestige.

And that got her to thinking about Aston. Her brother still had not returned from war. She'd received no writs telling her of his death but that didn't mean he hadn't succumbed to war. Often family remained unknowing if their sons or husbands were killed in battle. She prayed that he would return and when he did, he would find his home as grand as it had once been.

Kendra couldn't concentrate on the list and rose. She pressed her hand on the lower part of her back and ambled to the window casement to open the shutter. A brisk breeze blew at her face and whipped at her hair. The cold air felt marvelous on her face. She drew in the scent of the wintery, earthy dampness. As she gazed through the casement, she wondered what Magnus was doing at that moment and if he thought about her.

Probably not.

She grimaced to herself and realized that she had a difficult decision to make. If the clan mattered more to Magnus, she had to set him free. The last thing she wanted was to be last in the heart of her husband. If he ever showed up, she would have to tell him that he was free to rule his clan as he wanted but without her. His selfish attitude saddened her, but she had survived alone most of her life and she could well do so for the remainder of it.

Eventually, she'd forget about him. She'd be miserable but only perhaps for a short time. Her love for Magnus and his happiness overrode her own. She would go on and raise their child without him. Kendra vowed to love her baby with enough adoration of two parents. Though their marriage was contractual, she realized that she wanted and needed more from Magnus.

She needed him to care for her and to put her first in his heart. Kendra wanted him to love her, love her with all his heart, as much as she loved him with hers.

CHAPTER TWENTY-SIX

UPON THE RISE that abutted the field on the border of Cameron land, Magnus and his soldiers lined the ridge, side by side. Silhouetted and framed by the gray sky beyond them, Magnus hoped the Chattans hadn't spotted them from their land. Magnus peered below and his brows drew together at the sight of the short wall the Chattans had erected. There were no sheep in sight, and yet, the fact that they cut them off from their land irritated him. Magnus took the slope and his soldiers followed. When he reached the bottom, he dismounted and stepped to the wall. His men awaited instruction and their outrage was evident in their grousing and the harsh gazes upon their faces.

"I want this wall destroyed. Take every rock and toss it over the ravine. We will not make it easy for the Chattans to rebuild their wall again when the weather warms."

The mass of soldiers dismounted and ran to the wall. They took the stones the Chattans had used to build the wall and removed them one by one, carrying them to the crevice in the land. Magnus lifted a heavy stone and lugged it to the nearby gorge. He tossed it into what seemed to be a bottomless void in the land. No sound was audible when the stone hit the bottom of the abyss.

It took most of the morning to disable the wall. By the time they'd finished, the sky grew even more dismal with heavy clouds. On their ride home, fat snowflakes fell and covered the ground, their horses, and themselves. Their beasts pounded the ground with their hooves as they rode through the gate, flattening the snowy trail to the keep. His men assembled at the training field and readied to practice arms. Magnus flung his hand up in greeting at Wyren who approached.

"Is it done?" his brother asked.

"Aye, the wall is gone. We'll have to send the sentry to ensure the Chattans don't build another. The men want to practice arms but I deem they deserve a day off since they tarried all morn carrying heavy stone."

"I'll let them know," Wyren said and stepped to the edge of the field. He cupped his mouth with his hands and bellowed, "Men, ye are permitted the rest of the day to seek your leisure. Report back on the morrow unless I deem otherwise."

His men shouted with glee. Many of them gathered snow in their hands and tossed it at each other. The melee continued and Magnus was hit with a ball or two of formed snow. He chuckled and relaxed at the sight of his men enjoying themselves. He didn't leave the field and watched his men's mirthful entertainment and merriment.

Someone struck him in his chest with a snowball and he glared at Wyren, who chortled. "Ye are testing my patience."

"Why do ye not join in?" His brother tossed another snowball at him and guffawed.

"I detest the snow." Magnus marched forward to stand with Wyren. "I am putting ye in charge of the task of ensuring the Chattans do not build another wall. If ye need to post men at the border then do so."

"Why? Ye usually like to control such a mission."

He shook his head. "I mean to give ye more authority and will entrust ye to see to the matter. Ye are more than capable of handling the responsibility. In the future, I will delegate more important matters to ye, Jake, and others. 'Tis time I hang back a wee bit."

Wyren frowned at him. "*Och* why? It is because of Kendra? Do ye mean to go to her?"

Hearing his wife's name tensed his shoulders. "Aye, I do. As soon as this damnable snow ceases or lets up, I'll be taking Hayden with me. I'm not sure how long I'll be gone but I trust ye will see to the clan until my return."

Wyren set a hand on his shoulder. "I am gladdened to hear this, brother. Worry not for I will ensure all is handled whilst ye are gone." His brother bowed his head and marched off toward the field.

Magnus chuckled aloud at the sight of his men in a melee of snow being thrown to and fro. His soldiers' voices rose in mirth and their expletives shouted in aghast of being targeted. He joined in, knelt, and retrieved a bit of snow, formed it into a ball, and tossed it at Wyren. His aim struck true and landed in the center of Wyren's back. His brother turned and glared at him. Magnus shrugged but then bellowed in laughter at his brother's disgruntlement.

"It is good to see ye laugh," Jake said on his approach.

"There hasn't been much to laugh about recently."

"I should have been there to help ye take down the wall. Aye, Da told me where ye and the soldiers went this morn. Magnus, I trained hard to gain my comrade's respect and yours. Finally, I have succeeded in wielding my sword for the clan and am effective with my bow and dagger. Because of Ned, I am resigned to regain your respect and my comrades' once again…"

Magnus sighed at his brother's passionate speech. He understood how hard Jake had trained and knew the lengths he'd gone to, to effectively gain skill. He'd been the first on the field and the last to leave on many a day. Jake gave his all to training and Magnus had been proud of him.

"I told no one about what ye confessed to me, except for Wyren and Da." Magnus had only spoken to their direct family about Jake's involvement in Ned's death, and that he'd sought retribution in the name of their clan.

"Our clansmen must suspect something is amiss and most shun me. Mayhap it is the way ye avoid me. Ye cannot even look at me, can ye?" Jake used his boot to kick at the snow.

He was astute in that because Magnus had avoided him. The only reason he had, was because he was uncertain what to do about the situation. That Jake had to regain respect from their brethren disheartened him. He wanted to forgive Jake but that was easier said than done. In truth, he was obligated to banish his brother for lying to everyone. But Jake was a beloved member of their clan, well-respected, and a fierce asset to their army. It was hard to decide if his betrayal outweighed his worth as a clan member.

"I am still considering what to do about your wrongdoing. Ye were led astray by Ned, and I understand that ye sought to make him see he'd made a mistake before he was caught." Magnus kept a serious tone to his words and hoped his brother understood the position he'd put him in. "If ye were not my brother and I was laird, I'd have to punish ye for the killing of two of our clansmen even though they deserved their end. Ye should have come to me and told me what ye suspected."

Jake nodded continually. "Aye, I should have, *och* I was unsure how ye would react. I was closer to Ned than I ever was to ye. My whole life, you and I barely spoke two words to each other. But Ned, all I wanted to do was to protect him and give him a chance to turn back. He was always there for me, Magnus, when we were wee and others teased me. He'd protected me most of our childhood. Ye were never around and even though ye are the laird, I couldn't trust ye to help Ned. I owed him my allegiance. Our bond was strong."

Magnus flinched. It was true that he and Ned were close. He'd had little to no time to form a bond with Jake or Ned. But he understood why Jake would want to protect Ned. They'd been raised together and their bond was greater than any that Magnus had with his brothers. A regrettable feeling overtook him at such a thought. He'd wished he'd been given the opportunity to form such a relationship, to have an unyielding trust and connection with his brothers. But since he hadn't been fostered with them, they didn't know each other well enough.

"We Camerons do not take arms against each other even if deserved. There are ways to punish those who need it. But there are also times when killing a man is called for."

Jake took a step toward him and held out his hand. "Take my hand then before ye slay me and take my life. I deserve the punishment, brother, and I am ready to face it."

Magnus's chest twinged with pain at his brother's words. The last thing he'd ever do was to take his brother's life or harm him. "Ye took from me my right as the laird to enact retribution and to discipline those who beheld treason. I cannot banish ye or harm ye. In the future, Jake, ye need to come to me if ye find out someone is against us. We shall, all of us, collectively, decide what to do and take action."

"Am I forgiven then?" Jake clasped his hand. His brother's eyes shimmered with tears.

Magnus enclosed his fingers around his brother's hand, but pulled him into an embrace and pounded his back with affection. "Ye must prove yourself worthy of my forgiveness and when ye do, I'll have Wyren put ye in charge of a regimen of soldiers. Ye have earned the right to do so, but must rebuild that trust."

"I am grateful, Laird, for your pardon and I promise ye that I will regain your trust." Jake bowed to him and marched away.

Magnus was glad that was over with. He'd thought long and hard about how to handle his brother's overstepping his authority. Yet he had to admit that Jake possessed loyalty and that alone saved him from being banished. Of course, there was also the fact that his parents would never have forgiven him if he had banished Jake.

The men finished their revelry and sauntered from the field. Most had dampened garments from being pummeled by the wet snow. He too was cold and slightly damp from the snow that had hit him. He walked leisurely back to the keep, feeling lighter than he had in days. Magnus entered his bedchamber and rummaged through a trunk for a change of garments. He hurried to the kitchen and had the servants warm water for a bath. When the water was nearly filled half way in the tub, Magnus stepped into it and sank down. The heated water eased him and warmed him within a moment.

The door banged and he glanced up to find his brother Wyren strolling inside. "I told the men to stay within their cottages and the barracks on the morrow. It looks to be a heavy snow falling. We will probably need to stay inside until the snow lets up, and it might be days until we can take to the field again. When it does let up, I will have the soldiers clear the paths and distribute firewood to those who need it."

Magnus rubbed a soapy cloth over his chest. He continued to wash as his brother enlightened him on his orders to the soldiers. "I wish this snow would let up now because..."

"Ye wish to be on your way, aye?" Wyren sat on a stool and snatched a sweet roll recently taken from the oven and ate it.

"I miss her. She probably detests me for not coming to her sooner. I am uncertain what I will find when I finally do reach her—a sweet lass or a wrathful minx. The crux of it, is that I've wanted to leave straight away when I found out that she left. But with all the problems that I've had to deal with...and now I am further delayed."

"I feel for ye, brother. Wives are never easy to please. Marny often scolds me for naught but I cannot be angry with her because I usually deserve it. My advice is to confess your sins and beg for her forgiveness."

Magnus chuckled at the grimace on his brother's face. "Aye, I intend to, if I can get to her. It might take until spring if this horrid snow doesn't cease." He finished his bath and by then all of the kitchen servants had gone to seek their beds. After he dressed, he sat on the stool next to Wyren and ate a small bit of stew. "Are ye hiding here?"

His brother chortled. "Caught me, aye? Hale is fussy this

night. I suppose that I should go and relieve Marny for she's been dealing with the bairn all day. Ye might want to wait afore ye bless your lives with bairns because they can be difficult." Wyren shifted off the stool and headed for the door with a chuckle.

Magnus considered his brother's jest and reasoned he might be right. Bairns would come eventually, but he was content to wait a few years before he and Kendra became parents. He supposed it was in God's and the goddess's hands. He finished his supper and left the kitchen. As he crossed the thoroughfare between the buildings, he pulled his tartan tightly around him to ward off the coldness. That night everything would freeze for it was colder than he'd ever recalled.

The wind forced the door to close behind him when he entered the keep. Magnus headed for the great hall and collected a cup of ale on his way to the fire. He pulled a trunk near a chair and set his drink on it. Then he sat back and shifted his feet atop the trunk. He was about to close his eyes and take his rest when he heard someone's footsteps.

"Magnus, are ye asleep?" His mother's voice sounded.

He opened his eyes to find her standing near him. "I was about to be."

"I don't mean to keep ye from your rest but Jake just told me what ye decided." She took the chair next to his and rubbed her hands together, warming them. "'Tis so cold this eve." She seemed to be deciding what to say as she held her hands out to the fire. Finally, she said, "I want to thank ye for being so forgiving toward him."

"Of course I would forgive him. He is my brother and a damned good soldier for our clan."

"Can ye also forgive a mother who is undeserving?"

Magnus set his feet on the floor and leaned forward. "Why do ye say such a thing? What do ye need forgiveness for?"

His mother's eyes lowered. "For my brash behavior of late. 'Tis just I was so devastated by Ned's death, and then to learn what Jake did... I rebuked ye and I should not have. As laird ye had every right to act the way ye did. I should have held my tongue."

"I do not hold it against ye, Ma, so worry not."

"I never got to love ye like I loved your brothers. I never got to nurse your wounds when ye were a lad or dry your tears when ye got hurt. I was angry that ye were taken from me, ye being so young. Why did ye stay away?" She sniffled back tears.

Magnus was astounded by what his mother said to him. "I…I didn't think ye cared for me because ye allowed the elders to take me from ye. I thought ye cared more for my brothers than me, and so I…stayed away."

"I should have fought against it when they took ye and Wyren. I should have forced your da to stand up to the elders but me and your da understood the service ye were destined to. We did not want to interfere. I lost out on many good years with ye, son, and it saddens me." Tears gathered in his ma's eyes and she swiped them away with the back of her hand.

Magnus reached for her hand and held it tenderly. Then he rose and pulled her up into his embrace. "Do not weep. It hurts me to see ye so distressed. Ma, I wanted nothing more than for ye to nurse me and coddle me like ye did Ned and Jake. I am sure Wyren feels the same way. But ye are right, we were destined to put aside our wants and wills to serve the clan. I am not displeased by it now that I'm older. Ye have my forgiveness if ye accept mine."

"I am grateful for your mercy, and of course, I forgive ye. There should be no strife betwixt us, Magnus." She squeezed his body before releasing him. "I shall go and seek my bed now. See ye on the morrow?"

He nodded and leaned back as he watched her leave the hall. The conversation with his mother eased him but also beset him with a little melancholy. It was a long time in coming and they should have spoken sooner about the time he'd been taken from his parents' loving arms.

Magnus shivered a little, fetched a tartan from a trunk across the hall, and returned to his chair. He covered himself with it and leaned back. With his eyes closed, he was weary enough to fall asleep. He only hoped his troubles allowed him to rest.

More footsteps sounded in the hall. He ignored them and kept his eyes closed until he heard his father's voice. "Magnus, why are ye sleeping down here when ye have a warm bed above?"

His eyes shot open and he peered at his da. "I cannot sleep there. Not without Kendra. There are too many reminders of her there."

"What reminders?" His da took the seat next to him.

Magnus sighed and thought he'd never get rest if everyone insisted on conversing with him. "Reminders? Ah, well there's the bed we shared, her belongings, the manuscripts she went through for me. Da, when I last saw her, I was so angry with her because she…" He swallowed his culpability at being cross with Kendra.

His father peered at him inquisitively. "Because she what, son?"

"She entered the figures of our stores from the time Ned went missing. I had wanted to do it and she didn't ask for permission to employ herself as the steward. I said some rather unbecoming things to her and was harsh. Being there…in my bedchamber reminds me of how coarsely I treated her and I cannot get the vision of her dejected face from my mind. It was my duty—"

"Duty," his father said, cutting him off. "There is more to life than duty to the clan. Magnus, in all your training to become laird, the elders missed one important detail. That is, ye alone cannot do everything. Ye must rely on your clansmen and women, your direct family, but most of all, your wife. Your wife and children should always come first, then yourself, and finally your clan."

"I know that now, Da. Kendra tried to tell me that before she left. She told me to leave the clan's matters at the door when I entered our bedchamber. I deemed she wanted my attention but I acted borishly. She only meant to aid me and like an arse, I criticized her for doing so. I hope with all my heart that she forgives me when next I see her."

"Ye must find a way to meet her halfway. So ye intend to see her again? I thought that since ye had not left that ye were resigned to let her stay at her family's manor."

Magnus grunted at his father's assumption. "I wanted to leave but I still had to find out what happened to Ned and then there was the Chattan's interference. Now that I've solved the mystery of Ned's death and we've dealt with the Chattans… I vow to go to her but I'm despaired that she didn't leave me a missive or send one explaining…"

"No message has come?"

"Nay and that tells me that she is still wrathful at me. I await the snow to melt and then I shall leave. I grow weary waiting for the weather to break."

"It is hard to be separated from those that we love."

Magnus quailed at his father's conjecture but what he'd said was an utter truth. "I never got to tell her that I love her."

"Ye must do so when ye see her." His father smiled and nodded encouragingly.

"What if she doesn't love me in return?" Admitting such vulnerability was something he'd never thought to profess. He wanted Kendra to love him because he loved her with his entire being. Now if only he could find a way to prove it. And what if she didn't love him? The king had given her to him and she had no choice but to accept their marriage. If she didn't love him now, he'd get her to love him one day.

"There's no sense, lad, in staying here in the cold hall. Go on and seek your bed. Let the reminders be for the night. Cease being so hard on yourself."

Magnus agreed by nodding but he made no move to go to his bedchamber. He wouldn't sleep there until Kendra returned, he vowed so and wouldn't go back on his promise to himself. As he closed his eyes and drifted off to sleep, he envisioned her next to him, her bonny smile, and her soft touches.

CHAPTER TWENTY-SEVEN

KENDRA WADDLED ACROSS the hall's floor and reached the massive table in the center. "It is as beautiful as I remembered." She stroked her hand along the gleaming wood and smiled. "I am gladdened the hawker hadn't sold the table yet. My thanks, John, for arranging to have the men to bring it." Many memories were linked to the table: times spent with her father learning sums, eating meals with him and her brother when they were young, and quiet nights spent sitting together as her father spoke of his travels. How she missed those precious moments.

"I am pleased to serve you, My Lady." John stood near her and seemed apprehensive. "Shouldn't you sit? I fear you'll fall on your face."

"Are you saying that I'm large?" She scrunched her eyes at the soldier in mirth because he hadn't spoken falsely. She was as fat as a coo and just as slow. The girth at her waist encumbered her movement and she could barely walk.

"Ah, no, of course not, My Lady." John's face brightened.

"I jest, John, for 'tis true, I am as large as a coo. Just look at the size of me. I can bearly fit through the threshold."

Linet entered the hall carrying a basket of bread. "What are you doing out of bed? Kendra, you're supposed to be in confinement. Glorious God, you could've fallen down the steps. Am I going to have to watch you every moment of the day?"

Kendra smiled at her friend for her concern. "John helped me down the stairs and made certain that I didn't fall. And nay, you don't need to watch me."

For his aid, John received a glare from his wife. Linet set the basket on the table and settled her hands on her hips. "What were you thinking, John? She shouldn't have left her bed. Kendra, come along, we must get you back to your bedchamber."

"It's lonely there and I wish to stay here for a little while. When John told me the table had arrived, I had to see it for myself. I don't know why you are making such a fuss."

"Maybe it's because you are near to birthing your babe? Or perhaps it's because you can barely stand with the weight of that babe hunching your back? Am I the only one concerned that you'll have this baby in the hall?"

Kendra loved Linet for her worrisome mood of late. "I have plenty of time, more than a month or so before the baby is expected. Now cease nagging me. I just wanted to see the table. Can you believe the hawker still had it? I can almost see my papa sitting at it as he'd always done."

"I should think the hawker wouldn't have sold it since no one could afford to purchase it. At least, none in these parts. Why do you not sit, at least, so I don't worry. John is concerned as well for he is standing close to you and ready to catch you if he must."

Kendra rounded the table and continued to press her hand on the cool wooden surface. She loved the old table and what it represented. It was endeared to her. There was nary a mark to blemish its surface and its shine remained even after years of use. "Oh, nay, I need the chamber pot again. I vow this baby is pushing down so hard. I have to pee. Help me, Linet?" She held out her arm for her friend to take.

"I'll get the pot. You stay here," Linet said and hurried behind the buttery where they had stored a chamber pot. Her friend was kind enough to put one in every room of the manor since she'd had difficulty making it to her bedchamber even months before.

"John, be gone, and let us give Kendra some privacy."

John left after he inclined his head to her.

Kendra leaned on the table with the flat of her palms and drew a sharp breath. Her back ached furiously but she pressed herself upward and took a step toward Linet.

A noise came from the manor's entry and Gilda rasped as she reached the hall's threshold. "My Lady, you have a visitor. Ah, I think he must be your husband…" Gilda's eyes widened and she waited for Kendra to acknowledge her.

"My husband? I doubt very much that he is my husband. What does he want?" Kendra disbelieved her because it was doubtful Magnus would come. She gave up hope long ago, many moons before, that she'd ever see him again. If he hadn't bothered to answer any of her missives, why would he bother coming to see her?

"Ye," Magnus said as he stepped around Gilda. "Ye, wife, I want ye. It took me long to get here, Kendra, but I have finally arrived…" He peered at her with a frown.

"You came. I…did not deem you would." Kendra gasped as she felt a sharp pop deep inside her, and looked down at the floorboards at the puddle between her feet. "Linet, I…didn't…make it." A pain racked her back and she almost pitched forward. Embarrassed beyond belief, her face burned. She couldn't hold back and moaned when another pain came and it was much stronger than the last.

Linet held out her arm. "Oh, Gracious Lord! You've lost your birthing waters. Agnes warned me that might happen. We need to get you in bed. Take hold of me and we shall get you back upstairs."

"Birthing waters? What is going on here? Why are ye…? Are ye expecting a bairn? Ye appear to be—"

Kendra cut him off and held up her hand. "Do not speak it because I can only imagine what I appear to look like. Yes, I am expecting a bairn, Magnus, your bairn. Now move out of the way before I have this baby right here on the hall's floor." She huffed and tried to move around him but Magnus didn't move and blocked her path.

He scooped her into his arms. "Sweetheart, why did ye not send me a missive telling me that ye were having a bairn?"

Kendra closed her eyes at the disappointed tone of Magnus's voice. When she opened her eyes and took him in, she glared. "I did. I sent many missives, Magnus. I thought you ignored them or was…" She moaned and her body stiffened from the pain that wound its way up her spine. "Too busy to…respond. Pray, put me down, I can walk."

"I do not deem ye can, sweetheart." He shook his head and then leaned it against hers as he trudged up the steps. "What chamber is yours?"

She pointed at the door in the center of the hallway. "There. Did you?" Kendra panted lightly at the ache that slowly intensified.

"Did I what?"

Kendra drew in a sharp breath and clutched onto Magnus's shoulders when a pain came upon her. When it eased, she drew breath through her nose. "Did you ignore my missives?"

"I never received any missives from ye. Had I done so, I would have come sooner." Magnus reached the door and Linet rushed to open it for them. He turned sideways but even so, they barely fit through the opening. With light steps, he continued until he reached the bed and then set her gently upon it.

"Linet, you best fetch the midwife." Kendra peered at her friend and tried to smile.

"I will have someone fetch Agnes and shall not leave you for a moment." Linet pulled back the cover on the bed. "Worry not. I will take care of you."

Kendra shifted to the side and waited for her friend to finish. "Honestly, Linet, I likely have plenty of time. Go on and fetch Mistress Agnes. I'll be well enough until you return."

Magnus shot his gaze to Linet. "She's having the bairn now?"

"Seems she is, Laird Cameron. Kendra, let me help you get settled and then I'll go and fetch John to alert Mistress Agnes."

Linet pulled off one of her slippers but Magnus pressed her gently back with his arm.

"Linet, go and get the midwife and hurry. I'll see to Kendra."

Kendra wanted to call Linet back to her but her pains were coming quickly. She didn't know what to say to Magnus and being alone with him brought on a strange trepidation. "I can settle myself, you need not bother." She tried to lean forward to remove her other slipper but her wide girth prevented her from reaching her foot.

Magnus, with the gentleness of a lamb, removed her slipper. He turned and retrieved her nightdress. "Do you want to wear this?"

She nodded. Kendra shifted the material of her overdress so he could pull it over her head but it got stuck at her shoulders. Magnus pulled on the fabric and once she was free of it, he helped her redress in a light linen cotte.

"I missed ye and have so much to tell ye. *Och*, it'll wait. What can I do?" Magnus pressed his hand on her cheek and she closed her eyes at the solace it brought to her.

"Nothing at the moment. Did you find Ned's murderer?"

Magnus sat on the bedside and cupped her face with both his hands. He brushed his lips on hers, lightly touching hers with affectionate kisses. "I wanted to come to ye when I found out ye had left. I was sorry to hear of the passing of your da and wanted to be here to ease your mourning."

Kendra lowered her chin and huffed as agonized pain seemed to paralyze her. She couldn't speak but only moan. As much as she tried not to scream, her throat grew louder with each groan. The pains were stronger than she'd thought they'd be and she realized she might not be as courageous as she'd hoped to be.

"Easy, sweetheart. Take slow breaths. Grip my hand if ye need to." Magnus continued to hold her and when the pain eased and her breath improved, he pulled back his head and gazed at her. "If I could take your pain, I would."

She smiled at him and brushed his hair aside from his face. "I will bear it. It is my duty."

His thumb grazed her cheek but his face remained serious. "Ye are a brave lass."

Linet bustled into the chamber with Mistress Agnes following in her footsteps. The midwife appeared ready to take on the world. She smiled at her and gave a nod before setting her satchel on a nearby chair.

"My Lady Kendra, you be a little bit early but let us see where we are." She approached the bed. "You, sir, must leave at once. Be gone."

Kendra's heart tensed. She wanted Magnus to stay and was about to say so, but when the midwife grumbled at her objection to him being there, she kept quiet.

Agnes stood on the other side of the bed and shook her head. "This is no place for a man. You must leave. Go on. She's in safe hands with me. I have delivered many a baby."

"Don't leave, Magnus. Please, stay at least until I have the baby." She drew a deep breath and moaned when another wave of pain returned.

"I am not leaving," Magnus said in a gruff tone. "I'll await in the hall. Linet, send for me the moment I'm able to return." He leaned close and whispered in her ear, "Be strong, be brave, my love." With a light kiss to her face, he rose, turned, and left the bedchamber.

Kendra wiped at the tears in her eyes. Magnus had come and that alone made her weepy. She pressed back against the mattress when an intense pain forced her to yell. After it had passed, she whispered, "Linet, if I die…"

"You will not die." Linet sidled to the bed and grabbed her hand. She clasped it and Kendra squeezed it with force. "Speak no such nonsense. Now hold on, my friend, and we shall see this through together. Let Agnes see what's what."

Agnes bade Linet to help her remove her nightdress. Kendra lay back and continued to moan. She clutched the bedding so tightly that her fingers dug into her palms. "I cannot do this because I am a coward. Please…" She moaned with such force that it turned into a growl.

Linet shifted her face so she would look at her. Kendra groaned louder and tried to breathe, but it was difficult. "You are not a coward, Kendra. Mistress Agnes will tell you what to do and you will listen to her direction."

Kendra hastily wiped the tears that fell over her eyelashes. "I shall try… Aye, I will."

"Your baby does not want to wait. It shouldn't be too long now for he is coming fast." Agnes remained at the end of the bed and rolled two blankets and shifted them beneath her knees. "This will help ease your back pain."

"I cannot breathe. Open the window, Linet. I need air." Kendra tried not to scream when the next pain came, so she gritted her teeth and groaned furiously.

"Nay, do not open that window," Agnes said when she looked up. "We cannot risk evil spirits coming inside the chamber when the baby is born for it could enter the child."

"I do not believe such nonsense," Kendra said and tilted her head for Linet to open the window. "Open it, please, just for a moment or two. I need air."

"'Tis cold out," Linet said as a gush of cold air rushed through the window when she opened the shutter. "That's enough for now." She quickly closed it and went to the basin. When she returned to her, Linet put a cool cloth on her forehead. "That's it. You're doing well. Is she not a brave woman, Agnes?"

Agnes kept her focus between her legs and didn't respond to Linet's question. "I can see the baby's head. When you wish to, push, My Lady, push with all your might."

Kendra gripped the bedcovers, Linet's hand, and squeezed her eyes shut. She bore down and pushed with all her strength. Rumbling in her throat rose and her breath hitched. She forced her mouth closed and squeezed her eyes shut. A moment later, she heard the sound of a wail and she opened her eyes.

"Oho, a little lad, My Lady. He appears to be healthy." Agnes swooped the baby into her arms and wrapped him in a cover. "Lay still until I return to you and then we'll get you cleaned up." She took the baby and appeared to be cleaning him. She wiped his skin and smiled. "'Tis a handsome fellow, My Lady. You did well."

Kendra's eyes widened as she waited to see her baby. But then another pain came and she huffed. "Something is wrong... I feel it."

Linet hurried to Agnes and took the baby from her. She cooed at the baby and gently rocked him. "What is happening? Why is she still having pains?"

Kendra flailed her legs until Agnes rushed back to her and lifted the bedcover. She pushed her legs apart and held her still. Kendra thought something terrible was happening and that she might succumb to the pain. She felt weakened and gasped for breath.

Agnes's eyes rose and she pursed her lips before speaking. "Oho, there is another babe. I can see the head breaching you, My Lady. Take easy breaths and when you are ready, bear down."

Kendra thought she'd expire from the pain but she did as the midwife instructed and took slow breaths, almost panting from her exertion. She felt the intensity of the pain building and when it became unbearable, she pushed, grunting with all her effort. Agnes stayed seated with her head practically between her knees.

"I cannot do this," she said and huffed. "Make it cease." Kendra moaned and didn't think she could continue to push. Fear lodged in her throat and it overtook her will. She eased back and raised her chin. With her gaze on the ceiling, a sob caught in her throat. She cried and wept with a moan, knowing she'd failed. Exhaustion overrode her ability to heed the midwife and even so, she thrashed about the bed when the pains swarmed her lower back and legs.

Linet approached the bed and sat on the small space next to her. "Kendra, look at your son. Focus on him, for he's a sweet lad.

When the next pain comes, do your best. See him? Does he not look like his father?"

Kendra shifted her head to the side and peered at the baby. Tears rolled from her eyes and she sobbed at the sight of him. He *did* look like Magnus with a dark head of hair. She couldn't tell what his eyes looked like but they were dark. He was magnificent and winsome. Her heart burst with love for him and she wanted desperately to hold him.

When the pain came, she bore down and tried not to scream. It was close, though, and she bellowed loud enough to shake the rafters. Before she could catch her breath, her daughter entered the world and screeched like a hellion.

CHAPTER TWENTY-EIGHT

MAGNUS'S BREATH FORMED a cloud of mist. He couldn't stay inside the manor and listen to his wife's screams. He needed to distract himself from the plight Kendra was going through. On his walk about in the courtyard, he trailed along a waist-high stone wall. Stars speckled the night sky and a shimmer swathed the darkness.

He wasn't pleased to see the essence of the heavens because it reminded him that childbirth was a dangerous business. He prayed that God wouldn't call Kendra home and that she wasn't taken from him. Then he prayed to the Goddess Flora, for she would protect his wife. Magnus was being selfish and prayed to both deities—he couldn't lose her. He needed Kendra because his life would be meaningless without her.

Why hadn't he realized that until now?

A woman emerged from the manor and hurried toward him. He turned to face her, his heart thumping in his throat. "Ah, Laird Cameron, there you are. I'm Gilda, Linet's mama, and the maidservant to my lady Kendra. We met briefly when you arrived." She bowed slightly and smiled when she raised her face to his.

She didn't look like she had bad tidings to share. He took a deep breath because, he discovered, he'd forgotten to breathe. "Good eve, Mistress."

"I do not deem we have long to wait for Kendra was well into her pains. Seems your bairn wants to enter this world and is hasty." So she had no tidings at all, really.

Magnus nodded absently, hoping what she said was true. The thought of Kendra suffering tensed every part of him. He wished he could be there with her, supporting her, and assuring her.

"Are you hungry? I thought you might want a bite of supper?"

"Nay, I couldn't eat right now, but my thanks."

Gilda stepped beside him. "Do you mind if I walk with you? 'Tis the truth, I could do with a bit of air and to keep my mind occupied. I fear that I am as worried as you be."

He slowed his pace so the elder woman could keep up with him. "Do ye know how Kendra fares? Has Linet given a report? I am impatient for news."

Gilda shook her head. "None have left the chamber as yet, and I am certain you must be anxious to meet your baby. Agnes, the midwife, is skilled and has delivered many babies. Your wife is in good hands. My lady Kendra also has Linet with her. I thought it best to give them room to do their duty and I ensured clean cloths and freshly heated water were made and readied. I heard Kendra though for she's bearing the pain well."

"I cannot bear that she's in pain."

She clicked her tongue and shifted to gaze at him. "You must love her to have such concern. I too cannot bear it for Kendra has been akin to a daughter to me."

Magnus nodded and couldn't hold back his grin. He held out his arm for Gilda to take because he didn't want the servant to trip in the dark. "Kendra is unlike any woman I've ever beheld. When did she learn to be a steward?"

Gilda chuckled lightly. "Ah, so she has shown that side of herself to you? I have known Kendra since the day she was born. A few years after her mama passed, she asked her da to teach her counting and sums. It was her way of getting him to spend time with her. I fear that she was a lonely lass what with her da being away and her brother as well. She did what she could to spend time with them."

"So she had more than one purpose for learning sums?"

"Indeed, aye. Kendra usually has more than one purpose for anything she does. When her da became ill, she sold almost all the manor's possessions to find a cure for him. She used all the wealth and hired healers, bought potions, and even communed with mages and paid for them to cast spells to take away her da's ailment. But it was all for naught."

"Is that why Lord Graham accepted coins from Lord Heatherington for Kendra's hand?"

"Ah, so ye know about that too? Nay, Lord Graham wasn't in his right mind and would never have accepted Heatherington's offer had he been so. He wouldn't give Kendra to the knave but he must have taken the coins and misunderstood. Unfortunately, he lost the coins before Kendra could return them. She searched everywhere for them and finally found the coins and is now intent on returning the manor to its former glory. She despaired over it and tried to repay Heatherington but he said the debt had already been paid. Kendra didn't say so to me, but I assume you had something to do with that?"

Magnus wished Kendra had spoken to him about the missing coins. He could have eased her worry over it. "Aye, I gladly repaid the debt for her."

Gilda clung to his arm and peered ahead as she spoke, "You allowed Kendra to repair the manor and restore it. She's very pleased about that."

"It is a bonny home." Magnus hadn't ever seen such a small manor home like Kendra's. It had a grandness about it and yet held charm.

"Kendra worked herself to weariness tending to the manor after her brother left to go lend his sword to the English. She was alone, left to bear the responsibility when Aston went off to war. He needn't have gone, but he had wanderlust in his heart and in his feet. Still, that left Kendra to look after her da. She wouldn't allow us to help her. It was not only disheartening for her but also taxing. She took care of him when he ailed and ensured all those within the manor had enough food. We are devoted to my lady for her kindness and devotion."

"Aye, as I said, Mistress, she is an incredible woman."

"It does this old heart good to hear you proclaim such." Gilda tapped her chest. "She was distraught when you didn't come. But now you are here and I hope you mend her broken heart."

Magnus flinched and stopped walking when he reached the kitchen. Gilda released his arm. "I am resigned to do so even if it takes me until the end of my days."

Gilda smiled and bowed to him. She entered the kitchen without another word.

He ambled toward the manor's entrance. He had grown cold, walking in the frigid night. Magnus entered the manor and couldn't hear anything except for the crackle of the wood in the hearth. Kendra was no longer yelling and he stood still, listening hard and praying that she'd survived the birth and was well. He stood before the fire and warmed his hands waiting for someone to come to give him a report of her condition.

Noise from outside drew his gaze to the entrance of the hall. The sound of a horse's whinny and men's voices reached him. The manor's door creaked open and John entered the room. When he spotted Magnus he approached, and called out to him, "Laird Cameron, can I get you ale or wine?" John shook the barrel and lifted it. "I'll fetch another. This one is empty." He hefted the barrel and left.

Magnus's gaze shot to the steps when he thought he heard someone but it was probably a soldier or another entering the manor. A tall burly man stood at the threshold of the hall and grimaced at him.

"Who are ye and what do ye want?" Magnus hadn't seen the man before.

The man grunted and stepped forward. "I am Aston of Clan Graham. Who the hell are you, and where are my father and sister?"

Magnus felt the heat of his ire reach his eyes. After what Gilda told him, he detested Aston for his selfishness. The man gave no care about his family when he rode off to join with the Sassenach king. Magnus couldn't hold back his anger; marched to the man and struck his jaw with his fist. Aston staggered back a few steps, pressed a hand to his jaw, and continued to glare at him.

Her brother resembled Kendra with a head of long blond hair but his blue eyes were much darker than his sister's. His beard was unkempt and scraggly but Magnus supposed he hadn't taken care of it during his travels. As much as he wanted to lay the man flat, Magnus clenched his hands closed and remained where he stood.

John reentered the hall and set the barrel on the stand by the buttery. "Oh, Laird Cameron, I forgot to tell you that Aston arrived."

"Cameron?" Aston said to John and rubbed his jaw. "Who the hell is he, and why didn't you tell me he was in my hall?

Magnus couldn't shake his irritation. The man had the gall to instigate him, he'd give him that. "I am Kendra's husband. Ye remember her? She's the lass, your sister, who ye left to fend on her own, to tend to your ailing da, and kept this manor afloat."

Aston bellowed with laughter. "Kendra married you?" He shook his head as if he disbelieved him. "Why would she marry you, a Highlander? You speak a falsity, yes, you must."

The man insulted him which made Magnus want to pummel him, but he held firm and didn't move. Kendra would be displeased if he harmed her brother and so he kept himself from doing as he'd wanted—to give the man a blackened eye or a bloodied nose. Yet, he wanted to thrash him with every bit of his strength. "She did marry me, happily I might add, by the order of King Alexander. She is at this moment, giving birth to my...*our* bairn." Magnus couldn't help but put a wee bit of arrogance in his tone.

Aston's mouth hung open but then he closed it. "You had no

right to strike me."

Now Magnus bellowed. "Ye call that wee tap a strike? Ye best prepare yourself for your sister's anger for she must harbor intense ire at you for abandoning her." He didn't think Kendra would ever strike anyone, least of all her boorish brother, but Aston didn't know that. The man should grovel at her feet for his neglect. Then Magnus flinched because he too had been guilty of neglecting her. He had every intention of groveling for her forgiveness, though.

Linet entered the hall and reached him quickly. "Laird Cameron, Kendra is ready to see you now. You can go up."

He tried to ascertain by Linet's look how Kendra had fared but the woman just appeared weary. "She's well? And the bairn?" That was all he wanted to know at the moment. He hoped that she didn't have difficulty or hurt too badly.

"She is and did well. Prepare yourself, Laird Cameron."

His brows drew together at her words. "Prepare myself for what?"

"A surprise. Go on. Don't keep her waiting."

Magnus rushed to the steps, his heart pounding in his chest. He didn't care about whatever surprise Linet spoke of. He only wanted to reassure himself that Kendra survived, and if he was blessed, their bairn would thrive.

He hurried down the hallway until he reached her bedchamber door. With his hand on the door handle, he took a calming breath and realized the moment was at hand—he'd make his confession, beg her forgiveness, and praise her for putting up with him.

Magnus released a slow and steady breath and opened the door.

CHAPTER TWENTY-NINE

KENDRA HELD HER swaddled babies, one on each side of her body. The babies were a good size and she realized how blessed she was to have survived giving birth to them. The lass had barely any hair at all, but the lad had a full head of shiny dark locks like his father's. She tilted her head to smell the scent of the lad's hair. She smiled to herself and a sense of pride filled her heart.

When she glanced up, she found Magnus standing at the door staring at her. He quietly closed the door behind him and approached with silent steps. As he reached her, a grin widened on his handsome face. How she'd missed him. She dreaded the words she needed to say to him. Kendra decided that if he was going to continue to be laird to his clan then she would stay at her home and give him his freedom. Her decision nearly broke her heart when she considered it, but it was best not to have false hope that he would ever care enough about her to put her before his clan.

"There are two? Ye went beyond your duty, Kendra, for I would've been pleased with just one bairn." He chuckled and set a gentle hand on the lass's head then leaned forward and kissed the lad's hair. "Are ye well?"

"I am, Magnus. I cannot lie and say it was easy but I am well enough." Kendra had thought so many times about what she'd say to him when she saw him but the words seemed to vanish in her mind. She sighed and tried to shift upward.

"Do not move, sweetheart. Rest, for ye deserve it." He sat by her knees and reached to take a baby from her. "What have we? Lads, lassies, or one of both?"

"One of each. I cannot believe you stayed and thought you would return to your clan. I did not think you would stay because of the bairn." She sighed and wished she could tell him how much she cared for him, that she didn't want to lose him, and that she needed him.

His eyes found hers and he frowned. "Of course I stayed. Why wouldn't I stay?"

"You did not reply to any of my missives. I sent you three and not once did you reply."

Magnus's voice pitched, "I did not receive them, Kendra. Had I done so, I would have come even sooner. I regret now that I was delayed. Believe me, I wanted to come when I first found out ye had left for your home."

"I understand that your duty was to your clan. It shall always be. That is why…"

He pressed the baby against his chest, leaned toward her and set a light kiss on her lips. "It was wrong of me to put my clan before ye. I realized my error soon enough but then the snows came and I was unable to get to ye. Believe me, sweetheart, the last thing I wanted was to be parted from ye."

"I cannot leave with you, Magnus. Not if you—"

He pressed a finger on her lips. "I will not hear of such—"

"Let me speak, please, because I have thought about this for months. You are finally here and I can tell you that I cannot return with you. If your duty to your clan outweighs your care for me and your children, we shall stay put. I have been alone for so long and it won't matter if I remain so. Have no guilt over that. But I cannot bear being there amongst your clan with you traipsing about as if we don't exist. That is more than I can take." Kendra held back a sob that tore at her at admitting how she felt about his absence.

Magnus stood when the baby, his daughter, fussed in his arms. He gently rocked her and peered at her small face. Without glancing at her, he said, "I understand, Kendra."

"Then you shall leave us?" Emotion snuck its way into her words and she about wept as she spoke. At that moment, she felt more alone than she ever had.

"Nay, sweetheart, wherever ye are, that is where I shall be. Ye are my home. I am more than ready to be a husband, a friend, and a lover to ye, and a father to our bairns. It took me a long time to understand what my duty was and is to my clan, but I will not allow it to come betwixt us. Ye and our bairns are more important than any duty to my clan. All I need is ye and our children."

She sniffled back her tears. "I do not know what to say... Do you mean that?"

"Aye, I do. I came here with the intention of begging ye to forgive me and I wanted to tell ye that I..." Magnus retook his seat next to her and settled the baby in the crook of her arm.

"What? What did you want to tell me?" Kendra shifted their daughter and pulled her closer to her. She watched Magnus's expression and noted the weariness on his face. He looked tired and sad. That tightened her chest and she reached for his hand and held it. "You can say anything to me, Magnus. I want us to be truthful."

"I wanted to apologize about how harsh I was when I last saw ye. It was not that ye handled the stewart's duty that irked me, but that I failed to do it. My anger was more directed at myself but I failed to say that to ye when I had the chance. I want to tell ye that I love ye, Kendra. I love ye more than I can bear. Without ye, I am a man with no existence, no joy, no meaningful moments. I am nothing but...but his clan's laird. I want much more than that if ye are willing to..."

She squeezed his hand. "Look at me, Magnus." He shifted his gaze to hers and she peered at his soft greenish-brown eyes. "You are more than just a laird. You are the man that I love and have loved for such a long time. I vow that I have loved you probably since you challenged me to find you a stronger drink at the king's castle on the night we met."

"I was drawn to ye from that moment too. Mayhap I should send the king a message to thank him for such a gift." Magnus chuckled and his eyes shone with mirth but then he sobered. "I am undeserving of ye and well I know it."

"That is not true, Magnus, because you deserve to be happy. You *do* realize that the queen instigated our marriage. I never told you this but she said if I made you smile that night that you would be mine. I did more than that, I made you laugh."

Magnus chuckled again and nodded. "Aye, ye did. Ye were a wee bit brazen but no other lass affected me like ye did. I suppose then I should thank Queen Margaret instead."

"Oh, nay, you shouldn't. I don't think the king knew about her trickery. Let us allow the king to believe he made the matches." Kendra giggled and considered how angry the king would be to learn that his wife instigated relations between them without his knowledge.

"I remember what ye said to me that night. When that man knocked ye over and I caught ye. I asked if ye were falling for me and ye replied that ye might get me to fall for you too. Kendra, I beg ye to forgive me for not realizing sooner how much ye mean to me. I should have put ye first and not my clan. But all that is going to change. I dealt out my responsibilities to the clan and am giving myself more freedom. I only want to be with ye, to raise our bairns, and to have ye with me. Say ye will come with me when I return?"

Kendra released his hand and moved her gaze to the babies, first glancing at the lad and then the lass. "More than anything, do I want to return with you. But I will not have my son taken from me as you were taken from your mother. You may not know this but your mother has regretted not being the mother she wanted to be to you and has suffered. I couldn't bear that."

Magnus set his hand on her thigh and lowered his chin. "I know. My mother and I spoke at length about her regrets and mine before I left to come to ye. I agree, Kendra. No one will force us to part with our children until we are ready to let them go."

She felt a tear fall from her lash and it rolled down her cheek. With no free hands, she couldn't wipe it away. Kendra sniffled and tried not to weep but she wanted to cry at the joy she felt that Magnus had finally found his way home and opened his heart.

Magnus pressed her cheek with his thumb and smeared the tear there away. "Our son will be the laird to our clan one day, but he will be guided by me. And I vow to ye, he will not give up his childhood or be taught to be nothing but a laird, like I was."

"I am pleased to hear that, Magnus. If we do return to your clan, it shall be a while yet for we cannot travel. Oh, I just thought about the manor. Who will take care of the Grahams…? Perhaps we can ask John."

"Ye will need weeks to recover. Perhaps in early spring, we'll return. And have no worry for your clansmen and women… Your brother has returned." Magnus took the lad from her and held him up. "What a handsome braw lad he is, our son. Our daughter is a bonny wee lass too. Ye have done well, Kendra, aye for our bairns are beautiful." Emotion snuck into his praise.

"My brother… Aston has returned? When?" Kendra wasn't sure if she was happy to hear that her brother returned or not. He'd been gone for so long that she doubted she would even recognize him. And yet, she was gladdened to be rid of the responsibility of the manor and its servants. A little guilt twinged in her heart for thinking such, but she'd given more than any woman should to such an undertaking. The duty now lay at her brother's feet.

"A short time ago. I should tell ye that I struck him for he deserved a thrashing for leaving ye to fend for yourself all these years." Magnus cradled the lad and his eyes found hers. "What are we going to name these two?"

"I cannot believe Aston returned because I thought him long dead. Well, I am pleased that the Grahams will have their lord looking after them now. As to our children, I thought to name him Hugh after your grandfather and her Catherine after my mother. What think you of that?"

Magnus bent toward her and kissed her lips. "That is most pleasing, Kendra. My grandfather will be honored as would your mother. This pleases me greatly. Aye, Hugh, my wee lad, and Catherine, a great beauty like her mother—my children. I am the most blessed father."

"My thanks, Magnus, for coming to me. I am happy that you are here and that you love me. It is all that I hoped for." Kendra couldn't hold back her smile. Happiness filled her. Not only did Magnus come to her, but she had two beautiful babies to love, and a clan—the Camerons, a family that would endure hardships together like a family should.

He smiled and gave her another kiss. "There is no one I love more or anywhere else I would rather be than here with ye."

EPILOGUE

Eilean nan Craobh, Cameron Holding
Highlands, Scotland
Late April 1261

A S THE CLAN readied for another Bealtuinn Festival, Magnus happily directed the men to gather the seven sacred woods for the bonfires. A group of others collected the boughs for the doors and windows of the maidens within the clan. On the morrow, the great fire would send its blessings amongst the people and all would rejoice at the prospect of new life, a new growing season, and new beginnings. He looked forward to sharing a drink with his soldiers at the stone. With vengeance behind him, he would offer up his gratitude to the Goddess Flora for the unbelievable blessings he'd received.

Magnus sat upon the grassy land before the training field and watched Wyren train the soldiers. His brother regaled him with the tale of how Hale had finally slept through the night. He now understood what his brother had gone through because both he and Kendra were awakened throughout the night to tend to their bairns for many months.

Jake stood amid a group of fledglings, all of whom stared and appeared engrossed by what his brother was saying to them. His brother was apt at teaching the younger lads how to wield their swords, but even more than that, what honor and dedication meant to their clan.

Magnus held his bairn, Hugh, in the crook of his arm and was content to do nothing but watch the melee. Sigge, his faithful hound, lay beside him with his legs stretched out and his tail thumping the newly grown sprouts of grass. Magnus stroked his head contentedly.

He felt a hand on his shoulder and turned to find Kendra standing beyond him. She held their daughter. His wife had a way of tracking him down. Now she sat on the grass next to him and smiled. For a moment, he stared at her, taking in her beauty and the way her long blond tresses fell over her shoulders. Her blue eyes shone with love.

"Here you are. I thought you might have gone to visit your grandfather but one of the soldiers told me that you were here."

He grinned knowing Kendra kept abreast of where he was throughout the day. She still was wary about him leaving the keep without telling her. But he'd promised that he would never leave again without letting her know. Soon, she'd gain trust in that.

"Aye, I visited my grandda earlier. Our lad Hugh wanted to see the men tarry so we stopped for a short rest. I was just about to return to the keep. Ye look bonny this day, wearing my grandmother's brooch on your tartan."

Kendra beamed at his admiration, bumped her shoulder to his, and smiled. "I am gladdened you returned it to me." She paused, tilting her face toward the sun, and she sighed. "'Tis a beautiful day to be outside."

"Aye. 'Tis beautiful." He didn't look away but enjoyed the view of his lovely wife.

She continued, unaware of his rapt stare. "I received a missive from the queen. She and King Alexander returned to England with their daughter Margaret. We shall likely have a visit from them soon. She promised to visit us upon her return from England."

"I recall her saying that. Aye, well then, we should prepare the keep for their visit. They'll probably bring a good amount of followers with them. Do you think they'll betroth their lass right away or wait until she gets older?"

Kendra drew in an awed breath but then giggled. "I should warn Ellen to prepare and hoard as much foodstuff as possible so we are ready when they come. The king has probably already betrothed his daughter. I'm gladdened our children will not be political pawns. They won't be, will they?"

He shook his head. "Nay, not if ye don't want them to be. I hope that Alexander considers one of Haakon's sons for his daughter. It might very well be the thing to bring peace to the north—their marriage. Then we will not need to supply men for the war Alexander intends to start." Magnus had given thought to such matters, but if Alexander called them forth for war with Norway, he had no choice but to supply his king with soldiers.

"That would be good tidings. I fear the day you receive a missive from Alexander calling all to arms. Speaking of war… Do you think the Chattans will leave us be now that you dismantled their wall?"

Magnus grunted. "So far they have kept to their land and the sentry reports the Chattans have not rebuilt the wall. Now that spring is here, I suspect the Chattans will crawl out from under their rocks. We shall endeavor to keep the peace but Wyren says that we are more than ready to face any threat should we need to war with them."

"You will tell me if that happens?"

He nodded and hoped to avert war. With his life finally settled, the last thing Magnus wanted was to hail off to fight with the Chattans. He had too much to lose now. His lovely wife and sweet bairns needed him—a duty that he was more than willing to give himself to.

She pulled a missive from the seam of her overdress. "I also received a message from Linet. The news is disheartening."

"And what does your good friend say?" Magnus moved Hugh to his lap and gently caressed the babe's back.

"I am dismayed, Magnus, for she says that Aston sold our

manor to an English knight for a paltry sum. He's gone and left the Grahams to fend for themselves. I should have known he'd do something so dreadful. Aston is not the lad that I remembered from my youth for he is selfish and cares not about our people."

He bumped her shoulder with his. "Ye cannot fret about it, sweetheart. It was his to part with and he hasn't lived there in many a year. With ye and your da gone, he probably feels no connection to the land. Linet and John are welcome to come here if they are in need of a home."

Kendra leaned up and kissed his face. "You are kind to offer but Linet says she will await the new owner and if she must leave, she will come. Mistress Gilda won't ever leave the land. It's where she was born and where she will depart this world. Do not laugh for that is what she told Linet. Hopefully, the new lord will appreciate her."

Magnus envisioned the elder woman and envied the new owner of the Graham manor. Gilda worked tirelessly for those in the Graham clan. Although, his maidservant Ellen was just as capable.

Before he'd left the keep earlier that day, he'd helped his father move some heavy trunks to his parent's new cottage, Old Angus's abode next to his grandda's where Kendra's father had lived for a time. "My parents have settled in their new home. Ma says keeping a cottage will be easier than the fief." Magnus was gladdened they left the keep because truly they needed the room for the bairns.

"I am saddened they have gone, but at least they don't live too far away. And I'm certain that your ma will come by daily to visit the children."

Magnus chuckled at that. "Nothing will keep her from her grandchildren. My ma mentioned that she wants to have a welcome home feast for us. Will that please ye?"

Kendra's brows rose. "A feast? For us? I wouldn't be displeased by it. Why though? We have been home nearly a fortnight and the Bealtuinn Festival is on the morrow."

Magnus laughed lightly. "She wants to boast about her grandchildren. I will tell her to go forth with her plans and include our homecoming in the celebration. We should introduce our bairns to the clan and there's no better time. They are growing akin to thistle weeds. Hugh is much heavier than Catherine." He grunted when he lifted the bundle of his son in his arms as if he weighed as much as a stone.

She chortled at his jest. "Soon they shall be running us in circles. If we are going to have a feast, we should also honor the spring planting as well, not just our homecoming. I would like us to gather and have merriment more often. I never got to celebrate such festivals when I lived by the border. And I vow I cannot await the Bealtuinn because the last, was one I shall never forget." Kendra shifted Catherine to her breast and quieted while their daughter suckled.

The last May Day celebration they had attended was one he'd never forget either. When he and Kendra had joined in the forest, he was sure the Great Mother, Goddess Flora, had blessed them. Magnus leaned toward her and set his mouth on hers. He kissed her with passion and all the desire that swarmed within him. It had been too long since he'd enjoyed his wife's body. "Bealtuinn reminds me… How much longer do we need to wait?"

Kendra seemed to know what he was thinking. "All I can say about that is that tomorrow is Bealtuinn. Perhaps we can venture to the woods when night falls and be alone for a time."

"We certainly will not be alone. The woodland shall be filled with my soldiers and their maidens. Good, it has been too long since we have been together and I cannot wait to—" Magnus ceased his thought when a soldier shouted his name and he turned to see who called. Hayden approached but he held up his hand and signaled to his soldier that he wanted no interruption. Hayden bowed, turned, and retreated just as quickly.

"Shouldn't you find out what he wanted?"

Magnus grunted. "Nay, whatever it is can wait. I'm enjoying a moment with my wife and children which also reminds me…

My thanks for suggesting that Winston serve as the new steward. Ye were right, he has a way with figures and sums. I trust him implicitly to do the job."

Kendra giggled and leaned against him. "Your face was somewhat comical when you viewed the manuscripts in our chamber. I knew that you detested the chore and Winston showed interest when I asked him to help me. His wife is pleased that you have given him an important duty for the clan. Gloria hasn't ceased singing your praises."

Magnus had lingered by the training field long enough. He held out his hand to help Kendra to rise. "At least now Sigge stays with me and is not so traitorous. Although, my hound went missing when Winston went to the fields yestereve."

When he spoke of his pet, Sigge thumped his tail and got to his feet, stretched, and butted his head against his thigh.

Kendra took his hand and stood close to him. "Sigge is devoted to you, and well you know it. Have I told you that you please me very much, and I understand there are times when you must do your duty? I took you as my husband, Magnus, a laird with great responsibility."

"Aye, my sweet bride took a laird, but foremost I am a man with wee needs: only his wife who pleases him beyond sense and his sweet bairns. When I first beheld our bairns, I thought my heart would burst for love for them...and you. I thank ye for giving them to me. I am most content." Magnus's words thickened with emotion.

Kendra wrapped her free arm around him, leaned upward on her toes, and pressed a kiss on his lips. She whispered when she drew back, "I love you and always shall. As am I, Magnus, most content."

The End.

The End

About the Author

Read a Scottish or Medieval Historical Romance book by Kara Griffin and transport yourself to the mystical enchanting realms of the Scottish Highlands and Medieval Britain. Stories of noble swoon-worthy warriors and strong but sweet heroines will have you rooting for them as they encounter dastardly villains, political upheaval, and family dysfunction. Be romanced with sweeping tales of love and honor.

Kara Griffin has always had a vivid imagination and has been an avid romance reader since her early years. Inspired by her grandfather's heritage, she loves all things Scottish. From the captivating land to the ancient mysticism, all inspire her to write tales that make you sigh. With heroes, heroines, villains, and romance, there's always a Happily-Ever-After in her stories.

When Kara is not writing, she enjoys family life with her husband of 34 years, daughters, and five grandchildren. Living in the Pinelands of New Jersey, she spends a lot of time at a nearby lake, the Jersey Shore, and wooded areas of the Pine Barrons. She and her family are huge sports fans and cheer on the teams of the city of Philadelphia.

Website – karagrif66.wixsite.com/authorkaragriffin
Facebook – facebook.com/AuthorKaraGriffin
BookBub – bookbub.com/authors/kara-griffin
Amazon – amazon.com/stores/Kara-
Griffin/author/B006ZCH4PG
Goodreads – goodreads.com/author/show/1428371.Kara_Griffin
IG – authorkaragriffin

www.ingramcontent.com/pod-product-compliance
Lightning Source LLC
Chambersburg PA
CBHW070531310726
48976CB00002BA/599